Trinity's Child

Trinity's Child

William Prochnau

G.P. PUTNAM'S SONS/A BOSTON BOOK

NEW YORK

The author would like to thank the following for permission to reprint selec-
tions: Mayday Music/Benny Bird Music for excerpts from "American Pie" by
Don McLean, copyright © 1971, all rights reserved. Colgems–EMI Music Inc.
for the lyrics from "If" by David Gates, copyright © 1971 by Colgems–EMI
Music Inc., all rights reserved. Warner Bros. Music for lyrics from "Red Neckin'
Love Makin' Night" by Troy Seals and Max D. Barnes, copyright © 1981
by Warner–Tamerlane Publishing Corp., Face the Music, Blue Lake Music &
Plum Creek.

Library of Congress Cataloging in Publication Data

Prochnau, William W., date.
Trinity's child.

I. Title.
PS3566.R587T7   1983   813'.54   83-4595
ISBN 0-399-12777-1

Design by Constance Sohodski

Printed in the United States of America

To my beloved daughters,
Monica, Anna, and Jenny,
To whom I wish
I could have presented
A more hopeful world.

Author's Note

The characters in this book are fictitious, as are the events. Little else is. To believe that 0600 Zulu could not be the next tick on our clocks is to continue to be what we have been: a collection of fools.

WILLIAM PROCHNAU
Washington, D.C.
March 1983

I

The Zulu Minutes

One felt as if he had been privileged to witness the birth of the world, to be present at the moment of creation when the Lord said: Let there be light.

> —William Laurence, the only authorized journalist at Trinity, the first explosion of an atomic bomb

ONE

0600 ZULU

In Colorado stands a mountain called Cheyenne. The dark crag juts out of a high plateau in the shadow of Pike's Peak, where the Rockies break off abruptly into the endlessly flat expanse of the Great Plains.

In the late nineteenth century a schoolteacher and minor poet named Katherine Lee Bates traveled to the fourteen thousand-foot summit of Pike's Peak, gazing out across the incredible array of jagged crests and down across Cheyenne Mountain and the plateau into the bountiful plains. Her poet's eye saw purple-mountained majesties stretching endlessly in one direction, fruited plains reaching forever in the other. Her vision absorbed it all and more, seeing the manifest destiny of a young nation stretching from sea to shining sea. To Katherine Bates it was everything that made her America great, made her America the Beautiful, and so she wrote it.

Others came later and saw more. In the middle of the twentieth century, when America was at its most powerful and most afraid, others saw the Rockies the way the French saw the Maginot Line—as an impenetrable fortress. They were equally patriotic if less poetic than Katherine Bates. So they dug deeply into the bowels of Cheyenne Mountain, hollowed out her granite innards, and lived there. They stayed for decades, watching and waiting.

Over the years, the world inside the mountain took on a life all its own. Entrance was gained through a dank quarter-mile tunnel. At the inner end of the tunnel, twenty-five-ton vault doors were engineered so perfectly that a single man could swing them closed in less than a minute, shutting off the outside. The raw black rock surrounding the city seemed to weep moisture, rainwater and melted snow from the mountaintop taking exactly two weeks to seep through the four thousand feet of granite separating the dark cavern from Cheyenne's summit. The men of the city said that was ideal, two weeks being the time it would take to cleanse the air and water outside in the event of an exchange. The city itself, of course, was protected from the dankness. Barbers and teachers and generals and psychiatrists lived there. More important, so did computers. Computers need clean, moisture-controlled air. They also need stability. So the city was built on shock absorbers as tall as a man.

In the lee of Cheyenne Mountain, the little town of Colorado Springs thrived, such business being good for business. One of the nation's great golf courses stood on the plateau at the edge of Cheyenne. In 1959, as the hollowing began, a young man named Jack Nicklaus won the national amateur golf tournament there, driving little balls prodigious distances, sometimes four hundred yards, in the rarefied atmosphere of the high plateau. At nineteen, he became an American hero, and his career spanned the time that other men of his generation lived inside the mountain.

The people of Colorado Springs built one of the nation's great zoos on the side of Cheyenne. They had a joke about the zoo, being vaguely aware of Cheyenne's meaning. When the animals come marching out two by two, they said to each other, we'll know we're in trouble. But for decades, when the downtown sirens sounded in Colorado Springs, the people looked for tornadoes, not the animals.

Now, in this cold winter in the 1980's, night skiers were on the mountain, schussing unknowingly over the men in the nether regions. Far beneath the carefree skiers, the watchers were vigilant as always. On the inner walls of their Stygian city they had many clocks, so they could track the time simply in many other cities and places—Moscow, Omaha, Washington, Plesetsk, Tyuratam, Kapustin Yar, and, of course, the universal time of Zulu. The Zulu clock, showing Greenwich mean time, stood at 0600 exactly. Near it a sign asked: Are You EWO Ready? Near the sign hung an alert-status board, its unlighted codes reading, in order of readiness:

Apple Jack . . .
Lemon Juice . . .
Snow Man . . .
Big Noise . . .
Cocked Pistol . . .
Fast Pace . . .
Round House . . .
Double Take . . .
Fade Out.

Men with pearl-handled pistols guarded other men whose vigilance was tuned to computers with green screens, to printouts with endless sequences of numbers. The screens were tuned to orbiting satellites. The satellites were tuned to silos in far-off steppes, as well as to the oceans where Yankee-class Soviet submarines had been tracked to their silent runs much nearer to the shores of all of America's shining seas.

A general, the head of the North American Aerospace Defense Command, stood on a balcony above the watchers, watching. He was not always there, but these had not been easy days.

Below him, a Royal Canadian Air Force officer fiddled with a screen that had boxed the rough location of a submarine that had gone silent days earlier 175 miles off the Pacific coastline at Neah Bay, Washington.

Blip.

Early that morning, as a dull gray false dawn melded without shadows into the winter-white nowhere of the highlands outside Spokane, Washington, a dark jeep ripped through the featureless landscape to the whine of third gear at eighty miles an hour. The jeep, not quite standard issue, being Darth Vader black with a roll bar and metallic gold lettering stripped across the chassis to spell out the word "RENEGADE," left the vision of a charcoal smudge against the snow banked along the highway. Moreau was early for work. The Washington State patrolman, who intentionally stationed himself along the highway every third Thursday morning, understood that. He stopped Moreau anyway.

"Strategic alert?" he asked, familiar sarcasm but no intimidation in his voice.

"Strategic alert," Moreau replied coolly but not coldly.

The patrolman stared into the souped-up civilian jeep, his eyes first catching the spit-polish black jack boots, moving slowly up legs covered in fireproofed flight-suit khaki, hovering briefly on a chest neutered by a flight jacket emblazoned with lightning bolts clasped in a mailed fist, and settling finally on the face inside a white moon-man's helmet. The eyes blazed in blue almost too fiery for the dull gray morning. One shock of hair, shining as black as the polished finish of the jeep, sprouted from the corner of the helmet.

"World War III has waited for forty years, captain," the patrolman said as always. "It'll wait a few more minutes."

Then he waved her on, no more than ten seconds elapsing before he heard the Renegade whine past sixty on its way to Fairchild Air Force Base. At the gate Moreau did a snap salute to the young airman guard, his beret providing no protection against the subzero dawn air, his desperately suppressed smile no protection against the strange woman who flew strategic bombers and raced open black jeeps through mornings this cold. She glared at him because he did not play the game as well as the civilian cop.

Moreau took one last look over her shoulder at the sign which told visitors they were leaving the isolated nuclear base with its weapons that could vaporize most of the world's great cities. "CAUTION," the sign said. "You Are Now Entering the Most Dangerous Area in the World—the American Highway." She had grown up with those signs, loving them even more as she began to understand their subtle double meaning and crude rationalizing. Just like the public-service radio commercials which, as a child, had stimulated her more than the music they interrupted. "K-a-a-wack!" her favorite began with a thunderous sonic boom. "That," a stentorian voice followed, attempting to mollify angry citizens with cracked plaster, "is the sound of security."

It was 7:15 A.M., Spokane time, Moreau being the usual forty-five minutes early for the beginning of a week of round-the-clock duty at the Alert Facility. She cruised the base slowly, past rows of barrackslike buildings that remained World War II Air Corps nostalgic on the outside, turned computerized high tech with green screens and red screens and blipping targets inside. She took the Renegade up along a ridge above the flight line. Stretched out below her were long rows of the disarmed B-52's she used for low-level, radar-spoofing training missions. The

Buffs, they called them, for Big Ugly Fat Fellows, although she saw them as anything but that. She had copiloted Buffs now for six months and, this early in the morning, they sat bathed in surreal pea-soup yellow from the arc lamps that illuminated them against intruders in the night. The KC-135 tankers, with which her B-52's mated during midair refuelings, stood in another long line. They were squat and fat compared to the bombers—and much more deserving, she thought, of an unflattering nickname.

Then, finally, she went to work, parking the black jeep far down the flight line from the alert bunker. As a woman in the Strategic Air Command, Moreau had learned long ago that she could exploit the other side of the double standard that forced her to be better than almost anyone else. But Moreau also knew that not even she could get her Renegade jeep near the bunker.

She walked the last mile, luxuriating in the deep cold breaths she would miss for a week during the confinement of alert duty. Then she approached the barbed wire, the Cyclone fencing, the super sensors and the hidden SWAT teams that surrounded the half-buried home in which she would spend the next seven days and nights. At the first door, where galvanized steel webbing interlaced with scythe-hooked barbed wire, a sign read: "Deadly Force Authorized." Inside the door, she was trapped momentarily. The steel wire and webbing closed behind her, leaving her in a pen in which the second door would not open until she had been scrutinized further, cameras probing, sensors sensing, slit eyes peering through the guardhouse beyond her reach.

The second door opened, a guard materializing in front of her. He, too, wore a beret despite the cold. But he suppressed no smile. An automatic rifle, quite efficient at spraying deadly force, hung deceptively loose in his arms. A pearl-handled pistol jutted open-holstered from his hip. She moved past him, after he ran a metal detector up and down the inside of her legs in one of the few totally sexless acts she encountered in a job in which women did not report sexual harassment.

Off to her left, six jungle-camouflaged B-52's stood in an alert line, ice mist wisping off their long, drooping wings. These were armed, their bombs and warheads measured in both kilotons and megatons. White-tipped SRAM missiles protruded from the wings of two planes, including hers. Gravity bombs were tucked into the bomb bays. The four others had cruise missiles hidden in the bays. The planes were ready to go at a moment's notice. But they didn't fly. If SAC called for practice alerts, and Moreau could expect at least two during the week, she would race from the bunker, clamber up the hatch in her B-52's belly, scramble into the right-hand seat in the cockpit, help start the engines, check the codes, and turn off the engines. Such was life in the intensified cold war of the eighties. At one time, until the first stage of the cold war began to taper off in the late sixties and seventies, the B-52's had been kept armed and flying at all times. But fuel was too expensive now, and the planes too old, to keep the B-52's on airborne alert. So, two weeks out of three, the crews flew their practice missions unarmed. Then they came here for seven awful days, the sitting and waiting interrupted only by the howling klaxons signaling a practice footrace to armed bombers ready for the real thing that never came. Moreau walked up the ramp into the blockhouse—the ramp being inclined upward so the race out would be downward—and in to her day's work.

The day had gone well—first the routine crew transfer, the prisoner exchange, they called it; the usual briefing next, then three hours of target planning, and finally the late-evening down time in which the crews were on their own to study, to read, to think, to play games. It was during the down time—late, almost ten o'clock local time, 0600 on the clocks that read Zulu in her bunker—that Kazaklis penetrated her personally well-constructed defenses.

The general inside Cheyenne waited calmly, out of ingrained habit. His predecessors had had trouble with radar reflections off the moon, even flocks of geese over Labrador. Back in the early days, the geese had set off a full-scale alert, appearing to be a fleet of invading Soviet bombers. His troubles, he thought, were much more perplexing. His computers malfunctioned randomly. They didn't need moon reflections or migrating fowl. They blipped when they shouldn't blip, for no apparent reason at all. He often wondered if they would not blip when they should blip. He wasn't sure which would be worse, given the trouble the blipping had caused throughout his tenure inside the mountain. It made his few superiors in the Air Force very unhappy, irritated the President of the United States, and invariably caused a handful of senators to grumble on Capitol Hill until he went to Washington to let them tattoo his hide in secret hearings.

It also made the Soviets quite nervous and angry, but that didn't bother him. The senators bothered him.

By now he had his response down pat. Computers will be computers, he told them, like a father telling angry neighbors that children will be children. His computers had been sitting inside the mountain a long time, and in a way, the outside world had passed them by. If the senators wanted to do something about it, and it surely was their patriotic obligation, he testified, they would supply him with a new generation of computers the way any good insurance company would upgrade its equipment in the interest of efficiency and better business. When he told them the cost, with a flair that covered up his own sense of slight intellectual dishonesty accompanying all such testimony, the hearing quickly came to an end and he was allowed to return to his mountain.

So he waited.

Below him, the Canadian tapped at his green screen in agitation. In rapid order his screen flared with more activity, all from the same zone off Neah Bay and the Strait of Juan de Fuca. Blip. Blip. Blip.

Kazaklis was down to green out. He liked it there, down where the tension was greatest, the skills most needed. His mind was blank, his various other worlds excluded. He did not see the sign above that asked if he was EWO ready. He did not see the warning klaxons or the semihidden cameras. He did not see Moreau watching him with an ill-disguised mixture of disdain and exasperation. He did not see Halupalai, first staring blankly at the window's painted desert vista and then focusing sharply on Moreau and him.

Left five, fire. Blip. Left five, fire. Blip.

Essential to have a mind like his now. No room to fuck up. No room to think. Thinking caused fuck-ups. So his mind sent instant signals, unimpeded by the sludge of doubt, unsullied by love or hate, by good or bad, to the rawboned fingers that were so adept at so many tasks. Thinking would tell him that his adversaries were pulling him left, hard left, up against the wall, the canyon wall, where the odds were all on their side, not his, from which escape was possible but random. And unlikely. Thinking would tell him that now it was him or them, perhaps even bring in the emotion of fear. So his mind sent light-speed signals, ruling out thought about what training long ago had taught him.

Left five, fire; left five, fire. Blip. Blip.

The fingers deftly followed each command. They ignored the wall, ignored the known that his adversaries, desperate in their extremis, raced faster now—subsonically, supersonically, accelerating their offense, accelerating their defense, luring him toward the wall. Left ten, fire. Blip. Left ten, fire. Blip. One more now, streaking, drawing him along, his crew's fate, Moreau's fate, Halupalai's fate, Tyler's and Radnor's and O'Toole's, the world's, riding with him.

Left ten. His left index finger responded.

Fire. His right forefinger responded.

Blip.

It was good. So clean. So professional. He relaxed, ever so briefly. His taut shoulders sank, the fireproofed flight suit sinking with them. The double white bars of his Air Force captain's shoulder patch drooped, as did the lightning bolt, the eagle's talons, and the olive branch of the emblem on his right arm. He would not relax long, because they'd be back, a full squadron, and the chase would begin anew. He had accepted the inevitability of that long ago, just as he accepted the inevitability of succumbing. He was good, very good. He had to be. But he could not win. He could extend the period of survival. He could take far more of them than they could of him. His scores, indeed, often ran up toward 100,000, he was so good. The ultimate, he knew, was in the range of 1,000,000, in a far-off city on the shore of the deepest lake in the world. But he could not survive, not taking 100,000, not taking 1,000,000. In the end he lost, and he always would. Such was the system, and he accepted it. He was EWO ready.

Kazaklis felt so good, having survived green out flawlessly, that he began whistling exuberantly as he paused. *O beautiful, for spacious skies* . . . The tension oozed out, bringing the dull throb of a hangover just above the level of consciousness, reminding him also that he had played early into the dawn after the two-A.M. closing of the Boom-Boom Room in the High Pine Lounge near his isolated place of work. His fingers, as usual, had been quite adept at the after-hours play, too. He continued whistling at the brief intrusion of the thought. . . . *for amber waves of grain* . . .

Behind him, Moreau muttered audibly. Halupalai had fixed his eyes on the window vista again.

Kazaklis was aware of neither. The tension began to surge back, the silver captain's bars rising, the Strategic Air Command's lightning bolt stretching into an attack poise. The hangover ebbed, leaving him with a fleeting thought about the irritations of the PRP regulations. Officially, with the Personnel Reliability Program taken literally—which it was, being the regulation governing the fitness of those, like him, with hands on nuclear weapons—he was not EWO ready. He dismissed the thought. He was the best they had. They knew it; he knew it. He had just performed perfectly. On green out. Which *was* low level. Which was where he was supreme. Which was what it was all about, taking his big lumbering B-52 down on ground-hugging nuclear-bombing practice missions.

In his most recent practice run, Kazaklis had commanded his Buff for eight hours on night low-level, the ultimate test. He had gone out with the same slight nag, the Jack Daniel's gone from his system but his system not quite having forgotten the Jack Daniel's. He had flown after the same kind of mostly sleepless night with one of Spokane's awe-struck lovelies, different girl that time, but the fingers and other gear working just as deftly. He had found the target precisely, evaded the computer-simulated SAM missiles expertly. He had come back exhilarated. It had been his brain, sending those light-speed signals to his fingers, that moved his huge craft ten degrees left, five degrees right; moved the great plaything of his B-52 around western buttes and mesas and down long, narrow gorges that remained inky black until the moon peeped briefly over a ridge and glittered spookily off the snow below. Three hundred feet below, racing past at five hundred miles an hour. The moon also glittered off the canyon walls just beyond his wingtip. The walls flashed up above him, closed off in front. High terrain at twelve o'clock, Tyler radioed from below. The radio voice crackled. Ten degrees left, careening over the frozen riverbed, the moon gone now, the wall ahead disappearing into the black night, only the dim red glow of his radar screen telling Kazaklis it still was there, giving way to the safe tunnel of the river gorge that his brain told his fingers to follow. Red screens in darkness, better for night vision; green screens in daylight.

The screen was green now, the pause over, the garishly yellow computer letters disappearing, a formation of adversaries lining up, eleven across and five deep, moving to a hum-dum-a-dum narcotic beat.

Kazaklis came to full alert, although it took added effort. This part was tedious, just like the duty he had begun today. Dull. Sit and wait. Howling klaxons, the top-speed sprint to his nuclear-armed plane. Engines on. Sit and wait. Engines off. Just to show the Russians they were ready. Always. Then back to the alert bunker and wait. He wasn't in it for this. He was in it for low level and the sheer flier's joy of snaking the biggest bomber in the American Air Force down western canyons, granite just off his wingtips, his mind transforming the American deserts into the steppes of Russia, his imagination making the Missouri River the Volga or the Lena.

His fingers moved automatically, this being a trip of his trained mind, too—blip, blip, blip—carving out one row of adversaries, then another. Kazaklis long ago had broken down the adversaries' computer program, learned the secret of the count, filed away the pattern of their attack and all its variations. He had done this exactly as his SAC colleagues had broken down the computer programs of the heat-seeking SAM missiles that would come up at him, just as they had cracked the secrets of the MIG's he could expect north of the Beaufort Sea, just as they had probed and adjusted for the radar defenses he could expect near the entry point over the Arctic islands, Novosibirskie Ostrova. Exactly as the Russians, after more than thirty years, had learned and adjusted for every secret of the B-52. But he would never see the entry point, never see the deep lake so far inside Siberia. Not even if he went there, went for a million.

He was on the count, ready for the bonus shot at the command ship, when Moreau brushed past him. The distraction was minor, but fatal. Instead of the bonus shot, a lone adversary caught him just as his brain frantically signaled hard right. The explosion resounded through the computer screen.

"She-e-e-e-it!" Kazaklis exploded in unison with the machine.

He glared at Moreau.

Moreau's face wore the slightest smile of satisfaction.

"You, Kazaklis, are a fuck-up," the copilot said to the pilot, sensing that nothing could be more demeaning.

Kazaklis bristled instantly, the eagle's talons flexing. Then he grinned from ear to ear, knowing his crew member's vulnerabilities far better.

"And what you need, Moreau," he said through the gleaming white teeth that worked so well in the Boom-Boom Room, "is a good fuck!"

Moreau turned quickly away. The green screen flashed a computer message: Game Over.

Far to the south a young American lieutenant, new to the bowels of Cheyenne Mountain, watched the Canadian officer's screen in fascination, distracted from his own.

Blip.

The little spasm from the lieutenant's own screen, trained on a patch of ocean in the Georgia Banks off New England, caught the corner of his eye. Blip. Blip. Blip. Next to him, on a third screen, the blips emerged almost simultaneously off the Outer Banks of North Carolina. Another screen did a staccato dance from a patch of the Pacific beyond Catalina in Southern California.

The general watched his men cross-check computer printouts. But he knew what they showed—many zeroes, computer code for missile launches—and knew that already the printouts were being dispersed to more than one hundred strategic sites around the world, setting a preliminary attack conference into motion. This had happened 147 times in the past two years. He pushed a button that changed the alert code from Apple Jack to Lemon Juice.

The general sighed and shook his head slightly. Damned computers. And he waited.

In the alert room Halupalai stared into the window, but he did not see its western vista. Instead, he saw a handful of Dali clouds dancing beneath his feet far below over the verdant jungles of Vietnam. The gunner, oldest of the crew Kazaklis commanded, had retreated, as he often did, into the past. From the serenity of his tail bubble, the sky lay beneath him, the heavens everywhere but up. Gossamer wisps of cirrus floated just beyond his fingertips. Endless and placid, unearthly blue in its paleness, the sky surrounded and enveloped him. There was no bliss like this. Halupalai had found himself.

He could understand Gagarin: *I am eagle!* He could understand Borman approaching the edge of the moon: *In the beginning . . .* He was free. He was unfettered. He was alone.

Even the words, echoing preternaturally through his bubble, were part of the splendid solitude.

"Twenty seconds. Ready, ready. Now."

The words came from afar, not disruptively. They, too, were part of his realm, no tension to them. He watched for the first gray globule they signaled. It came quickly, followed rapidly by a stream. The bombs floated downward, wafting like gray feathers, tumbling gently through the cirrus, growing tiny and innocent and natural and good as they descended into the cotton-candy clouds far below.

Halupalai felt his world begin to tilt, arch gracefully on its side in a wide sweeping turn toward home. So well was Halupalai attuned to his world and its own special rhythms that he saw the first glint of the intruder almost simultaneously with the huge B-52's radar operator who sat with the rest of the crew far ahead of Halupalai's tail-gun bubble. Suddenly Halupalai's quiet world erupted into raw chaos. Still, he watched almost passively, fascinated, as the missile soared upward. Then he broke into uncontrollable rage. The intruder scarred his landscape, raped his world. His brown hands turned white in their grip on the fifty-caliber machine gun, the electric jolts of the gun pulsing through his arms as he fired and fired.

Halupalai's bullets impacted on nothing, the strafe racing invisibly into his heavens, randomly and futilely, never meant for an intruder like this. The SAM missile raced nearer, its outline growing more menacing as its outline clarified. The gunner fired relentlessly, without meaning or hope but in outrage and frustration at the sacrilege. The B-52 groaned in the desperate strain of its effort at evasion.

Halupalai stopped firing, his arms limp. He watched the missile race toward him, catching only a shark flash as it soared by toward the starboard engines, and he reached for the ejection lever that would cast him into the now hostile sky over Vietnam.

The explosion snapped Halupalai out of his reverie. He saw Moreau brush past Kazaklis, heard the thunderclap inside the green computer screen, heard Moreau's taunt and then heard Kazaklis thunder back. He relaxed, the tension gone from the memory of his ecstasy gone wrong.

Halupalai watched Kazaklis flash the toothy smile, the same one he used in the Boom-Boom Room to lure woman after woman to his side. He saw the commander slip another quarter in the old Space Invaders computer game which he played as relentlessly as Halupalai had once fired his gun.

The big Hawaiian also watched as Moreau turned and moved away, past the poker tables and chess sets, away from Kazaklis and the row of computer games in the game room the Air Force had provided for its bored nuclear warriors. She was framed briefly against the panoramic picture window looking out on a western plateau, pine trees blurring into the purple haze of a far-off mountain range, the sun setting majestically and spreading multi-colored rays across the land. He had lived this life so long that the window did not strike him as unusual. Curtains were drawn back to the edges of the scene. The fact that it was nighttime and midwinter, the window showing sunset and autumn, did not jar him. There were no windows in this hardened bunker, braced inadequately against megatons. The picture window was a painting, perfect in its three-dimensional concept, designed to give them all a homey illusion of reality. It did not strike him as odd. He did not think of it at all.

Moreau swept out the door, her head passing under the alarm klaxon. She retreated quickly toward her quarters after the pilot's remark, hoping she had not shown her agitation. She disliked him intensely. He was a woman-user, which put her at a distinct disadvantage, because she was a man-user. Not quite in the same way, but close enough.

Normally she kept her emotions under rigid control. Even with Kazaklis. Even knowing he was hung-over after a sleepless night and still could perform nearly flawlessly. It was immensely frustrating, knowing that Kazaklis could break all the rules and get away with it. It wasn't the game that had set her off. She felt superior to Kazaklis on that, because she had gone beyond him. It was his whistling, the infernally joyous whistling. Of "America the Beautiful," for God's sake. As if he indeed were saving the world as his butt swayed right, then left, in the rhythmic chase of the little aliens on his green screen.

Moreau had played the game, too—attacking it methodically and mercilessly. Early on, Moreau had broken the game's computer program and learned the secret of the count. Soon Moreau learned the secret of green out, the secret of moving in so tightly on your adversaries, allowing them to move in so tightly on you— just as she was trained to do skimming treetops in her giant B-52—that the adversaries couldn't see you, couldn't kill you. If you were good. It was a valuable piece of knowledge. But to Kazaklis that seemed to be the final secret and he had stopped

there, which was a telling shortcoming in Moreau's eyes. Moreau
had gone further. She had learned the secret of the narcotic. At
great cost. And with seemingly little practical value, which irritated Moreau further because she was in a very practical profession and she knew the secret of the narcotic was part of that
profession as well. Moreau had stopped playing the computer
game after learning the ultimate secret. She had not stopped playing her professional game after learning its secret. Knowing is not
curing. She thought briefly of her father. Then she hurried on
down the hallway to her room.

Inside, she sprawled across the bunk in the room she shared
with a woman tanker pilot. The room, deep in the bunker, was
different from the others. The fortress, the men called it. A fortress within a fortress. Her roommate did not like the way Moreau
had decorated it, particularly the picture of the medieval chastity
belt she had stretched across the door. Inside, the mock *Playgirl*
centerfold of Edward Teller completely confused the other
woman. As did the full-color photo of a mushroom Moreau had
planted between Teller's scrawny legs. Her roommate was complaining again, which, at the moment, Moreau didn't even want to
try to handle.

"Why don't you take that silly thing down?" the roommate
pleaded, gesturing at the mushroom.

"What have you got against a climax, dear?"

"Yours or his, Moreau?"

"Ours."

The other woman looked at Moreau blankly. She didn't get it.
An orgasm with Edward Teller? Sick. An orgasm with her? Not so
sick. But after living six months with Moreau, the tanker pilot was
quite sure that wasn't the meaning.

She did understand the map. Everyone had one of those. The
rest of the 92nd Bombardment Wing kept the maps in their
minds. Only Moreau had spread one above her bunk. Only a
woman could get away with that, enjoying the base commander's
discomfort every time he brought a visiting VIP into the fortress.
Women in the Strategic Air Command were a recent phenomenon, women in nuclear-combat B-52's very recent, and every visiting senator, every visiting newspaper reporter had to check in on
the ladies of SAC. They usually laughed at the chastity belt,
quickly averted their eyes from the mushroom between Teller's
varicose veins, and riveted on the map.

"An attack flight plan?" the most recent visitor, a senator from Vermont, had asked the commander.

"A joke, senator," the commander had replied uneasily. "A common joke. These are not easy places, the B-52 bases and the ICBM bases. Prime targets. We call them the First Good-Bye, Bull's Eye, Ten Strike."

He shot a withering glance at Moreau's passive face.

The map did contain a flight plan. It showed a B-52 heading north, up toward the pole and the adversaries beyond, then diverting and making a beeline for Tahiti. It was a common joke. Everyone had an island, and the big bomber, which could pull ten thousand miles with refueling, had the range. No one was serious, least of all Moreau, an Air Force brat raised on all this, with a SAC general for a father. General Moreau was retired now, but he had been something. Still was. The coldest of the cold warriors, the press had called him as she grew up. She knew another side. But he had been a looming national figure for a generation, a natural and more sophisticated successor to SAC's legendary General LeMay. She grew up determined to follow in his footsteps. Still, she delighted in exploiting the other side of the sexual double standard. The commander would never say a word to her about the map—not because she was General Moreau's kid but because she was a woman. She knew that. And she used it.

Inside the mountain, an orange light had begun flashing. The general stared at it, perplexed.

Beneath him, at a new bank of computers, still another watcher was flipping his screen on and off, then pulling the picture in tight for magnification. The screen showed flexing molars, like computer-game aliens. They represented silo doors opening at Polyarnny, the Soviets' northernmost—and nearest—land-based missile field on the Arctic edge of the Barents Sea.

The general flicked Lemon Juice to Snow Man and reached to his right. The last time it had gone this far, back in 1980, he thought unhappily, some idiot had slipped a training tape into the main computer bank. Nice exercise, scrambling fighter pilots north over Canada. Bad politics, with the Russians sending hostile notes and the general giving his least satisfactory performance before the Senate. His right hand paused briefly, his peripheral vision catching the three stars on his shoulder. This is no way to get the fourth, he thought.

Then his hand picked up the direct-line phone. He had many ways to communicate with Strategic Air Command headquarters in Omaha, far across the fruited plain. But the telephone still was best.

In the Fairchild bunker, Halupalai quietly watched Kazaklis begin another assault on the aliens. He knew that Kazaklis, the ultimate SAC jet jockey oozing all the near-perfect animal instincts that once had drawn the world to him, too, and Moreau, the kind of woman that always attracted Halupalai but whom he never could attract, were a somewhat dangerous combination in their hostility. He knew how many directions those sparks could fly, how many different fires they could ignite inside the claustrophobic confines of a B-52. He also knew a lot about the Personnel Reliability Program. After Vietnam, PRP had worried him. He was afraid it would get him, and he wanted to stay in the wonderful cocoon of his B-52, even though the exhilarating tail bubble was gone, victim of another technological advance.

He had gone the psychotherapy trip, required after his Vietnam experience, the depression was so deep. A potency crisis, natural to men in war, natural to a man who had found his only function to be not enough, the shrink had said. No sweat, pal. It will pass. But he had sweated. He wanted to be part of the post-Vietnam Air Force world. He studied PRP. He knew how it was linked to being EWO ready, how crucially the Air Force viewed the combination. He knew that men had been bumped out of nuclear missions because they were taking antihistamines or fighting with their wives. He knew that crews were expected to look for flaws in their buddies, to turn them in for the security of all, look for the little quirks that meant they might rebel or question too much or crack up around all the weapons, or simply not go at the moment of truth. He could quote at length from the regs of the Personnel Reliability Program established to maintain sanity even if the situation were not sane.

Halupalai had memorized Air Force Regulation 35-99, especially the section dealing with "Personality and Behavior Factors That May Affect Reliability." He recalled the category "Factors Relating to Thinking or Attitude." One of the first line items instructed the crews to look for "Arrogance—Individual assumes or presumes the possession of superior or unique ideas or abilities." Kazaklis at his Space Invaders game? Or the next line item: "Lack of humor—especially the inability to laugh at oneself, at one's mistakes or weaknesses." Moreau stalking away from the pilot's toothy grin? Halupalai himself, still dreaming about a weakness almost fifteen years old? Halupalai knew that Air Force Regulation 35-99 could get anyone in this bunker on one item or another. Or it could get none of them. He had memorized the PRP regs, run his life by them, so they would not get him.

Still, he also knew that Kazaklis, so cocksure of his own ability, passed. And he knew that Moreau, so steeled in her determination to cover the pensive side of her nature with Darth Vader jeeps and maps to Tahiti, also passed. Even together, two scorpions in the bottle of a B-52 cockpit, they made it. The Air Force was far more likely to bump Tyler for his family troubles, far more likely to come at Halupalai if he weren't careful. Kazaklis was safe; Moreau perhaps safer. They would never pull the trigger in paranoia; they would always pull it when ordered. You got to know people well in this kind of life—six people crammed into the tiny upstairs-downstairs crew compartment of a giant bomber scraping American rooftops in practice after practice for a suicidal low-level run into Russia.

At forty-four, Halupalai was far older than anyone else in the crew. Kazaklis was next at thirty-one; Moreau just twenty-seven; the others still younger. This was a youthful game. They kept him here only because he was a gunner, an anachronism who filled a seat, the only noncommissioned officer aboard the bomber. He knew he had less function now than he had in that most splendid world above Vietnam, where at least he had his bubble and the sky was beneath him, endless in its eternity. In the nuclear bomber he had been placed forward with the rest of the crew, no windows for him in either the alert facility or his airplane, his useless gun run by remote control and radar. Still, he was content with that, and careful with it.

It had occurred to Halupalai that he should put in for retirement. His twenty years were up. But what other world was there for him? Back to the islands, which he had left after high school, a muscular and sought-after prep football player, one of those Hawaiian wonders who had spun into glamour and success in the Coast Conference in the sixties? UCLA's headlines had eliminated any chance of that, especially when he became an All-American, the young blonds hanging on him the way they hung on Kazaklis now. Then his college glory expired into flaky real-estate huckstering and flimflam Southern California deals selling overpriced sports cars to the few aging alums whose memories yellowed more slowly than his scrapbooks. He joined the Air Force shortly before Vietnam really ignited, spurning the chance at officers' school to avoid any more disappointments. He also raced through three marriages with less and less likely women, all island-struck, starting with a UCLA cheerleader who was more attracted to the beachboy than the man in him. Now, in middle age, he knew where none of the women were, not even the fifteen-year-old daughter he had fathered so long ago.

Halupalai glanced around his bunker world, the one place, along with the tight compartment of his B-52, that he felt at home. Free. Unfettered. Alone.

He watched Kazaklis, his rear end swaying left and right with the descending adversaries. Above the pilot, Halupalai's eyes drew themselves to the sign that demanded: "Are You EWO Ready?"

Hell, yes, Halupalai told himself, he was EWO ready. On his nuclear uniformed upper arm, just below the mailed fist clutching lightning bolts, he wore another patch that showed he had flown 163 missions in Vietnam. He was the only one here who had dropped a real bomb, the only one who had seen a real SAM missile. EWO ready? Hell, yes, he was Emergency War Order ready. His eyes flicked past the sign to a row of clocks on which the hands edged past ten P.M. local time, past 0600 Zulu.

Two

Beneath Omaha, across the fruited plain from Cheyenne Mountain, SIOP and RSIOP hummed quietly in their clean-room niche around the corner and below the Command Balcony. The two huge computers were engaged in their usual mortal combat, deadly deities calculating the megadeaths they had imposed on each other, calculating the megadeaths they had absorbed, strategizing moves and countermoves in the great chess game they had played now for decades. SIOP, an acronym for Single Integrated Operating Plan, always won. SIOP was America, containing all the nation's nuclear capabilities on the silicon chips that ran the modern world. Each bomber was a data bit, as was each submarine and each intercontinental missile and each warhead that could be spewed out of each weapon. Cities were data bits, as were earth satellites. Armies were data bits, as were civilians. Even SIOP was a data bit, as was the President of the United States. RSIOP represented America's evaluation of Russia's system, with its own world broken down into bits. SIOP and RSIOP were practicing now, testing each other. But SIOP never lost a practice. Since 1958, when the United States Congress amended an appropriations bill at the height of the early cold war, it had been against the law to use federal funds to study nuclear surrender. That made it difficult for SIOP to lose, not knowing how to give up.

29

Over the decades SIOP and RSIOP had engaged in every conceivable kind of nuclear war. At the moment, SIOP was trying a game of chicken—moving nuclear detonations (nudets, they are called in the world beneath Omaha) methodically across Siberia toward Moscow. In this dance of the nudets, SIOP had moved past Ulan-Ude, and Moscow had not yet responded.

Omaha, the home of the Strategic Air Command, clearly has better computers than Cheyenne Mountain, the home of the North American Aerospace Defense Command. Omaha, after all, is the nerve center of the offense; Cheyenne merely the first outpost of the defense. Offense prevails in the world of Omaha and Cheyenne. In most other ways, however, the buried bunker at Omaha is not nearly as imposing as the city inside Cheyenne.

Unlike the bastion at Cheyenne, the Omaha facility is buried under just twenty-two feet of soil and concrete rather than four thousand feet of mountain granite. Rather than skiers frolicking overhead, the men of Omaha are covered by a broad green lawn manicured to funereal perfection. Instead of a long dank tunnel ending in a twenty-five-ton vaulted door, the Omaha entrance is through swinging office doors.

Inside the entrance, secretaries type methodically in small offices and men cluster around water coolers much as they would at Prudential Life. The first sign that this isn't an insurance company is the Strategic Air Command motto at the end of the entrance hallway: "Peace . . . Is Our Profession." The next is a rugged bust of General Curtis LeMay, the father of SAC, a man who believed that air power could win any war, a man who, in the sixties, said America should bomb Vietnam back into the Stone Age. When America didn't listen, he gave up his military career and ran for Vice-President on the George Wallace ticket. But most notable is the red telephone, encased in glass like a prized butterfly on a pedestal just inside the door. A small bronze plaque notes that this is the original red phone, donated by the Bell Telephone System in appreciation of its historical significance. The real phone, the line to the President, is downstairs. It is yellow. It also is dirty, as if the janitorial service dusts everywhere but there.

Downstairs, the atmosphere changes abruptly. A sign to the entrance of the bunker says simply: "No Lone Zone." That means no one can proceed alone, not even a general, not even *the* general. The guards wear ice-blue berets, pearl-handled pistols, automatic weapons, and stern countenances.

Beyond them is the Command Balcony, beneath which SIOP and RSIOP hum contentedly and an eleven-man staff watches a bank of other computers with screens not unlike those at Cheyenne. They can communicate with almost anyone, a radar watcher far north on Hudson's Bay or the pilot of the always-flying *Looking Glass* plane which would take command after the first missile struck Omaha. In addition to their small screens, the men of Omaha have six large screens, sixteen feet by sixteen feet each, at eye level with the Command Balcony. On those screens computer projections are more easily viewed by all, especially the commanding general of the Strategic Air Command.

The general, his four stars glowing fluorescently tonight, swiveled left and right in his overstuffed leather chair on the balcony. The general had just turned a pale, luminous blue, so luminous that his body radiated a ghostly metallic halo. The color washed his craggy face down to a sallow, featureless mask. Red lights, like tracer bullets laid against the powder blue of a battlefield at dusk, raced across his forehead.

He cradled the phone, one of several he had at his reach, including the grungy one which he had not touched. Having listened patiently to his colleague at Cheyenne, he now felt the pumping adrenaline ripple through his body. This didn't happen often enough, the phone flashing urgently, setting his underground empire on the combat footing that called for dim blue lights and red siren flashes calling everyone to attention. He liked it. He had his four stars. He was months from retirement. Taking political flak for computer malfunctions at Cheyenne didn't bother him.

This, not the decades of watching and waiting, was what it was all about. Of the scores of times that Cheyenne had set this in motion, only five had reached the stage where the exchange seemed imminent. Even during those five episodes the general did not quite reach the point where he had picked up the dirty yellow phone to the President. But he had felt the rest of the thrills, his anticipation far outrunning his apprehension. He had scrambled fighters, placed the nation he was sworn to protect on a war footing. He had felt what a marine must feel on a beach landing, and he had liked it. The general had missed the Second World War. His career had been full of political wars, nonwars, cold wars. The blue lights meant the real thing, and he liked it.

His fingers jabbed at the controls that would bring what he called the big picture up on all six screens in front of him.

In front of him the main screen fluttered briefly in a televideo snowstorm and then came into focus.

WELCOME
REP. BILLY JOE HARKINS OF ARKANSAS
HOUSE APPROPRIATIONS COMMITTEE
TO COMMAND BALCONY SAC HEADQUARTERS

Jee-zuz, the general muttered to himself. Visiting congressmen were the bane of all their existences. Billy Joe Harkins, here yesterday to play Dr. Strangelove war and sit in the general's chair, had been even dumber than most. Would you take time to pray? the Bible Belt congressman had asked the general. Jee-zuz.

"Get that mother-humper off the goddamn screen," he growled into the public-address system.

The screen dissolved quickly into snow again, then refocused on a large polar map looking down on the northern hemisphere. The view gave the general the pleasing feeling of looking down on the world. The god's view was flanked, on the other screens, by computerized characterizations of his missile installations, his B-52 bases, the Navy's submarines, and endless data about the activities of the adversary. But his eyes did not get that far.

Out of the polar map he saw computer projections of missiles crossing all American coastlines. He also saw that the flexing molars in Polyarnny had changed. They had become snaking white lines. He knew instantly where the white lines would end, and when.

The general shuddered for the first time since his wife had died. He quickly hit controls which moved his status from Snow Man to Big Noise and changed the preliminary attack conference, already under way, to an attack conference. He flicked a switch that interrupted SIOP and RSIOP just as RSIOP was about to respond to the nudets marching on Moscow, turning them to a different problem. He also picked up the grungy yellow phone.

The kid really had been a little bastard today. Tyler, struggling with former Budget Director Stockman's "The Up Side of Supply Side Economics," would have been having trouble anyway. But stacking the kid's antics on top of Stockman's obtusities, putting both together in the cramped and overheated library in the Alert Facility with the goddamn sign that asked him always if he were EWO ready, was too much.

The kid simply had been a little bastard. And his mother hadn't been much better. He was doing all this for them. The Air Force was paying for his master's degree in business administration. So he flew as a navigator aboard a Strategic Air Command B-52 every four days and sat in an overheated blockhouse one week out of three. It was called paying your dues. His wife knew that. Maybe he should chuck it all and become a salesman. Then he could be gone two weeks out of three.

His wife, of all people, should have handled it better. He could have been PRPed. Kicked out, as he had seen others get the ax for far smaller violations. Six months to go, six months to the degree he had been after so long, six months to the end of his second Air Force tour. Six months to out. And they could have nailed him on PRP. They still could. That would do it nicely, very nicely indeed.

He read the sentence for the fourth time and clapped the book shut, not able to handle it.

SAC showed some understanding of the pressures on a twenty-six-year-old father. It was prison, without conjugal privileges, but it wasn't like the submariners, who stayed at sea for months now in the new Tridents. This was one week out of three. SAC had built the little alert annex where families could visit briefly. They had placed the jungle gym and swings out back for the kids. And the boy came almost every day, a little wide-eyed kid who made his father swell with pride. The boy's bulging eyes riveted on the flying suit with its demigod symbols, the child-face painted with both awe and fear the way he watched the Ajax man swoop into a television kitchen, uncertain if the image was there to save or destroy his three-year-old world.

Tyler hadn't really expected the boy today. It was his first day on alert and a brutally cold winter afternoon, the temperature hovering just at zero. But there he was, a soft little ball wrapped in his snowsuit, and Tyler had swung his son high on the swings, coaxing him: "Take off, Timmie! Reach for the sky!"

When the time had come to leave, the boy had gone reluctantly and morosely. His mittened hand tugged against his mother as he toddled toward the barbed-wire control point, his snowball head craning back toward the retreating hulk of a father-hero returning to the blockhouse.

"Timmie!" Tyler heard his wife scream.

He turned to see the little boy romping toward him. Tyler froze, arms cocked angrily on his hips, and glared at the boy. The boy froze too, fleetingly, staring uncertainly at this other father. He turned and saw his mother racing at him. He bolted in panic, away from both of them, off toward the drooping wings of the airplanes his father flew. He skidded on a patch of ice, slid on his padded behind under a huge sagging wingtip, colliding with a wheel beyond which slender projectiles jutted. Suddenly a white form loomed above him. He heard his mother nearby, heard her land on the frozen tarmac too, the air whooshing out of her in a moan.

Tyler, who understood, moved more slowly toward them. He had watched the security patrol, a SWAT squad cloaked in winter-camouflage white, appear out of nowhere, training their weapons on the child first, the mother second. He saw one guard trip his wife, instantly spread-eagling her on the runway and placing a foot on her back, a sawed-off Italian riot gun inches from her head. He saw another guard's foot land on the boy, only slightly more gently, but firmly, with a riot gun directed at him, too.

Tyler edged methodically toward them.

"Cottonmouth," he said to the snowmen.

The foot came off the boy first, then off the woman, more slowly. Tyler picked up the boy and, wordlessly, struck him sharply on the rump. The boy's eyes filled with water that would not leak. Tyler handed him to his mother.

"You do not go near the bombs," Tyler said to her tonelessly.

His wife stared back blankly, stricken eyes saying nothing and everything.

Now, as it became almost time for lights out in the alert bunker, Tyler reopened the book and reread the sentence, still unable to handle it.

"Yes?"

The voice was groggy and slurred.

Jee-zuz, the general thought. He's drunk.

"Mr. President, we face an extremely serious situation. I have asked for a full attack conference. Under my authority, I have moved us from Cocked Pistol to Fast Pace."

"Cocked Pace?"

Jee-zuz.

The President represented everything the Joint Chiefs had wanted since the bleak days following Vietnam, the rise of OPEC, the humiliation of the hostages, and the Soviet adventures in Africa and Afghanistan. He had begun the development of a trillion dollars' worth of new strategic weapons, although their deployment was just beginning. He had sent the Russians into a cold sweat, yelping that this was the pathway to war. He had ended the last vestiges of detente with the Soviets. Good stuff.

"Mr. President, I know you are upstairs. But the line is secure. The call was moved, through standard emergency procedures, directly up from the Situation Room."

"Who is this?"

The general slumped slightly in his swivel chair. Who the blazes did he think it was? On the Command Balcony, the siren-red lights had stopped spinning. The room was still blue. The white lines out of Polyarnny had inched ahead. The lines over the coasts looked like the Fourth of July weekend at the O'Hare Traffic Control Center. The general did not like his most recent code name.

"Icarus."

The phone seemed dead, the silence was so leaden, although the general heard some babbling in the background. The President was beginning to make him very nervous, bringing back some old, nagging doubts. The general had dealt personally with four Commanders-in-Chief, briefing each of them on the complexities of this moment. Of the four, this President was the only one who had joked during the briefing. The others had been dead serious as they listened. One broke into a heavy sweat, left the room abruptly, and slipped into such a deep depression afterward that he spoke only to his wife for a week. But this President had listened in what appeared to be satisfaction and quiet confidence until they reached the communications portion of the briefing.

"Don't call us," the President had interrupted, grinning, "we'll call you."

Then he launched into what he called his hemorrhoids theory of history, mixing metaphors rather badly. All the best-laid plans of mice and men, he informed the general, could go awry because of one enlarged blood vessel in the wrong leader's rectum. Very irritating, that, enough to cause anyone to misread Sarajevo and stumble into World War I. The Secretary of Defense had blanched. The general had stumbled to a stop. "Don't worry, general," the President, attempting to make up clearly lost ground, assured him. "I'll keep Preparation H in every desk drawer."

The general waited an intolerable length of time, twenty seconds on the long row of Command Balcony clocks that had crept past midnight in Omaha, one A.M. in Washington.

"Icarus," the general repeated.

"Icarus," the President said.

"Mr. President, is your EWO there?"

"EWO."

Jee-zuz. The general paused in frustration. Then he added with a bite: "Your Emergency War Orders officer, Mr. President." He almost added: The man with the black briefcase who sits outside your bedroom while you're fucking, Mr. President.

Radnor returned from his daily thirty-minute session with the Alert Facility's barbells, slipping into the cafeteria two minutes after the scheduled ten-o'clock closing. A young Vietnamese, the only remaining attendant, shot him a briefly hostile glance—a look that said Radnor once again was keeping him in this crazy place longer than necessary—and continued rubbing down the stainless-steel counters. Radnor, caught up in a decision between pie or a doughnut, ignored the look. He chose the doughnut, bounced a single penny onto the counter, and retreated in his skivvies to a dimly lit government-issue lunch table. He draped his flight suit, from which he never could be separated, over a plastic chair.

The price was right, the radar operator thought, mentally thanking the Air Force for this little fringe benefit for a 168-hour work week without overtime.

The wall menu read: "Doughnut 1 cent, pie 5 cents, Blue-Plate Special (Chicken Cacciatore today) 35 cents."

Radnor, a freckle-faced twenty-five-year-old newlywed who usually chose apple pie, liked the Air Force. He had many reasons for that, not the least of which was his wife, Laura. If it hadn't been for the Air Force, they would not have met. He took a lot of joshing about being married to an Air Force cop. The base newspaper, the *Geiger Alert,* loved it—romance on the flight line and all that. The public press sensationalized it—"A Doomsday Romance," "Finding Love by the Megaton," and so forth. But he didn't mind, figuring he had found the most special woman in the world.

The Air Force had been very good about it, transferring her from the Minuteman missile base at Great Falls where they met and placing them both on duty here. Just a few years earlier, the Air Force would have turned purple and transferred one of them to Guam. But the times were changing. He knew that the other guys his age, middle to late twenties, were studying and using this as a chance to get advanced degrees and get out. But not Radnor. This was a way of life, a good way of life, important. And it was even better since he had met his wife, the cop.

Radnor made a mental note to ask Tyler if the incident with his kid had been planned. They picked some screwball ways to test flight-line security. But with a kid? Radnor was glad Laura had not gone on duty till tonight.

At times he really worried about her. That was another reason he felt a debt to the Air Force. She was a lot safer here than she had been in Montana guarding those isolated missile silos. That wasn't just a rationalization, either, of which he knew they all did their share. Sure, the missile silos and their underground command capsules were targeted with the biggest crater-makers the Russians had. That was the only way to take them out—dig them out in the craters. But, hell, Fairchild probably was spray-targeted with smaller but more warheads to get the Buffs before they got off the ground. So that wasn't the point. Radnor was career. He knew why they were here. To deter. As long as they were here, as long as the hardened silos were spread throughout the Great Plains and the submarines moving silently beneath the oceans, nothing would happen. That was the point of all this. If that wasn't the point, what was?

No, it was simply that her job had been damned dangerous in Montana. People were wacky over there. They went hunting with a thirty-aught-six in one hand and a six-pack in the other. Get those folks out there in the boondocks, where the silos were, and they took half-stewed potshots at the Minuteman security patrols. Just for kicks. It was nice having her here, near him, guarding B-52's, where all she had to worry about was the screwball drills and a few ban-the-bomb freaks trying to climb the fence.

Radnor took the last bite of his penny doughnut, wiped at the barbell sweat glistening off the freckles on his forehead, draped his flight suit back over his arm, and headed for the showers.

Icarus was mistaken. The President was not drunk. He had fallen asleep in his chair in the Lincoln Sitting Room on the second floor, watching a rerun of *Mission Impossible*. His wife was in Connecticut overnight after christening a new ship, and it was uncomfortably lonely in the White House. The ethereal image danced foggily in front of him now, Greg Morris setting an elaborate bug in the ornate woodwork of an old East European capital. The sounds meshed uneasily—cocked pistol, this tape will self-destruct, Icarus.

Icarus.

Greek mythology was not the President's strong point. His mind tripped woozily to the vision of a demigod flying too close to the true god, the sun. Icarus. Then he remembered. He came awake rapidly. Damn, he wished these guys wouldn't call him in the middle of the night. He had aides for this stuff. Still, he was embarrassed by his lapse and his mind raced in search of a smart line to recapture control of the conversation. Then, recalling his first meeting with the general, he discarded that thought and said alertly: "Sorry, general, you caught me half asleep. What seems to be the problem?"

The President thought he heard a sigh at the other end.

"Is your EWO there, Mr. President?"

"I'm sure he is outside the door. In all this time, I've only been able to ditch him once."

The President chuckled. The general did not.

"You need him immediately, sir."

"General, what is the problem?"

"We are at Fast Pace, sir. I am now moving us to Round House. It is in your hands."

"*My* hands, general? What is the problem?"

"Mr. President, we are in the secondary stages of a major attack, probably a Counterforce variation. SIOP is analyzing it now. Our defenses show a swarm attack by submarines, almost certainly Soviet, and a random attack by land-based ICBM's, certainly Soviet. We need your authority."

The phone conversation paused again, the President staring dully into the television screen as Martin Landau parked a false-bottomed getaway van over a Budapest sewer manhole.

"Defenses," the President said finally. "The computers again, huh?"

The President thought he heard another sigh, which he took as a sign of weakness. Getting no other response, he went on, adding a touch of anger to his voice.

"General, may I be candid with you? This is a shitty way to get a new set of computers."

"Sir!"

"How many times, since I became President, have those damned machines screwed up? Several hundred? How many times have they screwed up so badly we have gone to attack conferences? Five? Six?"

The general was getting truly worried. And angry.

"And how many times have I picked up this telephone, Mr. President? We have no time for this, sir. As you know from the briefing"—he paused slightly on that—"we have no time for debate, no time for thinking. We need your authority. This is real. This is Pearl Harbor."

"I don't believe it. I talked to the Russian ambassador today."

"I'm talking to SIOP. I trust him more."

"And what is your computerized adviser telling you, general? You woke me up at one o'clock in the morning with this crap. This is not new. What is SIOP telling you? Your career may be riding on it."

"My career, sir?"

Icarus looked at the huge map in front of him, saw the white lines inching farther out of Polyarnny. He looked at a side screen onto which the computers, very rapidly now, spewed out data showing one of the white lines attaining suborbital height over the Arctic Ocean. He watched the computerized data quickly reduce the margin of error on the missile's trajectory. His voice took on a brittle quality.

"Our defense system is telling me that a Soviet SS-18, carrying 2.5 to 5 megatons, has my name on it, Mr. President. SIOP is telling me my career will be over in twenty-six minutes."

The conversation stopped again.

"It also is telling me that a submarine-launched missile, fired off the Outer Banks, has MIRVed near Richmond. One of its multiple warheads, carrying forty kilotons, is directed at the vicinity of Washington."

The general's tone changed again, with a slight hint of puzzlement. "Strange. It's so small." Then the brittle monotone returned.

"The computers say the odds are fifty-fifty the target is the White House, thirty-seventy it is aimed at Andrews Air Force Base. Pentagon is a possible target but it is so near the White House the choice seems irrelevant. Depends somewhat on whether it is a ground burst or air burst. We can't determine how the warhead is rigged. It will arrive in four minutes, sir."

"Bullshit," the President said.

The President looked up to see his EWO, the ever-present man with the briefcase, switch off *Mission Impossible*. Standing near the EWO in the open door to the sitting room were the night duty officer from the Situation Room and the President's appointments secretary, the only one of his personal aides working late this night.

The water pelted O'Toole with a thousand Lilliputian fingers. His own Gulliver's hands pummeled the soap, turning the Ivory into a froth that filled his hair, whitewashed his huge shoulders, and invaded every bodily crevice with 99.44 percent purity. He was glad the Air Force provided Ivory. It reminded O'Toole that he hadn't come that far. The shower reminded him that he had.

O'Toole felt good. He almost always felt good.

Inside the Alert Facility, O'Toole took two showers a day, one in the morning and one, like this one, at night. He realized this was an idiosyncrasy, one which his buddies razzed him about. But they had not grown up in a three-room house with no running water, escaping to the Air Force.

O'Toole rubbed the soapy lather up and down his legs, working the Ivory into the warmth at the top of his thighs where he felt the familiar pleasure of lubrication as well as cleansing.

"O'Toole!"

O'Toole's spongy knees snapped into a near-joint lock. He dropped the Ivory.

"Cleanliness may be next to Godliness, you Mick prick. But you can't stay in the shower all night. Get your well-scrubbed butt out of there or you're going to have company. And you know what the Air Force thinks of asshole buddies."

O'Toole relaxed. It was Radnor, back from his barbell workout. Radnor was his pal. He hadn't seen.

"Hang on to your own sweaty dong, Radnor. And don't try

anything funny. I got a pal whose wife is a security cop here. She'd love to get a couple of hotshot SAC airmen on lewd behavior in a public—well, almost public—restroom."

The young Electronics Warfare Officer picked up the soap, placed it on the shelf, and let the shower spray begin to hose him down. He turned the water on ice cold, as he always did, to get that last jarring bit of stimulation.

The EWO opened the briefcase. The President seemed not to notice, staring out the sitting room's corner window where the white edifice of the Washington Monument stood frozen in the clear January night. The monument's tiny red eyes, beacons for the commercial aircraft at National Airport, winked at him in devilish mockery.

Like most Presidents, in moments of trauma he felt a sudden dislike for this house. It creaked with ghosts. He felt Lyndon Johnson here, during Vietnam, sleeping fitfully, jolted out of nightmarish dreams by the roar of aircraft approaching National, certain that the planes were bombing the White House. Johnson had lunged out of bed night after night, the huge Texas frame dripping sweat, and stared out the window at the same haunting red eyes.

The President gripped the phone tightly and stared into the monument's tiny Orwellian orbs. The Emergency War Orders officer spread a file in front of him.

No one had told him it would be like this. No one told him he would have to trust computers that didn't work half the time. No one told him he might have to make a decision in four minutes, not knowing if the computers were working or not, not knowing if some fool Russian or some fool American had run the wrong tape again, not knowing if SIOP or the general was out of control. Not knowing, for God's sake, if he ever would know.

He felt Richard Nixon in the house, with a different kind of trauma, gesturing almost hysterically to a group of congressmen who wanted him to quit. He could go into the next room, Nixon said, push a button, and kill twenty-five million people. Too low, the President thought. Nixon's figure was too low. Button, button, who's got the button . . . dammit, there is no button . . . dammit, you've got the button.

The appointments secretary placed a hand on his shoulder, squeezing slightly, seeming to nudge him, too.

The President sagged. He had pushed the Russians. Everyone knew that was the proper way to treat them. Push them and they backed down. He had run his entire life believing that, preaching that. It was gospel, part of his political liturgy. You didn't question truths like that. It was the wishy-washy Carters that got us into trouble, nibbled to pieces; the dilettante Kennedys with their first-step treaties.

He didn't understand. He had weapons so accurate he could lob them, as Goldwater had said years ago, into the can in the Kremlin. Weapons so awesome Russia could be a moonscape in half an hour. They couldn't possibly be so foolish. He didn't believe it. It had to be the goddamn computers. His palm had grown wet gripping the phone. But the voice at the other end continued.

"We need your authority, sir."

The words rang woodenly in his ear.

"Authority," the President repeated dully.

In Omaha, the general's hands had grown wet too. He was afraid now. Not of the white snake uncoiling out of Russian Arctic. He was afraid of the President.

"Time to earn your two hundred thou, sir," the general said coldly.

He almost added: Time for the Preparation H, Mr. President. But he already had spoken more icily, more disrespectfully to his Commander-in-Chief than he had ever dared during his long career. He also had moved the alert status to Double Take.

"We need your authority."

In the sitting room, the President looked around him. He saw the appointments secretary, an old friend and overweight political strategist who had advanced to the White House by virtue of his friendship and his penchant for remembering the name of every county chairman in the country. He saw the night duty officer from the Situation Room, a young naval commander he knew only as Sedgwick. He saw the Emergency War Orders officer, one of a faceless corps of shadows to whom he never had spoken, never so much as nodded. He was alone.

"The Secretary of Defense is not here," he said into the clammy phone. "The Secretary of State is not here. The head of the National Security Council is not here."

"They will not be there, sir. We anticipated this. SIOP has accounted for it. Confusion was expected. You do not have time for your advisers and you do not need them."

"A decision of this magnitude—"

"We do not need decisions, sir. We need your authority."

"To nuke Moscow? To nuke Kiev and Leningrad and Vladivostok? You don't need my decisions?"

"We've been through this before, sir. You don't have to make those decisions. SIOP will make those decisions. We need your authority. In the codes. In the EWO's briefcase."

"SIOP will make those decisions? A goddamn computer?"

"The goddamn computer has twenty-five minutes, sir. You may have less than four. The computer's brain registers data, evaluates alternatives several million times faster than your brain, sir. SIOP has all the options and has never lost."

"Because it's against the goddam law!"

"Because we decided long ago we did not want to lose. Because we realized long ago that a single man or a group of men could not react quickly enough to the options. We placed the options, determined by the best human brains of two generations, under the authority and understanding of eight Presidents, in SIOP. We placed the Russian options in RSIOP. It is all there—even, I'm certain, this rather strange attack sequence."

"Strange?"

"We're wasting time, sir. Your time."

"Damn you, general, I want to know what is coming at us. If anything."

"Sir, our readouts show a massive attack from submarines, directed almost entirely at our strategic-bomber bases. The exceptions are our Trident submarine base in Puget Sound, which is multitargeted, and the single small warhead directed at Washington. Soviet land-based silo doors are open, but only a handful of ICBM's have been launched. Their targets are Omaha, Cheyenne, and a token number of Minuteman installations at Malmstrom in Great Falls. Frankly, it is not a strategically sound attack. If I had more time, I would be puzzled."

The President paused, exhausted.

The EWO thrust sealed packets at him. The duty officer talked on a second telephone. The appointments secretary looked at him plaintively.

"We have to get you downstairs, Mr. President," the secretary said. "Quickly. Or aboard the chopper."

The President stared at him in disbelief. He heard the whump-

whump-whump of the giant helicopter landing on the South Lawn.

"Rat's ass bit of difference downstairs will make. And that chopper won't make it past those beady red eyes that are staring at me."

"You are not secure here, Mr. President."

"Secure? And I'm secure downstairs? The basement hasn't been secure since the fifties. It's about as secure as Omaha."

"Secure from surveillance, Mr. President. The phone line is secure. We are not certain about the room."

The President laughed, a harsh, crackling laugh. "You mean the Preme might be listening? That's rich. Well, fuck you, Preme."

The duty officer interrupted, holding the second phone loosely at his side. "A message is arriving on the direct teletype from the Soviet Premier, Mr. President."

The President's head started to spin. "What's it say?"

"Eyes only for you, Mr. President."

"Well, get the fucker."

"Two more minutes, Mr. President."

The President placed both his palms against his forehead, running his fingers roughly through hair that suddenly felt unnaturally oily. "Did you hear that, general?" he finally said into the phone.

"Yes, sir. Nastygram on the hotline. Shrewd buggers, aren't they?"

"What is your superbrain saying now about the Premier's earlier message for me?"

"Three minutes, twenty seconds to impact. Trajectory still uncertain. Wobbling slightly. Forty kilotons. Ground burst likely. Ten-ninety on Andrews. Still fifty-fifty on White House."

The President stiffened now, ignoring the trajectory and target odds, focusing on a nagging human question that SIOP never would compute. "I'll wait," he said.

"You'll what?"

"I'll wait, general."

"Mr. President, you are playing with the fate of millions."

"That's how I earn my two hundred thou, general."

"They're mousetrapping you."

"I'll wait."

Icarus paused, feeling the heat of the sun. "You will accept my resignation, Mr. President?"

"Strange time to run, general."

"Effective in twenty-five minutes, Mr. President. I want it on the record."

"The record. Very well."

"Good luck, Mr. President."

"Thank you, general. And to you."

"You fully realize, sir, that under my authority I launched the B-52's when I moved us to Double Take?"

"You what?! God damn you, general."

THREE

0608 ZULU

After two weeks working in this crazy place, the Vietnamese counter boy just wanted out of here as fast as he could every night. At ten o'clock sharp. This was a place of dragons and malevolent spirits. It had no soul. It was a place to play war. Crazy war. When the Americans had no place to fight a war, they made a place to play war. He would never understand them and he would never like this place.

The counter boy unlocked the cash register to add the last penny the American had bounced off his counter. He hurriedly locked the register again, still unhappy that the visitor had kept him here past the ten-o'clock closing. He rubbed one last smudge off the stainless-steel counter and turned to leave.

Down the hallway in the game room, Kazaklis kicked the Space Invaders game in frustration. "Fucking machine," he muttered. "Life's run by fucking computers that don't work." He kicked the machine again, watching the game flare in rebellion after eating his last quarter. He turned to catch Halupalai grinning at him.

"You laughing at me, you over-the-hill beachboy?"

Kazaklis leveled his heaviest stare at the gunner, but his eyes gave themselves away with their twinkle. He liked Halupalai. Everybody liked Halupalai.

"Or you laughing at Moreau? Got her a good one, didn't I, old buddy?"

46

"You're hopeless, Kazaklis. Why don't you let up on her?"

"Me?" the pilot protested. "Don't lay that one on me, pal. This joint's been like a damned sorority house since Moreau showed up."

"No, you'd like that. Your problem, captain, is that our hard-nosed Vassar copilot won't let you romp through her fortress like it was a sorority house."

"Worst mistake the Air Force ever made, letting broads into SAC."

"That's not what you thought when she first showed up."

Their eyes locked. Then the twinkle returned. "That's what broads are for, Halupalai. Typin' or screwin'. Wasn't much typin' to do around here."

"Not much of the other, either." Halupalai paused. "As it turned out."

"Fuck off, old man," Kazaklis said sharply.

Halupalai watched Kazaklis closely, for the pilot seemed genuinely irritated this time. "That's okay, Kazaklis," he finally said. "I evened it up for you."

"Yeah?"

Halupalai paused again, wondering briefly if he was being unfair to Moreau by continuing. He thought not.

"You know how point-blank she was when she first came here. Had to know everything about everything and everybody. She was a real pisser. But she learned how to fly the Buff faster than anybody I ever crewed with."

Kazaklis grunted.

"Well, after your little . . . uh, failure, Moreau comes up to me the way she does—sticking her chin out a foot and boring those laser-beam eyes straight through to the inside of my skull—and asks what's with Kazaklis. I say whaddaya mean. And she says, very seriously, 'Everybody's got a skeleton in his closet, Halupalai.' I says, are you serious, and she says, yep, she's serious, she wants to know what skeletons Kazaklis has got in his closet."

"No shit?" Kazaklis said, surprised.

"So, I look at her," Halupalai continued, "and say, just as seriously, 'I wouldn't open his closet door, Captain Moreau.' She asks why and I says, 'Cuz you'd be smothered in pelvic bones.'"

Kazaklis erupted into volcanic laughter. "Pelvic bones!" he roared.

"You know something, Kazaklis?" Halupalai continued quietly. "She laughed as hard as you just did."

Kazaklis stared at the floor and frowned. His lips puckered outward and his face took on that flagrantly fraudulent double image of little-boy pout and pool-hall hustle that Halupalai had seen so many times it no longer was fraudulent.

"She still walks around here like she's got cramps twenty-eight days a month," Kazaklis grumped without looking up. "You think you can trust somebody with nukes if they're on the rag?"

Halupalai went quiet, wishing he had not told Kazaklis the story.

"You old fart," Kazaklis said after a moment, his twinkling brown eyes lifting off the floor and out of their pout. "I think you're in love."

Halupalai said nothing. Not true, he thought sadly. He felt his stomach, once taut and flat, bulging against his flight suit. He felt his bronzed face tighten into furrows that never quite disappeared now. He felt old and he felt Kazaklis sensing it, too. Their moods changed simultaneously.

"Why don't you get out of this shit, Halupalai?" Kazaklis said abruptly. "How old are you? Forty-three? Forty-four? Been through Nam. Been in these airplanes for twenty years. Why don't you just retire and lay in the sun on those islands of yours? This is such bullshit. Sitting here in this godawful overheated bomb shelter waiting for something that will never happen and if it does we couldn't handle. Get out of it, man."

Suddenly Halupalai didn't like this at all. He could handle Kazaklis when he was deadly efficient or wildly, excessively escaping. He could handle the double image and the con. But he looked at Kazaklis now as if he had never seen him before. He was certain Kazaklis didn't even believe what he had said about bomb shelters and wars. That wasn't the subject. It was far more serious than that. It was personal and threatening. Halupalai sucked his stomach in hard. He forced his face to relax, flattening the furrows.

"Why do you stay, Halupalai?"

"Why else, captain, sir?" Halupalai grinned, forcing the smile and forcing the lighthearted sarcasm into his voice. "To keep this world safe from godless communism, captain, sir!"

And then the siren wailed.

Halupalai bolted out of his chair, started his scatback dash past the picture-window vista, and pivoted sharply under the howling klaxon. In the hallway he opened up his long-yardage sprint and collided with the terror-struck Vietnamese counter boy, sending him sprawling back into the darkened cafeteria from which he had been emerging. Halupalai did not pause. The clock was on him now. He had no illusions, no fears, about anything else. This was a drill. That was fear enough. Someone somewhere had a stopwatch on him. So he raced against it, against the others, against the unseen evaluators, against the looming end of his own usefulness.

In the shriek of the siren, Kazaklis heard World War Three. He always did, despite his words to Halupalai, and he wanted it that way. Some always heard drill, to keep their sanity. A few always heard more, to keep the adrenaline pulsing, to keep their speed at optimum. Kazaklis always heard more, and as he wheeled into the hallway, he trailed Halupalai only slightly. He knew Halupalai had to be first. He understood the Hawaiian's need. Still, he would not give him an inch, not lag a quarter-stride now to serve that need. If Halupalai got there before Kazaklis, it would be because Halupalai beat Kazaklis.

Moreau, lying on her bunk in a sleepy reverie, landed on her feet before her brain fully changed gears. Her roommate moved simultaneously, the reflexes automatic, and the two women wedged in the door before Moreau elbowed out first, ripping the chastity belt in the scuffle. Halupalai shot past. Moreau slipped in front of Kazaklis and broke into long, strong strides. Kazaklis cut off the tanker pilot, causing her to stumble.

Tyler, his head swimming in the money curves that would guarantee his family's long-term security, slapped his book shut. He jammed his feet into poised boots, tucking the laces without tying them, and joined the race. In the Alert Facility all minds, except one, were blank.

O'Toole shuddered. His heart leaped, his stomach sank, and he burst out of the icy shower without turning off the water. Radnor stood there, already pulling his flight suit rapidly over his sweaty body. Radnor glanced quickly, with no facial sign of sympathy, at his drenched crewmate. O'Toole caught the look, silently answering it with "Oh, shit!" in his eyes.

"You gonna have one very clean, very cold fanny, pal," Radnor said as he spun out of the room.

O'Toole grabbed a towel, discarded it immediately, seconds ticking away, and pulled his suit over his dripping body. He forced his wet feet, bare, into his boots, grabbed his socks and his underwear and his flight jacket, and started running. At the locker-room doorway he lurched after another towel for later, missed, dropped his socks, paused, forgot the socks, goddamn these drills, and stepped back up to full speed. He was scared, like a kid on the way to the dentist—not of the wrench of the dental pliers but of the quick stab of the needle. It was going to be balls-freezing cold out there. But he ran.

Outside the Alert Facility a soft mantle of powdery snow blanketed everything except the polished runways, the floodlit B-52's, and the bulbous brown tankers. Fairchild's darkened roads throbbed surreally in the undulating fog-light orange of the scramble signals. A few blue alert trucks sped through the burned light. All others pulled quickly onto the highway shoulders. In the tower a young air controller watched traffic screens monitoring flights at both Fairchild and nearby Spokane International. He quickly aborted an F-15 fighter-interceptor coming in for a touch-and-go landing. But he was drawn away from the flight-control screens to the other computers and their coded printouts. He had heard the sirens, seen his world turn flexing orange, many times before. But this time he paled, the acne on his twenty-one-year-old face turning scarlet against a mask gone white.

Icarus glanced sideways almost stealthily, feeling as if he were intruding into a valued colleague's soul. At his right sat Harpoon. The admiral. Suddenly the general wished he had come to know him better. His number two. They came and went so fast in this business. Odd job for a sailor, holed up down here running SIOP and the targeting staff. But his number two was always a sailor, always a submariner, a bow to the Navy's persuasive role in nuclear deterrence. Nuclear war, buddy boy, Icarus told himself. The game just changed. The admiral was white-haired and open-collared. His face was tanned and Marlboro-man craggy, a contradiction in a man who spent so much of his life away from the sun, deep beneath the sea, prowling. The red police-car lights of the Command Post whipped across Harpoon's forehead as his unrevealing eyes darted almost imperceptibly between the large missile-display screen and the row of relentless clocks. The clocks said six minutes past midnight, Omaha time; 0606 Zulu. Twenty-four minutes left for Omaha, perhaps two minutes for the President.

"Turn off the fucking red lights," Icarus barked into the P.A. system. "We know we got an emergency, for Christ's sake."

He turned squarely toward the admiral, eyeballing him across the bank of multicolored phones on the Command Balcony. He had to send the man out now, off in the giant *E-4* command plane idling on a runway just minutes away. Then the country would have at least two command planes up. Harpoon in the *E-4;* Alice, his friend and fellow general, already up in the always-flying *Looking Glass* plane. They would run the show after he was gone. That was the system. Harpoon also had another job—finding a surviving President. Any surviving President, most likely a successor. Harpoon turned slowly to face him and stared without expression at the general.

"It's time to go, admiral," Icarus said softly.

"The Navy doesn't like to abandon ship, general."

"This is my ship, admiral. You got a new one now."

"Still . . ."

"You don't want me to order you to do your duty."

"No."

The admiral rose, picked up the satchel at his side, gazed one last time down at the men below, and then snapped a salute. The general saluted back.

"Godspeed," Icarus said.

"God grace," Harpoon replied.

The general watched the sailor's ramrod-straight back move across the Command Balcony. The admiral tapped a young escort on the shoulder. Even now, twenty minutes before the No Lone Zone beneath Omaha would become most lonely indeed, the admiral could not move alone here. The two of them disappeared around the balcony's corner and the general returned his attention to the screens.

The admiral moved quickly now, striding into a tiny hallway and up to the vault door that sealed the post off against gases and biological spores. At one time, long ago, the door offered some blast protection. Not now. Man had moved beyond defense in that area. Two guards, dressed ranger-style in berets and ascots, stood barrierlike at the door. Holsters were unsnapped over pearl-handled pistols.

"Open it up," the admiral said.

"Sir," one protested firmly, the awe of military brass ruthlessly drummed out of him.

"Open it."

"Sir. I am not allowed."

"You been practicing practices, son," the admiral said without rancor. "The door will be opened." Harpoon gestured at the red cipher box behind them. "Zebra One, Charlie Six, Zebra Three, Alpha One-Niner." The guard fingered his sidearm, as he had been trained, then turned and punched the instructions into the code box. He looked up without expression and asked: "Code word?"

"Jericho." And the walls came tumbling, Harpoon thought.

"Jericho," the guard repeated in an emotionless voice. He turned and spun the wheel on the back of the door. The door hissed, then gave way. The admiral and his escort moved quickly through it into an empty hallway. The door hissed behind them, sealed again, for the last time now. The admiral glanced at an elevator door, decided against trusting technology tonight, and headed for the stairway, choosing the short walk to the surface. He took the stairs two at a time, followed by his escort. At the top, he met two more stern guards.

"ID, sir," the first said.

The admiral unsnapped the sealed plastic card from his shirt pocket, handed it to the young man, and watched as the card passed first under ultraviolet light and then through an electronic authenticator.

"Right hand," the guard said.

The admiral laid his hand on a plastic square. He thought he felt the probes tickle but knew that was his imagination.

"Code."

"Jericho."

"Your card, sir," the guard said, returning the ID. "The alert truck is at the door."

The admiral wheeled away, then paused briefly to look back at his escort. "You can't go," Harpoon said.

"I know, sir."

"You can't go back, either."

"I know that, too, sir. Maybe I can find a good gin-rummy game in the cafeteria. Stakes ought to be out of sight tonight."

The admiral looked deep into the young man's face. There was no fear in it. "Good luck, son," Harpoon said. He turned away from the young man quickly and began sprinting now. "Shove it up their commie asses, admiral." The voice trailed off behind him. He ran down the office-hallway entrance to SAC headquarters, past the bust of Curtis LeMay and the glass-encased red phone, and stiff-armed the outside door.

The cold air and the undulating orange alert lights hit him simultaneously. The orange lights played discolike on the neutered mockup of a symbolic Minuteman missile planted for tourists in the snow-covered front yard of the base. The missile seemed to point toward a heaven lost, and momentarily his mind tripped into disarray. The colored lights of a proud nation caromed off a different white symbol reaching toward a different heaven. He shivered, not from the cold but from the flash of the memory, a honeymoon many years ago. It had seemed the right place, the right time; Washington, Fourth of July, after his graduation from Annapolis. He and his bride sat on a Virginia hillside across the Potomac on a muggy night so unlike this one. The world lay at their feet, as did the majesty of a nation he would serve, the rockets' red glare splashing off the Washington Monument, dancing among the flags circling its base. They held each other very close. Life with a submariner, months away beneath the sea, was not going to be easy. Never say good-bye, she said as the sparks of the last rocket faded.

Now she was asleep, alone four miles away in a mock-colonial home too large with their only son grown and gone. He shook his head, ducked it under the open doorway of the blue alert truck, and said, "Bust ass."

The President stood impatiently in the Situation Room, surrounded by oppressive gray file cabinets filled with background reports on trouble areas and the latest twenty-four-hour summaries of activities in every nation in the world. He was two floors below the Sitting Room, one floor directly below the Oval Office, having come here hurriedly in his bathrobe, but not for the security his staff had urged on him. He came for the telegram. He glanced at the clock: 0606 Zulu.

The telegraph operator, an Army Signal Corpsman wearing a forced look of detachment, handed the message to his bathrobe-clad Commander-in-Chief. The President began reading quickly.

"My dear Mr. President," the telegram began. "By now you are aware that my government has launched a limited number of nuclear weapons at your country. The missiles are selectively destined for targets which will inflict minimal damage on your nation, its civilian population, and even your military resources. Your wisdom, at this delicate time, can minimize the consequences of this event, which the mistakes of both of our nations have made inevitable. I pray that this may not be another of those mistakes. . . ."

The President let out a low whoosh of air. Mother, he thought bleakly, I'm dealing with a mad general, a rampaging computer, and now a commie religious nut who prays while he nukes me. The paper began to shake in his hand.

". . . While your warning system undoubtedly has described the attack which is about to arrive, I want absolutely no misunderstanding. We have struck all your bomber bases. There is no way to make a nuclear attack palatable. But these are the least reliable, most vulnerable, and most expendable of your forces. They also cost us billions to defend against, and we no longer can afford the cost. We have launched token attacks against a few Minuteman installations, away from population concentrations, and an attack on your Trident submarine base. These attacks show the obvious: all your targets, like all ours, are vulnerable. Omaha and Cheyenne Mountain will be destroyed. Your command facilities are undefendable, as are ours. I have attempted with great effort to limit civilian casualties. This has not been entirely possible, because your system has allowed civilian populations to thrive around strategic targets. We have never understood that peculiarity of your system. So be it. There is one final element. A single small warhead has been directed at Andrews Air Force Base. My generals promise me it will do little damage beyond the base. The target is symbolic, Andrews being the base from which you normally would leave Washington. We know you have other departure routes, just as you have command facilities that will take over from Omaha. I opposed the inclusion of this target, but in achieving far greater gains for both our nations, I was forced to compromise. Some of my colleagues demanded the inclusion of an intimidation factor. I doubt you will be intimidated. It will do you no personal harm. . . ."

The President knew every eye in the Situation Room was on him. He did not like the feeling. He fought to control the shaking. Why? And why this way? His mind floated woozily back to his Inauguration Day and the ride up Pennsylvania Avenue with his predecessor. He did not like the man he had beaten and did not particularly respect him, a feeling he knew was mutual. The inaugural ride had been mostly silent. Then, as the procession made the final turn toward the Capitol, the outgoing President finally broke the silence.

"What would you do if, the moment you took your hand off the Bible today, the Soviets hit you with a BOOB attack?" The question was quiet and serious.

"I'm sorry, sir," he had replied, not sure he had heard.

"If the Russians hit you with a BOOB attack?"

"A what attack?"

"A BOOB attack."

He had turned away from the crowds outside the limo and met eyes that bored in on him, the way he felt other eyes boring now. "Afraid you've got me there," he replied, the crowds smile still on his face. "Thought I'd been briefed on 'em all. What the hell is a BOOB attack?"

"Bolt out of the blue. No warning at all."

"We both know that's the least likely scenario." The President-elect didn't like his predecessor's tone. This was *his* day, dammit. "Guess that's why they gave it that acronym, huh?"

"Don't kid yourself. You don't have the space to kid yourself now. We say it's the least likely because it's the only one for which we can conceive of no humanly acceptable response. Therefore it won't happen. We're very good at rationalizing. Everything nuclear is a rationalization. The Japanese started World War II with a BOOB attack."

"This is different. This is nuclear. Only a boob would do it."

"Maybe. We ended World War II with a BOOB attack. A nuclear BOOB attack. The Soviets reminded me of that many times. And don't kid yourself about our wonderful propensity for acronyms. For most of our political lifetimes we've been living with a nuclear policy known as Mutual Assured Destruction. If each side has enough to totally destroy the other, neither side will use it. Nice rationalization, that one. Nice acronym, too. MAD."

The President-elect had stopped smiling and stared eye to eye with the man he was succeeding. Then he broke into a grin again.

"Well, at my age, I don't think I'll let boobs keep me awake nights," he said, and turned to resume waving to the crowds.

"That's too bad," he heard over his shoulder.

The conversation had confirmed his opinion of the man he had defeated. The man was damned rude.

O'Toole collided with the raw outside air last but at full stride. The first icy assault froze the hair inside his nostrils, then seared the inside of his lungs. Jackhammer pain racked his head. Icy darts jabbed through the soles of his boots, slicing at the nerves in his wet feet. His brain, overwhelmed by the sensory overload, went blank as he careened down the out-ramp, only his instincts and training propelling him after his crewmates.

Near the wingtip, Moreau edged past Halupalai, lung fog billowing over her shoulder. Kazaklis moved past, too, enveloping the Hawaiian in their mist. Moreau scrambled up the belly hole first, clambering up the inky stairwell toward the hypnotic lure of the dim red glow of the cockpit lights two levels above. Kazaklis entered next, his groping hand landing high on the inside of the copilot's leg before reaching the railing.

"You bastard," Moreau spat over her shoulder.

"Move it, Moreau," Kazaklis shot back. "I've felt better thighs on a Safeway fryer."

That wasn't true. But he had been regretting the foolishness of his move on Moreau for six long months now. There were plenty of pelvic bones. And she knew damn well there was nothing sexual about a stray hand in the chimney of the B-52. Not with the clock running.

Moreau cursed herself silently. She was having a bad night. She knew the hand had strayed accidentally. She could have saved herself a lot of grief six months ago. But she wasn't a grief-saver. And when he came at her with that Captain Shazam of the Strategic Air Command crap—the same line, she imagined, that rounded the heels of every female in the High Pine Lounge—she had shrieked in laughter. Not that any line would have worked. Moreau had been on the Kazaklis trip herself, matched him conquest for conquest, she was sure. But she had stopped a year ago, looking for a better hold on a very shaky life. Like everything she did, she also stopped with a totality bordering on obsession. She hadn't been with a man for more than a year, ending the earlier obsession with what might have been the consummate sex act in the history of SAC. In a No Lone Zone. Well, she hadn't violated security. She sure as hell hadn't been alone.

At the top of the stairwell, Moreau glanced sideways at the code box on the jump seat and hurried forward to the right-hand seat. She pulled the white helmet over her head, adjusted the radio to all five channels. Kazaklis, immediately behind her, slipped into the left-hand seat and did the same, his mind as far from their flare-up as hers now.

"Ignition," Kazaklis said in a crackling, radio-warped voice, which Moreau echoed. Then the pilot's sinewy hands, covered in fireproofed gloves, began manipulating the eight white engine throttles between them and Moreau began the methodical activation of other instruments. The engine roar gradually accelerated.

Kazaklis glanced at the luminous dial of his watch and mentally complimented himself. They had made it very quickly, under three minutes. Then he began to chafe, waiting impatiently for the codes. He turned and peered into the dark recesses of the back of the compartment. There, over the locked code box, he

saw two vague forms. One, Halupalai, he thought, grabbed the
other, O'Toole, and shook him violently. He saw Halupalai's arm
rear back and then plunge forward toward O'Toole's face.

"Codes!" Kazaklis said angrily into the radio. "Have you fuckers
gone crazy back there? Codes!"

The President's appointments secretary shook him gently by
the elbow. "Finish it, Mr. President," his old friend said. "There is
so little time." It was only then that the President realized his eyes
had drifted away from the telegram. His aide smelled of bourbon.
Lucky fellow.

". . . It is of epochal importance that you understand my ra-
tionale and recognize that this is not an act of aggression. Two
weeks ago the Politburo voted to mount a full Counterforce attack
against all your military and strategic targets simultaneously, with
a second assault poised against your cities if you responded. It was
the attack my country's military leaders have advocated for
years—sudden, preemptive, and total. You would not have survived. We would not have survived either, although not all in my
government agree with that assessment. I was able to delay that
action. But I have merely bought us a brief moment for one last
effort to halt the madness. Our meeting in Vienna was a similar
effort. It failed. The misunderstandings ran deeper than my
worst expectations. What you apparently perceived as my weakness was in reality an effort to warn you how fragile was the
balance of the debate within my government over the threat of
your massive arms buildups. The failure of Vienna tipped that
balance. The cost of matching you weapon for weapon is far too
great for the Politburo faction that sees our social fabric ripping
because of the immense investments we made to draw even with
you in nuclear weaponry after the Cuban debacle. The cost of
allowing you to proceed unmatched is far too great for the faction
that believes we cannot ever be at bay again as we were during the
1962 crisis. I must say that I see the point of both factions. I think
we all, the leaders of both our nations, knew that someday something would have to give. . . ."

Something would have to give. . . . The President read hurriedly,
but part of his mind drifted to his triumphant return from
Vienna and the summit meeting with the young, new, and pre-
sumably inexperienced Soviet Premier. On the flight over, the
Secretary of State had badgered him for hours about being tough.
The Soviets, the Secretary had said, are like burglars who walk

down a hotel hallway trying every door until they find one unlocked. Lock every door on them, Mr. President. During the summit conference, the Premier had surprised him. He had almost
pleaded with him to back down on the weapons buildup. The
President had stonewalled, as prompted, telling the Premier to
loosen his grip on Eastern Europe if he wanted to talk arms re-
ductions. On the return flight the Secretary gloated ecstatically.
This was a complete affirmation of the administration's policy.
The new toughness had left the Soviets in an American policy
pincer movement. The Soviets were trapped with an ailing economy, the Secretary beamed, and the Vienna meeting had forced
them to make choices among escalating arms costs, the relentless
ruble drain needed to prop up the satellite nations, and the increasingly tense internal pressure for consumer goods demanded
by a deprived citizenry. Now something would have to give, the
Secretary enthused, and it could even be the Soviet system itself.

". . . I confess, Mr. President, to a persistent fantasy. I had fan-
tasized that proliferation of nuclear weapons among other nations
was a good thing. Perhaps two less stable nations, with small arsenals, would use their weapons first and take the monkey, to use
your idiom, off our backs. Perhaps a million people would have
been killed, but the horror would bring both our nations to their
senses. We had no such luck. The monkey remains on our backs,
his claws dug in deeply. At best, now, we can become the symbols
that my fantasy would have passed on to other nations. To be
blunt, Mr. President, you have three choices, only two of which
are acceptable to us. You can accept the damage and we will stop,
the world divided between us as it is now. Like you, I am a politician. I cannot imagine my political system allowing me to accept
that choice, as clearly as we would prefer it. Your second choice is
to respond with a limited counterattack that inflicts upon my nation a similar amount of military damage and other losses. We will
accept that, provided the world's spheres of influence remain the
same and the arms increases cease. Our calculations show that you
will lose six to nine million persons in our attack. We will accept a
similar loss. It is a tremendous price to pay. But perhaps it can
serve as the symbol my fantasy would have granted to Riyadh or
Islamabad. Perhaps, without ending all our aspirations, it can
show all factions in both our nations the madness of the game we
have been playing. The losses are huge, but smaller and more
survivable than the world's losses in earlier wars. It has a certain
raw logic—considerably more than your third choice, which is not

acceptable to us. You will be under tremendous pressure, as was I, to respond massively. If this is your ultimate choice, my government already has decided to reply in kind, even before your missiles land. I pray now, Mr. President, that the distrust is not total and that, through the pain of the next few minutes, you make the decision that can bring this to a less-than-perfect end, but an end."

Halupalai slapped O'Toole hard, very hard, the snapping impact of the blow cracking through the rising engine noise like shattering glass. O'Toole did not flinch. Halupalai's eyes adjusted slowly to the red night lights of the cramped upper crew compartment. At O'Toole's side, just below the code box, the young airman's underwear and flight jacket lay in a discordant heap. O'Toole stood woodenly over the box, his hands clasped between his legs, as if to warm them. Halupalai struck him again, his open hand whipsawing back and forth across O'Toole's face.

"Mama," O'Toole mouthed through the noise, his hands pulling up quickly, then dropping helplessly at his sides.

The noise from the B-52's eight jet engines rose in a whining crescendo. Halupalai's mind cartwheeled in a jumble of thoughts. What was the matter with O'Toole? In the dim light he could barely see him. But this was such a routine function—a simple, simultaneous key turn with separate keys, then an elementary working of separate, but simple, combination locks. They had done it scores of times together, quickly and efficiently providing the data that enabled Kazaklis to say no-go and shut down the engines. Now Kazaklis was cursing at them on the radio. But O'Toole wasn't even wearing his helmet and couldn't hear the curses.

Halupalai hit him again, a high blow above the cheekbone, and the Hawaiian felt a sharp splinter nick at his hand. His vision sharpening, he saw that O'Toole's eyebrows were frozen white in ragged shards of ice. Halupalai winced for the poor bastard. He'd been in the damned shower again. He had to get out of here fast. But no one was getting out of the B-52, which was as cold as the freezing outside air, until the code box was open.

"Gunner!" Kazaklis rasped into Halupalai's earphones. "Maybe you'd like a Russian heat-seeker up your rosy-red patooie? Get the codes! Now!"

Briefly Halupalai bristled. "I'm dealing with a block of ice back here, commander," Halupalai snapped. "O'Toole's soaking wet, frozen like a damned side of beef. I can't get him to move."

"Kick him in the balls. Do something. O'Toole, you son of a bitch, if Halupalai doesn't kick you in the balls, I'll come back there and you'll never use those precious jewels of yours again."

"He can't hear you, sir. His helmet's off."

"Jesus. Hook him up."

Halupalai jammed the white helmet over O'Toole's unmoving head and attached the radio joint.

"O'Toole? Can you hear me, you icon-worshiping Irish potatohead?"

"Mama," O'Toole replied.

"Oh, Jesus wept," Kazaklis groaned.

"As well He might," Moreau added.

"Shut up, Moreau."

"You're the aircraft commander, commander."

"And what would you do, copilot?"

"Go back there and warm him up, one way or the other."

"That'll be the day."

Moreau unsnapped her shoulder harness, pulled off her helmet, reached in a pocket for the standard red-filtered penlight, and wheeled out of her seat. The tiny beam of light wobbled toward the two dark figures a dozen feet away. Approaching Halupalai, she motioned for his helmet. Then she turned on the immobile pillar of O'Toole.

"Lieutenant O'Toole," Moreau snarled, her voice grinding like a penny in a vacuum cleaner. "We are in combat conditions. Give me the key."

O'Toole stood mesmerized by the steel-blue eyes glinting out of the soft red halo of Moreau's helmet. His lips began to move wordlessly.

"The key." The penny rattled up the vacuum tube.

"Suh . . . cur . . . uty," O'Toole mumbled. "Security vi . . . lay . . . shun."

"Then do it yourself, lieutenant. Do your duty. Now. Right now."

"Mama," O'Toole reverted.

"Jesus," Kazaklis interrupted. "Kick him in the gonads. I'm not kidding, Moreau. Kick him in the balls."

Moreau edged closer to O'Toole, slid the helmet visor down so her head was almost fully encased, and placed the penlight on her chin, shining the red rays up inside the visor. Halupalai took a step back at the vision.

"Give me the key," Moreau repeated, her voice turned softly singsong.

O'Toole stared, his eyes widening in fear.

"Give me the key," the haunting rhythm of her voice insisted.

"Angelus mortuorum," O'Toole murmured.

"The key, lieutenant," the words danced.

He gave her the key, his ungloved hand touching hers with the burning bite of dry ice.

"Give me the combination."

He mumbled a short, simple sequence of numbers.

Moreau then tugged at Halupalai, bent over the code box, and they entered the keys, turning them simultaneously. She nodded at him and they spun the twin combination locks. The top of the square gray box popped open and she reached in for two code folders. She handed one to Halupalai, pulling at him so his ear was near her mouth.

"Strap him in," she shouted above the full pitch of the engines. "We'll get him out of here soon."

Then she threaded her way through the dark, narrow walkway back to her seat. It was as cold as a meat locker in here, she thought. Colder.

The President's eyes lingered on the end of the message. He struggled with the urge to hand it to someone. Of the group surrounding him, he was not sure to whom he should hand it. Sixteen hours earlier he had sat in this same room with the Secretary of State, the Secretary of Defense, his national security adviser, the head of the CIA, all the king's men discussing all the king's horses—the missiles, the submarines, the top-secret plans to deploy laser weapons in space. The next meeting was scheduled in eight hours. He chuckled, without mirth. Bit of a wait, considering the circumstances.

He looked up and saw the young duty officer, Sedgwick, staring at him strangely.

Something would have to give . . .

The words surged through the President.

Shrewd buggers, aren't they . . .

The duty officer held the phone.

No humanly acceptable response . . . Therefore it won't happen . . . Don't kid yourself . . .

The duty officer's eyes pleaded.

Won't lose any sleep . . .
The duty officer placed the phone in his hand.
That's too bad . . .
The duty officer lifted his hand to his head.
That's too bad . . .
The duty officer shook his arm gently.
"How long?" the President asked bleakly into the phone.
"Forty-five seconds," the general answered.
"The warhead is aimed at Andrews." The President's words seemed to come from outside him. "Surgical ground burst. Symbolic."
"Horse pucky," the general said angrily.
"The missile is aimed at Andrews."
"I doubt very much the missile was aimed at Andrews," the general said, biting off each word. "I know it will not land there. Its trajectory already has taken it beyond Andrews."
"The missile is aimed at Andrews."
"This is no time for delusion, Mr. President."
The President's shuddering stopped. He had to believe. No humanly acceptable response. His mind cleared.
"Put SIOP on this problem," he said to the general. "I want a responsive attack designed as closely as possible as a carbon copy of the Soviet attack. Take out all the Russian surface-to-air missile bases, or some equivalent, plus token ICBM installations and a submarine base. . . ."
The President paused, ever so briefly, just long enough for Icarus to understand that his leader grasped the nature of the next trade, a knight for a knight, Icarus being his knight.
"Take out their primary command facility." The President grew giddy at the simple brutality of the trade, flippantly adding, "Drop a little one, surgically, into the can in the Premier's dacha in Sochi."
The President shook his head sharply.
"Sorry. Forget that. Put the same kilotonnage coming at Andrews on Vnukovo Air Field outside Moscow. Leave the rest of their strategic system intact. Under no circumstances is the scenario to kill more than nine million Soviet citizens. Not one more. Do you understand?"
The President could feel the hostility seethe through the silence.
"Do you understand?" he repeated sternly.
"Mr. President," the general said coldly, "you are being conned

on a level unprecedented in human history. The disaster will be equally unprecedented, your role in it parallel to that of Nero's foolishness."

The President sighed. "General, I will hear no more of this. I want the response designed immediately. Instruct your computer. When the response is programmed, I will activate the codes through the civilian authorities and the Joint Chiefs, who will transmit them to you instantly, as the law requires."

The President handed the phone to the duty officer with a look far more persuasive than any military command the young naval officer had ever received. The President, seconds away from the answer to part of his riddle, slumped into an armchair in which he had been briefed daily on tribesmen crossing far-off frontiers, on British ministers jeopardizing NATO secrets through liaisons with European heiresses, and countless other international crises, large and small. He closed his eyes. In the background he could hear the Premier's words repeated mechanically into the phone. A teletype was clattering. He took absolutely no heed of either. He held a small blue-and-red card, encased in plastic like a fancy credit card. It said "Sealed Authenticator System" and contained various coded numbers and letters. It identified him as the man who could unloose the weapons. It rested loosely in his limp hand.

Two minutes after Harpoon emerged from the bowels of Omaha, twenty-two minutes left on the clocks Icarus watched, the blue alert truck squealed to a stop on a darkened runway outside SAC headquarters. The engine roar of the giant *E-4* command plane, a specially refitted Boeing 747, deafened the admiral. He glanced quickly at the words "UNITED STATES OF AMERICA" stripped across its side. It was an exact replica of the plane that might still be waiting for the President at Andrews.

The admiral leaped out of the truck, scurried up the stairs into the plane, and snap-saluted a handful of Air Force officers waiting near the hatch. He said nothing, hurrying toward the front of the windowless plane, double-timing it up a spiral staircase to the quarters a President would use. He looked at a bank of multicolored phones and a small table inside a square of four blue swivel chairs. He sat down, placing his satchel to the side, and picked up a white phone with twenty-two button lights. He pushed one, connecting him to the pilot, a major who wore a black eyepatch. "Get this bird moving," he said.

He paused for a second, trying to get the chill out of his bones.

Then he picked up a yellow phone, with buttons connecting him to the outside. He punched one. "Diogenes," a voice responded instantly, although the voice was a thousand miles distant in a bunker buried beneath the winter-brown horse country of Virginia. "Harpoon," the admiral said.

"The list is tentative."

"Come on, I know that."

"Looks like Number Eight."

"Jesus, that far down?"

"Afraid so."

"Location?"

The admiral listened carefully and frowned. "Good for him," Harpoon said after a second. "Not so good for me."

"Maybe you won't need him."

"Maybe."

The admiral hung up the direct-line connection to the civilian Presidential Successor Locator, an underground unit that coordinated the location of potential successors with missile-impact areas. He knew the first Soviet submarine-launched missiles were just now landing. He also knew the successor locators had to make their calculations before all the missiles, especially the ICBM's, landed. Afterward would be too late. Communications would go. The locator probably would go.

Number Eight. Good God, for a limited attack, we're going to lose one helluva lot of bigwigs. He tried to remember which Cabinet officer was eighth in the constitutional line of succession. Then, without coming up with an answer, Harpoon felt the huge aircraft lift ponderously off the strip and away from Omaha.

Kazaklis flicked the red terrain-monitoring radar on and off again in front of him. The computer converted the handful of ground personnel and the flight hangars outside the plane into sharp-edged pinnacles that moved from right to left across the screen, like a wildly gyrating stock-market chart. When the ragged obstructions reached the left edge, they reformed and raced left to right. He could read their crazy jumble the way a concertmaster reads musical scores, catching every inflection. In the corner he checked the elevation reading for the Fairchild runways, coordinating it to sea level on another altimeter.

"Two. Four. Five. Seven," he said.

"Two. Four. Five. Seven," Moreau repeated, reading the numbers off her own instruments.

"Los Angeles moratorium?" he asked.

"Angelus mortuorum," she replied brusquely, not liking the interruption of the routine.

"What the hell is that, college girl?"

"Grade-school Latin, commander. It means 'angel of death.'"

Kazaklis glanced sideways at Moreau's ghostly image reflected in her red radar screen. He laughed. "So you put the wrath of the church in our haunted Irishman. Spooked it out of him. Not bad. I figured you'd like the ball-breaking approach better."

"Fuck off, Kazaklis. We need to get the poor bastard out of here. You're the one who thinks all this is real every time we're out here. Get your fucking job done."

"You'd better think it's real, angel. It's simpler that way. That means the missiles are on their way down. And you, death bird, have the codes."

Kazaklis returned to his routine, hunching over the yellow clutter of his flight-panel lights, nudging the engine revolutions carefully, checking the flaps, spinning past scores of routine oil-pressure, water, fuel, altimeter, oxygen gauges he normally would be doing in tandem with Moreau. Hastily he ran a final check on the bright yellow squares at his right, just beyond the throttles. "Bomb Doors Not Latched," read one. "Bomb Doors Open," read the next. "Bomb Doors Not Closed and Locked," read the fourth. The third, which remained dark, read: "Bombs Released." One by one the yellow lights blipped off as he secured the doors. He felt tense, but good. From the babble coming from outside the plane he could tell that despite the trouble, he remained in flight sequence. First. As squadron leader.

"Code check ready, commander," Halupalai's formal voice cut in.

"Code check ready," Kazaklis repeated.

Halupalai began methodically. "Zero. Zero. Alpha. Hotel. One. Nin-er. Zero. Three. Quebec. Nin-er. Quebec."

Kazaklis repeated the calls carefully, punching each into the new decoder to which Omaha flashed the sequence during each alert. The hair crawled on his arms.

"Sequence two," he requested of Halupalai.

"Zebra. Zebra. Zebra. Six. Zero. Two. Nin-er. Nin-er. Fox-trot."

Kazaklis froze. Something was wrong. Sequence two was one digit off a go. They never made them that close, unless SAC was into one of its cockeyed new PRP tests.

"Copilot," he ordered. "Recheck sequence two."

"Zebra. Zero. Zebra—" Moreau began.

Kazaklis interrupted her instantly. "Code word!" he demanded of Halupalai.

"Trinity."

Gawd, the pilot's mind raced, thirty years of daily code-word changes, and he got Trinity.

"Voice confirmation," Kazaklis said into the direct channel to the tower. "Sequence one, go. Sequence two, go. Code: Trinity. Confirm."

"Confirm Trinity," a solemn voice, touched with a Bronx accent, replied. "Confirm go."

Inside the Buff, the radio went deathly silent. Then Kazaklis placed his hands on the throttles and began the crew check.

"Copilot ready?"

"Ready," Moreau replied.

"Nav ready?"

"Ready," Tyler responded.

The voice from the control tower cut in, its tone hysterically different. "Go! For God's sake, man, go! Get your bloody ass out of here. Go! Go! Go! This one is no shit!"

The voice almost wept. Kazaklis stopped the crew check and hit the throttles. He was calm, feeling the dance of danger he loved.

"*Melech hamafis,*" the tower voice whispered.

The words sailed past Kazaklis. He was rolling now, the engines growing deafening in their roar.

"Any questions?" he radioed to his crewmates, the tone commanding and nonchalant.

"Any jokes?" he asked.

B O P H U . . .

The President opened his eyes slowly.

T H A T . . .

He strained to focus, lost everything in a blur, then focused again.

S W A N A

The lettering, in large black capitals, formed fuzzily in front of him in a slightly skewed, dream-world eye chart reading vertically. His legs felt leaden. His head seemed propped high on a soft pillow. He tried to move and felt the pillow ripple like Jell-O. He turned and immediately became violently sick. His head rested on his appointment secretary's belly. A huge gray file cabinet, still locked tight with its contents marked "TOP SECRET" in stark red, lay across his old friend's face and chest. Red also seeped out from beneath the cabinet, rivulets edging across the pillow toward the President's head. He tried to wrench away, but Bophuthatswana, and years of American intelligence on the tiny all-black African nation, pinned his legs to the floor in a similar gray cabinet. Sedgwick, the duty officer, was pulling at the file cabinet to free him.

"Hang tough, Mr. President," the duty officer said. "Have you out in a minute."

As Sedgwick heaved at the file cabinet, the President scanned the Situation Room. His last formal briefing here had been confident and absolutely secure, with elaborately locked doors sealing off the rest of the world. Now the chairs were scattered about, the conference table cracked, files scattered, the main door sprung closed, jammed on its hinges. Pieces of acoustical ceiling wobbled loosely above him, as if caught in a breeze. The Zulu clock was frozen on 0608—eight minutes past one in the morning. Still, the room was far from destroyed. In one corner the Emergency War Orders officer stood unruffled, his suit hardly mussed, his black briefcase intact. He wore his usual blank expression. Others were moving about the room methodically.

"So where'd we get it?" the President asked.

"Not exactly sure," Sedgwick replied, finally rolling the cabinet off his legs. "Somewhere northwest of here. Definitely not southeast at Andrews. Not close. Not far. Coupla miles."

"Why are we alive?"

He immediately regretted the question, for he knew his old friend, who seemed to be the only casualty, was not. A wave of dizziness hit him. But his mind was clearer now. He struggled painfully to pull away from the body.

"Take it easy, Mr. President. The explosion was relatively small. I think they were telling the truth about a ground burst, which, as you know, digs a big hole but concentrates the damage. Not like Hiroshima. They were trying to be surgical. That's for sure."

"So we've got a big hole a couple of miles from the White House. What else?"

"Well, unless it landed in the park, it had to strike a residential area, upper Northwest Washington probably. Out near the cathedral, I'd guess. Maybe as far as Chevy Chase, but I doubt it."

"And killed a lot of people."

"At this time of night, probably fifty thousand, maybe more.

Hard to say. The big apartment buildings absorb the shock wave fairly quickly. That's why we're okay."

The President did a quick mental tally. The area was old, established Washington. He had lived there as a young congressman. He guessed a fourth of the Congress lived in the area. So did several members of his Cabinet. And a helluva lot of the national press corps, he thought ruefully. They loved the old oak-lined streets, the quick access down Connecticut and Wisconsin avenues to the power centers of the capital.

"What's upstairs?"

"We haven't been up. Part of the old place must be standing. But the concussion would have made quite a mess."

"Was I out long?"

"No, just seconds, really. Can you move your legs? They don't seem to be broken."

The President struggled to his feet. He felt as if he had been trampled by a horse. He tried not to show it. He also tried not to show the fear.

"What's next?"

"Communications are out. Briefly. The long lines are down, naturally, but the patch will be through quickly. We'll have Omaha back up any second. We could go downstairs to the shelter. I don't see much point, frankly. We really should get you out of here."

Sedgwick paused. Then he added: "You have an interrupted message from the Soviet Premier. It was arriving as communications went down."

The President sighed. "Give it to me."

The telegram was brief.

"Andrews missile malfuntioning. Deep regrets. Target military. Repeat: Target Andrews. All at stake in your belief in my intentions. Our combined will crucial. Other unexpected complications causing . . ."

The message broke off there. The President rubbed his temples, his head swimming again. A minute ago he had seen nothing to lose in waiting. Deep regrets. Good God.

"Omaha's back," Sedgwick interrupted, handing him a phone.

"Hello, general," the President said numbly. "The Preme sends his regrets." He instantly wished he had begun the conversation differently.

"I'll bet," Icarus responded caustically. "His little con didn't work. He overshot Andrews by thirteen miles. The blast wave rolled right up Rock Creek Park and took out Walter Reed. My father was there."

"Sorry," the President said, truly feeling it.

"It's irrelevant. He was sick. He was a soldier. A father should die before his son. The hospital wasn't the target. Andrews wasn't the target. You were the target. Our little wonder weapons aren't as surgical as we like to think. You can't do brain surgery with a nuke. Especially a Navy nuke. You are very lucky, Mr. President. You get what I won't—a second chance."

"A second chance?"

"SIOP is now developing a more appropriate response. There have been some unusual developments. The Premier has got a lot of problems. You get a second chance to save the world from those bastards, Mr. President."

The President glanced around the Situation Room, his memory playing tricks, conjuring up a rhododendron garden he had planted as a young congressman at a happy first Washington home along a quiet street shaded by pin oaks.

"Save the world," the President repeated. "I think we have a different vision of that, general."

Kazaklis felt the Buff's power gush through him, its swept-back wings becoming his wings, its immensity his immensity, its surging fuel his rushing blood. The altimeter, racing up the thermometer stem at the edge of the radar screen, seemed to monitor his adrenaline, too. He heard his voice say flaps up, wheels up. He saw the adrenaline climb to five hundred feet, one thousand, twelve hundred, fifteen hundred, and soar further. He became the Buff. There was nothing else.

For Moreau, PRP ruled as it should. She flew mechanically, robotlike, following the flawless lead of Kazaklis in equally flawless precision. Flaps up, wheels up.

Behind her, the now calm voice of the Fairchild air controller cleared the second B-52, then the third and the fourth. The quietly nasal echo of his farewell probed for an escape from her subconscious. But thoughts did not escape. Moreau's mind was on autopilot. She searched the dark night sky for other aircraft, as she always did on drills. She fine-tuned the moves Kazaklis made, as she always did on drills. Somewhere, the knowledge rested that the air controller's strange farewell was for her. But it was bracketed, closed off, shut away along with the hidden memory of her friendship with the young kid from the Bronx, the speeding drives through the desert that had terrified him so, the black jeep careening through canyon-road turns, barreling across dunes. The drives had stopped, although the big-sister/little-brother friendship had not, after a magnificent autumn day, an Indian-summer sun bleaching the desert with the dancing heat rivulets of one last mirage before winter. Moreau unleashed all the power of the jeep in a rapturous race through the open sagebrush. She dug into deep sand unexpectedly, spun wildly, flipped, banged the roll bar violently into the desert ground, and landed wheels down. She came up squealing in delight, grinning from ear to ear. The kid's face went bloodless. "Melech hamafis," he said quietly. It was some time before she learned the meaning of the Yiddish phrase, and it did not penetrate now. This is a test. Z-n-n-n-n-n. This station is conducting a test of the Emergency Broadcast System. Z-n-n-n-n-n-n-n.

The whine cut into the PRP-induced veneer around Moreau. It was an alarm whine, routine enough, too, but beckoning her to take control of the climbing bomber from a pilot preoccupied with other tasks. Still, it startled her and her body jerked almost imperceptibly.

She turned and saw Kazaklis reaching for the lead-lined flash curtain. He tugged at the dirty-gray screen, drawing it across his side of the cockpit window. Moreau made no move to pull her curtain, completing their isolation from the night sky and the last of the outside world. This was a drill. It was against regulations to fly with the nuclear blinds drawn on a drill. She had never pulled the curtain. The whine stopped.

"I've got it now, copilot," Kazaklis said. "Pull your curtain."

Moreau looked at him strangely.

"Draw your curtain, copilot."

Moreau exploded. Her words, vibrating in her own helmet, seemed to echo back at her. "Are you nuts, Kazaklis? We've got commercial jets out there, ranchers landing their goddamn Cessnas and Comanches at Spokane International. This brute is a bug-squisher. I'm not pulling the screen in a drill. No way!"

The dull throb of the headache, which Kazaklis had been subduing all day, crept into the pilot's forehead. He wasn't sure if it was Jack Daniel's or Captain Moreau, and he didn't care. "Draw . . . that . . . screen."

Moreau tightened.

"Take the plane, copilot," Kazaklis said, his voice abruptly calm. He lunged out of his seat and reached across the cockpit toward the second curtain. In the closeness, Kazaklis fumbled across Moreau, his gloved hand accidentally catching her in the left eye before grasping the curtain. He felt the plane nose downward as the copilot dropped the controls, pulling her hand over the eye. Kazaklis wrenched at the curtain, succeeding in closing all but a final narrow gap. He struggled back to his seat and pulled the plane upward again.

Moreau was mute, furious at both herself and Kazaklis. Her left hand remained riveted over the eye Kazaklis had struck accidentally. Her right stretched forward to close the gap in the curtain, her one eye fixed on the full winter-white moon she moved to eclipse.

The white moon burst. It burst into a sun, then into ten thousand suns, and the rays washed out the cockpit red. Moreau's eye remained transfixed on the aura of the curtain crack. She was a child again, her father showing her the beauty of the sun's evening rays—Jesus rays, he called them—filtering through pregnant clouds. Then the rays were brighter than Jesus rays, brighter than any sun rays filtered or unfiltered by any cloud. And she saw nothing but white, even after her hand closed the curtain.

"What the hell was that?" Radnor's startled voice came from below.

"Melech hamafis," Moreau answered placidly.

"Mama," O'Toole said. *"Angelus mortuorum,"* he added.

"Knock it off! Everybody!" Kazaklis ordered.

"The kid was trying to tell me," Moreau murmured.

"Moreau . . ." Kazaklis was almost pleading with her now.

"In Yiddish."

"Moreau. Stop babbling. I need you now." His voice had no anger in it, just desperation. Kazaklis turned toward his copilot. She turned toward him.

In the haunted red light of their new cocoon, one of Moreau's eyes peered at Kazaklis in the blazing challenge of its usual unearthly blue. The other stared in dead white. Neither asked for help.

"The kid told me, *Melech hamafis.* The king of death is in the room. He was warning me, saying good-bye."

"Moreau . . ." The pilot's words trailed off. He knew Moreau had felt little if any pain, that the light had quickly burned away the optic nerve. But he didn't know about the rest of her head, and he did know what was coming next.

"PRP's back, Kazaklis," she assured him, the monotone almost as vacant as her eye. "Let's get on with it."

Moreau reached forward and gripped the controls. She also knew what was coming next. She braced herself for the wave.

"Alice here," the baritone voice responded immediately.

"Icarus," the general said unnecessarily, the black phone into which he was speaking connecting only two points—the Command Balcony and the *Looking Glass* plane. "Harpoon's launched."

"I know, sir," the general in the *Looking Glass* replied. "We watched him on radar."

"God damn you!" Icarus exploded. "If you're watching us, you're too damned close to Omaha. I need at least two of you up there, general."

For a moment the phone between the underground post and the flying command post seemed dead, only the low hzzzzzzzz of the radio connection speaking to the contrary. Icarus closed his eyes and took a deep breath. He didn't want to chew on this man. He was too good. The country was very lucky it had him aboard the *Looking Glass* on this night. Sheer luck of the draw, too. Every moment since February 3, 1961—through cold wars with the ultimate adversary in Moscow and hot wars with the pests in Hanoi, through detente and confrontation, through Geneva negotiations and vitriolic speeches at the UN—the *Looking Glass* had been in the air, ready to take command instantly when Omaha went. The fleet of *Looking Glass* planes was outmoded now, modified old Boeing 707's crammed full of communications gear and a battle staff of twenty. But they still served their purpose, eternally vigilant, one always in the air, rotating on eight-hour shifts with the incoming crew up before the outgoing came down. And always with a general officer aboard. But a general of this man's caliber drew the duty no more than once a month. Top-notch. Friend of his, friend of General Moreau's.

"We're okay, sir," Alice interrupted the silence.

"I'm taking a lot of shit from the politicians tonight."

"No apology necessary."

"Apology? You ever hear me apologize to anybody?"

"Just once, sir."

"Bullshit."

"To Moreau."

"No way."

"Well, you were just a pup."

"No way!"

"General, you almost took his wing off."

"How do you remember that?"

"You almost took mine off, too. You were a little eager for a routine strafing practice."

Icarus grunted. "I *was* a pup then. Don't remember any apology, though."

"Well, you and Moreau cussed each other like longshoremen for twenty minutes first."

"Yeah. Then what'd I say?"

"You stuck your chin about an inch from his, standing there on the runway, and said: 'You're right. I was wrong. I apologize. Fuck you.'"

The hzzzzzzz returned. On the Command Balcony, the general averted his eyes from the battle staff. The eyes moistened ever so briefly. Then he chuckled. "Ivan's probably mousing us," Icarus said.

"Probably," Alice replied.

"You let 'em know my one failing in thirty years, asshole."

"Yeah. Just another soft, decadent, capitalist general waiting for his pension and a hundred thou a year at General Dynamics."

"Well, if Ivan's listening, he knows the same thing we do. Every one of his Model T missiles is missing by a country mile. What you think of that, Ivan? A fucking country mile."

Hzzzzzzz.

"Those cretins always did have trouble with anything fancier than a screwdriver," Alice responded.

Hzzzzzzz.

Beneath Omaha, Icarus looked up at the sixteen-foot-missile-display screen. He saw the one with his name on it arching down out of suborbit, edging over the Canadian wastes. It was not missing. High above, flying farther away from Omaha at 42,000 feet, the *Looking Glass* general looked at the same data being relayed to him. Bull's-eye.

"Cretins," Icarus said.

"Cretins," Alice said.

The phone conversation paused briefly.

"Moreau's kid is on alert duty tonight," Icarus said without emotion. "The girl. At Fairchild."

Alice thought a second. "He'd probably prefer it that way."

"Yeah," Icarus said. "You getting all the data? The SIOP data?

Missile-impact projections? The submarine missiles have begun to impact."

"Yes, general."

"My clock says nineteen minutes."

Alice looked at his watch. "0611 Zulu," he said, preferring to mark time that way. Icarus was looking at his execution date. Alice felt uncomfortable—as if he were running away, being up here.

"Even all these misses are gonna knock the shit out of your computers and radio gear."

"I know, sir."

"Might be hours before you get the stuff back up."

"We're good, sir."

Hzzzzzz.

"Yeah, I know you are. It's gonna get busy around here. I'll try to get back up to you with a couple of minutes to go. Harpoon, too. Give you both a last good read. If I'm not arguing with some piss-ant politician."

"Just be your usual diplomatic self, sir."

"You can count on that."

FOUR

To Halupalai, the wave was mystical, almost metaphysical. His earliest memories, those spellbinding image warps of infancy, etched the wave in some magical place in his mind. Even before he could speak, he toddled down to the sandy beach to watch it for hours, entranced. It emerged from the sea, swelling hypnotically until the little boy's neck craned high to watch the sunlight filter through the perfect prism of its curl. Then it crashed, thundering with the infinite power of nature, and sent swirls of foam and churning coral bits and little messages from distances undreamed washing up around the boy's naked feet. He could imagine no power greater. Soon his father taught him how to meld with it, not conquer it, for that was futile and wrong and ungodly. He learned to slice through its awesome strength, his body a spear, and swim far out beyond into the peaceful cradle of the sea. There he would bob for an entire afternoon before returning, stretching his young body rigid to ride the curl. Still later, he learned how to ride inside the curl, caught within the prism of dancing, holy light. He took endless voyages inside the curl, respectful of its power, worshipful of the halo of green-white radiance surrounding him. One day his father took him to the island of Oahu and they traveled north to the remote beach called Makaha. The boy stood mesmerized. The wave rose out of the

75

ocean like a mountain, taller than the palms, taller than the houses. It loomed four, five times as high as anything he had seen on Kauai. The water roiled like a devil's caldron at his feet. He looked up at his father, his eyes asking in both fear and expectation: Is this the next test? His father shook his head no. This was for fools and haoles, mainlanders who believed they could control all forces. A dozen years later, however, Halupalai came back, a high-school boy full of beer and the playful challenges of a California-born schoolmate, a haole who had conquered every wave from Malibu to San Onofre. Halupalai caught the curl of a thirty-footer, riding it flawlessly and ecstatically, never feeling such exhilaration as he pulled himself from the whirlpool tug of the caldron moments later and threw himself on the beach. His friend never came out. They found him later, his spine snapped clean where the curl had landed on it.

As the light invaded the B-52, Halupalai sat with his back to the cockpit. O'Toole sat alongside him. Halupalai closed his eyes instinctively, but even so, even with his back turned, the light was so strong he could see the veins in his eyelids twist like rivers on a roadmap. Just as instinctively, he reached for the ejection lever, as he had in Vietnam. But he pulled his hand back abruptly. He braced himself. He did not want his hand on the lever when this wave hit.

Up front, Kazaklis began counting even before he looked at Moreau. He continued to count as his own flash-shocked vision fought to focus on her one vacant eye. He ticked off the seconds as he implored her to help him push their aircraft higher, higher.

Three . . .

Four . . .

The Buff was tough. But he knew it broke, sometimes under natural forces they still didn't understand. More than once Kazaklis had felt the godawful shudder, heard the thunderous crack of the B-52 in whiplash, as he roared low over mountain ridges where powerful wind currents collided and clashed.

Five . . .

Six . . .

The Air Force kept the occasional crashes as quiet as possible. But Kazaklis heard. And Halupalai heard. And they both knew another Buff's back had been broken, snapped clean by the same kind of roiling forces that cracked a man's back in the ocean surf.

Seven . . .

Eight . . .

Kazaklis did not know what would happen now, for this would be no natural force and no man had ever felt it, no aircraft had ever been subjected to it. He knew only that survival was ninety percent luck of the draw, ten percent him. He would play the ten percent and climb, climb.

Nine . . .

Ten . . .

Moreau pulled with him, thank God for that. It would take both of them. He squinted, trying to readjust his eyes to the red light. The altimeter read 8,500 feet, 8,600.

Eleven . . .

The blast wave arrived with no noise interrupting the engine drone. But Kazaklis felt as if he had been hit in the gut first, then clubbed by a street fighter. The impact hurled him forward into the pinched embrace of his seat harness, then whipped him back. He could feel what he couldn't hear—the B-52's wings groaning under the immense stress. Groggily he fought to keep the plane climbing.

"Get the nose down, Kazaklis!" Moreau's steely voice hammered through the pilot's haze. "Dammit, you're going to stall us!"

Fuzzily Kazaklis concentrated on the air-speed gauge. It read under Mach point-five, about 325 miles an hour, two-thirds of the climb speed just seconds earlier. The horizon indicator seemed to have been blown completely out of kilter, showing them at a thirty-five-degree angle of attack, nose up, tail down. The altimeter was at ten thousand feet and still rising. It made no sense at all. His training told him the blast wave would drive the plane down, not up.

"Gauges malfunctioning!" Kazaklis shouted.

"No. Nose down!"

He ignored the copilot's dissent. The air-speed indicator dropped to Mach point-four, yellow alarm lights flashing like bonus lamps in one of his pinball palaces. He ignored them, too—little liars nuked—and held on as if he were strangling the wheel. Mach three-point-five. Kazaklis, following his instincts, was doing everything wrong. Pain stabbed at his forearm. He turned to strike back at Moreau, who had judo-chopped his right arm to loosen the grip that threatened to put them in a fatal stall. She sat hunched over her wheel, nudging the nose down. Mach three-point-seven. Then the aftershock hit, the wave sending a quiet shudder upward through the pilot's feet, and then again, twice more, rapidly, pocketa, pocketa, massaging his back like magic fingers in a cheap motel. All three aftershocks were soft, feathery, gentle—and telling. Kazaklis withdrew his upheld arm, took the wheel, and helped Moreau get the nose down.

"Jeezuz," Kazaklis muttered absentmindedly, "that was closer than a tit when you're screwin'."

"Missionary style," Moreau said blandly.

Kazaklis cocked an eye at Moreau, as if he had lost track. She stared straight ahead, but he laughed anyway.

"Only way I know how, copilot. I'm just a country boy."

"Uhm."

They leveled the plane out at 10,500 feet and then quickly adjusted it back to a steady climb rate.

"Well, I owe you one, Moreau," Kazaklis said.

"We're even, commander. One airplane for one eye."

Moreau's voice was steady. Kazaklis looked at her again to see what he should read into that one. But there was no way of telling. She still stared straight ahead.

"Okay, let's find out what happened," Kazaklis changed the subject. "It's still a long way out of this sonuvabitch." He switched to all channels. "Navigator, this is the pilot. You guys comfy down there?"

For a moment there was no answer. Then Tyler came on, his voice flat. "Scope's messed up."

"You sure? Ours are working now."

Tyler's voice turned brittle, his words biting with challenge. "Goddammit, I said my scope's messed up!"

Down below, the navigator and radar operator sat side by side at small desklike radar consoles in the windowless well hole of the navigation compartment. Alongside Tyler were the stairs leading topside to the other four crew members and behind the stairs a small open space leading to the locked hatch into the landing-gear hold and then the catwalk around the bomb bay. The light always was red here, even in daytime. The place was a closet, claustrophobic, and the pervasive red lighting pulled the walls in even closer.

Since the flash, which had bounced down here like an errant strobe light, Radnor had been transfixed by his radar screen. It was focused tightly on the area in front of the aircraft. The screen had flared with the flash. But now it was normal, except for a little more snow than usual. And an ugly red splotch, pulsing like a jellyfish, that crept out of the corner, partly on the screen, partly hidden beyond its range. But the radar was working.

Radnor looked over at Tyler, whose screen was set on a wider field, yielding a picture in a cross-hatched fifty-mile radius around the plane. Tyler's screen showed snow flurries too, but it also seemed to be working. The navigator had not moved, his eyes glued to the screen. Radnor leaned toward him for a closer look. His jellyfish, reduced on the broader field, looked like an amoeba under a microscope. Then the circling arm of the radar passed over another amoeba, and another. Radnor felt a sob catch in his throat. The color in his face faded, the freckles throbbing like painful welts in the red night light. Mechanically he did distance calculations. He pulled back away from Tyler's screen, tears welling in his eyes. He waited, fighting back the tears, swallowing the sob out of his voice. Then he spoke to Kazaklis. "Three detonations, commander."

"No!" Tyler shrieked the rejection.

"One slightly below us, maybe five miles ahead, fifteen degrees south. The others are behind us, air-burst altitude, due east . . ." Radnor's voice broke briefly. Then he added, "Roughly twelve and sixteen miles now."

"No. No." Tyler sounded calmer now, but insistent. "Radnor's wrong. My screen's a scrambled egg. I don't see that at all."

Radnor tried to place a reassuring hand on Tyler's shoulder. Tyler savagely pushed it away.

Up front, Kazaklis motioned Moreau to go on private once again.

Moreau spoke first. "Tyler hasn't got much to go home to," she said quietly.

"Dead center. One on the base and one on the town."

"Bastards."

"This ain't tiddlywinks, pal. What would you have done? Hit Grand Coulee Dam and tried to flood us out? They wanted to catch us on the ground. It almost worked. So they kicked us in the butt with two that should have caught us, and almost got us with a misfire. . . ."

"Almost . . ." Moreau said pensively, rubbing an eye that neither saw nor hurt.

Kazaklis ignored her now. His mind searched through his options. He had at least three problems, and one—the radiation, about which he could do nothing—would have to wait.

"What would you do if you were a submarine commander and your job was to take us out, all the way out?" he thought aloud.

"Hit us again in thirty to sixty seconds," Moreau replied. "In case I missed, in case somebody escaped, in case my warheads detonated each other. Submarine missiles are not that accurate. And they're fratricidal."

"That's right. They probably sprayed us with a dozen warheads, most of which killed each other. So if you were sitting out in the Pacific guessing ten minutes ago, where would you have dumped the next load?"

"West. They knew we would take off west. And north. Where we're turning."

"Right . . . and wrong. We're turning south."

Moreau chuckled for the first time since takeoff. "Tahiti," she said. "The senator from Vermont would love it. For all we know, he's President by now."

"No palm trees for you, Moreau. I gotta loop us around one big hot mother of a cloud. Percentage baseball. And you've gotta see if there are any friendlies still flying with us. Check Radnor and then try to find the rest of the squadron."

Moreau felt the big plane bank sharply left. Percentage baseball, indeed. That's what Kazaklis said every time he took a risk, and this was damned risky—brushing them up against a very radioactive cloud on the chance they had outguessed a Russian submarine commander. They had already taken one dose of radiation, God knows how large a dose.

"We need a REM count," Moreau said.

"You're not glowing in the dark yet, Moreau."

"Get off my back, Kazaklis. We need to know how much radiation we took."

"Not now, we don't. It's irrelevant, isn't it? It's a ten-hour trip. You're gonna live long enough. We'll check it if we get out of here. Right now, I'd rather know if we have any friends with us."

Radnor already had started looking, and he was confused. "Beats me, captain," he told Moreau. "I can see only one aircraft on my screen. It's big enough to be a B-52. Could be commercial, but he's sure in a strange place. Half-dozen miles behind us, very low, heading northwest."

Moreau changed radio channels.

"Polar Bear cubs, this is Mama Bear looking for strays," she said. "Do you read? This is *Polar Bear One* looking for *Polar Bear Two.*"

"Hello, Mama Bear." The voice, scratched by radio static, carried a strong Texas imprint. "Nice to hear yore voice. This is *Polar Bear Three.* Ya-all lookin' for us, too?"

"You're way off course, *Polar Bear Three.*"

"Not suhprisin'. Nope, not a-tall suhprisin' to hear that."

"Polar Bear Three, do you have problems?"

"Might say so, Mama. Couple."

"Can we help you?"

"Don't rightly think so, thanks. Ya-all get to write the manual for World War Four, underline the part about pullin' yore screens, hear?"

"You're blinded." Moreau felt a tiny pang of dread.

"Flyin' this old Buff by braille, Mama Bear."

"Hang in there, will you, *Polar Bear Three?* That's not the end of the . . ."

Moreau stumbled. *Polar Bear Three* chuckled.

"Li'l slip there, Mama Bear. Hope yore right. But I think that's ya-all's problem now. Not ours."

"There's a lot of desert out there, *Polar Bear Three.* We'll talk you down."

"Goddammit it, Moreau!" Kazaklis exploded into the radio. "We aren't talking anybody anywhere!"

"Calm down, commander," *Polar Bear Three* said quietly. "We'll respectfully decline. We already talked, and none of us feels much like wanderin' around in the desert for a few hours, stumblin' over mutated prairie dawgs. We didn't get very far from home. Dunno how the plane held together. Marvel of American technology. Thank the boys at Boeing for us. Old pappy's not so good at flyin' blind, though. 'Fraid I wobbled us right through the edge of the cloud. We took about two thousand REM's."

Moreau shuddered. The crew of *Polar Bear Three* had taken a massively lethal dose of radiation. In a hospital, they'd be dead in a few days. They weren't going to a hospital.

Down below, Radnor began shaking like a leaf. He had never heard of anyone taking that much radiation. In front of him, the jellyfish was growing, enveloping almost half his screen.

"We got our seein'-eye dogs down in the basement," Radnor heard *Polar Bear Three* say. "They didn't take the flash, lucky boys.

And they's hot—pardonin' the 'spression, Mama Bear—to trot far as we can git after the bad guys."

Radnor's bones suddenly ached. He knew the two men, down in the dark basement of *Polar Bear Three,* just like he and Tyler, had been protected from the blinding flash. He also knew nothing except distance could protect them from the radiation. His skin felt prickly, as if just below the surface the white blood cells were munching away at the red. His head throbbed. His eyes ached. The jellyfish grew, as Kazaklis neared its edge.

"Think we'll just mosey on north and see how far we git," *Polar Bear Three* continued serenely. "We don't make it, ya-all do us a favor? Get those mutha-fuckahs for us. Pardonin' the language, Mama Bear."

The jellyfish pulsed almost off the wingtip.

"Commander!" Radnor screamed.

Almost simultaneously, Radnor's screen flashed, flaring wildly, and then flashed again, completely washing out the jellyfish.

"Radnor?" Kazaklis responded.

Again, there had been absolutely no motion in the plane. Radnor, embarrassed that he had panicked, took the briefest moment to compose himself. Then he said: "Nudets, sir. At least two detonations."

Kazaklis began counting. "Where?"

"Dunno. Screen's flaring again."

"Lemme know." Kazaklis sounded so calm Radnor's embarrassment deepened.

Five. Six.

"Polar Bear Three, this is Mama Bear," Moreau continued. "Do you read me? Do you read me, *Polar Bear Three?"* She heard nothing but static.

Seven. Eight.

Halupalai saw the curl of the thirty-footer forming, feeling the mix of fear and exhilaration. He poised for it. He reached over and placed his hand on O'Toole's.

Nine. Ten.

"Screen's settling."

Eleven. Twelve.

"Detonations north," Radnor said, struggling to pick through the electronic riot of his screen. "Twelve miles. Fifteen miles." The jellyfish was receding, and others, more distant, were forming.

Kazaklis stopped counting at thirteen. He relaxed briefly. His taut shoulders sank, the double white bars of his shoulder patch drooping with them, as did the lightning bolt, the eagle's talons, and the olive branch. He began whistling, *Oh beautiful, for spacious skies* . . . Some seconds later, the first quiet little ripple of vibration moved through the Buff, then the second, pocketa, pocketa, magic fingers nursing the pilot's temples. . . . *for amber waves of grain* . . .

"Little more practice," Kazaklis said jauntily, "and we'll have this down pat."

Moreau looked at him strangely. *"Polar Bear Three,* this is Mama Bear," she said urgently. "Do you read, *Polar Bear Three?"*

"I don't think I'd bother, copilot," Kazaklis interrupted.

"Polar Bear Three, this is Mama Bear," Moreau insisted.

"You see any airplanes down there, radar?" Kazaklis asked Radnor.

"I can't find him, commander. The screen's still kinda cluttered."

But Radnor knew, as did Kazaklis.

"Polar Bear Three! Polar Bear Three!"

"They were heading straight into the detonations, copilot. They're better off. Do a radiation check on us."

"Polar Bear Three . . ." Moreau's voice trailed off. She slumped in her seat, rubbing her white eye. Then she began checking the radiation equipment.

"We took fifty to a hundred REM's on launch, commander, sir," Moreau said brittlely. "Maybe two hundred, probably one-fifty, passing the cloud. Commander. Sir." Moreau felt perversely sorry she couldn't tell Kazaklis he was glowing in the dark. The dose would make them nauseous in a few days, but not seriously, and probably long after they would have to worry about it.

"Well," Kazaklis said cheerfully, "sounds like we're all gonna get a little dose of the Russian flu. Everybody get their shots?"

"Commander? Would you turn on the heater? It's colder than a witch's tit down here."

It was Tyler. Maybe he's shaken it off, Kazaklis thought. He switched on the heater, having forgotten the routine chore in the turmoil.

Fear the goat from the front, the horse from the rear, and man from all sides. At the end of their single unproductive meeting the Premier, his gray eyes staring unblinking as the translator repeated the words in English, had suddenly popped the old Russian proverb at him. The President remembered bristling, intentionally tightening every facial fiber to stare back sternly. That sounds like a threat, Mr. Premier. The Premier's face had sagged into hound-dog sadness, Russian fatalism seeming to mold consternation into a face that would give but not yield. A threat; ah, yes, I suppose it is, Mr. President. To both of us. We now return to our world of men. Do you think we can control such a place?

Icarus interrupted the President's brief musing, answering a previous question. "How the hell can I explain what the Chinese did, Mr. President? Frankly, I think they did us a favor. I just wish their hardware had been a little better."

Icarus was down to eight minutes and he was not happy. He did not want to bother with this part. The President did. He was trying to get some grasp on a tangle of far-off events that made no sense. He needed to understand. One set of American missiles was on its way, at his instruction. But he still had a decision to make. A big one.

"But Pakistan, for God's sake," the President replied. "Pakistan has been allied with China longer than anyone in Asia."

"We're reasonably certain that was an error, a stray. A lot of mistakes are being made. Not only overseas."

The President let the last comment pass. He felt penned in, like a steer on the way to slaughter. Every new bit of information seemed to poke at him, cattle prods urging him this way and that, but always toward the same end.

"And the Russians have not yet responded to the Chinese?"

"They appear to be moving troops across parts of the Chinese border. It is difficult to determine. It is not exactly our most pressing problem here at the moment. The Soviets have not responded with heavy weapons."

"Heavy weapons. You mean nuclear weapons, general. They took a nuclear attack from the Chinese and did not respond."

"Mr. President, the Soviets have had less than five minutes. You've had almost twenty. The Chinese weapons were very crude. Of the forty-nine Soviet divisions the Chinese tried to hit along their border, I doubt a dozen were destroyed. Everybody in the world with a two-bit space satellite is watching this. The Chinese saw an opportunity and took it. It was semisuccessful."

"Semi. I'll bet that word sells well in Islamabad. The Pakistanis are not the most stable lot. The missile landed in the outskirts of the capital?"

"In the Indus Valley, toward Peshawar. Our assumption is the Chinese were trying to loft one over the mountains toward Alma Ata or Tashkent. I think the Paks misunderstood."

The President started to laugh, uncontrollably. "Misunderstood?" he gurgled. "Jesus. I'll bet they did." The President felt woozy again, his skull echoing, his brain rubbery.

"Misunderstood badly, sir. They've launched aircraft toward Delhi."

The President focused sharply and stopped laughing. "The Pakistanis have nuclear weapons." It was not a question.

"A dozen, maybe more. Elementary devices. Gravity bombs. They have no missile-delivery system."

"So we have to assume those are headed for New Delhi?"

"The Indians seem to be making that assumption. The Indians and the Paks aren't exactly friends. India has placed fighter interceptors in the air. And tactical bombers."

"And they also have nukes."

"That we know, sir."

"Good God, it's like a damned summer cold. One sneeze and everybody catches it."

The President closed his eyes and massaged the bridge of his nose between two nervous fingers.

"Almost everybody," Icarus said bluntly.

"What's that supposed to mean, other than another shot at my manhood?" the President snapped back.

"It means it's time to sneeze. Everybody's snorting except us, the Brits, and the French. The Brits, as usual, are waiting for us, poor fools. The French, I'd guess, don't know which way to point their missiles—at us or the Soviets."

"Everybody?"

"The Israelis," Icarus acknowledged.

"The Israelis," the President repeated.

"Well, what would you expect the Israelis to do? They've got planes flying in every fucking direction. They sent us one message: stay out of our way."

The President's head throbbed. The noise did not help. He glanced over at the sprung door. Bluish-white tongues of fire, jets from acetylene torches on the other side, sliced steadily around the remaining hinges. He could hear a muffled commotion and occasionally a muted pop-pop-pop, as if light globes were bursting.

"Why don't they just blow the damn thing?" the President snapped at the duty officer.

"We don't want the briefest communication outage now, sir. They're almost through. The Secretary of State's on the other side."

"I know he is," the President said bleakly. He wanted to see the Secretary about as badly as he wanted General Patton reincarnated in the Situation Room. In fact, in their brief conversation a few moments ago, the Secretary had sounded like General Patton, ready to swoop in to save the civilized world.

The door gave way with an unexpectedly quiet thump and half a dozen Secret Servicemen swept through, their stubby Italian machine guns tilted toward the ceiling. The Secretary strode through the doorway purposefully, in a tuxedo, followed by a handful of combat-dressed marines with carbines. The President suppressed a grim chuckle.

"Looks like all the burglars are coming through locked doors tonight, huh?" he greeted the Secretary.

The Secretary started to salute and caught himself in mid-gesture. "What was that, Mr. President?" he asked, confused by the half-caustic reference to his own description of the Soviets.

"Nothing." The President shrugged. "What's it like out there?"

"The best of worlds, the worst of worlds," the Secretary replied very seriously.

Oh, Christ, the President thought. "Can you be a little more descriptive?"

"The buildings near here are surprisingly intact. The White House, not exactly a hardened facility, is damaged but standing. Windows broken, lot of flotsam kicking around. Your helicopter was blown into the trees along the East fence. I've brought in another. Andrews is six minutes away. Now that you've launched the second attack, I'd suggest we move there immediately and board the command plane."

The staccato popping noise, much louder now, caromed sharply through the open door. The marines stiffened and turned. The President's body jerked, his nerves shattering like crystal.

"What the hell was that?!"

"We are having some minor trouble above ground," the Secretary replied matter-of-factly. "The civilian population is somewhat panicky."

"What do you mean, somewhat panicky?"

"It's controllable. I've deployed two companies of marines, as well as the Secret Service and normal guards, on the White House grounds. Some of the civilians are coming over the fence."

The President heaved a great sigh.

"A nuclear weapon has exploded in your nation's capital, Mr. President," the Secretary said, his words suddenly jaggedly edged. The President saw a glint, a glint he had seen before, in the Secretary's eyes. He looked at his Cabinet leader closely and saw, for the first time, why he was so intensely disliked by so many people in and out of his administration.

"Frankly," the Secretary continued, "I'm surprised you didn't launch before the weapon landed. The opportunity is golden. But not everyone is taking it as calmly as you."

"Calmly," the President said. "Mr. Secretary, the world is acting like an hysterical medieval nunnery. Everyone has gone mad. The only calmness I detect anywhere is in Moscow, I'm surprised to hear myself say."

"Calmness, foolishness," the Secretary said. "The Soviets' uncertainty has proved to be our opportunity. It has allowed us to unload our silos in the equivalent of a first strike. With moral justification and without the condemnation of history. It will alter the balance of power for centuries."

"Mr. Secretary, your trousers are bulging," the President said without smiling. "It is not becoming to a man of your stature."

The muscles flexed in the Secretary's face. He said nothing.

"I haven't launched a second attack yet."

The Secretary's face turned grotesque. He took two quite military strides toward the President, looming up against him. The two men stood jaw to jaw, one in his bathrobe, the other in cummerbund and black tie. Neither budged.

"Mr. President, this is . . ." the Secretary sputtered. "This is . . . treasonous!"

"Sir," the President replied evenly, "the Vice-President is in Sacramento, which has a SAC base in its suburbs. We have not been able to contact the helicopter that attempted to remove him. The Speaker inopportunely chose this time to visit Peking. The president pro tem of the Senate lives in an apartment at the Shoreham Hotel in Northwest Washington. You may be, as they say, a heartbeat away from the presidency. I am, however, finding you uncomfortably close at the moment. I do not need another hysterical nun."

The Secretary's hands opened and closed slowly at his sides. He stared in disbelief and condescension at the President.

"Mr. Secretary, I suggest that you turn around, sit down, and allow me to continue with my duties. Omaha has about six minutes."

Slowly the Secretary of State backed away. He lowered himself into a tattered chair, training his glazed stare on the President. The President turned away from him and sat down again, speaking into the phone he had been holding loosely at his side.

"General, sorry about the brief delay. The Secretary of State has arrived to assist me. Give me an update, please."

"We've had a detonation in Damascus. And several in southern Africa. We hadn't been paying much attention to the southern hemisphere. Only the South Africans have weapons there. One of the explosions, however, was inside South Africa."

"That's one way to solve apartheid."

"Everyone seems to be solving their problems, sir."

"Yes."

"Except us."

Icarus had changed moods dramatically. To the President, he sounded disconsolate, like a general assigned to a desk in wartime.

"General," he asked, "do you allot no credibility whatsoever to the possibility that the Premier's intentions are exactly as he stated them?"

The President ignored the grunt from behind him. On the phone, Icarus sounded almost despondent. "Mr. President, must we go through this?"

"Yes."

"I allot none. If I did, wouldn't an attack on our missile silos have been much more reasonable, much more humanitarian? They are far more isolated than the bomber bases. Far fewer civilians would have been killed."

"General, I don't think you believe that. Such an attack would have left us almost naked. Unfortunately, we can afford to lose the people more than we can afford to lose the ICBM's. The Premier knows that."

"Mr. President, as God is my witness, it does not make any difference. It has gone too far."

"So, what does SIOP say about the solution to our problem?"

"SIOP has composed a relatively simple two-part sequence," the general responded eagerly. "The computer recommends launching half our ICBM force from alternating silos. The target would be Soviet silos. The plan has several advantages. If the Soviets respond, even their computers will be hard put to determine which of our silos are empty and which are not. They will be required to deplete a large part of their ICBM force attacking our missile sites, half of which will be empty. If they do not respond, we will have destroyed a significant part of their land-based missiles."

"And how does our little Russian toy, RSIOP, say it would respond under the circumstances?"

The general paused. "RSIOP," he said finally, "cannot read what we have to assume is extreme political confusion in Moscow at the moment."

"How would RSIOP respond, general?"

The general paused again. "In a politically normal situation," he began slowly, "RSIOP predicts a major launch of Soviet ICBM's—perhaps half their land-based arsenal."

"The targets?"

"Double targeting of the missile fields, all NATO installations in Europe, the remainder of the military targets in the United States . . ."

"And?"

Silence.

"Cities?" the President asked.

"More than likely," the general replied.

The President closed his eyes once more. His mind felt rubbery again. Damn. He forced himself to think. One ICBM warhead from either of the superpowers could destroy any city in the world. Utterly.

"And the second half of SIOP's sequence?" the President asked.

"If the Soviets respond while our first missiles are in the air, we launch the rest of ours. At other military targets—and some cities, for maximum effect. I believe you know from your briefings what the normal sequence is after that—the programmed pauses for bombers and submarines, the wait to see what they do. . . ." Icarus paused. He did not want to go into detail about the problems with communications, preserving a chain of command, all the imponderables about which the President had been briefed but for which no one had certain answers. He saw no choice in the decision. He did not want to clutter the issue. He continued on a positive note. "Even at the end of such an exchange, we would be in a vastly superior military position. The Soviets have used part of their submarine resource. We have not. You also must understand the Soviets are able to launch such an attack at any moment without action by us. You have an opportunity to deter part of that."

The President's eyes remained closed. He suddenly felt a greater affinity for the Soviet Premier, a man with the same problem he had, than he did for the men around him. He wondered if the Premier, ensnarled in his own trap in some Kremlin hideaway, felt the same pressures he did, the same doubts, the same certainties. He wanted to believe him. Knock the crap, off, bucko. The soppy liberal crap. His mind spun. Did it make any difference? He tried to calculate what already was lost or doomed. Little towns like Utica and Colorado Springs, where the Chambers of Commerce published proud brochures about economies thriving on the magical multiplier effects of defense spending. Cities like Seattle, where men had built missiles for decades and sublimated that reality in the more soothing reality of ranch homes and Winnebagos and Chris Crafts. Farm towns like Omaha that forgot over the years that something else had taken root in their soil. Places like Spokane that the world seemed to pass by but suddenly remembered this morning. "Three minutes, sir." Little submarine weapons. Toys. Weapons fifty times that size were arriving from Polyarnny, *three minutes,* in Seattle, Omaha, Colorado Springs. Thousands more were waiting. "Sir." He had gone to most of those places, thanking the patriots who worked there to keep America secure. He had asked them to do more. To build more. To deter. Now, to deter, he had to use what they built, use the patriots, too. He felt trapped, trapped by his own rhetoric, trapped by a liturgy never questioned. He had talked about limited nuclear wars, heard rational men argue persuasively in this room that such wars could be won. Now the world had at least five limited nuclear wars under way. "Mr. President." Should he let Icarus go? He shuddered. There was no more time for thinking. He was drifting again, the doomed steer prodded, numbly, dumbly, too many little electric shocks, down the last narrow chute. *A world of men. Do you think we can control such a place, Mr.*

President? Apparently not, Mr. Premier. "No, we cannot," he mumbled, barely audibly, in answer to the Premier's question.

Through his daze he heard a shuffling noise behind him. Then the thunder knocked him from his chair again. His eyes opened to gaze up at a sign that asked: "Are You EWO Ready?" He nodded automatically, still clutching the phone. He reached for the blue-and-red card that had skittered out of his hand in the fall. He beckoned for the Emergency War Orders officer, whose face remained blank.

Then he turned to look behind him. The Secretary of State lay sprawled on the floor over a carbine he had wrested from a marine. Every other weapon in the room was trained on the Secretary's body. Most had been used. The eyes above them twitched nervously. Wondering if they had chosen the right target, the President guessed sadly. He maneuvered painfully to position the phone. "General?"

"Mr. President?" the general replied uncertainly. "We seemed to have a brief communications problem."

"Yes, briefly."

"Mr. President, the Russians launched more land-based missiles thirty seconds ago."

The President wondered if Icarus was lying. Did it make any difference? In less than three minutes his communications system would be in such disarray he might not be able to respond at all.

"At the Chinese or us?" he asked.

"We can't tell yet." Icarus sounded despairing. Then he added, with a bite: "Is it really relevant?"

Relevant. Good God. *Control such a place?* The President slumped, as if in surrender. He began speaking very quietly. "I will go with SIOP. We will do it in the prescribed fashion. We have an assistant secretary of defense and the chairman of the Joint Chiefs in place in the Pentagon. The order will be issued through them. It will not take long." The President barely heard the last word from Icarus.

His mind had floated a far distance away now. He took the briefcase from the Emergency War Orders officer and handled the details as routinely as he had signed milk-support bills, reading a quick code sequence from the Sealed Authenticator System card that identified him and let the Pentagon know they were dealing with the real thing. The real thing. He shook his head. He

looked up and saw the duty officer, the man he knew only as
Sedgwick. The President had pain in his eyes.

"Do you think the Premier was sincere?" the President asked
the junior naval officer.

"Don't torture yourself, Mr. President," the young man replied.
"We have to leave right now."

"Do you?"

"I doubt it. The idea was childlike. Impossible."

"Childlike. Yes. Maybe that's what we needed."

Sedgwick draped a Navy greatcoat over the President's bathrobe. He could feel the shuddering even through the heavy wool.

"And Alice said to the Queen," the President said in a detached
voice, "'One *can't* believe impossible things.'"

Sedgwick, worried, looked around for help.

"And the Queen said to Alice, 'I daresay you haven't had much
practice. When I was your age, I always did it for half an hour a
day. Why, sometimes I've believed as many as six impossible
things before breakfast.'"

The voice of Icarus scratched into the radiophones of his two
airborne command posts.

"You got the SIOP battle-order changes? Alice? Harpoon?"

"Instantly, sir," replied Alice. He was flying the *Looking Glass*
east now, away from Omaha and the missile fields to the west and
north.

"Clear as a bell, sir," replied Harpoon. He was taking the giant
E-4 south with its staff of sixty men and women.

"The new target projections in the Soviet Union?" Icarus asked
calmly but quickly. "Our launches? Successes? Failures? Alice,
does your board show Quebec Three at Minot?"

Inside the *Looking Glass,* the general hurriedly scanned his computer data. Quebec Three. Minuteman launch Control Capsule.
Seventeen miles northwest of Minot, North Dakota. SIOP orders
to the two-man crew: launch five of the ten missiles under their
command. Data: none launched.

"Fizzle," Alice said.

"The hell it was a fizzle," Icarus said. "They chickened out.
Override the lily livers and launch 'em from the plane."

"General," Alice said, "I need those orders from a National
Command Authority."

Hzzzzzzz.

"You looking at your clock, old buddy?" Icarus asked blandly.
"Yes, sir."

"Override 'em."

Inside the *Looking Glass,* the general paused just briefly, the low hzzzzzz becoming a roar. He thought of the oath he had taken so long ago. He thought of the briefing on electromagnetic pulse he had received so recently in Albuquerque and knew Quebec Three's missiles wouldn't go if they didn't go now. He thought of the two young airmen sitting in the tomb of their command capsule outside Minot. Cowards? Rebels? He thought of Icarus in his doomed blue tomb beneath Omaha. The orders were illegal but logical. He turned and gestured to a colonel sitting several seats away. "Sam," he said, "Quebec Three at Minot." The colonel flitted quickly through the combination on a red lock box. The general did the same. Each pulled out a key. Each punched in a code. Each inserted a key. "Three . . ." Alice said. "Two . . . one . . . mark." They turned the keys simultaneously. The data board changed, showing five more launches in progress out of the frozen prairies. Alice sighed.

"Geronimo," Icarus radioed upward.

Alice looked at his watch. 0630 Zulu.

"Your computers show the projected impact areas in the United States?" Icarus asked.

Alice ran his eyes across the computer data. He frowned, pausing again, even more briefly this time, as his eyes landed on the puzzling sequence of missile launches—first the limited Soviet attack, then our limited response, then the craziness around the world, then . . . why the devil had we let half our ICBMs go in response to a small Soviet retaliatory attack on the Chinese? A fuck-up? Murphy's Law—If something can go wrong, it will? Something he didn't know? He shook his head slightly and looked at Sam.

"Alice!" Icarus barked into the phone.

Sam's face was impassive.

"Affirmative," Alice replied.

"Print 'em out. You aren't gonna have your computers long."

"It's been done, sir."

"Old buddy?" Icarus said hurriedly to Alice. "You see General Moreau again, you tell him any apology that ends with 'fuck you' ain't an apology."

Alice felt his baritone voice catch, but he covered it and hurried. "He won't hold you to it, sir."

"Happy hunt—"

Alice heard no hzzzzzzzz. Just a snap, like a twig breaking. And silence. He cradled the phone. Good-bye, old friend, he said silently. Then he heard the noises. Low popping sounds. Subtle electric crackles. Grunts from his surprised crew. He looked down the aisle of the *Looking Glass* plane and saw his computers flaring and dying, the men and women of his battle staff shouting futilely into radios that didn't work.

To the south, in the more sophisticated *E-4*, Harpoon also heard the twig snap and saw the lights blink out on all his multicolored phone consoles. He felt the same tickling sensation he had felt on the palm-print authenticator. But again he knew it was his imagination. The plane did not even ripple in flight. He had felt nothing. So this is EMP. They knew a lot about nuclear effects, but very little about electromagnetic pulse. All they knew was that, unlike most nuclear effects, the massive power surge from EMP passed harmlessly through humans. It ate communications gear instead, moving thousands of miles in microseconds. He had a helluva mess to clean up inside America's premier communications plane.

Sedgwick reached under the President's arms and hoisted him to his feet. Then he pushed him forcefully toward the Situation Room exit, following a detachment of Secret Servicemen over the flattened door and up the stairs. On the first floor they moved quickly, maneuvering around broken plaster and shards of glass, an occasional overturned chair, a fallen chandelier. At the Oval Office the President fought to a stop. The door was blown open, the great windows shattered behind his desk. The office was dark, illuminated only by twenty-two pinpoints of light from the phone console hanging powered, but powerless, over the side of his desk. Sedgwick pushed him on, past the Cabinet Room and finally through the broken French doors leading out to the Rose Garden. The din staggered him.

A jungle roar, thousands of voices, guttural, primal, ugly, enveloped the White House. He could hear the angry scourge of metal on metal, cars scraping, colliding, ramming on Pennsylvania Avenue. Horns blared everywhere. Gunfire popped far off and then, in bursts, nearby. Through the awful sound the President heard the familiar whumping of Nighthawk, another in his fleet of Sikorsky helicopters. He strained to see its reassuring outline. A few lights shone brightly, eerily, in the city. But all were doused on the White House lawn. The Secret Servicemen crouched around him, Sedgwick forcing him to hunch down too, and then the group started into the void.

Gunfire suddenly cracked several yards away from them. Tracer bullets raced across the grounds, briefly freeze-framing in Roman-candle red the figures of men clambering over the East Gate fence. The skeleton of his first helicopter was frozen there, too, gutted and wrapped around a winter-stark oak tree. Then the tracers, green, yellow, red, swept back toward them. Sedgwick hit him first, smothering him, and he felt another body, and another, pound him into the frozen ground. The air whooshed out of him. He heard grunts and a high-pitched ping! ping! like violin strings snapping. "Shit!" someone shouted. He elbowed at Sedgwick viciously, struggling for air.

"Take it easy, sir," Sedgwick said. "Just stay down."

"Who are those people?" the President demanded, gasping for breath.

"People, people, sir." Sedgwick shrugged. "Who knows? Scared people, angry people, spooked people."

"But they've got automatic weapons. Tracer bullets, for Christ's sake!"

"Mr. President, the city of Washington is better armed than most armies. You know that. You can buy a bazooka in a pawn shop across the river in Arlington."

"The American way," the President said tonelessly. Then his voice firmed up. "It's the American way, by God. Help them defend themselves in this moment of peril."

Sedgwick remained silent.

"Why are they shooting at me?" the President asked, his voice ebbing.

"You've got the last train out of town, Mr. President. They just put a couple of holes in it, though."

The agents crouched low in a circle around them. One talked urgently into his radio. "I know that, goddammit," the agent growled. "Do you want him dead or alive? No, he does not have his vest on! He's got his bathrobe on. Yes, I understand." The agent edged up to the President. "We don't have time to wait this out," he said. "Can you see the chopper, Mr. President?"

The President turned his head toward the whump-whump-whump, picking out the shadow perhaps fifty yards away. Above the helicopter, the tiny red eyes of the Washington Monument winked at him, mocking him. "Yes," he said to the agent.

"The marines are gonna open up in a few seconds. We're gonna run. Head down. Full speed. No stopping. Run. Understand?"

"Yes."

"Can you do it?"

"Yes."

"Let's go, Mr. President." It was Sedgwick. "Now!"

Guilt seized the President. His wife. In the past thirty minutes he had not asked about his wife. His nerves were bursting. He wanted to sleep. The world exploded again. He ran. At the bottom of the helicopter ramp, he stumbled. Two agents caught him and shoved him roughly, like cops with a drunk, up the stairs. Sedgwick held his arm. At the top a hand reached out and pulled them inside and the chopper immediately swept upward.

The two remaining agents pushed him into a rear seat and left him. Then Sedgwick careened into a seat across the aisle. The helicopter banked sharply over the trees, and out the window the President saw the omnipresent monument flash by as they headed for the familiar course down the river to Andrews. At the Fourteenth Street Bridge he gazed numbly down over a tangle of cars, hopelessly snarled in the desperation to head south. Across the river, fires burned on the runways at National Airport, smashed planes scattered across the broad tarmac.

"Lear jets," a voice said. "Every lobbyist in town tried to get out at the same time."

The President looked up slowly. An Air Force colonel leaned over him. The President remembered the last word Icarus had said to him.

"Geronimo," he replied to the colonel.

"I suppose so, sir," the colonel said uncertainly. "The chairman of the Joint Chiefs is attempting to meet you at Andrews. He instructed me to inform you that our attack was carried out. Omaha went three minutes ago, Cheyenne thirty seconds later. Command has been assumed by the *Looking Glass* plane."

"Alice," the President said. But he was not thinking of the general. He was thinking of impossible dreams.

"Sir." The colonel looked at him strangely. "It will be transferred to you, of course, if we reach the national command plane at Andrews."

The President's eyes stared, unfocused, at the colonel.

"The Soviets launched again, sir. Shortly after our response to their attack on the Chinese . . ."

A numbing electric spasm rippled through the President. *Their attack on the Chinese?* The colonel handed him a large tumbler of Scotch and continued.

". . . Soviet ICBMs and a second shot from their submarines off the East Coast. We have to assume Andrews is targeted by the submarines. You can rest assured we retaliated, as you ordered."

The President downed the Scotch, closed his eyes, and appeared to go to sleep.

Kazaklis held the plane on its southerly course till it was well beyond the cloud, then began a slow, banking turn west again. The altimeter read twenty-seven thousand feet and climbing. Soon he would bank the plane again, north this time, toward the Positive Control Point far ahead above the Arctic coast of Canada at which they would get the final orders to go in. Kazaklis felt good, very good. He had done his job well. By now he had placed the rest of the squadron far out of his mind. They would have separated soon anyway, this being a loner's job, no security to be gained from the cluster target of a squadron. The Buff would go in low and alone, the loneliness being its security. Kazaklis guessed the target would be the primary, although they had practiced for six different Siberian cities. In his mind's eye he could see the course as if he had flown it a hundred times, which, indeed, he had—in simulation. He could see the Buff's white belly melding with the ice floes of the Arctic, ducking around the danger of the SAM base on the frozen coast near Tiksi, racing south over the snow-covered tundra, crisscrossing the Lena River, hiding at three hundred feet in the Verkhoyansk Mountains, breaking out low over the larch forests that hinted at the beginnings of civilization. . . .

"It's red-neckin' *twang! twang!* luv-makin' *twang! twang!* time . . ." The voice pounded into the pilot's helmet, a scratchy electric guitar clawing at his eardrums.

"What the hell is that?!"

"Listen to the whippoorwills *twang!* how they sing *twang! twang!* Just like us, doin' their thing! *twang!*"

"Psywar!" Kazaklis thundered. "Fucking Russians are trying to psyche us!"

"Conway Twitty," Moreau replied calmly. "Tyler's trying to convince us."

Kazaklis clasped his helmet in both hands, as if he were trying to smother the earphones. "Ty!" he bellowed. "Ler!" *twang! twang!* "Ty-fucking-ler!"

"Tyler's picked up a radio station," Radnor said from below.

"Get that fucker off!"

"I knew you guys were wrong," Tyler said serenely as Twitty's twang wound down. "They're alive down there. It's a drill. All this is simulated. Just like everything else."

"*Oxy!*" a new voice shrieked across the void.

"Jesus."

"I can tell you where the acne-causing bacteria are!"

"Jesus."

"All over your face—lurking, festering, pimpling all over your face!"

"Oh, Jesus."

"Where is your next pimple to be or where is it not to be? That is the question! Wash with new Oxy Wash!"

"Ty . . . ler. Damn you!"

"It's a drill."

"Hel . . . lo again. This is Crazy Eddie, stickin' by the phone so you're never alone. On big-boom night. Hang right in there, kids, at the dial with style—Kay . . . Oh . . . You . . . Double-You!—in humpin', jumpin' Coquille, Oregon!"

"God damn you, Tyler, get that off."

"They're playing music down there."

"Oregon, you diddle-brain! It's some stoned disc jockey in Oregon!"

"It's a drill," Tyler said confidently. "Pretty fancy one, isn't it?"

Kazaklis paused for a moment. His thoughts riveted on Oregon. Then he exploded.

"They're dead, damn you, Tyler! Your wife, your kid, everybody we left behind. Dead, dead, dead. Got that? Dead! You're alive and you got a job to do. Do it. And turn off that fucking radio!"

The radio went silent, as did the rest of the plane.

"What an asshole," Moreau said after a moment.

"Conway Twitty or Crazy Eddie?" Kazaklis asked.

The first lurch of the helicopter caught the President by surprise, snapping him out of his grogginess and throwing him half out of his seat toward the aisle. Sedgwick caught him. "Fasten your belt, sir," the young naval aide said. "It's going to get rough."

The President looked at him uncertainly. In the disarray of the last few moments his mind had taken refuge in the safety of just another routine *Nighthawk* flight to *Air Force One*. Ahead were more speeches, more parade caravans, with "Hail to the Chief" greeting him at every public pause.

"We're not going to make it to Andrews, sir," Sedgwick said. His voice had a slight note of alarm, but the President failed to perceive it. "Just strap yourself in." The President felt the young aide shove his shoulders back into the seat and pull the belts around him. "We're diverting, sir, making a run for it."

"Run?"

"It's safest, sir."

"President doesn't run."

Sedgwick looked into the President's uncomprehending face. He sighed but tried to hide the emotion by turning away. He fastened his own belts and gazed out the porthole window. Below him the blackness was nearly total as the powerful helicopter cut desperately back across the slum warrens of Southeast Washington. A few lights shone in the void—careening auto headlights, a small fire, the electrical dance of a loose power line. The blast effects had not reached this far. The psychological effects had. As had the power outages. The chopper raced across the District line into the middle-class suburbs of Maryland, but nothing changed below. This was going to be very close. Sedgwick's skin crawled.

Across the aisle, the President also stared out the window. He didn't understand the blackness beneath him—the little popping fires, the headlights racing toward each other like more tracer bullets and then poofing out, orange flames merging the two. The scream of *Nighthawk One*'s jet-assisted engines drowned out the whump of the chopper blades. He craned his neck back toward Andrews. What the hell were they doing? God, he was tired. His eyes paused on a full winter-white moon hovering above the dark horizon. The moon burst. It burst into a sun, then into the light of a thousand suns. It was very beautiful.

The President felt a powerful arm catch him behind the neck, shoving his head down into his lap. Over the searing whine of the engines he thought he could hear Sedgwick counting. He saw only the pure whiteness of the moon. An eternity seemed to pass. Then he felt the second lurch, and briefly he free-floated in the night's first heavenly serenity. Then he heard the screech of tearing metal overwhelm the engine whine. Then he heard nothing, the presidential helicopter breaking in two as the blast wave wafted it like a leaf into a stand of naked pin oaks.

Moreau helped Kazaklis level out at forty thousand feet and complete the turn north. Then she unsnapped her helmet strap and tried to relax. In front of her the control panel was a bee's hive of honeycombed yellow lights bathed in a red that seemed normal. She lazily panned across the controls until she came to the empty picture tube of her radar screen. She shivered. Staring back was the mirror image of a familiar face altered. The face was strikingly attractive—Moreau knew very well she was attractive— but the geometry was wrong, the symmetry slightly skewed. Staring out of the red screen was a still near-perfect image, but it had one powerful eye and one that looked like it had been copped from Little Orphan Annie. She chuckled mirthlessly. She was enough to spook anyone. Suddenly she thought about O'Toole.

"Hey, you crazy Irishman," she radioed into the back of the compartment, "how you doing back there?"

No answer returned.

"O'Toole?"

In the back, Halupalai lifted his hand off his crewmate's closed fist. "He's dead, captain."

"Dead?" Moreau's voice trembled in an incredulous whisper.

"Hypothermia . . . shock . . . heart attack . . ." Halupalai's voice was hollow and lost. "Who knows?"

"Shit, we needed that," Kazaklis interrupted. "We really needed that."

"Sweet Christ, Kazaklis," Moreau said, more in pain than anger.

"Cleanest corpse in the Air Force, I'll say that."

"Kazaklis!"

"Don't Kazaklis me, copilot. Now we got a stiff in the back and a wacko in the basement. What do you think about that?"

Moreau paused, a long pause. "I think you got a lot to learn about life, Captain Shazam," she finally said. "You think you can do it in ten hours?"

Kazaklis ignored her. He stared into the flash screen, still thinking about Oregon, which a very long time ago had been home.

II

North Toward Nowhere

We are all born mad. Some remain so.

—Samuel Beckett

FIVE

0730 ZULU

On summer mornings, the good mornings along the south-western coast of Oregon, the mist billows out of the Pacific like death's breath, does its ghostly dance over the dunes, and scuds into the low coastal mountains, where it stops, trapped and surly, hovering in the hollows like a shroud so the sun doesn't come up till midafternoon. The fog wisps in steamy images out of moss so primeval, so lush and verdant and deep, a big man can bury an arm up to the elbow and not get his gnarled fingers on the roots. It clings to the dropping boughs of phallic firs pointing toward a heaven obscured in gray, muted shadows above. It drapes itself over the wet, broken hulks of fallen forest titans that rest, rotting and fertile, in a somber double vision of death and rebirth. For if you look closely through the dim murk of the jungle-forest you can see, with the right eyes, of course, the seed for another epoch's coal, another epoch's oil, another epoch's man—hard, tough, and mean, a survivor who will come back to pick at the few treasures this passing era left behind.

Not that the new man will be any harder, any tougher, any meaner than the men who roamed here most recently. The hard land of the Umpqua and the Coos and the Coquille breeds tough men and always will. A boy learns his manhood and other lessons early.

As a small child, Kazaklis had loved it. Even in the most dismal of the rotting hollows his child's fantasies took trips into the distant past where prehistoric pterodactyls swooped through his murk, giant lizards slithered in and out of his own dark pools. And if his young mind turned just right, and he saw with the right eyes, he could see into the future, too. Not his future, but some realm afar—when the hard men did come back long after he was gone. In his child's way, he saw eternity in the woods—the endless turning of a rebuilding earth. His pa—Big Kazaklis, they called him, for he was as hard and tough and mean as any survivor who would ever come back—saw the same things and tried to teach the kid. But the lessons ended, and the kid's visions, too, one somber morning in the woods when the boy shot his pa. Whomp. Just like that. Aimed at the balls and hit him in the thigh. Whomp.

It was the second shot fired in the Oregon mist that morning, the first coming from Big Kazaklis, although few took account of that later. The first shot caught a startled buck just right, slamming in behind the shoulder exactly where it should and dropping the deer in its tracks. Perfect, except it was the kid's buck, promised to him that very morning as Big Kazaklis drank four-ayem coffee laced with Jim Beam. Got my first poon and got my first buck afore I was twelve, Big Kazaklis had said, and so will you, bub. But the kid froze—cow-brown eyes staring into frightened cow-brown eyes just like his, and even at eleven he felt it was eternity's trade, which he couldn't make—and so his pa fired instead. Humiliation flooded through the boy, having failed the hard man's test. Tears mixed with frustration and anger and hurt. He turned on his old man and fired wildly at his pa's manhood, missing through the blur, missing the balls. Big Kazaklis flailed backward into the crutch of a Douglas fir. Then he laughed, being as hard and tough as the woods. They walked out together, the big man propped on the small boy, leaving the buck behind, leaving a few pints of the old man's blood to fertilize the moss and the tangled timbers in the gray garden of the future.

At the trailhead, where a rusted old Ford pickup sat hugging the bank of the South Fork of the Coos, the boy shoved his old man into the passenger side and gunned the ancient truck backward up the rutted hard pan of the river road onto the highway. Had someone been watching, all he would have seen was the giant figure of a man propped against the passenger door and two intent cow-brown eyes framed inside the steering wheel as the

battered Ford clattered fifteen twisting miles into the town of
Coos Bay. Kazaklis bumped it down the main drag of the port
town, past the penny parking meters and the drunks lying in the
rain, past the whorehouses and the chug-a-tugs with their flotillas
of raw logs, past the Sportsmen's garish neon and the freighters
stuffed with Yankee wood for Japanese mills, and on up the road
to the hospital.

Big Kazaklis piled out first. He lumbered, ghost-faced, through
the hospital doors, and stopped, bear of a man, legs parted for
much-needed balance, one leg being faded-jeans blue and the
other cranberry red. He ripped a soaked three-bandanna tourni-
quet off and waved it once at a dumbstruck nurse.

"M' boy got hisself his first buck!" the old man thundered.
"Hope he's better at huntin' poon."

Then he rasp-roared a laugh and keeled over flat on his face.
Moments later, the boy looked up at the new figure towering over
him and, no flinch at all in his eyes or his voice, said: "Had it
comin', old bastard."

The deputy sat through the afternoon and then the night with
the boy, the kid not saying another word, not sleeping a wink,
either. In the morning, when the doctor came out and said the old
coot was making it, three pints of blood being what he lost, Kazaklis stood up and marched down to see him, the deputy following, instead of vice versa.

"What the kid tell ya?" Big Kazaklis grunted at the deputy.

"Told 'im ya had it comin', ya old bastard," the boy interrupted.
He stood, arms folded over his chest, staring down at Big Kazaklis
with eyes neither sorry nor hateful. Just certain.

"Didja, now, bub?"

"Yep."

For a full minute the deputy watched the two of them stare at
each other. The coast mountains had seen three generations of
these men, four if you counted the young one coming up. Nothing changed in them, except the Greek. The Greek seemed to
wash out generation by generation, diluted by a string of young
blond wives who washed out, too, turning fifty before they turned
thirty. One boy to a generation, no girls and no brothers, as if that
was all the Kazaklis women could find the soul and the source to
deliver up. And maybe it was. The deputy was glad he didn't have
a blond daughter. Damned glad.

The kid kept on staring at his old man, feeling the tears well up

again, and the anger flare, too, because Big Kazaklis stared back
with a half-smile. His old man could see through him, and he
hated it, so he willed the tears away and jutted his chin out at him
instead. Nobody was going to see him cry. Ever.

Big Kazaklis came home on the same kind of day he left, the
mist oozing out of the roof moss atop the weather-beaten house a
dozen miles up the Coos, the escalating rain just beginning to
overwhelm the moss like a soaked sponge and drain, plop-plop,
down from unpainted eaves. He stood in the doorway, braced
powerfully on a cane that looked more like a weapon than a
crutch.

"Well, bub, think yer grown up 'nuf fer the rest? Huh, bub,
huh? Tell yer ma you 'n me got some business t'do. Tell 'er to run
into town and see 'er folks. Then head upstairs. Man."

In the noontime murk of his room the boy did not wait long.
Nor was he surprised when Nikko, the raven lady from the
Sportsmen's card room, entered. Nor when the talons of her shel-
lacked fingernails picked quickly away at the buttons of her silken
black shirt, exposing the hint of apricot breasts in the shadows;
nor when the talons advanced to the Levi Strauss buttons of his
jeans; nor when they scampered farther. It was part of a ritual
never described, poon, but always sensed. The surprise came
when the talons did not advance to the faded Pendleton plaid of
his shirt, did not advance to the zipped hinges of the raven lady's
clinging black trousers. The surprise came, as it had in the woods,
as it had when the buck fell suddenly, when Nikko descended
suddenly, too, her clothed body matching his clothed body, her
nudity his nudity, but not matching at all.

"It's wrong!" he shrieked in dismay, pounding tight fists into
the back of black-clad hips swaying unused in front of him.

"Not long," the singsong canary voice cooed, pausing just
briefly in her chore. "Big Kazaklis say not long first time."

Then, in the spurt of his half-lost virginity, it didn't feel that
wrong. But it did. There was no warmth to it, no more warmth
than there was along the Coos.

Over the next years, as the boy learned far, far more about the
mysteries of poon, he stood regularly at the window of the Sportsmen's Club, nose pressed steamily to the glass as he watched Big
Kazaklis in the metallic blue light of the card room, one gnarled
hand on red Bicycles flicked to him by Nikko's talons, one gnarled
hand wrapped around an Oly, the beer hand occasionally slipping

around the felt-covered table to grasp a slender raven's thigh. And he felt failed—gypped, too—as he had in the woods. He also knew he had to leave this place.

The old man took a long time seeing that the bout with the buck, and the bout with Nikko, too, were truly bad mistakes. But the time came, maybe a year later, when he finally got the boy back out into the once-magical woods. It was a day when the heavens opened and the water poured out of the sky, as the old man put it, like the gods was drinkin' beer and peein' on 'em.

The kid looked up at his pa through the peek hole of an ancient and oversized poncho, November rain flooding down its green rubber sides. He wore sullenness in his eyes, though the old man could only sense it, not see it through the sheets of icy water cascading out of the bleak sky and tumbling down the limbs of the giant tree they used for partial shelter.

"Need ourselves a fire, bub, that's what we need, huh, bub, huh?"

The kid's cow-brown eyes reverted to their ancestral black. His boots were filled with ice water. He was soaked down to his Fruit of the Loom. He looked about him, and all he could see, as far as the eye reached in the gloom, was wetness. They stood in a rain-forest hollow. The shadowy hulk of giant trees lay rotting, their backs grotesquely broken where they had fallen decades ago. It was a dismal swamp, the kind of place in which he had floated through those childhood fantasies until he had been broken of all their allure. He said nothing. To make a fire here was to spark flints in a rain barrel.

"Come 'ere, bub," the old man said, pulling the kid toward the decayed body of a fallen fir wider than the boy was tall. His knobby fingers dug into the wet crud, sending giant beetles scrambling, grabbing one with a deadly pinch and thrusting it toward the boy. "Bear food. Kid food, too, if'n ya needs it." Then he dug further into the flaky corpse of the tree, prying out a glob of sticky amber-colored pitch.

The old man molded the pitch, planted it in a scooped-out trough beneath their shelter tree, and surrounded it with soaked fir needles. With one match the pitch snapped magically into flame, the needles steaming for a second and then crackling too. Expertly, Big Kazaklis added drenched twigs, then wet sticks, and finally soaked logs, the flames from one layer sapping the water out of the next. In a moment the boy was warm, in twenty minutes dry, even with the rain still pelting his poncho.

"That big rottin' tree's always gonna be there, bub, with pitch to keep you warm and bugs to keep your stomach full, if'n ya needs 'em. Remember that. Some things is eee-ternal, always there for ya, like the mountains."

The boy stared at the crumbling home of the beetle and the pitch. It was truly a miracle to build a fire in the rain, to create warmth in the cold, and his father had done it. But he could no longer give his pa any satisfaction in the woods.

"Nope," the kid said quietly. "It's gonna rot away and be gone. Just like you, Pa. Just like me." The father looked at the son as forlornly as he could show, because he knew that somehow he had driven the dreams out of the kid—that the boy, barely turned twelve, no longer saw the past or the future. He only saw the present, and that truly was sad, even to Big Kazaklis.

"Oh, yer right about that, bub," his pa said. "But yer wrong too. Don't know if yer ever gonna unnerstand."

Polar Bear One passed into Canada east of Penticton, droned north over the Caribou Mountains of British Columbia, and sliced across the corner of Alberta on a course toward the two immense frozen lakes of the Canadian Northwest Territories, Great Slave and Great Bear. The next hour passed more rapidly than any of the crew expected. PRP cluttered their lives with chores, leaving little time for inward trips, those being risky.

Kazaklis picked up a few radio transmissions from other aircraft, all civilian, most of the calls coming on the emergency frequency but none of them coded JIMA 14, the B-52's identification for military emergencies. Most were only marginally coherent and Kazaklis answered none. He received no military communications and he slapped a total ban on listening to ground radio. He did not need any more Crazy Eddies or Conway Twittys, and surely not from Coquille.

Kazaklis ordered O'Toole's body placed downstairs behind Tyler and Radnor in the little basement walkway leading to the sealed-off bomb bay. It was the only place in the small crew compartment of the huge bomber where six feet of now-excess baggage could be stowed relatively inconspicuously. Radnor came up, skittishly, to help Halupalai carry the body.

The PRP psychiatrists, had they been aboard for this ultimate laboratory test of their wisdom, would have observed Tyler with fascination. He ignored the entire proceeding. He did not draw his eyes away from his radar screen as his crewmates struggled to get the body down the ladder flanking his seat. He did not turn once to look at the corpse as it was stretched out behind him. He remained quietly unconcerned, as if the reality of one touchable body was simpler to handle than the vision of distant millions. That was the opposite reaction from the one predicted by the psychiatrists. They said the unseen millions would be more tolerable than looking death in the eye. Psychic numbing, they called it; a lesson from Vietnam that the shrinks concluded would be far more useful in the big war.

Tyler went about his business, watching his screen, charting and plotting, mouthing bland course corrections to Kazaklis. He was the perfect, efficient, no-nonsense navigator, a tribute to the system. He said nothing more about the super con of the mock destruction of his home and family, nothing more about the hoax of this most elaborate practice mission. Nor did he utter a single word indicating he had changed his mind. He engaged in no small talk with Radnor, his seatmate in the basement. He did his job. That was the beauty of PRP. It worked even when it didn't work.

The presence of O'Toole's body had a much more profound effect on Radnor. He found himself looking over his shoulder regularly at the placid hulk of the man he last had seen in the shower at Fairchild. O'Toole's feet pointed toward Radnor's back, his face hidden just beyond the bulkhead interrupting the radar operator's line of sight toward the hatch door. So Radnor saw two V-angled boots, two legs, and the beginning of a torso. No more. The body was bathed in the plane's red night lights, a routine red that now took on a hue of malevolence for the first time in Radnor's career.

Tyler wasn't helping matters either. Once, as Radnor drew his eyes back away from O'Toole's body, he saw Tyler reach reverently forward and carefully touch the little Kodak icon he had pasted above his radar screen, one finger caressing a cherub's cheek, another seeming to tousle the glossy image of fine blond curls. Radnor could see Tyler speaking softly, a loving incantation to the baby-blue eyes that had filled with tears on the frozen runway such a short time ago. Radnor shuddered. He wanted to scream at Tyler: *Take it down, damn you. Take it down.* Tyler bothered him almost as much as the nearness of O'Toole's dead figure. The whole thing gave him the jitters, conjuring up undesirable thoughts about Spokane, Laura, and the world he had left behind forever. Radnor kept no icon of his own. He didn't need one, Laura's face being riveted into his mind. He sobbed briefly. Then, as trained, he called on PRP to push those thoughts back down. It was not easy. But he was kept quite busy.

Upstairs, Halupalai now occupied the rear of the topside cabin alone. Had it not been for O'Toole's demise, Halupalai would have been the most dangerously exposed to wrong thoughts. He was the one about whom the psychiatrists—had they been perched in some dark corner of the nuclear bomber, watching, watching, as Halupalai's mind often had envisioned them—would have been the most worried. He simply had nothing to do, being the guardian only of the remote-controlled Gatling guns 150 feet behind him in the tail. That left time to think, and thinking truly was dangerous. Kazaklis handled that problem.

"Halupalai?" the pilot asked shortly after the gunner returned upstairs. "You think you can handle O'Toole's tinker toys for us?"

"You bet, commander," Halupalai responded excitedly, his enthusiasm briefly running away with him. "I've sat next to so many O'Tooles I've forgotten most of their names and faces." The sergeant immediately felt an overwhelming surge of guilt. He had forgotten many faces, but not O'Toole's, which leaped tauntingly into his mind's eye now. His voice trailed off. "I think I can do it, commander," he added.

Kazaklis took no heed of the mood change. "Congratulations, lieutenant," he said. "You may have the first battlefield commission of this here war . . . or whatever the hell we're into."

Halupalai paused again. "I'll take the job, commander," he said. "You keep the bars."

"You sunburned beach bum!" Kazaklis thundered. "Holdin' out for captain on me, huh?"

Halupalai gazed into the blinking red-and-yellow instrument panel in front of him. Fleetingly the roar of the madding crowds echoed again, the adulation of the California girls tickled at his loins, the succession of three wives clung to his arm and then detached, the great green turf bleached into seedy car lots with overpriced Mercedeses. Twenty years ago he turned down a commission, his own quiet acknowledgment that a college degree in off-tackle slants had brought him more grief than gain.

"Holdin' out for sergeant, commander. Don't need the lonely burden and all that."

Kazaklis chuckled. "You're never gonna get ahead in this world, sarge." He motioned for Moreau to take the wheel and, with both hands, lifted the cumbersome white helmet off his head, replacing it with a headset. In the pressurized cabin the heavy, hot helmet was necessary only at moments of risk—takeoff, landing, low-level, combat, and, of course, during the raw tension of air-to-air refueling. So Kazaklis placed it now to his left, just behind the innocently obscure red lever that armed the nuclear weapons. The plane had three such levers, one at each crew station. All three had to be pulled to activate the weapons. His hand brushed past the lever as he reached into the side pocket of his flight jacket and extracted a mangled pack of Camels.

"Watch the match," Kazaklis said automatically as the cupped light flared briefly in the dark cockpit.

"Afraid you'll blind me, commander?" Moreau asked blandly.

Kazaklis drew deeply on the stubby little cigarette, the red-orange ember melding into the safety of the night lights, and tried to ignore her.

"Those things'll kill you, Kazaklis," Moreau pushed on. She knew Kazaklis always stowed a carton of Camels in his alert bag—along with the candy bars, the first-aid kit, the radio beacon, the .45, the cyanide pill, and other essentials, including Russian rubles and Chinese yuan. She laughed a trifle loudly.

"Think you're funny, huh?" Kazaklis snapped. "That's a real ho-ho, Moreau. Anybody tell you about the union rules when they let you in this outfit? We get a cigarette break. A silent one."

"Well, well. Little touchy tonight? You were ready every time the siren went off. Remember?"

"Just can it, Moreau."

"I was laughing about the rubles we've got stuffed in our bags. Great piece of American ingenuity. Nuke 'em and buy your way out."

"I brought international wampum, Moreau. Camels and Hersheys. What you got to sell, pal? Or should I ask?"

Moreau stiffened. "God damn you, Kazaklis," she said after a moment. "You really are an asshole."

Kazaklis sighed, then pulled long and hard on the Camel, its ragged bite diverting the headache throbbing lightly at his temples. His mind darted erratically but calmly through what little he knew of the night's realities. Nuclear weapons, he knew, had been used in anger or error for the first time since Nagasaki. He knew Spokane was gone. He presumed Seattle was gone for the simple reason that he had picked up no air-traffic calls as he had moved past the fringe of the city's commercial landing patterns. He knew part of his boyhood home, Oregon being a state without strategic targets, was at least functioning and might be for some time, panic aside, because the prevailing westerlies would keep it out of the normal fallout pattern for days. But the frozen subarctic wastes over which he was flying revealed little more. The President could be alive and frantically negotiating. He could be dead. Hell, he could have started it and be orbiting in the National Emergency Airborne Command Post. The *E-4*. "The Flying Fuehrer Bunker," *Rolling Stone* had called it years ago, and the name had stuck in the black, barroom humor of the bomber pilots.

"Achtung!" Kazaklis snorted.

Moreau looked at him strangely, but his gaze held hard and blankly on the flash curtain.

The *Looking Glass* plane, the flying SAC command post, almost surely was flying. Kazaklis had no illusions about the latest political fad of limited nuclear wars. So he assumed what had happened in Seattle and Spokane had happened all over the United States. Still, the *Looking Glass* had to be flying. Not a moment had passed in more than two decades without a command post aloft over the Midwest, ready to take control when the land bases went. It was possible the *E-4*'s, the President's giant command plane at Andrews and the carbon-copy aircraft at Offutt in Omaha, were caught on the ground. It was almost impossible to take out the *Looking Glass*. It had been airborne and he should hear from it. Soon. But his more immediate worry was the refueling planes, not one of which had made it away from Fairchild. An alternate could be waiting for them, out of Eielson in Alaska or perhaps Minot in North Dakota. But the radio hadn't peeped. Without a refueling rendezvous, they had enough fuel to get in but not out. Moreau's little joke about the rubles, his about her pretty fanny, wasn't so funny.

Kazaklis grunted unintelligibly.

Moreau stared straight ahead, ignoring him this time.

Even the refueling problem was irrelevant. Of all the grand theories that had failed tonight, Kazaklis knew that he and the four others in *Polar Bear One* now were about to test the most dubious theory of all. That a thirty-year-old B-52 could somehow worm its way unseen into the heart of Russia and get out again. He knew the odds on that one—one hundred to one at best. This night, his throbbing skull told him, was not at best. He already had one dead crewman and another who was psyched into a jack-off world all his own. He could only guess about refueling tankers and communications. Of the six Buffs on alert at Fairchild, his was the only one still flying. That meant, he was sure, that of the hundred Buffs on alert tonight, maybe twenty were in the air. And that meant four thousand SAM missiles, plus countless fighter-interceptors, could pick away at twenty SAC bombers. The PRP psychiatrists would work him over good for that thought. The intercontinental missiles, they would counsel reassuringly, already had destroyed almost all the SAM bases. That's what they're for. Sure thing. So now we get to wander through fifteen hundred miles of radioactive fallout. The shrinks never answered that one. Are you afraid? they asked instead. No, Kazaklis was not afraid. But PRP had not freeze-dried his psyche to the point where he had any illusions. He knew, as all the bomber pilots knew, that once it went, it went. He knew that, for God and country, he now was a rational suicide. Contrary to the public's vision of nuclear war—one poof and it's all over—he now faced a ten-hour drone into Russia with sheer boredom and raw tension alternately ripping at frayed nerves and eating at trained minds, one threatening to drive them all nuts if the other didn't. His chore, as commander, was to hold them all together while they rationally committed suicide.

"Banzai," he said, grinding out the cigarette after the stub began burning his lips.

"Pardon?" Moreau said, her voice still reeking with anger.

"I said you're right. I'm an asshole. Report me to the Equal Rights Commission. But don't forget to tell them you're a pain in the asshole." He stared into the curtains. "And give me a fuel reading."

Moreau glared at him. "Two hundred ninety-three thousand pounds," she said curtly.

The pilot seemed not to hear her as he moved the plane across Dawson Creek in northern British Columbia, then veered it slightly eastward, putting it on a bearing almost due north toward Great Bear Lake.

The plane remained at forty-four thousand feet, an efficient if easily tracked altitude. The pilot assumed the Russians were watching them, but that was irrelevant. Coming over the Pole, any of the major cities in the Soviet Union were possible targets and the Russians could only guess at their destination. Although Leningrad and Vladivostok were five thousand miles apart on opposite Soviet coasts, *Polar Bear One* could reach either city with an arrival-time difference of no more than half an hour. The Russians would be expecting a Western-based plane to go for the Siberian coastal city with its array of military targets. It so happened that neither Vladivostok nor Leningrad was their primary. But the time for diversion, for hiding in the weeds at low level, would come later. Their progress was methodical and scrupulously planned, taking them slowly, speed not being one of the Buff's virtues, toward a rendezvous point where a tanker would or would not be waiting.

"Roger, two hundred ninety-three thousand pounds," Kazaklis repeated the fuel reading.

Almost half-empty, Kazaklis thought.

More than half-full, the shrinks in his mind replied.

Enough to get to the primary target and limp, perhaps, a few hundred miles away into the Siberian wastes, Kazaklis thought.

More than enough to make the low-level raid on the great dam on the Angara River, take out the industrial complex at Irkutsk, and destroy the troop placements and nuclear reactor at Ulan-Ude, the shrinks replied.

Not enough for the escape to the northern Chinese city of Tsitsihar, Kazaklis thought.

"Wishing you hadn't elbowed in front of my roomie, commander?" Moreau broke into his reverie.

"Are you EWO ready?" Kazaklis replied.

"Peace is my profession, commander."

"Flying off valiantly to save the American way, huh?"

"Hamburgers, baseball, and vaginal sprays, commander."

"Flavored?" Kazaklis asked.

"You like relish?" Moreau parried innocently.

"Never tried it," Kazaklis continued.

"Thought you'd tried everything."

"Oh," Kazaklis rebutted in mock surprise, "you meant hamburgers."

"Your mind's only in one place, Kazaklis."

"You think the Russkies targeted 'em?"

"Ground zero at Golden Arches? Ending the record at sixty billion burgers?"

"No, no, no. Hitting the strategic stockpiles of mountain-flowers fragrance."

"It sure would turn the American way upside down."

"You mean right side up."

Moreau gave up, the anger dissipating in a slow, rumbling laugh. "Kazaklis, I don't know where you were hatched. But you're a sketch. A real prick. But a sketch."

Kazaklis changed the subject abruptly. "Are you afraid, Moreau?"

Moreau turned and looked at him, her one good eye piercing through the red lights and framing the pilot's clear, serious face. He stared back, his brown eyes steady and unsmiling. "No," she said.

"Why are you here?" he asked curiously.

"To be with you, you charmer, you," Moreau purred, although cat's claws scratched through the softness. "Could there be any other reason?"

The psychiatrists would have nodded in satisfaction. Tension was good for PRP. Diverting. Even the loss of O'Toole was good for PRP. The dispatching of O'Toole gave Halupalai something to do with his time. And while Kazaklis and Moreau sniped at each other in their station up front, Halupalai played alone with his new toys in the now lonely station at the rear of the upstairs compartment.

The big bomber carried various defense systems, none of them giving SAC crews a great sense of comfort. It carried heat flares that might, just might, draw a Soviet missile away from the hot exhaust of the B-52's engines. It carried bundles of chaff, a sophisticated form of the same tinfoil that World War II pilots used to confuse early radar and some joyriding teenagers used to confound cops in their highway radar traps. Packaged in the right patterns, it might, just might, temporarily distract an attacking MIG. It also carried powerful radar-jamming equipment the Soviets had been breaking down regularly, and the Americans had been upgrading as often, in a thirty-year cat-and-mouse game of technological escalation and counterescalation. The defenses were the responsibility of the Electronics Warfare Officer, who, as the PRP psychiatrists would have put it, was now inoperative. PRP people didn't like the word "dead." Icarus was inoperative. So was

O'Toole. But not Halupalai. In fact, Halupalai was having the time of his life.

With a verve he hadn't felt since those ancient touchdown runs, the big Hawaiian raced to the rhythm of his new sport. He fired several decoy flares into the void over British Columbia. Hot damn! He wished he'd had those in Nam! Once again he saw the gray intruder racing up out of a bed of cotton-candy clouds far below. Once again he saw the finned threat scar his magnificent landscape, rape his serene world. But this time the shark flash of the Russian missile darted away from the engines of his Buff and suckered into the heat of the flare instead.

"Whoo-o-e-e-e!" Halupalai exulted, and Kazaklis looked back over his shoulder with a silly grin at the joyfully swaying back of the old man of the aircraft.

Halupalai's mind raced with fervor. This was good stuff! No more rat-a-tat pop guns for him! Now he knew why the kids, even big kids like Kazaklis, stood glaze-eyed in front of the blip-blip of the computer games while the Amazon Lady and her ancient pinball technology flashed forlornly alone in arcade corners. Now he understood why the generals loaded up their fighters with so many computer toys the pilots couldn't handle them all. This was fun! This was the future! At the console in front of him he rambunctiously triggered a quick combination that dumped several dozen bundles of antiradar chaff from the belly of the cruising bomber. Broad Slavic faces, bubble-framed in the cockpit canopies of their MIG interceptors, frowned in dismay as they twisted their supersonic fighters this way and that in chase of phantoms. Hot damn!

"Bandits! Bandits!" The voice, startled and panic-stricken, burst through the radio channels. "On our butt! We got bandits all over our butt!"

Halupalai froze at the emergency call from below. Then a cackle shattered into his earphones.

"Halupalai's playing with the tinfoil, Radnor," Kazaklis said, his voice bubbling with laughter.

"Damn you, Halupalai," Radnor said, embarrassed again.

"I gotta practice," Halupalai said sheepishly.

"Gum wrappers, Radnor," Kazaklis interjected. "You just got attacked by a squadron of gum wrappers."

"Oh, shit," Radnor said, running his hand through sandy hair above a freckled face that had turned red without the assistance of the night lights.

"Well, whaddaya think?" Kazaklis continued. "Did the American taxpayer get his money's worth out of the great tinfoil race? Or do we still have a Gum Wrapper Gap?"

Radnor remained silent.

"Come on," Kazaklis insisted. "It's the greatest untold story of the cold war. The taxpayer spent billions closing the bomber gap, the missile gap, and the window of vulnerability. He needs to know. How about the gum wrappers?"

Needing the relief, Moreau suddenly cut in. "We spent millions," she said, "probing the secrets of SAM missiles captured by the Israelis."

"Slipping CIA moles into Russian electronics plants," Kazaklis added.

"Sweating Soviet defectors in safe houses all over the Washington suburbs," Moreau pushed onward.

"Seducing East German scientists with voluptuous blonds trained in . . . well . . . radar technology," Kazaklis continued.

"All to stay ahead in the escalating tinfoil race," Moreau said seriously.

"All to find out if the gum wrappers worked," Kazaklis intoned. "Well, Radnor? Come on, this is crucial. This is a need-to-know situation."

Radnor stared sullenly at his fluttering radar screen. He had been through the joke about the Gum Wrapper Gap before. But he wasn't feeling funny.

"Well?" Kazaklis insisted again.

"I dunno, commander," Radnor replied dully. "It startled me. To tell you the truth, it looked like we was being swarmed by a flock of starlings."

"Hmmmm." Kazaklis pondered. "Messy little buggers, aren't they? Crap all over everything. Well, gang, foiled again."

"Ohhhh," Moreau groaned at the pun.

"Well," Kazaklis said, "it's pretty tough to make a bunch of gum wrappers look like the biggest bomber in the world."

Halupalai grunted this time, not liking the put-down of his new responsibilities.

"That's okay, Electronics Warfare Sarge," Kazaklis said. "Next time try Spearmint."

"Or Dentyne," piped in Moreau. "At least it'll smell better back there in the locker room."

Halupalai laughed. So, finally, did Radnor. The omnipresent shrinks, always aboard in the spirit of their works, would have been pleased. Humor was good for PRP. Distracting. Helped make the system work.

Halupalai returned to his chores. The tinfoil was designed to fool fighters. Now he cautiously tested the powerful radar-jammer that should blind ground tracking stations. From forty-four thousand feet the electronic rays poured silently and unseen for hundreds of miles down and out from the B-52, blanketing the Canadian wilderness beneath them.

In the basement, next to Radnor, the navigator was talking to his son. *Reach for the sky, boy!* Tyler's fingers reached out toward the wide blue eyes, gently stroking the child's pink cheek. *The sky's yours, Timmie. Daddy will take you there, where you can fly high, proud. . . .* Below the photograph, Tyler's radar screen erupted in a frenzy of crazily jumbled signals and his temper erupted, too. *Irresponsible sonuvabitch!*

"Dammit, Halupalai! Knock that horseshit off! You'll screw up every civilian air controller from Edmonton to Juneau. They'll roast our royal rears when we get back!"

Halupalai instinctively turned off the jammer. Then he wondered why he was taking orders from Tyler. Then he shrugged it off. No one offered a joke. No one said a word, and they flew on silently, northward.

Kazaklis rarely went into the woods again. He held tough in school, mainly to avoid being dragged off with his old man. In his spare time, he took to cruising the pinball emporiums, then the pool halls, then the back-room poker games. Pretty soon they said the kid could tune a flipper, palm an ace, too, the way his old man could read the woods. He came back to the weathered old house on the Coos late each night, long after Big Kazaklis was shaking the rafters with that Jim Beam snore. By the time the kid was sixteen they said he could hustle a fiver out of anyone in Coos Bay, just as he could hustle the shorts off anything female. Almost anything female.

Sarah Jean was a wisp of gossamer, her golden curls flouncing down over tight teenage breasts the way they did in those slow-motion shampoo commercials. She carried him into another

world, as if she held the magic to draw him out of the murk of the
Coos and into Clairol's fantasyland where the sun always shone,
the flowers always bloomed, and a soft wind always tousled the
high grass of perfect meadows just as it tousled perfect curls.
Sarah Jean was too flawless for poon—how his pa chortled at
that—and the closest the captivated kid ever came to her shorts
was the tender touch of hands, the tentative move of a sinewy arm
over a cashmere sweater. Never had he held anyone—anything—
in such awe.

For most of his last year at high school, Sarah Jean drew him
out of the pool halls and the card rooms. He watched her at the
football games, the princess of the Coos, a cheerleader, the tight
breasts bouncing as she leaped—*rah! rah!* Then it was the basket-
ball games, where she also leaped—*rah! rah!*—the slender thighs
spreading exuberantly in a winter cheer. But she was too good
and too pure for the usual spread, and the thought barely invaded his mind. He did not go with her to the proms and the sock
hops. His pa's old truck was not good enough for that and he
understood, just as he understood when she went with others.
That would change, just like the poon, when they finally left the
sullen Coos. Together.

For months it went on, with I love you returned by I love you,
with long unwatched drives in the rattletrap old Ford truck and
longer walks down the majestic dunes where the mist always lifted
for Sarah Jean. With her, he recaptured his vision of the future.
At the shore they would walk to the highest dune and they would
sit, amid the sand ripples and the rustling reeds, dreaming and
staring far out to sea, into tomorrow, into the escape they both
wanted. They would lie back and watch the jet contrails carry
other dreamers to distant alabaster cities, knowing that they
would be carried away too. Together.

It was the night before graduation that Sarah Jean told him.
They stood on the dunes, the sun setting in a brilliant spring
evening, and she said she was not going with him. She would
make the trip into the world with the president of their class—a
kid with glasses, for God's sake; but a kid with a scholarship to
Stanford, a sure ticket out—and they would be married the next
week. Kazaklis stared into the falling sun and knew the reason was
his pa's old truck, no ticket that, but he turned toward her anyway
with cow-brown eyes dying and disbelieving.

"Why, Sarah Jean?" he asked, his words strangled in pain.

"Nothing is forever," she said simply, and the sun sank.

"Why not?" he begged, but the pain broke his voice and he couldn't wait for an answer because the tears were welling and he couldn't let her see them. He couldn't let anyone see. So he ran. To the truck. He clattered up the river road, past the old moss-covered house to the trailhead, leaped out and raced into the woods, where it was raining. And he built a fire in the rain, using pitch as his pa had taught him—damn his pa—and he sat through the night, crying.

The next night he graduated, miracle everyone said that was, and took a hustled twenty down to the Sportsmen's and laid it on the felt in front of Nikko. Her talons flicked the Bicycles at him, his fingernails deftly nicking a few edges, and the twenty turned to fifty. Which he pushed across the felt, knowing it was twice the price. The next morning, at the house on the Coos, the raven lady's clinging black trousers were hanging from the antlers over the door. Pinned to the kid's trophy was a note saying he was joining the Air Force because he didn't want to get drafted and muck around in the woods in Nam the way he had mucked around in the woods of the Coos. The real reason was that he wanted to ride the jet contrails. It was a long while before Kazaklis learned that Sarah Jean's first baby had been born just six months later. He never allowed himself to see wisps of gossamer again.

The radio silence became oppressive. For thirty minutes none of them spoke to each other, except for the occasional monotone course corrections from Tyler. And nothing had come in from the outside.

Moreau, even though she had been through this dozens of times before in long droning practice runs, felt fidgety. She squirmed in her seat, shifting against the discomfort of her parachute pack and finally relenting against the weight of her bulbous white helmet, lifting it off so her jet-black hair spilled over the fireproof green of her shoulders. She ran an ungloved hand through the hair, giving it a finger comb, and arched her back to loosen the taut muscles.

It was an inadvertently sensual show and Kazaklis cast a side-long glance at her, surreptitiously, as if he had caught her in the shower. Without the helmet, she was a woman, all right, and a pretty one, he had to admit. Her face had a soft glow in the red light and the one blank eye gave her what Kazaklis suddenly saw as a mutated beauty, as if she had been transformed from moth to butterfly.

Shake your head, Kazaklis. Bitch to witch is more like it. Last-woman-in-the-world syndrome.

Moreau, pensive and restless, suddenly broke the silence. "We gonna make it?" she asked, not seeking confirmation as much as conversation.

Kazaklis chuckled. "Wull, uh, golly gee, I dunno, ma'am," he mocked her. "You think we have time?"

Moreau's face snapped left to glare at him; then she merely shook her head in despair. "Kazaklis, I think you'd go to the Last Supper with your fly open."

"You shock me," the pilot replied gravely. "There *are* limits."

"I'm glad to hear that."

"That was a men-only outfit, Moreau. The way it was meant to be."

"Jesus."

"You know your history."

"Well, we're making it now . . ." Moreau abruptly caught herself, trying to avoid that trap again. "History, Kazaklis, making history."

Some of the bravado seemed to drain out of the pilot's voice as he replied, "Making it or ending it."

The plane bumped, a good solid whack of clear-air turbulence, and Moreau automatically reached forward to reset the flashing yellow Master Caution light. She sagged back, pulling at a strap that was pinching at her chest, and saw that Kazaklis didn't notice this time. He seemed lost in thought.

"Do you care, Kazaklis?"

"I'm trained not to care. Just like you, Moreau. Just like all of us. PRP *uber alles.* Six little, six little, six little robots, flying off to war."

"Five little robots."

"Yeah."

"You ever think much about PRP?"

"Only when the colonel stares into my bloodshot eyes at oh-eight-hundred."

"Like today."

"It's such bullshit. Who got the only B-52 off the ground at Fairchild?"

"I don't mean that part. Not whether you should show up in the morning swallowing aspirin with Listerine. Not the part about writing letters to your congressman or fighting with your husband."

"Wife. The regs say wife."

Moreau ignored him. "The sanity part," she continued. "The part that's designed to make sure that insane men won't throw the switch and sane men will."

"You want insane men doing it?"

"You think sane men *would* do it?"

Kazaklis, the commander, flinched. He looked at Moreau very carefully. Then he gurgled up a slow, mad cackle and flamboyantly placed his right hand inside his half-open flight jacket. "Josephine, *ma chère*," he said in a brutalized French accent, "Pearee is yours for zee bidding, Moscow mine for zee taking."

"You tried that once before, Nap," Moreau replied caustically. "In the winter. Froze your pecker, as I recall, giving half the feminine population of Paris a badly needed rest."

"A rest? *Chère*, my poor *chère*. How little you knew in those days. How, my dear Josephine, did you think I thawed it out?"

"Okay, okay, okay. PRP's working just fine. It's got you acting like Napoleon and Tyler acting sane. I'm not sure which worries me more. We've got ourselves an Earth-to-Mars case in the basement. He's really spaced out."

Kazaklis looked nervously at the radio-channel dial to make sure they were on private, a channel which other crewmen could, but rarely did, interrupt.

"He's numb. He's denying. And he's functioning. That's the way it's supposed to work."

"I'll remind you of that when he wakes up. Meanwhile, Halupalai's too spooked about his own future, about getting too old to do all this, to do any thinking at all. Too old. Now, that *is* funny. And Radnor's too mesmerized by his oath to God and country."

"That's PRP, pal. Five little robots, programmed differently but heading in the same direction, flying off to war." Kazaklis, the commander, paused for a moment. "Or is it four?" His voice went flat and strained.

"You'd love that, wouldn't you, macho man?" Moreau pronounced it Match-O, with a bite. "Got your hand on your forty-five? No, PRP's got me hooked, too. Proving I'm one of the boys, just as Match-O as Captain Shazam."

"There, along with Maggie Thatcher and Indira Gandhi, goes the theory that rule by the womb will save mankind."

"But that's what we robots five are doing, commander," Moreau said. "Remember?"

"Saving mankind from the Red Menace," Kazaklis responded. "Better dead than Red."

"We're deterring war, Kazaklis. Did you forget?" She added the last line with a bite. Kazaklis sat silently a moment, then laughed. She turned away abruptly, angry again.

"Reminds me of my first SAC briefing." Kazaklis ignored her, continuing to chuckle. "Colonel gave us the full works—failure of deterrence, men, means the failure of our mission! We are here to prevent war, not fight it. But one of the new guys pops up: 'Does that mean if it all starts we don't have to go?' Jesus. You'd think the Russians had just infiltrated a commissar onto the Command Balcony. The colonel wriggled like he had a SAM up his behind. 'Son,' he said, the others being men, of course, 'are you on Dristan?'"

"And you never saw him again," Moreau said.

"Nope."

"Probably the sanest one in the room. You tell him nuclear war is insane. So the world goes nuts and he asks if it's sane or insane to go nuts with it. Not exactly an illogical question."

"Sanity is what everybody else is doing, Moreau."

"Right. Like Jonestown. Nine hundred little robots marching up to the Kool-Aid barrel. Like the arms race. Crazy to build fifty thousand nuclear weapons. But if everybody else is doing it, it's crazy not to build them. That means mass suicide is sane. It's crazy to do it, but if everybody is doing it, it's sane. Right?"

"You think too much, college girl," Kazaklis said. Suddenly he didn't like this. At all.

"Getting a little close to home?"

"You on Dristan?" the commander asked, his voice betraying no humor at all. "Be careful. PRP would give you the hook right now. Pull your ejection lever."

"When we get back, you can report me to PRP while I'm turning you in to the Equal Rights Commission." She paused. "Dristan. You never did understand the narcotic, did you? Pumping your goddamn quarters into that goddamn machine. You got better. It got better." She paused again. "Who won, Kazaklis?"

Kazaklis looked at her curiously, then very carefully. He wanted her to stop. Now. But Moreau, caught up in it all, went on.

"Remember Yossarian in *Catch-22*? Only sane man in a crazy world. So sane they thought he was crazy. He didn't want to fly his B-25 on any more of those World War II suicide runs. So he told the shrinks he was crazy. And why do you think you're crazy, Yossarian? Because I don't want to fly anymore. Then you must be sane, because it's crazy to want to fly into flak and Messerschmitts. You mean you think I'm crazy but if I'm crazy enough to want to stop flying I must be sane because it's crazy to want to fly? That's right, Yossarian. Catch-22."

"Next," Kazaklis said wearily, "you'll tell me B-25 spelled backwards is B-52."

"Very shrewd, Kazaklis."

"I think you'd better shut up. Now."

"Oh, don't worry, commander. PRP's working. The five little robots are droning mechanically along. We're all heading for Irkutsk on the Doomsday Express, each for our own individualized, preprogrammed reasons. Me too. PRP's ingenious. PRP's the Catch-22 of World War III. Commander. Sir."

Kazaklis tuned her out. Damn her. This was a new side of her. Unexpected. But he blamed himself for playing along with her too long. Everyone was spooking. Even he was spooking.

The plane hit another pocket of clear-air turbulence. *Thwack!* The big bomber shuddered. Moreau efficiently pulled on the wheel, flicked out the Master Caution light, and did a routine sweep of the instrument readings.

She's all right, Kazaklis decided. Her way of venting. Everyone in the plane could use some venting, but he didn't want the rest of the crew hearing hers. He switched to all channels.

"This is your captain speaking," Kazaklis said brightly. "On behalf of Strangelove Airlines and your flight crew I'd like to welcome you aboard our Stratocruiser flight to Irkutsk, with possible intermediate passovers—little pun there, folks, heh-heh, for our Jewish passengers—in Leningrad, Moscow, Vladivostok, and other scenic Soviet cities. Our estimated time of arrival in Irkutsk is ten P.M., local time. Barring local air-traffic problems, folks, and you, heh-heh, know how pesky those can be . . ."

The pilot's mind was racing in one direction while his words moved in another. Damn, he wished he would hear something.

From Omaha, from the Pentagon, from the *Looking Glass*. From the tanker. From somebody.

". . . As you may have noticed, we have been experiencing some mild clear-air turbulence. Absolutely nothing to concern you, of course. For those of you who are not familiar with our safety procedures, however, I wish to point out that the little red lever to the left of your seat is not an armrest. I repeat, the little red lever is not an armrest. . . ."

He knew he wouldn't hear much in any case. Just orders. Go or don't go, although there seemed little doubt about that one. And where. That could always change.

". . . From time to time I will point out some areas of interest along our flight path. At the moment, we have just passed into Canada's Northwest Territories. Those of you on the right of the aircraft would have a magnificent moonlight view of frozen Great Slave Lake. On the left the panorama of the Mackenzie Mountains, and beyond them, the romantic Yukon, would also be stunning. If we had windows, heh-heh. . . ."

PRP wouldn't want them to know what had happened back home. PRP wouldn't want them to know if they were expected to penetrate Russia against full defenses or massive clouds of fallout. Not yet. PRP would want them to be five little robots.

". . . Now, folks, please settle back, enjoy your flight, and if our charming stewardess can be of any assistance to you, please call on her."

Kazaklis bowed grandly toward Moreau.

"Coffee, tea, or Kool-Aid?" she said sweetly into the open mike.

God damn you, the pilot mouthed silently over the droning engines. Kool-Aid. Jonestown. Suicide. Damn you, Moreau.

Far to the south, inside the *Looking Glass*, the isolation also was getting to Alice. Not the smell of the sweat. Not the tediously weaving figure-eight flight pattern in which the pilot had placed them high over the Midwest. Not even the mind's vision—ruthlessly subdued—of the huge pockmarks he knew had been gouged into the dark prairies below. It was the frustration of being gagged, of being inside a command aircraft that could not command.

More than an hour ago, in the last frantic minutes before Icarus had gone, Alice had sent out a flurry of orders, some of them quite unusual. Hurried messages to Greenland and into the Canadian wastes, desperately setting up links between his few surviving B-52's and the still fewer tanker planes that seemed scattered in all the wrong places. He also had sent a single supersonic FB-111 racing far ahead of the B-52's to test America's new air-launched cruise missiles and, more important, to test the Soviet coastal defenses long before the Buffs would get there. But now Alice had no idea what good the tests would do, what the links would accomplish. Since the sizzles and snaps of the electromagnetic pulse, Alice may have been in command. But he was a commander who was deaf, dumb, and blind.

Forlornly he looked down the narrow aisle of the converted old 707 jet. Panels had been unhinged from switchboards to get inside at burned-out wiring. Teletype machines, supposedly the most secure standby for this moment, sat dismembered. The tops were off almost all the computers jammed into the plane's small work space. His battle staff of twenty had jackets off, sleeves rolled up, sweaty foreheads poked inside the innards of wounded computers. Circuit boards littered the floor of an airplane usually scrub-brush clean. He stared into his black phone with its white light that now refused to blink.

Slowly Alice rose from his swivel seat and moved toward Sam. He laid a hand on the colonel's shoulder, feeling the wetness seep through a rumpled blue shirt as the man removed his head from the bowels of an open computer. "Anything?" Alice asked.

"I don't know, general." The colonel brushed an arm across his forehead. "I thought I had it back a minute ago. Then it just flared and went down again. I'd like to get ahold of the frigging egghead who said we could protect an airplane against EMP."

Alice forced himself to act the commander. "We knew the pulse would raise hell, Sam." He squeezed the colonel's shoulder. "We'll get it back."

"I know, sir. Sorry if I sounded down."

Down, Alice, thought. Good God. How else should the poor bastard sound? He turned and returned to his seat, glancing at a large paper wall map covered with multicolored targets. They would get it back, Alice thought. But they had so little time. How the devil could he run a war if he couldn't talk to anybody? And where the devil was Harpoon, who was supposed to snatch the man who really had to run this war?

*   *   *

Still farther south, in the *E-4*, Harpoon had more elbow room, but no more of anything else. He moved slowly, his white hair marking him regally, through compartment after compartment of the much larger plane. The men and women of his staff withdrew their heads and hands from similarly gutted computers and communications equipment, casting pained looks at the admiral. He nodded at them confidently, disguising his emotions, and moved on.

Like Alice, he had spoken to no one outside since the sizzles and snaps. Like Alice, he had sent out a flurry of desperate messages before the pulse struck them. Unlike Alice, he now had more to worry about than getting his communications gear working again. He had to get the man. And Harpoon was more confident about the first than he was the second.

In the final frenzied moments before the EMP wave, he had rousted a contingent of Secret Service agents working on a counterfeiting case in Baton Rouge, a city that had not been struck. He had tried to patch a radio call through to the potential successor forty miles outside the Louisiana city and cursed the communications system when he couldn't get through. He then had worked out a rendezvous time, cutting it very close considering the panic the agents had described on the ground. He had checked and rechecked the runway dimensions at the Baton Rouge airport and knew the extraordinarily heavy *E-4* had no business putting down on them. He had issued orders for the dispatching of all available troops to the airport when the Secret Service agents told him the rioting quite naturally centered there. But he had no idea whether those orders got through.

Harpoon emerged from the neutered satellite-tracking compartment into the curved outer hallway of his command plane, returning a snap salute from a one-star Air Force general. Their eyes locked briefly, transmitting an unspoken message of despair, and they began to move past each other wordlessly.

Abruptly Harpoon stopped. "Where are we now, general?" he asked. "Precisely."

"Just north of Texarkana, sir."

"The pilot's keeping us away from Shreveport?"

"Christ, yes, admiral. The Russians kicked hell out of Barksdale Air Force Base. The fallout's pretty mean."

"Yes." Harpoon suddenly felt very tired. "We'll get to Baton Rouge early."

"Very." The general looked at Harpoon anxiously. "We'll have to orbit quite a while. We can't go down and wait."

Harpoon said nothing.

"We shouldn't go down at all, admiral," the general volunteered cautiously. "This baby would have trouble handling those runways under ideal circumstances."

Harpoon's eyes flashed at him. "We're not fighting this war without the Commander-in-Chief, general."

"He might not even be there."

Harpoon's eyes drifted.

"Who's he going to command, admiral?" the general asked softly.

Harpoon's eyes returned to his fellow officer and remained on him implacably. "We're going down for the man."

On the ground, not too far beyond Harpoon's approaching command plane, a young Secret Service agent cradled a submachine gun as he crouched behind the half-open door of an armored troop carrier commandeered after rioters had disabled his group's helicopter. "Spray them," his superior said. He looked uncertainly at the senior agent. Two of their eight-man contingent were already dead and one other was wounded. They were no more than twenty miles out of Baton Rouge. Ahead of them, on State Route 77, the road was barricaded by perhaps a dozen locals and three battered old cars.

"Spray them, dammit." The voice was insistent.

The young agent unloaded his Uzi into the three vehicles. A wisp of smoke rose from the middle car. He heard groans. A rifle shot snapped back from the barricade, its bullet pinging off the top of the armored door.

"Okay, everybody open up," the senior agent ordered.

The country road erupted in a thunder of automatic gunfire. The middle car broke into flames. The others began smoldering in the light rain of the Louisiana night. The thunder fell off into a brief silence and the senior agent bellowed, "Now! Move it!" The armored car gunned toward the barricade, then cut to the side and clipped the fender of one of the smoking cars before rumbling onward into the blackness.

Kool-Aid. In the cockpit of *Polar Bear One*, Kazaklis still was glaring at Moreau, who smiled back innocently, when the outside world clattered in at them for the first time in an hour.

"JIMA 14, JIMA 14." The voice, laced with the raspy twang of western Canada, scratched its way into the cockpit. "This is Klickitat One. I see ya up there, Yank, but I don't hear ya. Aincha got a few words for a cold and lonely Canuck?"

"Who the hell is Klickitat One?" Kazaklis asked Moreau.

"Beats me. Some rattled bush pilot?"

"No. He's on our emergency frequency. He must be a radar-watcher at some fire base. He knows he shouldn't be calling. Check the book. Fast."

Moreau shuffled quickly past the reams of Siberian flight charts on her right and retrieved a two-inch-thick book. It was well-worn and marked in faded black letters: "Procedures—Top Secret." She thumbed immediately to the right page. "Ask him 'How's fishing?' she said.

Klickitat One replied immediately. "Through the ice. Grayling and northern pike."

Kazaklis looked at Moreau and she nodded. "Reply: 'Walleyes not biting, partner?'" she said. Kazaklis gave the acknowledgment.

"Oh, Yank, I'm glad it's you," the voice responded. "After two hours of this, and everybody gettin' drunker'n a skunk over at Ruby's in Yellowknife, I thought I was seein' thangs. You're a Buff? Just one of ya's?"

"This is *Polar Bear One*," Kazaklis replied, ignoring the rest.

"Out of?"

"Come on, Klickitat. What's goin' on?" Kazaklis asked angrily. "We're on an open channel."

"Strange doin's, *Polar Bear*. Sorry. But I need to know. Snow Bird or Cow Pasture?"

Kazaklis paused unhappily. The Canadian radar-watcher, sitting in some lonely outpost on the shores of Great Slave Lake, had just given him the code names for Minot and Fairchild. Shit, he thought. Forty years to plan this, and we're playing British commando games.

"Cow Pasture," Kazaklis spat into the radio.

"You're it," the voice crackled up out of the frozen tundra below.

"That's nice, real nice," Kazaklis said. "Wanta say bye-bye now?"

"Got a message for you, *Polar Bear. Elsie's* had a change in plans. She's been waiting for you at the corner of Ninth and Easy streets. Got that? Easy Nin-er."

"Easy Nin-er," Kazaklis repeated.

Moreau thumbed rapidly through the book again, tracing E down to nine, and nodded at Kazaklis. "Smack dab on the Arctic Circle, commander," she said. "At 124 degrees west."

"Funny way to make a date," Kazaklis continued with Klickitat. *"Elsie*'s choosy, Yank. She's the only girl in town."

"What made you the matchmaker, Klickitat?"

"Dunno for sure. Maybe you're the only lad."

"And *Elsie*'s too shy to call me herself?"

"Her phone's not workin' too well, *Polar Bear.*"

"Why didn't her old man call?"

"Dunno. Lotta phone trouble tonight."

Kazaklis drummed his fingers on the two upraised white throttles numbered four and five, finally hammering at them so hard the inboard engines gunned in acceleration. Moreau grabbed at the knobs and quickly pulled them back into pitch.

"Goddammit it!" Kazaklis roared at Klickitat. "I don't think I believe you! This is so damned far down the contingency list it's barely in the book."

"Don't God-damn me, Yank," Klickitat replied evenly. "This is your fuss. Your people planned it, not mine. Your people built all the toys, not mine. We just happen to be your friends, passin' on a message. Take it or leave it, bucko. Then I'm gonna sit back and wait for the ash to start fallin'."

Kazaklis took a deep breath. Then he spoke more calmly, breaking out of the lingo. "Klickitat," the pilot said, "the book says you're real. But you know the game. I gotta take my orders from command authorities."

"Great theory, Yank. But their phone seems to be off the hook."

"I just don't believe the Russians took out everything, including the *Looking Glass*. It just isn't possible."

"Well, I'll tell ya, Yank, on one of those middlin' days, when you look up at the sky and can't quite figure out which way the weather's goin', you got two choices. You can look up and say it's partly cloudy. Or you can look up and say it's partly sunny."

The conversation paused briefly.

"Now, I can look back south, Yank, and try to figure that out," Klickitat continued. "I can say there ain't nothin' left a-tall. Or I can say the Russians beat things up a bit but made damn sure they took out your communications. You don't need to look up EMP in your book, do ya?"

"Nobody knew what it would do."

"They had a pretty good idea, Yank. One big boom, maybe two, a hundred miles above the prairies would send out enough voltage to burn out damn near every vacuum tube and transistor in America."

"The command plane was hardened against EMP," Kazaklis said.

"Nobody knew what it would do," Klickitat mimicked Kazaklis. "But take your own choice. I do know it ain't all gone. My short-wave's still pickin' up radio stations. Odd places. Iowa. Oregon. West Virginia."

"Well, what are they saying, for Christ's sake?"

"Oh, not sayin', Yank. Just playin'. Ballads. Blues. Lot of John Lennon. Got myself one of your Moral Majority preachers. Blamin' it all on abortions. Kill and ye shall be killed. Appreciated that, I did. Surprised you ain't listenin'. Disciplined bunch, you guardians of democracy."

Kazaklis loosened up. "We switched off on a commercial for Oxy-5."

"Excedrin Headache number seventy-nine didn't do much for me, either."

"Okay, Klickitat, I guess I got a date on Easy Street."

"One more thing, Yank. Think I'd haul ass if I was you. *Elsie*'s motor is runnin' and she's low on gas."

"The refueling plane is running out of fuel?" Kazaklis asked incredulously. "You got any more partly sunny news?"

"Oh, she's got some in the tank for you, *Polar Bear One*. Just not enough for the both of you. She was cruisin' around on a practice run when all this happened. That's why she's the only girl in town."

"God. So when's the date?"

"Twenty minutes. Like I said, think I'd haul ass."

"Haul ass? She's forty minutes away."

"I got her headin' south soon as I picked you up on the screen. Intersecting courses, assumin' you know how to navigate that beast. Date's on. Twenty minutes."

Kazaklis shivered. Refueling in midair with a troubled tanker. It was bad enough on a normal mission. But he was out of choices. Partly sunny it was.

"Thanks, pal," the pilot said. "Run on over to Ruby's and have a drink on me. Jack Daniel's."

"Naw. I can use the overtime. Somebody's gotta watch the Pole for you guys. Don't think you need any Red Stars comin' over the top just yet. Thumbs up, Yank."

Kazaklis felt the shiver run through him again. "Thumbs up, Canuck," he said.

Eternal vigilance, Moreau thought bleakly.

Six

In the New Mexico valley the Spanish called Jornada del Muerto, the journey of the dead, the heat storms roil out of the south, sucking up the dead mesquite and the fine sand particles in a choking desert wind that moves quickly through the wastelands and buffets finally into the deep-purple walls of the Oscuro Mountains. It started here, and even as a ten-year-old making an only partly understood pilgrimage with her father, Moreau knew that.

It was a forbidding place. The sandstorms could etch the skin off a foolish man. But by now, in the late sixties, the storms contented themselves with etching his relics instead, most of the foolish men having left long ago. In the loneliness, the winds carved at the stark, sun-petrified bunkers into which the desert rats darted for shelter at the first far-off whisper of the wind or visitors. The antelope bounded into the deepest purple clefts of the Oscuros. The buzzards, black scavengers of all desert foolishness, lifted themselves ponderously and reluctantly off the twisted scarecrow crosses, the Trinity crosses, from which the last men to work here draped their hearing wires a generation gone. The rattlers were the last to leave, catching the final rays of a sun that burned with the white-hot luminescence of dry ice. They slithered quickly into the snug safety beneath the rotting floorboards of

133

man's most conspicuous relic, the old adobe house known as the McDonald ranch. Standing in the middle of the desert's hostile isolation, miles from any neighbor, the ranch house could be a testament to man's unceasing efforts to challenge and control nature's most unruly elements. But it isn't. In the old adobe house he assembled the first nuclear explosive and then moved a few miles past the buzzards to unleash those elements.

The sands had stopped now and the freckled young Army lieutenant swung the jeep to a bumpy stop among the greasewood scrub growing like weeds in the McDonalds' abandoned yard. The child eagerly hopped out first, racing straight for an old windmill which tilted precariously from neglect, dry skeletons of tumbleweed clinging to its ankles. The general went next.

The general was a strange cluck, the lieutenant thought, taking a kid to a place like this. But General Moreau was one of the cold war's living legends and the lieutenant imagined all such people were strange. He watched as the father tenderly took his daughter's hand. But General Moreau walked as if he had the child in one hand, the world in the other. He cut an imposing, intimidating figure, befitting a legend—walking ramrod straight and unswervingly, his coal-black hair infiltrated by the first bristling strands of iron gray, his eyes frozen blue in their certainty. The lieutenant wondered briefly if he held the world's hand as tenderly. The general made the lieutenant nervous. He accurately sensed the man wanted to be alone with his daughter, as if he had some private lesson to impart. But the young officer hurried after his two wards.

"What you want to see is in here, sir," the lieutenant called out, cursing himself for what he thought was a squeak in his voice. He beckoned them back toward the sagging ranch house. "Watch your step. The porch is gone now."

The general's eyes paused on him in silent intimidation and then swept past. The girl, long-legged, skinny, and lithe, bounded around him and darted through a door swinging loosely on one hinge. He started to warn her, then thought better of it. It was a father's place, dammit, to caution his kid against risks. The general said nothing and the two of them followed her into the empty living room.

She stood entranced. The windows were long gone, the panes ground by the desert winds into the dust from which they came, so that not even a glass shard remained. The ceiling rafters hung in cobweb shadows. The hardwood floors, once the pride of the McDonalds, were a swamp of dry-rot traps beneath which, the lieutenant knew, the rattlers still were curled up from the storm.

"You can almost feel the ghosts in here, can't you, general?" the lieutenant volunteered. "Oppenheimer, Fermi, Szilard, Bethe. Even those who are still alive seem like ghosts. Haunted by what they did. Getting senile, I guess." The lieutenant hesitated, trying to think of something to please the general. "Too bad," he added. "It was mankind's greatest scientific achievement."

The soldier moved gingerly across the floor, leading them into a second, smaller room.

"Critical mass room," he explained. "Built the bomb—called it the gadget—up at Los Alamos, but this is where they got it ready for the test. Put the hemispheres together by hand. With a screwdriver. Imagine that. A few months later, when they were getting the Bikini bomb ready back up at Los Alamos, the screwdriver slipped. Guy reached in and pulled the spheres apart with his bare hands. Saved the barn, but he sure was a gone goose, even though it took nine days. Hair fell out, so they said, and his bones just turned to pulp. Helluva way to go."

The lieutenant could see the general's back stiffen. Jesus, he was really blowing this.

The girl seemed oblivious to the tension between the two adults. She stared transfixed, as her father should have known a child would, at a far wall on which initials were carved crudely.

G. J. Loves J. J.

The general had been here before, not at the beginning but as a later visitor to the shrine. The initials left him vaguely uncomfortable. The ranch had been ignored for years, but it had remained deep inside the Army's top-secret White Sands Missile Range since the end of the Second World War, surrounded by miles of untracked desert which, in turn, was surrounded by guards and fences and sensors. But G. J. and J. J., two unknown kids, had slipped through all that, come in here and carved their own memorial on one of man's strangest monuments. You had to be a determinist, believe in man's ability to control events, to do what General Moreau did. The initials seemed so random, so unlikely. General Moreau did not like random events.

"Who was G. J., Dad?" the girl asked, brightly curious. "Did he make the bomb?"

"Made J. J., more likely," the lieutenant blurted out, grinning at the father. The joke was a mistake. The general turned and stared hard and steely-eyed at him. Without another word, the flustered young escort saluted, turned on his heels, and hurried out to wait in the hot jeep.

The girl squeezed her father's hand. She held him in total awe. But he held her in awe, too. She was nature's grant of immortality, his only child, his only tie to the future, especially now that his wife was gone. He intended to give her that future intact. He also wanted her to take some responsibility for it, as he had taken it on himself. The two of them sat down on weathered old packing crates which lay broken open, the faded transit instructions still visible from the summer of 1945. Masking tape hung like flypaper from the ceiling where the physicists had sealed cracks against the blowing sands. The place looked as if the men had fled after their work was done, the girl thought, not bothering to clean up after themselves.

"The lieutenant isn't very smart, Dad," she said. "Live men can't be ghosts."

"They can lose faith," her father replied. "That can make a ghost of a man."

"Is that what happened to the men who made the atomic bomb?"

"Some of them. The men who worked in this room before you were born left a terrible burden for the world. I don't envy them."

The girl frowned. She didn't understand. She knew her father carried the same burden; that, in fact, he carried atomic bombs around in his airplanes and directed men who sat underground with huge missiles with bombs on top of them.

"Why don't we just throw them all away, Dad?" she asked with the crystalline logic of a ten-year-old.

"It's too late for that, Mo." Her father's voice carried the slightest touch of sadness, the first she had heard since her mother died. "The men can't take away what they did in this room. They can't uninvent what they invented. Now it's up to the rest of us to learn to live with it. Most people choose to ignore it. I choose to deal with it, the only way I know how."

"I'm going to die from it, aren't I?" There was no alarm in the girl's words. Just ten-year-old certainty.

"No!" The reply was an order, more sharp and stern than the eye command to the lieutenant, and the girl was taken aback, as if she had failed her father.

"That's what all the kids say, Dad," she continued cautiously. "They're afraid of it. They said the world is going to blow up and we're all going to die. Sometimes I have to fight with them." She loved her father too much to tell him the fights were over him. But he knew.

"I'm sorry, Mo," he said, his eyes drifting toward G. J. Loves J. J. "I'm sorry your friends are afraid. I'm sorry you have to fight. I don't know if you can understand this yet, but fear is my job. It's my job to keep everyone so afraid no one will ever use these bombs again."

"How long do you have to do it, Dad?" she asked, eyes down, her small, fine hand picking at the old bomb crate.

"Forever, honey. Eternal vigilance, President Kennedy said. After me, someone else and then someone else and then someone else. Forever, into infinity."

The girl continued picking at the crate. She remembered a talk with her mother, just before she died. How big is the universe, Mom? Eternal and infinite, her mother had answered. How big is that, Mom? Forever, child. But it must have some end, Mom. Don't think about such things, child, because they have no answers and they will drive you mad. Her mother had sounded very sad.

"Mom said infinity can drive you crazy, Dad."

Her father stood up very slowly and led her back to the jeep for the short, bumpy ride to the site of the Trinity explosion itself.

A solitary buzzard circled slowly ahead of them, then settled on one of the stubby Trinity crosses beyond the outer fence. Two fences surrounded the crater, the first with a sign that read "DANGER—RADIATION," the second warning that no one was to stay inside longer than ninety minutes without protective clothing. The lieutenant opened both gates and led his visitors toward the center.

"What kind of radiation count are you getting these days?" the general asked.

"It's still hot," the young man answered, looking uncomfortable. "But less than a chest X ray if you don't stay too long. The crater doesn't really look like much now. Somebody bulldozed dirt into it years ago. The dirt settled, so you get this shallow dip like a saucer. After the explosion, the crater was green as an emerald. The heat fused the sand into green glass."

"Brighter than a thousand suns," the general said absentmind-edly.

"The glass still works its way to the surface," the lieutenant went on. "Trinitite, the scientists named it. Maybe we can find a piece for your daughter."

At the center of the depression, the lieutenant stopped. "Just a pile of dirt now, sir, but this is ground zero. Everything vaporized here. The scientific gear. The steel tower. The concrete footings. Hard to imagine we make them hundreds, thousands of times more powerful now."

The girl kicked at the dead dirt in search of a piece of the green glass.

"The only part of the original crater is over there," the lieutenant said, pointing at a low weathered hut that resembled a chicken coop. "They wanted to save it for the scientists. But nobody goes there now. Roof's falling in. I guess we've got enough places to study this stuff now. We've dropped a helluva lot of 'em since Trinity."

"Why did they call it Trinity, Dad?" the girl asked.

"I don't know, Mo. Dr. Oppenheimer named it."

"But Trinity means the Father, the Son, and the Holy Ghost," she said, puzzled.

"Yes," her father replied distantly.

"Did they think they were making another God?"

The general didn't answer. He stared into the dark recesses of the Oscuros, against which the fireball and the mushroom had been framed. General Moreau had seen his own mushrooms, and his mind drifted now to Oppenheimer's thoughts on that morn-ing in 1945. At first the physicist had seen great beauty, and he recalled the lines from an ancient Hindu epic: "If the radiance of a thousand suns were to burst at once into the sky, that would be like the splendor of the Mighty One." Then Oppenheimer had recalled the next lines of the epic: "I am become death, the shat-terer of worlds." The general sighed.

"I don't know, Mo," he said after a moment. "I really don't know." The wind whistled quietly in the desert. Ahead of him the lieutenant was pawing at the dirt for a souvenir for his daughter. He turned to get her, and she was gone.

"Mo!" he screamed, putting the lie to the image of total, steely discipline. He sprinted toward the sagging chicken-coop shelter. Through a gaping hole in the roof he peered down into the dark greenness. His daughter sat on the emerald floor, shuddering, her hands holding the broken remnants of a trinitite slab she had just crushed over the head of a rattlesnake. He leaped in, grabbed the girl, and thrust her out, following quickly.

In the hot desert sun the girl stood trembling, eyes brimming with tears, one hand still full of her broken green prize.

"I was afraid, Daddy," she whispered, struggling to control a sob. "He tried to bite me."

"He was more afraid than you," the father said, covering his own racking fear. He drew a deep breath, forced a broad grin, and scooped her into his arms. "Eternal vigilance," he said.

She looked up at him reverently, the fear lost now in pride over belonging to a father who, to her, was half-god and who would, although she did not know how at the time, forever change her life. Behind them, the lieutenant rolled his eyes upward, catching the arcing shadow of the buzzard, which, as was its way, had lifted off the Trinity cross and circled now. Eternal vigilance, he thought.

"After you," the girl said softly, "I'll do it, Dad."

Kazaklis reached for the radio dial, switched it to intercom, and bent over halfheartedly for his helmet. He brushed against the dirty flash curtain, jarring it into a slow, heavy ripple, and forgot the helmet. He called downstairs. "Okay, navigator, give me a course correction for an intercept point in twenty minutes. You heard *Elsie*'s coordinates, 124 degrees west at the circle?"

No reply returned.

"Tyler?" Kazaklis said.

"Timmie?" Tyler said.

Kazaklis turned toward Moreau, his look despairing. He took his right hand off the controls and rubbed it abrasively up the side of his face, as if he were scouring a frying pan.

"Tyler!" he ordered.

Below, Radnor looked curiously at his buddy. Tyler's eyes were riveted again on his son. Cautiously Radnor reached over and nudged the navigator's arm. Tyler turned slowly toward the nudge, but his eyes seemed focused far beyond the tight walls of their compartment.

"You want me to do it?" Radnor quietly asked.

Tyler seemed puzzled. "Do it?" he asked.

"The commander needs a new course to the IP," Radnor said as unemotionally as he could manage. "Did you get the coordinates?"

"Oh, sure," Tyler said blandly. "From the ground. Boy, this is a strange one, isn't it? From the ground. This one's really strange."

"Tyler, you want me to do it?" Radnor was getting worried, and his voice reflected it.

Tyler suddenly exploded. "You do your job, Radnor!" he lashed out. "I'll do mine!" Then, just as quickly, his face changed from fury to intentness. He hunched professionally over his console, worked out the course change, and radioed up to Kazaklis: "Ten degrees left, sir. Maintain altitude. Radar contact approximately twelve minutes."

Radnor briefly watched Tyler, who seemed completely normal now, and then turned back to his own console, the corner of his eye catching O'Toole's red boot before his gaze settled back on the hypnotic rhythm of the radar arm sweeping methodically across his screen. The young airman's wife broke through his defenses, a haloed image now of an always smiling, always bubbling woman, always gushing about their future—the two kids they wanted, a boy and a girl; a house with lots of land somewhere in the Big Sky West, their own American dream. And growing old together. He marveled how this young woman, whom he loved so dearly, could derive so much pleasure from the dream of growing old together, sometimes fantasizing about the joys of having grandchildren before they had children.

"Hey, Radnor," Tyler said. "I'm sorry I jumped all over you. This one is just kinda getting to me. You know?"

"Yeah, I know, pal. Me, too," Radnor said.

"I'll be glad when it's over."

"Me, too."

Tyler's voice abruptly turned exuberant. "You know what I'm gonna do when we get back? Buy Timmie a bike! Every boy oughta have a bike, don't ya think?"

God damn.

"Don't you really think so?"

God damn. Timmie is only three years old. Is. God damn. Was. Radnor's mind was beginning to spin now. "My wife wasn't on duty today," he said.

"I know."

"That was real tough for the boy out on the runway. It wasn't a drill, was it?"

"I dunno." Tyler's voice went dull.

Radnor groped for words. His mind felt waxen. "My wife . . ." He stumbled. "Laura must feel rotten about it."

"One hundred twenty-four degrees west . . ." Tyler said.

God damn. Radnor shook his head violently. He forced the haloed image out of his head. He would be glad when this one was over, all right, even though he had no doubt how it would end.

Upstairs, Kazaklis completed the course maneuver and looked at his watch, the luminous face staring back at him like a jack-o'-lantern. 0830 Zulu—12:30 in Spokane, two and a half hours into the mission. Good God, 150 minutes. The shrinks talked about delayed-shock syndrome, the flip-outs coming months or years later. But they never could simulate this one, try as they might. Everybody tried, especially after we started talking about fighting it instead of deterring it. His memory froze on a television news clip he had seen a few weeks earlier, with some civil-defense bureaucrat testifying before Congress. A congressman asked him how you hardened an industrial plant against nuclear attack. With bulldozers, sir. Bulldozers? With an attack imminent, sir, you plow dirt over the essential machinery. Dirt? It enables the machinery to absorb a higher level of psi's, sir. What? Pounds per square inch, sir, during a detonation. And after the detonation? We dig the machinery out, sir. Who the hell is "we"? The survivors, sir. And what do these patriotic survivors do for electrical power after a couple of megatons has flattened Pittsburgh? Kazaklis remembered that the bureaucrat looked at his inquisitor as if the congressman had a brain the size of a wart. The bureaucrat, after all, had *studied* this. Sir, the civil-defense man said, do you realize that if we strung together all the automobile batteries in Pittsburgh we'd have enough power to run U.S. Steel for *two* years? He had a vision of ant brigades of Russians, one brigade plowing dirt over the factories in Irkutsk right now, the other wiring automobiles together. Lots of luck, comrades. He sighed.

Dammit, he had a few wires to string together in his airplane. Yossarian, huh? Those guys went through forty to fifty missions, skies black with flak, before it was bananas time. But his crew got it all compressed into ten hours, with no Betty Grable pinups to go back to, nothing to go back to. The eggheads could do all the planning they wanted, line up the bulldozers and the PRP shrinks, and there still was no way to figure human responses to this one. No way at all. Hell, so far they had had the easy part. Except for their little minuet with the nudets at the beginning, this had been two and a half hours of droning, dull flight. Maybe that was the problem. It was too dull.

"Copilot," Kazaklis said brusquely, "get on the horn and see if you can pick up *Elsie*. She's less than four hundred miles away."

It wasn't going to be dull much longer. Refueling was enough to make anybody sweat blood. Then they'd be near the PCP, the positive control point at which they had to wait for confirmed orders to go in. Then across the Arctic ice. Then the coastal defenses of Russia. And after that . . .

Moreau adjusted the radio frequency and put out the call. "This is *Polar Bear* calling *Elsie*. Do you read? Date's on, sweetheart. Do you read me, *Elsie*? This is *Polar Bear One*. You ready for the dance? Acknowledge. *Polar Bear* calling *Elsie*. Do you read?"

Moreau's hand involuntarily jerked to her ear at the squawk of static. A jackhammer of sounds, bz-zuz-zuz-eeee-eowwww-eee-zzzzz-zap, pounded her eardrums. The static broke intermittently with a babble of disconnected words, ". . . bear . . . extreme . . . condenser . . . breakaway . . . effort . . ."

"I think we're being jammed," Moreau said to Kazaklis.

"No," the pilot replied. "Klickitat got through. They're receiving but patching their gear with Band-Aids. Tell 'em we understand, we have an IP in sixteen minutes, and we want to refuel at thirty-four thousand feet. We'll pick 'em up on radar soon." He thought quickly. The two aircraft were closing on each other at twenty miles a minute. "Tell 'em to try again in five minutes."

This is going to be some refueling, Kazaklis thought. *Elsie*'s running out of gas and can't talk. Tyler, who's absolutely essential to this high-wire act, is downstairs talking to Timmie. And the Russians, if they've got anything left at all, could be watching and listening. Moreau finished the message and switched to private. "This is gonna be real fun," she said. "I think you ought to let Radnor handle the refueling navigation."

"Nope."

"Tyler sounds like he's ready for the farm."

"Maybe he's Yossarian," Kazaklis said sarcastically. "The only sane one left."

"Well, that's an idea worth pondering," Moreau said, and Kazaklis immediately wished he had kept his mouth shut.

"We're going to make this airplane function," the pilot said stonily. "We got a long way to go. We're already down one. We need everybody and we're going to use everybody. Tyler's okay when the heat's on."

"Sanity and insanity," Moreau murmured, ignoring the pilot's words. "How many Minuteman launch-control officers do you think turned the keys? We've got a hundred launch capsules, two men to a capsule, ten missiles each. That's two hundred men with one thousand ICBM's. How many would you bet launched their missiles?"

Kazaklis felt the anger well up. "Moreau, I'm not getting into this shit with you again. I don't care if you're wacko, I'm wacko, Tyler's wacko, or the President's wacko. We're going to do what we were trained to do. Right now that means refueling this bird."

Moreau ignored him again. "My guess is 197."

"You're wrong on that one," Kazaklis snapped. "PRP made sure of that. It took simultaneous key turns. So it might have been two and it might have been two hundred. It sure as hell wasn't 197." Again Kazaklis wished he had bitten his tongue. Moreau was mousetrapping him into another one of these screwball conversations.

"My bet's still 197."

"Forget it."

"Yeah, I figure 196 launched just like nice little robots should. Two figured out a long time ago, talked it over in some bar like your Boom-Boom Room, that they wouldn't do it. And in that one other capsule two guys had their own little World War Three. Number 199 turned right on schedule. Three, two, one . . . mark. Number 200 sat there and stared at the Missiles Away light and froze. No go. He couldn't do it."

Moreau paused. Kazaklis wouldn't play. Moreau took his straight-man line anyway.

"So then what happened? Number 199 took out his handgun. That's what they've got them for. To use on each other. They weren't expecting a commie invasion sixty feet under those wheatfields. So Number 199 points the forty-five at Number 200 and says: Turn the goddamn key. Number 200 looks at his buddy and shrugs: It's all over, gumdrop, so let's give the mamushka in Kiev ten hours to pack before the Buffs get there. Ka-*pow!* War's over for Number 200. Omaha overrides his key and the missiles go anyway."

Moreau paused again. Kazaklis was seething and she could feel it.

"Now, the ultimate question is: who was the sane one? Number 200? He tried to give the mamushka, plus a million or so, an extra ten hours. He ends up dead and the mamushka does, too. Number 199? He followed his training, killed a million commie devils and one buddy. And if he's lucky—or unlucky, depending on your point of view—and the Russians missed his capsule, he's sitting down there now in a twelve-by-twelve bunker staring at a dead man. He gets to stay down there two weeks, you know. Those are the orders. Two weeks to let the fallout settle, then dig your way up to what's left of Montana."

Moreau felt Kazaklis staring at her. She turned and looked into eyes so angry they glinted.

"Moreau," he said very slowly and almost menacingly, "I'm going to tell you something I didn't think I'd ever tell you. You are a good pilot. An excellent pilot. You are better than·anyone else I've ever had in the right-hand seat. You probably saved this aircraft when the first bombs went off. You also are a bitch. I never wanted you here. I wish you weren't here now. But I never thought you'd fuck up, mentally or physically. You are fucking up right now."

He stopped for a second, then continued.

"I cannot make it in or out without you. You cannot make it in or out without me. We can be Number 199 and 200. We've got the equipment, too. It's your choice. But I don't want to hear another word of this pop-psychology shit. It's down-to-business time. Understood?"

Moreau was silent for what seemed an eternity. She wasn't afraid of the pilot's .45. She wasn't afraid of the refueling, the Russian interceptors, the SAM's, or the low-level run over Irkutsk. She was afraid of the logic. She knew Kazaklis was right and she didn't look at him as she finally spoke.

"Understood, commander," she said, not making an excuse of how difficult it was to lose her religion, all her belief in the rightness of her dedication, in one brief wail of a klaxon. "I'm sorry. No more mind-fucking. I'm with you one hundred percent. Mind and body." She stopped abruptly, and swiveled a quick and challenging look at him. "Kazaklis, *please* don't smart-aleck that one."

Kazaklis chuckled, an honest, straight, relieved chuckle. "No, *sir*," he said. "I won't. Tonight I'm going to need both. A mind and a body trained like yours. I'm going to need them badly." He paused. "Thank you, captain," he added.

The two of them could feel the tension flow out of the cockpit of the giant bomber. Then the radio started squawking and the tension was back instantly, but of a different kind. Even through the static, the anxiety in the voice from *Elsie* crackled like sparks from a broken power line.

"*Polar Bear! Polar Bear.* Do you read, *Polar Bear?* Acknowledge. Closing on your position. IP estimated nine minutes. Do you read, *Polar Bear?*"

The voice was female. It also was urgent and brittle, but not frightened.

"Read you loud and clear now, *Elsie,*" Moreau answered. "*Polar Bear* here." The incoming voice had been so taut and clipped, she added, "Are you Mayday?"

For a moment only the strange radio sounds of the Arctic night—huzzes and snaps from the aurora borealis, whoosh warps from the nearby magnetic pole—danced into Moreau's headphones. The sounds mesmerized her, tapping a momentary Morse code of guilt against her eardrums. She asked herself if she had been as professional as this pilot, a woman, too, flying in circles for hours now, waiting for them, following a duty that doomed her. She didn't answer herself.

"Thank God in heaven," the radio finally whispered in relief. "We found you."

Moreau asked: "Repeat. Are you in a Mayday situation?"

"Negative, *Polar Bear.*" The voice was loud and clear this time. "Not yet."

Moreau looked over at Kazaklis, who seemed deep in thought. His face was furrowed, his eyes staring over the instrument panel into the dull gray of the flash curtain. For no apparent reason he reached forward and ran a finger down a curtain crease. Suddenly Moreau knew what he was thinking. They had to see for this one. She rubbed her good eye, her only eye, and cursed herself for the involuntary display of weakness.

"*Elsie,* we need a precise rundown on your condition." Moreau thought her voice sounded hollow.

"Precision isn't our game tonight, *Polar Bear.* Our fuel gauges are bouncing like jumping beans. We might have 100,000 pounds. We should be able to make a precise connect. But I tell you this: we gotta get that probe in the womb fast. No foreplay. This one's gotta be slam-bam-thank-you-ma'am. How much jizz you need?"

Moreau turned to Kazaklis, who looked unnecessarily at their fuel gauge and shrugged.

"All we can get, *Elsie*."

"Okay. Now, get this and get it good." The voice turned to stone. "When I say breakaway, I mean breakaway. No questions. No good-byes. No screw-ups. One of us is going in anyway. Screw up and we take you with us."

"We read you, *Elsie*," Moreau said. "Thanks."

"That's what we get paid for," the tanker pilot replied tonelessly.

"Well, *Elsie*," Moreau continued, trying to sound upbeat, "you got the biggest runway in the world below you. Great Bear Lake oughta be frozen twelve feet thick."

"Oughta be," *Elsie* said. "At sixty below zero. But this big baby ain't a glider, honey. And you hotshots got the ejection seats. Not us. It's a little chilly down there for a San Diego girl anyway. And the nearest hot tub is in Fairbanks." The radio went silent for a moment, only the haunting huzzes and whooshes echoing in Moreau's ears. Then *Elsie* added flatly: "Was in Fairbanks."

"That bad?" Moreau asked painfully.

"That bad," Elsie repeated simply.

"Damn, I'm sorry." Moreau's words sounded hollow.

"Don't be," Elsie replied with a tinny nonchalance. "In a way, it makes all this easier. We were on our way back, couple hundred miles away, when it went. Looked like the northern lights. Didn't believe it at first. So we started on in. Then we got the call from the *Looking Glass*."

Kazaklis cut in. "What did the *Looking Glass* tell you?" His voice was urgently curious.

"Oh, Lordy, a male voice. How nice. Had me worried there for a minute. It's bad enough for the last one to be a flying fuck. But for a while there I thought it was gonna be with another broad. That's adding insult to injury."

"The *Looking Glass*," Kazaklis repeated.

"Said go for the IP and wait. Orbit and wait until we found you or ran out of gas. So we been waiting."

"That's all?"

"That's it. Haven't heard a peep since."

"Seven minutes to IP, two minutes to radar contact," Moreau cut in. "Estimating arrival zero-eight-four-niner, Zulu."

"Roger, *Polar Bear*," *Elsie* said. "We got a little housekeeping to do here. Let's get back together on radar contact. Commander?"

"*Elsie?*" Kazaklis came on.

"We were flying a routine proficiency mission. The *Looking Glass* also ordered my B-52 to head south."

"South?" Kazaklis sounded puzzled.

"To pick up armaments, I guess."

"I'll be damned," Kazaklis said absentmindedly. But it made sense. At least the B-52 was aloft and safe, which most of the bomber force almost certainly was not. "Must be figurin' on a long war."

"Yeah, twelve, fifteen hours at least."

Kazaklis stifled a chuckle. He decided he liked *Elsie*.

"Now, listen, commander." The tanker pilot's voice turned deadly serious. "We're going to stick with you down to the last drop. There's no way you're gonna get all the fuel you want. But breakaway means breakaway. Got it? Coitus interruptus, pal. On the first word."

"Got it, *Elsie*. Back to teen time."

"No, this is kiddie time," the refueler said solemnly. "Anybody who'd let this stuff go is loonier than Captain Kangaroo."

"Yeah," Kazaklis said. "See you soon, mate."

"Propositioned at last. Okay. *Elsie* out."

For the next minute no one said a word in *Polar Bear One*, as each crew member steeled himself in his own private way for minutes of sheer terror. Moreau felt her nerve endings begin to scream beneath the unheard din of the engines. She took her left hand and clenched her right elbow, pulling the hand tightly down toward the wrist as if to force the nerves back down where they belonged. Ironic, she thought, that this moment would produce more palpable fear than the bombs going off. But she could feel the fear in the plane, wisping up out of the basement, spreading to Halupalai and then edging forward into the cockpit. The bombs had come at them out of the blue—theoretical death dancing in unseen particles that might be eating at the marrow of their bones, rolling shock waves that could crush them or massage them, take your pick. But this was no theoretical terror. This was known. And there was no one in the B-52 who wouldn't admit to being petrified with fright the first time they went through a midair refueling, and few who would deny being scared stiff each time since.

In the *Looking Glass*, Alice flinched. The white light had suddenly begun blinking at him. He stared at it, mesmerized. The blinking continued insistently.

"General, for Christ's sake!"

Alice flinched again, turning to look vacantly at Sam. The colonel's eyes were riveted on the light.

"General!"

Alice shook his ruddy head, as if to clear it. He reached slowly for the persistent phone, lifting it gingerly. "Alice," he said cautiously into the speaker.

"Harpoon," a voice crackled instantly back through the void.

Alice slumped over the phone, the tension oozing out of him. "Jesus," he muttered. "Sweet Jesus."

"No, old friend, but we might need His help," the phone voice replied. "Do you have anything working?"

Alice relaxed, and shook his head ruefully. He gazed down the aisle. His eyes stopped on his chief communications officer, a chunky young woman. She was intently prying into the bowels of a teletype machine with a hairpin.

"Harpoon, you old sea dog, we're patching things together with hairpins." Alice paused and winked at the communications officer, too roguishly from one officer to another, too blithely for the circumstances. "Had to be some reason for letting women into the Air Force."

Harpoon chuckled—his first laugh, half-laugh that it was, since 0600 Zulu. His crew was using everything available, too, amid curses and whistles of amazement at the damage a few high-energy pulses could do to the best communications equipment a technological society could produce—and had spent billions to protect. Slowly, very slowly, some of the gear was coming back. "Did you ever dream EMP could be this bad?" the admiral asked his Air Force counterpart.

"I dreamed a lot of things, Harpoon."

"Yes."

"You getting anything from the ground?"

"An Arkansas radio station. Some good hillbilly music."

"Hmmph. We got Kansas. They're still quoting cattle prices.

Did you know on-the-hoof is down to seventy-one bucks a hundred?"

The phone seemed to go dead for a moment, cracks and pops mockingly interrupting the silence of the two men. Then Alice continued. "Crazy, isn't it? It's so random. We knew EMP would knock out damn near everything. It musta burned out every power grid in the country. I can't even find a staff sergeant down there. But I get a goddamn cowboy quoting yesterday's cattle prices . . ."

"A tape recording . . . an alternate generator . . . some warp in the effect . . . we didn't expect to understand it." Harpoon paused. "But there's still a helluva lot of people alive down there. . . ."

Alice suddenly banged a beefy hand down on the desk-console in front of him. "Not for long, dammit! Not if we can't talk to anyone!" Alice thought he heard a sigh over the phone.

"Okay," Harpoon said. "So what have you been able to do? Can you talk to the bombers?"

"You kidding? Maybe in an hour or so, using the ultra-low-frequency trailing wire. It's the only thing that seems to be working halfway right. We haven't exactly got an armada up there anyway." Alice shook his head at the thought of the number of B-52's that had been caught on the ground. He looked questioningly down the aisle at a major. The major nodded affirmatively. "We may have found an eye," Alice said into the phone. "That'll help."

Far to the south of the *Looking Glass,* Harpoon thought a moment. So some of the camera satellites had survived. That would help. "What about refueling?" he asked.

"A few tankers got off. We had a handful of others up on training missions. We got through to them, and some ground stations, before the EMP explosions. Some of 'em will be able to rendezvous with the bombers. We had to use the by-guess-and-by-golly plan." Alice swiveled in his seat and stared at a wall map of the Soviet Union. "And what the hell would you suggest I tell the bombers?" Alice asked tensely.

"I'm afraid that's your job, Alice," Harpoon said evenly.

The tension erupted. "The hell it is!" he shouted into the phone. "It's the Commander-in-Chief's job! And gettin' him's your job! What the hell are you doing? Taking the scenic route?"

"I have an appointment in sixty-plus minutes," Harpoon replied emotionlessly.

"Sixty-fucking-plus minutes!"

"Alice," Harpoon said, the first sign of irritation creeping into his voice, "the man was out in the boonies. We have people after him. I got the word the same time you did. They said it would take four hours. You want me to put this big bird down on that runway and wait? How long you think I'd last?" Harpoon paused, sympathetically, but for emphasis. "Then you could have the submarines and the bombers."

Alice slumped again over the phone. The submarines. Jesus. "I'm sorry, Harpoon," he finally said. "Bad night."

"Yes, bad night," the admiral's voice huzzed back. "I want him as much as you do, Alice." Then the two officers disconnected, the *Looking Glass* continuing its slow orbit over the plains, the *E-4* moving over the Mississippi River north of Baton Rouge.

"Radar contact!"

"Ready, Tyler?" Kazaklis asked.

"Hell, yes. Let's get this refueling done right." Tyler sounded aggressive and blasé at the same time. "Then we can move on to the low-level and get this harebrained stunt over."

Moreau looked over at Kazaklis. The pilot stared back, his eyes saying nothing. He reached into his flight bag for a big red bandanna, the kind he once wore in the Oregon woods. Moreau's skin prickled again.

"We have to open the flash curtains," he said.

"I know," Moreau said. She also knew that, at night, a nuclear explosion fifty miles in front of them could take her other eye. She also knew that, once again, Kazaklis was playing percentage baseball. Odds were the Russians would not come at them now. But the planes were sitting ducks and Kazaklis was covering his bet. He wrapped the red bandanna, doubled and redoubled in tight folds, over his left eye and tied the kerchief behind his head. If the odds were wrong, there would be one good eye left of the four in the cockpit of *Polar Bear One.*

Kazaklis reached across and pulled the dirty-gray curtain. So did Moreau. The night light streamed in and the white radiance of endless snows reflected fluorescently up at them. Moreau blinked at the brightness. It was a wonderland—and very threatening.

"Helmets!" Kazaklis said into the intercom. "Okay, *Elsie*, sweetheart, we are at one nautical mile and starting our climb," Kazaklis drawled into the radio. "You look beautiful up there, baby, just beautiful."

The tanker did look beautiful, Moreau thought, hypnotically beautiful. By rote she helped Kazaklis maneuver the bomber up toward the illuminated underside of the KC-135. Her good eye was frozen on the tanker. In reality the two huge aircraft warily closed on each other at near-identical speeds of five hundred miles an hour, the bomber climbing steadily. But the illusion was far different. The tanker, framed in white night lights, seemed slowly to descend on them like a space platform, the glare of its lights blotting out the Arctic stars.

"Looking good. Stand by for half-mile."

Still, it was the breakaways that took your breath. Suddenly your stomach was falling up. But in the illusion, only the surreal white platform moved, taking off straight up, escape-velocity-rapid in the mind's eye, like a *Star Wars* mother ship accelerating into inky space. Tonight it wouldn't be that way. The tanker might do anything. Barrel roll, snapping off a wing. Sag back into their faces. Nose over on top of them. Moreau shuddered.

"All crew on oxygen."

Moreau turned away from the descending lights. Beyond Kazaklis, out the left window, the moon was setting below them now, a giant yellowish ball perched between two white crags in the far-off Mackenzie Mountains. She flinched, her last moon vision suddenly invading her memory, and snapped her head right. In the crystalline night, she could see forever. Below her, snow and ice, glowing in the Arctic moon-set, stretched flat and endlessly to the horizon. The southernmost arm of Great Bear Lake, clearly outlined, snaked off to the northeast toward the main body of the great frozen lake. Below them the tundra, unmarked by a hint of civilization, ebbed and flowed softly, Sahara-like, in windblown snow dunes and rippling white eddies. Suddenly lights flared far off the wingtip. Moreau lurched toward the flash screen, then slowly pulled her hand back. For God's sake, she told herself, calm down. Even the northern lights are spooking you.

Kazaklis appeared not to notice. "Closing now," he said. "Nudge it right. Nudge!"

Moreau snapped her full attention to the front of the aircraft. The platform was almost on top of them, the immense refueling probe hanging from the tanker's midsection, the probe's green-lit nozzle hovering no more than a dozen feet in front of the windshield. It swayed—inches right, inches left—like a snake's head poised for the strike. Moreau flinched again.

"Doing just fine. Little left. Little down. Careful, now. Careful! Up a bit!"

The snake passed over their helmets.

"Now!"

Clunk! Moreau felt the angry wrenching of metal, heard the grinding steel teeth lock onto the huge phallic probe just inches behind her head. The great plane heaved, its wings shuddering, and then it began a slow, groaning undulation up and down in rhythm with the tanker. Kazaklis felt the tendons in his arms stretch to the ripping point. Moreau watched her knuckles turn dead white on the wheel as, together, they fought to mate the Buff to the bulbous plane above. The tanker's tail loomed almost directly over their heads, visible and threatening through the overhead windows. But behind them the probe settled into place and the JP-4 jet fuel, lifeblood, began to surge from the tanker into the B-52. Kazaklis relaxed somewhat, took one hand off the wheel, and looked at his watch. It showed 0852, twenty-three minutes since they talked with Klickitat. Good. It was damned good.

"Beee-yootiful!" Kazaklis radioed above. "*Elsie,* baby, you did great!"

"Yeah," *Elsie* responded. "Not bad for a dame, huh?"

Kazaklis turned toward Moreau and winked a grotesque wink, made even more bizarre by the Sinbad look of a pilot with a red bandanna wrapped diagonally over the other eye. He grinned. How the hell did he ever get surrounded by women, working women, in this business?

"Not bad for a dame, *Elsie,*" he acknowledged. "Not bad at all."

"You looking up at me, commander?"

"Right up your . . ." Kazaklis paused. "Right up at your lovely frame, *Elsie.*"

"Yeah, I know, you dirty old man. Look a little farther up. You see that red on my belly?"

Kazaklis moved his eyes up the white undercarriage of the tanker until they fixed on the blinking red beacon.

"Looks like it's working fine, *Elsie,*" Kazaklis said, puzzled why the pilot would be worried about her beacons.

"That's what I'm worried about, ace. I'm a black widow tonight. Don't you forget that. A red-bellied black widow. You know about black widows, mate?" *Elsie* placed an extra edge on the last word.

"Run across 'em, *Elsie*. Deadliest of your species."

"Gender," she corrected him. "A little black lady spider, with a red spot on her belly. Known for killing the daddy."

"Right after screwin'," Kazaklis said flatly.

"Right after screwin', mate."

Moreau tightened her grip on the wheel. This was certain death for the crew of *Elsie*. And for *Polar Bear One?* A midair collision, at worst. For a few extra hours, at best. Assuming something else didn't get them. Which was a big assumption. What did that add to the chances of a suicide mission? One percent? Doubtful. Training was driving them now. Moreau wasn't sure this was percentage baseball. Neither, apparently, was Kazaklis.

"You sure you want to go down to the last drop?" the pilot asked *Elsie*.

"Nervous?" *Elsie* asked.

"Serious."

"What are your chances of getting in now?"

"Next to zero."

"What are your chances of getting out?"

"Zero."

"What are your chances of getting in with more fuel?"

"Next to zero."

"And out?"

"Next to zero."

"We'll go down to the last drop, commander." *Elsie*'s radio voice crackled but did not crack.

Kazaklis stared vacantly up at the tanker, briefly fixing on the ghostly vapor trails streaming out of her four engines. The exhaust poured out steel-mill-hot and then froze, snap, into ice-crystal fog faster than the eye could see. He remembered teenage jet trails that had seemed to go on forever. Now he had to watch them snap out again. "You got balls, *Elsie*," he said, and only he seemed to notice the choke in his voice.

"No, commander," *Elsie* replied. "They issued us everything but those. What we got, if you want to get schmaltzy, is our duty." Then she added, with a wry chuckle, "And if you want to get technical, we got our orders—empty the pump, *Polar Bear*."

"Okay," Kazaklis acquiesced. The pilot could feel the anxiety building. Everybody was scared stiff, including him. "What's your best fuel estimate?"

Elsie's voice returned firmly. "Eight minutes. Ten minutes."

"How do you plan to break away? Without power, you can't go up and you could belly in on top of us. We can't go up through you."

"I ought to be able to hold it level for a moment," *Elsie* replied. "If I can't, I'll nose it down slightly. If that doesn't work, I'll put it in a spin. Left. Got that? Left."

Moreau had a nightmare vision of tangled wings. But she also knew what a spin meant to *Elsie.*

"Got it," Kazaklis said.

"You put the brakes on and dive. Fast. Got that?"

Kazaklis paused and thought hard. Percentage baseball, he sighed silently. He switched to the intercom and radioed downstairs: "Keep your mother-lovin' eyes peeled down there. We've got the window open and don't need visitors." Then he spoke to *Elsie* again. "We got it, *Elsie.* Your soulmate on my right will handle that part."

Moreau looked at Kazaklis in surprise. He reached up slowly and pulled away the protective bandanna. Then he locked both eyes on the contrails from *Elsie's* four engines and didn't say another word. Nor did she, as her arms locked on the controls just as firmly.

Moreau last visited her father at Christmas, a month before the flight of *Polar Bear One.* It was a spectacular holiday of all-day skiing and crackling evening fires with rare steaks and rarer brandy high in the exhilarating alpine air of the Rockies near Steamboat Springs. He had retired there, with four stars, choosing the mountains because he loved them and Steamboat Springs because it was just near enough to keep his distance but also make his occasional lectures at the Academy in Colorado Springs.

It had not been an easy year for her. Finally, they had put her in a bomber where she was determined to be. Her father had sent congratulations, no more, when she got the assignment at Fairchild. Those first months had not been calm and she had lain awake night after night with pounding migraines for which she could not find relief because PRP would find the migraines. And then there was the men thing, the flamboyant, compulsive, self-destructive men thing which she had stopped, cold turkey, like a nun, a nuclear nun, almost a year ago.

So Steamboat Springs had been a tonic. Her father was in his sixties, the strands of iron gray turned to a sheath of steel. But he still stood ramrod straight, still forced her to her physical limits as they raced through the deep powder of this cold winter's early snows. The only sign of age was in his eyes, the radiant blue having faded some, the riveting gaze occasionally drifting into a distant other world.

On the last day, they skipped the skiing, walked the snow-banked streets, stopped for Riesling and cheese in an overdone Swiss chalet, and then headed back to their A-frame condo.

The fire seemed brighter that last night, the brandy more heady. Moreau looked at the man, whom she worshiped and after whom she had patterned her life, and knew that if an oedipal complex existed for women, she had it. They both got a little giddy and a trifle silly as the fire burned down, the brandy taking them into the high clouds which provided such ecstasy for them both.

"Are you happy, Dad?" she asked suddenly.

His eyes turned perceptibly gray, and then moved away from hers to stare into the fire. "Happy?" he repeated, as if it were a question he never had been asked. "I suppose happiness is not one of the goals I set in life."

"No. You only set one real goal, didn't you?"

"Preserving mankind? Sounds terribly pompous now, doesn't it?"

"No. No, it doesn't. It sounds incredibly beautiful. Like you. And you gave that to me." Moreau looked at her father and saw that not only had his eyes faded, but his face turned sallow and gray now, too. Her heart fell and she took her brandy snifter, clattering it loudly off his in an attempt to regain the silliness and giddiness.

"My God, you are something, old man," she said brightly. "I could go for you. Did you ever think how remarkable it is we never thought of incest?"

Her father turned back toward her, some of the glitter returning to his eyes at the ludicrous perversity of the thought. "Well, Mo," he said blandly, "you never brought it up."

"Father!" she exploded in laughter. "You old bastard, you! The original male chauvinist pig! I never brought it up, huh? You old phony!"

They reached for each other in a bear hug that was sensual beyond measure, sexual not at all.

"Oh, we've practiced incest for almost thirty years now, Mo," he finally said. "Incest of the mind."

"Some people call it mind-fucking." Moreau laughed, and her father withdrew again.

"I know," he said, and the words were painfully forlorn.

"Hey, wait a second, Dad. Let's start over."

"I want you to stop, Mo."

"Hey, hey, hey. I was kidding, Dad. You know that. Remember me, the skinny little kid with super-Dad?"

"I want you to stop flying. It isn't going to work, Mo. We're losing."

Moreau sat in stunned silence.

"Not to the Russians," he continued, "although this administration scares the be-Jeezuz out of me. Driving the Russians to the wall, where they're most likely to lash out. But that isn't it. We're all losing. We're losing to the bomb. It's become too big, too pervasive, too matter-of-fact and ingrained. We're failing, Mo. And you and I are the pawns. We always have been."

Moreau stiffened.

"I don't believe this. Not from you. Remember the ten-year-old kid you took to the Trinity site? Remember the lieutenant and his haunted scientists? Come on, Dad. Eternal vigilance. What's the alternative? You said it yourself: the danger is in losing faith in ourselves."

"Remember the initials at the McDonald ranch?" he asked.

"G. J. Loves J. J.," Moreau answered noncommittally.

"The random event. Two kids who walked unseen past hundreds of Army guards, climbed over a six-foot fence past trip wires and sensors, crossed miles and miles of desert, probably with missile tests all around them. Two unknown kids we'll never know. Into that room, not even knowing what it was. Probably had a six-pack of beer and screwed their eyes out. Carved their initials in Oppenheimer's wall and then walked back out again. The random, unlikely, impossible event. Part of the human cycle. And it's going to get us. We're going to lose."

"I don't buy that," she said stiffly. "We made it through your life, while you carried the torch. We'll make it through mine. And

then the next. Just like you said. We're like dry alcoholics, Dad.
We can't afford to fail. They take it one day at a time. We'll take it
one life, one generation at a time. Now it's my turn."

"There's a big difference, Mo, and you know it."

"No, I don't know it," she replied angrily.

"Dry alcoholics fail all the time, Mo, and it's one poor soul's sad
tragedy. He doesn't take all of AA with him."

"So what's your answer, Dr. Oppenheimer?" Moreau asked hostilely.

"I don't have one, dearest daughter," he said sadly. "I simply
know I was wrong, that nothing goes on forever. I simply know
that I want you to get rid of those gray phalluses you pack around
with you and find one life-giving one of your own. I want you to
settle down and try to find, for as long as you can, what I never
was able to give your mother."

Moreau stared into the fire. She had not known, until she began
college, that her mother had committed suicide.

"Sorry, Dad," she said. "It's a little late."

"Very late," he said.

Moreau's arms felt numb from her fingernails back over the top
of her shoulder blades. In front of her the yellow dials of the
instrument panel wobbled like birthday candles and she flexed
and unflexed her jaw muscles to keep her eye in focus. Her head
throbbed violently. She had not turned since the conversation
stopped. How long, in God's name, had it been?

Across from her Kazaklis could feel the water, a mix of sweat
and eye-ache tears, flood under his visor, down over his oxygen
mask, and drip into his lap. *Elsie*'s contrails blurred-in the visor
fog and he brushed at the protective plastic shell fruitlessly. In
frustration he wrenched the visor back up inside his helmet, mopped at the wetness with his glove, and sorted out the four jet
streams again. He glanced quickly at his watch. 0903 Zulu. Eleven
minutes. Jesus. How the hell had Moreau held the plane that
long? It was like being on the rack. Minutes were hours. They had
taken less fuel than he would like, more than he had expected.
But this was moving beyond both physical and psychological toler-
ances. And it had to be worse above them in the tanker. The
percentages were turning. Fast. *"Elsie!"* he rasped. "You wanta
break it off? Maybe you can ride the fumes down to the lake."

"Negative. We're gonna play it out. Might be the gallon that gets you to Paris, pal." The tanker pilot's voice sounded as tight as an overtuned violin.

Kazaklis turned to Moreau. "How you doing, copilot?"

"I'll make it. Keep your eyes on the road." She didn't sound any better. Kazaklis was worried. They were taking this too far.

"Thanks for the juice, *Elsie*," he radioed. "You did great. It's time to do it the easy way."

"Hang in there, commander." *Elsie*'s voice was tinny again. "You'll thank me later."

Kazaklis felt the slightest shudder, saw a dark puff from the tanker's number-four engine, and then just three contrails.

"*Now!*" he screamed. "*Breakaway!*"

"*Breakaway!*" *Elsie* shouted in panicky unison. "*Breakaway! Breakaway!*"

Two contrails. One contrail. The tanker wobbled precariously.

Moreau heard a violent scraping behind her, then a tremendous clanging crash at her side. She turned instinctively right and saw the ugly head of the refueling probe bounce away from the metal window strut near her ear and then scratch slowly across the Plexiglas. *No sparks!* her mind shrieked; oh, God, *no sparks!*

Down! She could hear Kazaklis yelling, ghostlike, far, far away. *Down! Take her down!* But she already had begun to take the B-52 down. Fast. At the first scream she had automatically nosed the plane into a dangerously deep dive. Her ears were ringing. *Down!* The yellow Master Alarm light glared angrily at her. Out the window she could see *Elsie* pulling in the probe. One engine still sputtered. But the tanker slowly settled back on them, the leading edge of the tail section barely above their cockpit.

"*Elsie*, get your nose down!" Kazaklis shouted. "Your tail's on top of us!"

Slowly the tanker's nose eased over, the tail came up, and *Elsie* slid into a shallow dive. For one long, agonizing moment the two aircraft moved in almost parallel dives, no more than one hundred feet apart, and Moreau stared horrified into the winking red beacon in the tanker's belly.

"It isn't going to work, *Elsie*," Kazaklis said in a low, haunted message to the tanker.

Silently, as if on orders, *Elsie*'s right wingtip arched up. And then she spun, like a fighter plane, wingtip over wingtip, to the left and out of Moreau's sight. The copilot felt the B-52 shake as the tanker's tail scrambled the air currents in front of the bomber's left wing. Then Moreau slowly began to pull their plane level.

"Jump, damn you!" Kazaklis said in a final plaintive order.

"They can't, commander," Moreau said quietly.

"No," Kazaklis replied.

"They knew that."

"Yes."

Kazaklis reached over and pulled the curtain again, shutting out the world.

Below, in the navigation quarters, Tyler watched his screen in silent fascination. The tiny image swirled downward like a dead mosquito. Then it appeared to strike the ground. Poof! Damnedest thing. It seemed so real. He looked up from his screen with a troubled, puzzled expression. It had seemed *too* real.

Radnor could feel the eyes turn toward him, but he refused to look back at his crewmate. Up the stairs, in the rear of the topside cabin, Halupalai slowly released his hands from an ejection lever turned clammy wet. He swiveled his head and looked into the forward cabin. The vacant redness enveloped Kazaklis and Moreau again, the night sky gone, and all Halupalai could see was the back of two white helmets trained, straight ahead, on the closed curtain.

In the cockpit, not a word was exchanged for minutes. Kazaklis had retaken the controls and Moreau tried to will some vitality back into her lifeless arms, some sense into her benumbed head.

"Nice job," Kazaklis said to her, his monotone barely discernible.

Moreau did not respond immediately. "Do you think you could have done that?" she asked.

Kazaklis paused too. Their words seemed to be lobbing back and forth like tennis balls caught on a stop-action viewer. "I suppose so."

"What *Elsie* did."

"I know."

"Took guts."

"Guess so."

"Guess so?"

"Don't really know what it takes, do we? Life comes along and hands us one and we react."

Moreau slumped in exhausted exasperation. She had neither the heart nor the energy for anger. "You guess so," she said with lifeless weariness. "Life comes along. You react. How can you write those people off that way? What does life mean to you, Kazaklis? Do you even think about it?"

His words came back without emotion. "Life's a game, Moreau," he said. "A game you play the best you can."

"Good God," she murmured. "A game. And what if you lose?"

"You tell yourself you were playing the Yankees," he said blankly.

The silence went tomblike. A long while later, Kazaklis glanced sideways at Moreau. She sat stiffly in her seat. He wondered which of them was better off now, although that was a matter of very small degree. Was she, this strange woman, his chance partner who had believed in something and had it all come apart? Was he, who had believed in nothing and had it all come true? He glanced at his watch and saw it was past one A.M. in Oregon, these not being Zulu-time thoughts. His old man would be up in a couple of hours, lacing the morning coffee with the usual Jim Beam and heading into the same eternal woods as if this were just another day, with the fallout, if it had reached the Coos this soon, being just more hay-fever pollen. He saw Sarah Jean . . . and the contrails flick away one by one. Briefly he wondered if this abrasive, perplexing woman sitting next to him was as fraudulent in her life cover as he was in his. He snorted quickly, inhaling the thought and the tears, and radioed downstairs, asking for a fix on their Positive Control Point, the last stop sign the Air Force left for them before the plunge low over Russian tundra.

Far behind *Polar Bear One,* on the ground in the damp drizzle of the woods of Louisiana, a man in jeans, a yellow chamois shirt, and a down vest watched a group of shadowy figures approach him. He knelt nervously behind a soggy fallen tree, holding a double-barreled shotgun trained on the newcomers. He had used the gun in the past hour. Life had been a bizarre and unexplainable hell since the far-off but near-blinding midnight flashes during this damnable camping trip. Since then, people had gone crazy, and the man had defended himself.

Through the murk, he saw the group of men carefully advancing on him. They held small sawed-off weapons, and the man shivered. He shakily pointed the shotgun at the first shadow and fired. He heard a grunt and the shadow fell. The other shadows faded into the protective cover of the woods. Suddenly the woods thundered with the fire of automatic weapons and the branches splintered above him. He cowered deeper into the semiprotection of the log.

"I'm a federal Cabinet officer!" he shouted, cursing himself for a voice that sounded squeaky with fear.

"Throw your weapon out," a disembodied voice responded.

He paused uncertainly.

The woods thundered again and the spray of wood chips showered him again, closer this time.

"Secret Service!" the disembodied voice said. "Throw your weapon out. Now."

The man looped his shotgun up over the log, but kept himself protected. He heard crunching footsteps nearing and looked up to see men in bloodied business suits pointing stubby gray submachineguns at him. "Identification," one said curtly. He reached for his wallet. "Hold it!" the voice commanded. "I'll get it." The figure reached over and extracted the wallet, examining it carefully. The man in the jeans heard a sigh of relief from above him. "The Condor is caged," the figure said over his shoulder to the others, and the weapons were lowered.

The leader of the Secret Service agents beckoned to a man who did not seem to belong with the group. He was short, fat, and carried a small black book. "Do your thing, judge," the agent said, "and do it fast."

The ceremony was over in seconds, the man in the jeans so woozy he was not sure what he had pledged to do. Then the lead agent took him by the arm. "Mr. Secretary . . . Mr. President . . . we have to get you out of here in one helluva hurry."

Hundreds of miles to the northeast, in an inky blackness somewhere in Maryland, Sedgwick opened his eyes slowly and painfully. It took him a moment to adjust to the near-total darkness. As his eyes focused, he first saw the jagged, twisted metal of the rear section of *Nighthawk One*. It appeared to have been sheared off only a few feet in front of his seat, and the rest of the chopper was nowhere to be seen. He panicked and turned abruptly to look at the passenger next to him, a sudden surge of pain causing him to faint again. After a moment, his wits seeped back. He turned more slowly this time, saw his companion hunched forward exactly as he had been when the chopper started down. He reached over and grasped the man's wrist, seeking a pulse. At first, in his grogginess, he missed it. Then he felt a slight but distinct pump . . . pump . . . pump.

SEVEN

0930 ZULU

"They got the fuel, general."

"Enough?"

"Marginal."

"And the tanker?"

"Crashed. Near Great Bear."

In the *Looking Glass,* Alice turned away, squeezing the major's shoulder. He glanced at the row of clocks on the far cabin wall, his eyes quickly passing Moscow time and Washington time and Omaha time. Zulu time read 0930, three and a half hours after the first exchange. Since the conversation with Harpoon, more of their communications had come back up. But not nearly enough. He moved across the narrow aisle to another member of his battle staff.

"Your boys?"

"One of 'em got a few minutes from a tanker out of Thule."

"The tanker?"

"Down in Baffin Bay."

"And your other Buff?"

"The tanker out of Goose Bay is still chasing him. Don't particularly want the B-52 to slow down. Looks like they'll rendezvous near the east coast of Greenland, north of Iceland. It's hairy."

"Yes." Alice's voice was tired and he turned toward his old friend for the summary. "So what do we have, Sam?"

"Less than fifteen still flying, sir. Half of 'em refueled. Three or four more will get the fuel. The rest will have to go in with what they have."

"Did the FB-111 make it in?"

Sam looked at Alice strangely. They had made a guinea pig out of the supersonic fighter-bomber, sending him in too fast to probe the Soviet defenses for the B-52's. "That wasn't a fair test, general."

Alice said nothing. Fair. Damn you, Sam. That's why we've got generals and that's why we've got colonels.

"He never was meant to fly supersonically all the way," Sam continued. "Little spurts, yeah, for evasion and the final run, sure. Not all the way. He was slurping gas like a Ferrari."

Alice still said nothing.

"At Mach two-point-five, eighteen hundred mother-humpin' miles an hour, he damn near got there. He launched the new cruise missiles off Hope Island, made it through the Soviet perimeter, and did a helluva job evading the MIG's over the Barents Sea."

Alice stared vacantly past the colonel at his communications officer, a short, stocky woman perspiring as she still worked frantically to patch together the tools of their control. He couldn't remember her first name. Why did men want to mate when their world, little world or big world, seemed terminal?

"He was approaching the coast of Finland, west of Murmansk, on a straight shot at Leningrad. He was running out of fuel. It was slow down or flame out. He slowed down. We think a MIG rammed him."

Alice turned back toward Sam. "So what did we learn?" he asked.

"We learned that, coming straight in, there still are enough MIG's to stop an armada. We can surmise that some of our electronic-warfare gear, the jamming equipment or the chaff or something, worked better than expected or the MIG wouldn't have needed to ram him. We learned the cruise doesn't work. At least in this environment."

The general's entire frame seemed to sag. "Eggheads," he said wearily. "Remember all those four-hundred-dollar suits and alligator briefcases parading into the Pentagon from Seattle and Fort Worth and Long Island? Christ, some of their slide shows would have put Coppola to shame. Bright little farts, weren't they?"

"It was a great theory, sir. A fifteen-hundred mile cruise missile, launched offshore from a bomber, its computer memory following maps of riverbeds, mountains, bridges, television transmitters. Error probability ninety feet. Aim at home plate and you won't miss by more than first base. Terrain trackers. Somebody forgot the first whomp would change the terrain."

"So what do we have?"

"With the cruise launches from the FB-111? They're going bananas. Running around in circles. Hitting mountains. Nosing into the tundra. One of 'em is heading for Stockholm. It's only four hundred miles off target. Don't guess we'll get the Peace Prize for that one." The colonel looked at Alice. "It means the B-52's will have to go all the way in. Use the gravity bombs."

The general turned away and stared up the aisle of the command post. His staff had done a remarkable job, considering the damage done to both the hardware and the outside atmosphere needed for men to communicate. Of the forty-three different communications systems he normally had at his command, three or four were working intermittently. Only one seemed to be working consistently—the ultra-low-frequency system operating through a five-mile-long copper-wire antenna trailing out of the back of the airplane like a fishing line. He always figured that one would be the survivor. Unfortunately, it had its limitations. The frequency was so low and so slow, he could tap out no more than a few words a minute. On a teletype.

Still, the early chaos had settled down to an eerie routine aboard the *Looking Glass.* He could sense a bizarre fascination among his people as they slowly gathered data about what had worked and what hadn't, what had survived and what hadn't. From the *Looking Glass,* the general thought ruefully, he had at least a blurred view into the new world he had temporarily inherited. He had already decided he didn't want his inheritance or the responsibility for the next steps. He moved forward where the colonel was scrolling—Christ, they had him *thinking* computer talk—through tracking maps.

"Sam," he said, "what the hell is going on with Harpoon?"

"Beats me, sir," the colonel replied. "I think he's getting ready to put down in Baton Rouge. That's where the man is supposed to be, if everything worked right on the ground. God, it's high-risk. First of all, there are mobs all over every surviving airport in the country."

"Troops deployed?"

"Several battalions."

"But it's the other opposition that worries you?"

"Hell, yes. Nothing visible. But we can't see beneath the Gulf of Mexico."

The general stared into the screen. "Pull me on the Buff, Sam," he said.

"Polar Bear?"

"Yes."

The screen flicked through a maze of fluttering projections and then settled on a map that boxed part of Alaska, the northernmost reaches of Canada, and the edge of Victoria Island. A small white cursor stood stationary just millimeters shy of the edge of the continent and the beginning of the Beaufort Sea and then the Arctic Ocean. The cursor edged forward, as the computer adjusted to the plane's flight path, and then stopped again. The B-52 was almost on top of its PCP, the Positive Control Point at which the bomber required further orders from Alice before making the ultimate commitment to go in.

"Do you want to call them, sir?" the colonel asked.

"No!" the general replied in a voice so stern he startled himself. "Goddammit! No!"

The drone of the eight straining engines went unheard by the five people inside *Polar Bear One,* the din of their own silence overwhelming the mechanical noise. Only Radnor broke the quiet. "Request permission to leave station, sir," he radioed upstairs. Good God damn, Kazaklis thought. This is the second time in ten minutes Radnor, whose bladder had held through twelve-hour practice missions, had asked to come up to use the head. "Granted," the pilot grunted. Kazaklis understood what this was. The tension of the rendezvous with *Elsie* had given way now to a dull, nagging anxiety that crept slowly down the spine and then bored inward to settle, like an ulcer, in the stomach. With Radnor, it seemed, the anxiety was settling a little lower. Where the hell was the *Looking Glass?* The waiting was worse than the action.

Omaha Beach syndrome, the PRP psychiatrists hot-wired into the pilot's brain. Your crew is over the side now, commander. Cut away from mother, cut away from their world, their safe ship. Off in a bobbing ocean limbo between a reality understood but left behind and a new reality they can't comprehend. Don't want to comprehend. The beach, commander, the alien beach. Make it real for them, commander. Limbo is dangerous.

Fuck off. Wire your postmortem crap into somebody else's head. Game's over.

Aha, commander. Can't handle the end of the world? What does the end of the world mean to you, commander? A father, a mother, a girlfriend? A childhood lake where the rainbow bit, leaped, dived, and fought young hands? A fire in the rain? Those misty Oregon woods where child's eyes saw pterodactyls swoop on webbed wings and older eyes see them swooping again? Is that your lost world, your new world, perhaps? Pterodactyls swooping again? Have you lost a song? A dream? A memory? You can keep the memory, commander. But memories are dangerous now, devil children of the mind. Revenge is safer.

Kazaklis pulled at the lumbering airplane. The Buff seemed to struggle against him, a friend no more, its wings no longer his wings. He prodded it higher, through 40,000 feet, then 45,000 feet into the rare, thin reaches of the stratosphere where each pound of fuel would yield a few more miles. But the drag of the SRAM missiles, tucked under each wing, tugged against him. The weight of *Elsie*'s last precious gift rebelled against him. He was a behemoth now, a half-million pounds of gas and weapons and machines and flesh and blood and minds and memories and one useless body blissfully immune to the PRP threats of fathers and mothers and lovers and dreams and songs and lost lakes of a world gone. *Careful, commander.* The aircraft's sluggish. *Who's sluggish, commander?* Weighted down. *Omaha Beach syndrome, commander.* Fuck off. *You're over the side too, commander.* An old girlfriend. Thanks, mind invader. How are you, Sarah Jean? Are you at all, Sarah Jean? Kazaklis shook his head. Go away, girl-image. Gone-image. But seventeen-year-old blond curls tumbled past milky cheeks, over soft shoulders, down around firm breasts hidden, forbidden, beneath a pompon sweater. *Coos Bay! Rah! Rah!* Got yerself a little blond poon, has ya, bub? Shut up, Pa. Best get the poon, bub, cuz that's all yer gonna get from that one; mite too fancy, that one. Pa said you were too fancy, Sarah Jean. Halupalai was driving Kazaklis nuts.

"Goddammit, gunner, go back and sit down!"

The Hawaiian, bending over the telegraph machine behind the pilot's seat, jerked upright at the unexpected violence in the words.

"You're pacing up and down like a goddamn expectant father," Kazaklis spat.

"Just looking for the message, sir," Halupalai said defensively.

"We oughta have the message by now. We only got two hundred miles to go."

Kazaklis let his shoulders droop. The waiting was driving them all crackers. Where was the *Looking Glass?* Where was the message giving them passage through their control point, confirming their targets, revealing the codes to arm weapons? Halupalai, assigned the job of decoding the instructions, had been moving back and forth between his seat and the telegraph since the refueling. Kazaklis suddenly felt guilty. He didn't like blowing at Halupalai. Nobody liked getting angry with Halupalai.

"Hang tough, Pops," he said soothingly. "Go on back and sit down. The doc will be out soon enough. And he'll tell you it's a boy."

Halupalai slouched back toward his rear seat.

"It's a boy," Moreau mused, "a goddamn boy."

Kazaklis bristled again. "Don't tell me you're gonna start the Gloria Steinem shit. Not now."

"Settle down, commander," Moreau said evenly. "Little jumpy, aren't we? History was getting the better of me. Not penis envy. After they tested the first bomb at Trinity, they sent Truman a coded telegram in Potsdam. Just like the one we're waiting for. 'It's a boy,' the message said. 'It's a girl' meant the bomb was a dud."

"Thanks for the history lesson," Kazaklis said sullenly. "Maybe ours will say 'It's a person.' Then we can guess."

Moreau didn't reply at first. It's a girl, Harry. Sorry, Mr. President, a bomb without a cock. No blow-jobs for the Japs. No phallic club to hold over Uncle Joe Stalin. No need for strategic penetrators plunging into Mother Russia. No need for the big hard ones buried in the womb of America's prairies. Man's ultimate failure, Mr. President. It's a girl.

"No," she finally said. "Ours will be a boy too, Kazaklis."

"Yeah."

"You ever wonder where we'd be if it had been a girl, that first one?"

"Still fightin' the Japs door to door."

"Come off it."

"Omaha Beach syndrome."

"You okay?"

"We need to do a little mission planning."

"We don't even have a mission."

"Mission planning!"

Very shrewd, commander. Now you're being the commander, commander. Keep them busy while they're in the landing boat. Keep yourself busy.

"Okay, heroes, we're gonna do a run-through on Irkutsk," Kazaklis heard himself say to all crew stations.

Downstairs, Tyler turned toward Radnor. "Jesus Christ, Kazaklis is really something. Mission planning. To Irkutsk. Jesus. Guess that's why they think he's such a hotshot. He takes everything so serious."

Radnor turned his head away. His stomach gnawed. Please be quiet, Tyler.

"Not me. Tell you that, Radnor. I'll never take this stuff so serious. This is a stepping-stone for me. I'm getting out as soon as I can. Use the Air Force, that's what I say. Let 'em get you that master's degree and get back outside to a nice quiet, sane life quick. That's what I'm doing. No more war games for me. No sirree."

For the first time, Radnor thought Tyler sounded as if he were trying to convince himself. The thought made the radar operator still more nervous. He had to get away again. "Request permission to leave station, sir," he radioed up to Kazaklis.

Why, Sarah Jean? Nothing is forever. Why not, Sarah Jean? "Pee in your frigging boot, Radnor!" Moreau looked at Kazaklis and thought his eyes glistened. But that, of course, couldn't be, and the commander quickly lowered his visor.

"Is the *E-4* down, Sam?"

"I think so, general."

"No radio confirmation?"

"Christ no, sir. They sure as hell don't need to send up any beacons. We got one big sitting duck on the ground in Baton Rouge right now and there still are plenty of hunters around."

"Subs."

"We had no trouble taking out the ones they used in the first exchange. They were gone in minutes. We also caught a Delta-class sub in the harbor near Havana. The commander must have been sound asleep or chasing Cuban fanny in town. But we lost track of one Yankee-class boat a coupla days ago after he went silent off Haiti. And we know there were a couple more off Venezuela about the same time. We sure as hell can't find them now— or do anything about it if we could."

"It's a damned risky landing."

"I don't know if I would have taken the chance, general."

"We've still got a little document called the Constitution, Sam."

"Yeah, I know, sir. But are we even sure we got the right guy?"

"Sam, old friend, right now you are flying around in a world without an ionosphere. You are flying over a country that doesn't have fifty functioning computers. Nobody said nuclear war was going to be an exact science. The last word we got from the Presidential Successor Locator, two minutes before it and most of the successors went, said he was the highest-ranking likely survivor. The plan said don't fart around, get the most likely. And get him fast." Alice paused. "Bird-watching in rural Louisiana was a pretty good place to be when the bubble burst."

"Jesus, is that what he was doing?"

"He was on an inspection tour of a game-management area. Camping out overnight to please the nature-lovers."

"You're kidding."

"No. I'm not. That was his job, Sam."

"God. A couple of hours ago his biggest problem was understanding the mating habits of the red-billed osprey. I wouldn't want to be the first guy to brief him on the forty thousand target options in SIOP."

"The man's got a much bigger problem than understanding SIOP, Sam. And a decision to make."

"Fast."

"Very fast."

"The Secretary of the Interior. Whew."

"Eighth-ranking in the constitutional order of succession, Sam. President of the United States. Your Commander-in-Chief."

"Okay, kids," Kazaklis said jauntily. "We're at the dateline and I'm takin' her down."

Moreau felt the adrenaline surge through her, washing away the lingering aches of the refueling. Below her, in her mind's eye, as she had a dozen times in mission drills on the ground at Fairchild, she could see the twisted crags and soulful spires of Arctic Ocean ice floes rising up toward them. She could almost feel the huge drooping wings of her bomber, her strategic penetrator, strain against heavier and heavier air as they dropped lower and lower, beneath the radar, beneath the eyes of their adversaries.

"Ready offense?" Kazaklis asked.

"Ready," Tyler responded.

"Ready, defense?"

"Ready," Halupalai answered.

"Position, nav?"

"One hundred eighty degrees longitude, seventy-seven degrees north."

"Entry point?"

"Landfall, one hundred forty-six degrees east, seventy-five degrees thirty minutes north. Asian landmass, one hundred thirty degrees east, seventy-two degrees north."

"Right on, nav," Kazaklis acknowledged, his voice chipper. "Hokay, radar, we're at two hundred feet. In the weeds, pal, and whadda we got for obstacles?"

"Landfall, no problems, sir," Radnor replied. "Straight in over Faddeevski Island, thread the needle past Kotelny. High point on Kotelny, 1,227-foot hill starboard. Approach the landmass over Laptev Sea, with a feint straight at Tiksi. Break it off, taking a heading due south over the gulf, and tiptoe through the foothills of the Verkhoyansk Mountains back toward the Lena."

"Sound like you been here before, radar. Hokay, defense, the natives are a little restless down there. What you see?"

Halupalai fumbled briefly. In front of him lay O'Toole's charts, looking like a new set of plays for the Rose Bowl.

"Early-warning radar stacked throughout the islands," he said, beginning slowly. "Jamming now. Missile batteries, Kotelny. Our problem. Decoys, chaff dispatched. SIOP says forty percent chance Tiksi destroyed in first wave. If not, our problem. Heavy radar concentrations, major SAM batteries. The feint will draw them out, unless they think we're a decoy for the others coming in behind us."

"The others," Kazaklis said. "Yeah. That would be nice."

"If they see us," Halupalai continued.

"That's what you got all those toys for, defense."

"Yep. Tiksi is the biggest problem. Past the village, heading down the gulf, we got one more major battery of missiles near our entry point at Nyayba. Jamming. Decoys if necessary. Sharp eyes down below, please."

"That's you two in the basement," Kazaklis said.

"Got it," Tyler said.

Halupalai paused again. He could see the gray shark of the SAM racing up at him. His hand involuntarily went to the Gatling-gun trigger. He shook his head. "Then we are in the mountains," he continued, "and the threat is MIG's."

"Also requiring sharp eyes down below," Kazaklis added. "Got your eyes open down there, radar?"

"Wide, commander," Radnor answered.

"Okay, sarge," Kazaklis said to Halupalai. "Not bad, coming off the bench. We're in the mountains now, huggin' and hidin' for a while. Three hundred feet and eyes on the ridges, please. If we got anybody watchin' up above, assumin' our guys missed a satellite or two, we're headin' on a course for . . . ?"

"Vladivostok," Tyler answered.

"Or maybe the Petropavlovsk submarine base on Kamchatka," Kazaklis acknowledged. "Shifty little buggers, aren't we? So we pivot . . . ?"

"At one hundred twenty-six degrees east, sixty-five degrees north," Tyler said. "Right, twenty degrees."

"And we're into the wide-open spaces. Tundra. Down to one hundred fifty feet. You might let me know when we see the tree line. Larch scrub first, pine forests next. No pine needles in the intakes, please. Other obstacles?"

"Mountains about halfway," Radnor replied. "High point, Mount Purpula. Five thousand, three hundred twenty-six feet. Eight-hundred-foot television transmitter at Vitim."

"Then we're in the woods again," Kazaklis continued, "and coming up on the lake."

The lake. Moreau saw the frozen shore approaching, as she had in countless dreams. Holy Baikal, the Russians called it, the majestic ocean. They said it contained one-sixth of all the fresh water in the world—a saltless inland sea stretching four hundred miles long with barren nine-thousand-foot mountains jutting up from its western bank. She saw the lumbering bomber roar treetop level over the great lake's deserted northern shore, kicking up powder snow off the ice, and her pulsing adrenaline turned to clammy sweat.

"Decision time," Kazaklis went on. "Who makes it?"

"SIOP," Moreau said. "Hours ago."

"If SIOP, in its computerized wisdom, said the dam at Bratsk is still standing, we get a little side trip," Kazaklis said. "We hop over the Baikal Mountains, lay a SRAM down on it, and scoot. Question of American pride. The Russkies say it's the biggest dam in the world. We get to personally put Grand Coulee, right outside good ol' Cowpatch, back on top."

Kazaklis paused for a second, a shudder passing through him.

The pilot's chin edged forward and he began whistling softly. *. . . for amber waves of grain . . .*

Moreau looked at him curiously.

"Opposition?" he asked.

"Surrounded like Fort Knox," Halupalai answered. "SAM's, MIG's, antiaircraft batteries. Unfriendly place."

"Yeah. Let's hope we don't have to make the visit. Hokay. We're huggin' the foothills of the Baikals now. Still a long haul in."

"One hour," Moreau said.

"Almost one hour," Kazaklis confirmed, "and then we make the turn up the Angara River and . . . ?"

"Irkutsk, forty miles," Tyler responded.

"I got it in the weeds now. Ticklin' your rumps down there?" Kazaklis didn't expect an answer. "Targets, offense?"

"In the outskirts, we gotta loft a SRAM over the top at the oil refinery upriver at Angarsk," Tyler said. "And then two more SRAM's at the oil fields."

"Mobil will thank you eternally, nav," Kazaklis said. He felt shaky. His chin edged farther forward to cover. . . . *for purple-mountained majesties . . .* "And Irkutsk. Targets?" . . . *above the fruited plain . . .*

Tyler floundered. "Targets?" he asked. Irkutsk was the target. "Satellite-tracking station, heavy industry, machine-tooling plants, electronics, Trans-Siberian Railway . . ." Tyler's voice trailed off. He had never been asked that question before.

"Population?"

"Kazaklis!" Moreau protested.

"Just under a million," Tyler responded. His voice was firm now, a game being a game. He felt better. His voice sounded better.

"Yep," Kazaklis said. "Irkutsk gets the big banana. Gravity bomb. One megaton. Ground burst. Low level. Approaching. On the racetrack . . ."

Moreau began to protest. Then the adrenaline began pulsing again.

"On the racetrack," Tyler repeated.

"Switch lights on," Kazaklis said. "Pre Em lights on."

"Entry plus two-niner-zero," Tyler said. "Calibration, two-niner-zero. Midpoint two-four-zero. Exit two-eight-zero."

"I.P. two-two-two-six."

"Winds, twenty knots."

Moreau sat mesmerized.

"Coming up on sixty seconds," Tyler said. "Ready . . . ready . . . Now!"

"Hokay," Kazaklis said. "Heading into bomb run. Straight down Karl Marx Street."

"Coming up on twenty seconds," Tyler said. "Ready . . . ready . . . Now!"

To Moreau, the silence seemed to go on forever.

"And?" Kazaklis demanded.

Silence.

"And?!"

"PUP!" Moreau responded urgently, automatically leaning forward to begin the Pull Up Pushover procedure that would arch the hydrogen bomb up slightly on its departure, giving them a few extra seconds' escape time.

. . . *America! America!* . . . Kazaklis whistled. "Bomb away," he said serenely. . . . *God shed his grace on thee* . . .

Moreau saw the bulbous weapon hover briefly beneath the open bomb-bay doors, saw the drogue parachute unfold to slow it on its short descent, saw it land in Karl Marx Street where people could stare at it for the few seconds before the time release activated. Then she saw the moon burst again. She started to tug at the controls. Her eye caught on the bomb-release lights, which were out. Her gaze fixed on the altimeter, which read 46,000 feet. Then she settled back in her seat and returned to the reality that they still were high over Canadian tundra, rapidly approaching their control point. Practicing. A recital. Damn you, Kazaklis.

"Bye-bye, Irkutsk," Kazaklis said in a strangely quiet voice. "Bye-bye, mamushka," he added, his voice almost inaudible.

Moreau felt a sudden wave of unexpected sorrow. She turned toward the pilot, watching his shoulders sag, his left hand sliding limply off the red bomb lever, his right slipping disconsolately from the wheel onto the throttle control box between them. Instinctively she slowly placed her hand on his. Neither spoke and Kazaklis let the copilot's hand remain on his briefly. Then he pulled his hand away and began asking for the vectors for the course change that would take them to the other big-banana target, the city of Ulan-Ude.

"General, they're seventy-five miles from their PCP."

Alice stared into the panoramic world map lining one wall of the battle-staff compartment of the *Looking Glass*. He did not look away.

"Sir, we don't want them wasting their fuel orbiting and wait-ing. Doesn't make sense. Certainly not now."

When Alice first had come aboard the *Looking Glass,* as a young pilot twenty years ago, the map had jarred his senses—although not for the reason it caught the attention of most first-time visi-tors. He had examined it for minutes before realizing what was wrong. The Eurasian continent, not the Americas, occupied the center of the huge wall map. Every map he had seen since child-hood placed the Americas in the middle of the world with Eurasia stretching to the right until it stopped abruptly and arbitrarily somewhere beyond the Urals. Then the eyes had to swing far left to pick up the great landmass of Asia as it moved eastward across Siberia and India and China toward the center, America. It was a year later, during a tour of the Far East, before he realized no one else in the world drew maps the way Americans did.

"They're minutes away, sir. We might have to try several fre-quencies to get through the crud in the atmosphere."

On the *Looking Glass* map a seam ran through the center of the Asian landmass, creating an artificial ridge in a straight line south through central Russia past Afghanistan and Pakistan. Bombay was in the middle of the hump and then the ridge continued through the Indian Ocean to Antarctica. Even here, the general thought, we had to cut and paste to bring our world view into line with others. But it wasn't conformity, like Americans begrudg-ingly adopting metrics, that dictated the change in the *Looking Glass* map. The *Looking Glass* wanted the target in the middle. All the targets. He pondered, only briefly, whether his Russian coun-terpart flew high over the ruins of Omsk or Sverdlovsk, staring at a pasted ridge of Middle America—Winnipeg on the hump, and Sioux Falls and Wichita and Oklahoma City and Corpus Christi, cut away from the edges of the world and glued together so they could become unglued now.

"Where is their PCP, Sam?" Alice asked. "Precisely."

"About seventy miles northwest of the old DEW-line radar site at Tuktoyaktuk. Over the Beaufort Sea."

"You're kidding. Jesus Christ. What genius planned that one?"

Alice looked back at the map. The Asian landmass, including China—just in case world politics swung again as it had so often in his life—was covered with clusters of small colored dots. Areas of interest, the battle staff called them. Red for ICBM fields, blue for troop concentrations, yellow for submarine and bomber bases, black for oil fields and industrial sites. And green. The damned green dots. He shivered at the thought that it might be time to take the green out and that he might have to give the orders.

"What's with Baton Rouge?" he asked.

"Still on the ground, sir. No radio contact."

Alice sank deeper in his chair. What damnable twist of fate had placed him aloft tonight, one of the random eight-hour shifts he drew no more than once a month? Fleetingly he envied his boss—the commanding general, code-named Icarus. Quick, simple, reflexive decisions. No right. No wrong. No thinking. Then a quick, simple good-bye and carry on, a burned-out huzz on the phone in the *Looking Glass,* and no second thoughts.

"I shouldn't make this decision, Sam. I'm not even sure it's legal."

"It's legal, sir. Under PD 58."

"Screw Presidential Directive 58 and its blasted nuclear-command line of authority. It puts me in charge only if there's no constitutional successor around. We may have a President on the ground in Louisiana."

The general looked at the colonel wearily. They had known each other many years.

"I don't want to make this decision, Sam."

"I know, sir."

"I'm not sure if it's right."

"It's debatable, general."

"Goddammit, Sam, I know it's debatable! That's the point!"

"Bye-bye, Ulan-Ude," Tyler repeated exuberantly. The navigator grinned from ear to ear. Radnor tried to ignore him.

"That doggone Kazaklis," Tyler continued. "He's so good at this, he just makes it feel real. Man, I could feel us down there in the weeds, skimmin' over the tundra, cutting through the mountains. Just plain fun, that stuff. Couldn't you feel it, Radnor? This big baby romping down Baikal, couple hundred feet over the ice, and coming in on Irkutsk. Ready . . . ready . . . Now! Ka-*whump!* And then Ulan-Ude. Ready . . . ready . . . Ka-*whump!*"

Radnor doodled with his pencil, making meaningless marks on a chart.

"I mean, Kazaklis is better at this than they are. They're doing their damnedest to make this real. But when it comes to games, our boy has 'em all topped. He's really doing this in living color. He almost had me believing it."

Radnor's thumb pressed, white-knuckled, against the center of the pencil. It snapped, sending a painful sliver-spear up under his thumbnail. He slammed the broken pencil down and turned angrily on Tyler, fighting back the urge to grab him, shake him, shout at him. He forced himself to relax and speak quietly.

"You gotta wake up, Tyler. You just gotta." Radnor paused. "This *is* real."

Tyler stared back at Radnor, a grin twisting across his face. He reached across their work console and put his arm on Radnor's shoulder, as if to comfort him.

"Hey, old buddy, this is getting to you, isn't it?" Tyler said calmly. "Hang in there, will ya? That wasn't real. Look at the altimeter. We were at forty-six thousand feet the whole way. We were just talkin' it through, the same way we do in the alert room."

"Mission planning!" Radnor shouted, angrily pushing Tyler's arm away. "Damn you! Wake up! Yeah, we were at forty-six thousand feet. Over Canada. Planning a mission. A real mission, dammit!" Radnor's voice suddenly turned to quiet pleading. "Please, Tyler."

The grin faded off Tyler's face. "Radnor," he said, pulling his arm back, "if you gotta believe this bullshit to do your job right, go ahead. I don't need it."

Radnor's body wilted in frustration, his eyes catching the red V of O'Toole's boots. "Tyler, look behind you. Is that real?"

"O'Toole screwed up," the navigator said, refusing to turn his head toward the corpse. "I feel as bad about it as you do."

"The missiles, Tyler. We got kicked in the butt by nudets. We almost packed it in. You saw it on your screen. You felt it. *Polar Bear Three* packed it in. The whole squadron packed it in. Fairchild packed it in. Spokane packed it in."

"Simulated." Tyler's voice turned icily even. "They can simulate anything. You know that. It's more war games. And when we get back, Radnor, they're going to rate us on how well *you* handled it."

Radnor slumped forward, forlornly taking his head in his hands. Maybe he was buggy, not Tyler. He felt his buddy's hand on his shoulder again, shaking him gently.

"Hey, Radnor, look at that, will you?" Tyler tapped at the radar screen in front of him. "What does that tell you?"

Radnor looked at the radar screen and the jagged Arctic coastline passing beneath them. Good God, how could Tyler ignore that? They didn't come up here on drills. They could run into MIG's. Soon.

"We're at our PCP," Tyler said, jabbing at the center of the screen. "Now, how come we don't have orders to pass through the control point?"

"I dunno," Radnor said dully. "Communications maybe. You know what a few dozen nudets will do. Punch holes in the ionosphere, so you got nothing to bounce high-frequency radio beams off."

"We got low frequency."

"Maybe it's EMP. I dunno, dammit! Maybe they're changing targets on us. Maybe nobody's back there. I dunno."

"We haven't got any orders, 'cause it's a game. It's all another highfalutin, fancy war game, Radnor. That's why we haven't got any orders."

Radnor looked at Tyler and felt downright afraid of him. Tyler smiled back warmly, reassuringly. Radnor braced himself.

"Tyler," he said very quietly, "it is real. It is very real. Your wife's gone. Your kid's gone. We're not going back, 'cause there's nothing there."

Tyler's eyes narrowed hostilely, causing Radnor to shiver. Then the navigator's expression changed again, becoming pained. "I don't know why everybody has to lay that one on me," he said. "It's cruel, Radnor. Very cruel."

"Tyler . . ."

"You guys act like I'm screwing up. Have I screwed up? So they're trying to make this one seem like the real thing. Another goddamn PRP test. Nothing to go home to. I'm playing along. I'm doing my job. I'll pretend. But do I keep telling you that your wife is dead? Do I? And Timmie? Huh? It's cruel. It's very cruel."

Radnor turned away. He slowly pulled the sliver from beneath his thumb and then concentrated on his radar screen to distract himself. The coastline slowly inched away from them. The screen seemed fogged, and he reached for a tissue to clean it. The fog did not want to go away.

"Nav!" The commander's voice cut into the downstairs compartment. "Are we on our PCP?"

"Dead center, commander," Tyler radioed back firmly.

"Shit," Kazaklis said. "Okay, we're gonna put it in a slow orbit."

Tyler looked over at Radnor and smiled smugly. Radnor took out a second tissue and rubbed at his screen.

Upstairs, the commander's fingers began an agitated drumbeat on the white engine throttles. "You take it, copilot," he said to Moreau. "Throttle her back just above stall speed and put her in a goddamn circle." Moreau began the maneuver without comment, banking the plane to the right. "Assholes," Kazaklis said, fidgeting angrily in his seat. "So this is what we're going to do with *Elsie's* gas. Bastards! God damn those bastards!" The Master Caution light flashed at Moreau. She pushed the lighted yellow button and it flickered, then came back on. She checked the aircraft's speed and pushed the button again. It blinked off, then came back on. She ran her eye quickly over the controls, saw no problems, and decided to ignore it. Gremlins, she thought. You get used to that in a thirty-year-old airplane. A high, staccato pinging entered her earphones. She looked quickly at Kazaklis, who stared back at her, perplexed.

"Radiation!" Halupalai cut in. "We're in radiation! The detector's jumpin' off the scale!"

Kazaklis spun around and saw Halupalai hovering over the small black radiation detector.

"Shut the vents!" Kazaklis shouted. Moreau lurched forward at the switches.

"Oxygen!" Kazaklis ordered. He stopped for a second, thinking.

"Can you guys see anything downstairs?"

Radnor stopped rubbing at his screen.

"It's just a blur, commander," he said woodenly. "A fuzzy blur."

"Where?"

"All over the screen."

"Shit."

"Fallout," Moreau said.

"Thanks."

"From a strike on the radar stations."

"Thanks again."

Kazaklis and Moreau sat mutely for a moment, the ping echoing in their helmets.

"I'm gonna have to take a look," Kazaklis said. He reached forward and pulled at the corner of the flash screen. He froze in awe and horror. Then he gasped. Out the cockpit window, the Arctic air pulsated red. Kazaklis felt his skin creep. The air seemed to dance, tiny crystals glowing and careening off each other in electric spasms. The redness swept at him in relentless ghostly waves, like the fog over his boyhood dunes.

"Good God," he whispered. Then he yelled, "Full throttle! Get us out of here!"

"Where?" Moreau could barely hear her own voice.

"How the hell do I know? North! They didn't blow up the whole damn Arctic Ocean!"

"General, *Polar Bear One* has gone through her PCP."

"Gone through! On whose authority?"

"I don't know, sir. I don't imagine the northern coast of Canada is a very comfortable place to orbit right now."

"Fallout?"

"It must be floating all over the place up there. The Russians took out every radar installation, Canadian and American, on the Arctic coast. By now the fallout is floating wherever the winds took it."

Alice thought briefly. "Make it official."

"Sir?"

"Send them through."

"Through to where, sir?"

"Just through, dammit! I don't know where."

"Winds!" Kazaklis demanded.

"Eighty-five knots," Tyler responded. "Southerly." The navigator paused. "Westerly now," he said. "Ninety-five knots."

The big bomber bumped violently, groaning under the new pressures. Moreau's left hand manipulated the throttles, pushing the aircraft to full power, while her right fought to hold it steady against the swirl of the shifting winds. Kazaklis peeked tentatively around the corner of the flash curtain. He looked like a spying spinster, Moreau thought—a spinster whose forehead was popping beads of nervous sweat. Moreau caught her first brief peephole look at the surging red poison outside. She turned away quickly.

"Where is Tuktoyaktuk?" Kazaklis asked desperately.

"One hundred ten nautical miles behind us," Tyler replied.

On the pilot's forehead the little beads turned to globules, then to streams. Kazaklis slapped at his helmet to try to stop the pinging whine pounding at his temples. Through the corner of the window he stared into a sky throbbing in spasms of deep scarlet, fading to a hot red glow and then to softly dancing electric pink before the wave of scarlet rushed over them again. He saw no opening.

"Jesus," he sighed.

"Komaluk?" Moreau asked.

"Good Lord, Jesus."

"Komaluk?" Moreau repeated. "Is it Komaluk?"

"Oh, God in heaven, it's a horrible sight. Red fucking crud rolling at us in waves . . ."

"Commander." Moreau sounded remarkably calm. She bit off the urge to tell Kazaklis he wasn't glowing in the dark yet. She knew the early-warning stations had been hit. But it was hours ago now. "The vents are closed. It's three hours old. We could fry an egg on the wing. Inside, we're okay. For a while. Let's figure out where it's coming from and how to get out of it."

Kazaklis turned away from the window and looked at his co-pilot. His eyes were wide and frightened like a cornered doe's. Almost instantly they turned their opaque brown again, cutting off the view inside to the self he protected so vigorously.

"Just remember to hose down this brute when we get to Pear-ee, Josephine," he said.

Moreau stifled a smile and said nothing.

"Komaluk, huh?" Kazaklis wondered aloud. "Maybe. It sure isn't Tuk. Tuk's floating around someplace, too, but not here. We flew straight over it without a whimper, and the winds didn't blow it out to sea."

"Komaluk sits on a peninsula," Moreau said, "the last radar site before the Alaskan border."

Kazaklis started to reach for the charts and then radioed down-stairs instead. "Nav, give me a reading on Komaluk Beach."

"Due west," Tyler said.

"That's it." Outside, the haunting red sky, a maze of ionized particles, seemed to mock him. Komaluk Beach. A handful of ancient shacks, equally old radars, a supply plane twice a month, *Playboy* centerfolds and a pillow to get you through a nine-month winter. Forgotten by the martini-drinkers in Washington. Never known, in thirty years of cold war, by the people who paid the bills. A dozen men, freezing their gonads, watching, always watching. They still watched. Dust to dust, cold dust to hot dust, spar-kling red atoms of eternally vigilant men taunting him for thanks—thanks for the extra minute, thanks for the extra sec-onds. Fucking Russians. Well, you said it, pal. This ain't tid-dlywinks.

"Thanks, guys," Kazaklis said.

"Sir?" Moreau asked.

"I said ninety degrees left. Quick."

"At Komaluk?" Moreau asked, puzzled.

"Komaluk's coming toward us, copilot—frying the eggs on your wing."

"North's just as safe, commander," Moreau protested. "Maybe safer. This cloud can't be too wide."

"Through our control point? The general's daughter wants to take us through our control point?" Kazaklis said sarcastically. "Highly provocative action, copilot. The Soviets might consider that an act of war."

The commander's voice sounded very brittle. Moreau banked the huge plane left. She shrugged. They already had passed through their control point.

"Message, sir."

Alice looked up, startled, pulling his eyes away from the green dots scattered across the middle of the world.

The colonel handed him a small piece of telegraph paper, its edge torn as it was pulled hurriedly off the decoding machine. The message from Harpoon, dangerously exposed far to the south in Baton Rouge, read: "CONDOR NESTED."

"Thank God," the general said. But he knew he could not breathe too easily until the message read: "CONDOR ALOFT." He turned back to his map, briefly wondering what perversely wry and lost soul had come up with the code names for the event they never expected to happen. Looking Glass, Alice, Icarus, Trinity, Jericho. And Condor, powerful, ominous, lord of all it surveyed. Last of a long and proud line, almost extinct now.

The din inside the pilot's helmet became thunderous, pounding at his temples, numbing his reasoning the way too much Jack Daniel's did. He was losing it, dammit. He shook his head and stared into the great waves of red, looking for an out. One minute. Two minutes, three minutes, four. The sound pounded deeper into his skull, into the pons, the cerebellum, the cerebrum itself. The neutrons from his own brain, punished by the sound as they had been punished by the bourbon, emitted more slowly now, reducing his respiration, his heart action, his circulation, his reaction time. Five minutes, six. Red waves, ghosts. A dozen men true, winking at him in a red night, their souls divided into a billion particles, crimson and ruby, scarlet and pink. His neutrons slowing, theirs racing. Why would dead men dance while he ebbed? Shake your head again, Kazaklis.

"Thirty years of eternal vigilance."

"Come again, commander?"

Kazaklis shook his head.

"You okay, commander?" Moreau asked.

"Ten degrees left," he said sluggishly.

Moreau moved the bomber left again. Kazaklis watched an ice-white beacon edge toward the nose of the B-52. Then, suddenly, the beacon turned to a shimmering star, the redness washed away over the wings, and the sky opened again into a black and familiar panorama. Kazaklis slowly let the curtain slip back into place and sagged back into his seat.

"We're out of it," he said. He felt an arm on his shoulder and turned numbly around. Halupalai hovered over him with a confused look on his face. In the background Kazaklis could hear a new din and it took him a moment to realize it was the audio alert for an incoming message. Halupalai handed him a small piece of paper.

The pilot examined the code-garbled lettering, turned to look into Halupalai's blank face, and then examined the encrypted message again. Behind his ear, the telegraph clattered. The message was so brief he did not need his code book to unravel it.

"Where's the rest of it?" Kazaklis asked.

"That's it, commander," Halupalai answered. "The machine's sending bomb codes now. To arm the weapons."

Kazaklis stared unseeing into the flash curtains. His bedeviled brain felt like mush. Something was wrong. The world behind him was not functioning properly. He had the sinking feeling everything was out of control. The message made no sense. He reached for the code book to confirm what he already knew. Finished, he looked back at Halupalai.

"Did you decode it?"

"Regulations, sir. Three of us have to confirm it."

"How do you read it?"

"Same as you, commander."

"Dammit, Halupalai, tell me what you read."

"Proceed. And you, sir?"

"Proceed."

"Proceed?" Moreau interrupted. "Proceed where?"

They ignored her.

"Take it down to Tyler."

"Tyler?"

"Tyler! The navigator has to confirm it."

Halupalai disappeared into the back of the compartment. Kazaklis sat waiting.

"Proceed where?" Moreau asked again.

"Something's screwed," Kazaklis said.

"Commander!" Moreau asked more urgently.

"We got your message, copilot. No boy. No girl. It's a person. Tyler? Do you read that?"

"Yes, sir."

"Well?"

"It says proceed, sir."

"Confirmed."

"Sir?" Tyler asked strangely. "Proceed where?"

Kazaklis turned his head away from Moreau. His eyes lingered briefly on the red bomb lever and then focused on the pouch of navigation charts at his left. In those charts the route to their primary target—across Faddeevski Island and toward Tiksi, through the Verkhoyansk Mountains and along the Lena River, down the frozen shore of Baikal and back up the loop toward Irkutsk—was cross-hatched into one-kilometer squares. A generation of satellites and several generations of spies and tourists and Soviet dissidents had mapped every isolated grain elevator and tower, every mountaintop and missile battery a ground-hugging bomber might find troublesome, no bug-squishing wanted. Behind him, in the storage bays between the pilot and the gunner, similar charts were filed for every inch of the Soviet Union—and China. On the chance the Yellow Peril decided to become perilous again. He had charts of every railroad crossing and gravel road from Shanghai to Sevastopol.

"How the hell do I know?" Kazaklis roared. "Just proceed!" And the groaning bomber, nudged by Moreau, banked blindly north again.

In the *Looking Glass,* the colonel nudged the preoccupied general. "Opposition, sir."

"Where?"

"Everywhere. Coming out of the Leningrad-Moscow corridor at the Buffs. Coming out of Siberia." He paused. "Coming out of the Gulf."

"The Gulf?" Alice swiveled an alarmed look at Sam.

"Submarine launches. From the Yucatán Channel near the Cuban coast."

"Christ. What do the missile trajectories show?"

"Looks like they've targeted Baton Rouge."

Alice slumped. "Condor?"

"Harpoon's got some kind of trouble on the ground."

Alice slowly turned back toward his map. He ran his eyes over the green dots. They clustered around Moscow and Leningrad, then became random and isolated as they spread across the expanse of Russia. Smaller clusters at Plesetsk and Tyruatam. Single dots here and there. Command posts. Leadership bunkers. Places where men plan wars. Turn them on. And off. The general allowed the air to whoosh out of him. Opposition. You aren't making this any easier, comrades.

In the dark of the Maryland night, Sedgwick had a small fire going. But the cold still worked through to the marrow of his bones. The rear section of *Nighthawk One* lay nearby, where it had settled after ripping away from the rest of the chopper in the blast-wave crash and sliding down into this black gully. Far off, Sedgwick could hear strange sounds. But in four hours the sounds had not come closer. He had no idea where he was. He could see no lights. It was as if they had dropped off the edge of the world, and yet he knew he could be no more than a dozen miles from Washington.

On the other side of the fire the President lay quietly under several blankets which Sedgwick had spread over him after pulling the unconscious man from the wreckage. The President had been out since—only an occasional groan or a painful grunt letting the young naval officer know his Commander-in-Chief was still alive. Sedgwick stared at the bundled form. The President's labored breathing caused the blankets to rise and fall ever so slightly. Sedgwick knew he had to get the man out of here soon or the blankets would stop heaving. But he didn't know how.

III

THE GRAND TOUR

Every civilization must go through this. Those that don't make it destroy themselves. Those that do make it wind up cavorting all over the universe.

—Dr. Theodore B. Taylor, a
theoretical physicist who
abandoned bomb-making

Eight

Outside, incandescent flares floated slowly downward like wounded fireflies, spreading the harsh white light of phosphorous through layered levels of the southern night's drizzle and smoke. No more than one hundred yards from the *E-4*'s wingtip, Harpoon could see the outlines of an overturned and smoldering half-track. The periphery line had been set there, with the shadowy outlines of men crouching behind it and other troops stretching into the darkness on both sides. Beyond, the airport terminal building was burning, orange flames licking into the void and casting different shadows on milling masses of pushing, shoving forms. A quiet, low moan rose and ebbed in the distance, undulating in a haunting sound that cut through the impatient whine of the giant aircraft's engines. This was a safe area, more than 150 miles from the nearest nuclear detonation. The pop-pop-a-pop of automatic-rifle fire, then the quick clatter of a not-too-distant machine-gun burst, snapped Harpoon back to the job at hand. Beneath him, slightly below the only open hatch of the rescue plane, men shouted at him. Harpoon leaned down toward a ramp that did not quite reach the high door of the plane. He grasped a hand that slipped immediately out of his grip, forcing him to reach down a second time, clasp the wrist, and hoist the man the final few feet into the darkened doorway.

187

Harpoon probed through the gloom for a look at the man he had hauled aboard. "Mr. President?" he asked tentatively. The man breathed in heavy wheezes. "Barely," he replied with great effort. "Just barely."

"Are you injured, sir? Do you need assistance?" Harpoon signaled a nearby Air Force captain.

"No, no," the man replied. His voice sounded very shaky. He started to droop against the bulkhead and the captain rushed to prop him up. "No!" he snapped. "Just get the others so we can get our tails out of here. Before the whole consarned state of Louisiana rushes us!" The captain drew back.

"How many others?" Harpoon asked.

"Four."

The admiral craned his head out the door into the half-light. On the platform, several feet below, two rotund figures clambered desperately to get aboard. Two less frantic men stood behind them, their backs to the plane, their obscured hands occupied. A group of men in combat gear, their automatic rifles turned outward from the aircraft, shuffled uneasily on the stairs. In the distance Harpoon heard the sharp crack of high-powered rifles, deer rifles, and then a burst of popping return fire, military issue. Near the half-track an airport fuel truck burst into flames, the flare of the explosion capturing a camera-flick image of men and women charging the periphery. He wheeled on the captain. "Get those four aboard and seal this bird up fast," he ordered.

Harpoon took the elbow of the dark figure next to him and felt a shiver run through the damp cotton of the man's shirt. The presidential successor withdrew his arm quickly, as if to hide any hint of fear. Don't cover it, Harpoon thought. You'll need every ounce of fear you can muster, you poor bastard. The admiral had no idea who he was getting—couldn't even remember his name, he had been buried in the isolated subterranean world of Omaha's war-gaming computers so long. Just Number Eight, the Secretary of the Interior, code-named Condor. Harpoon was tired, overwrought, and edgy. He also was severely disillusioned four hours after he had seen his computer games become real life. All he knew was that he badly wanted a man with a healthy dose of fear, a dose as potent as his own.

"No time for pomp tonight, sir," he said. "Would you please follow me?" The man edged gratefully away from the door and followed the tall, white-haired military man down a hallway toward dimmed lights. It was a strange aircraft aisle, its contours second nature to the admiral but disorienting to his companion. On one side the wall bent concavely, being the inner side of the aircraft's outer shell. No windows looked out. Instead, occasional windows looked inward from the aisle's other wall. They were thick panes through which the successor peered curiously at bee-hive compartments of men and women laboring with such preoc-cupation that they seemed totally unaware of the jungle world out of which he had just emerged. Their jungle, through which they struggled without a glance at their new leader, was a tangled maze of wires, cables, loose data boards, and crippled computer hulks.

"Lord A'mighty," the man said wearily, "ol' Harry Truman said he felt like a bale of hay landed on him. Must say I feel like I got the whole barn."

"Afraid so, sir," Harpoon replied, his impatience yielding to sympathy. "Maybe more."

The man still peered in the window, his back to the admiral. "How bad is it?"

"Bad."

"We losin'?"

Harpoon paused. He didn't know how to answer.

"I asked you if we were losing." The drawl disappeared from the man's voice, a bite replacing it. From the back he looked like a cowboy. As the drawl faded, however, the cowboy appearance dissolved with it. Even dirty and rumpled, Harpoon observed, the jeans were a bit too stiff, the outdoorsman's shirt a touch too new.

"I'm not sure that's the issue, Mr. President," the admiral volun-teered cautiously. "You need to be briefed."

"Not the issue?" The man spun on Harpoon, his face shimmer-ing white in the hallway lights. His hand moved reflexively to his forehead, rubbing at dried blood that was not his own. "Believe me, mister," he said firmly, no drawl left at all, "winning and losing are the only issues. I don't need a briefing to know that."

Without a further word, the two of them resumed their walk down the corridor, around a corner, and up a spiral staircase where Harpoon opened the door to the baby-blue presidential compartment, directing the man, then the others, toward seats inside.

Losing. Harpoon had known fear—that skin-crawling moment of sheer panic when a submariner feels the awesome power of the sea pressing down on him, his delicate mesh of men and machines failing. But he had never known anything like this, a fear that settled in the marrow and stayed there, gnawing. The world had built a similar mesh of men and machines, holding back a power far more awesome than the sea in a fragile balance that could never fail. It had failed and the mesh was unraveling like a dime-store sweater.

Harpoon had always had nagging doubts, sometings raging nightmares, about a survival system that called for a never-ending balance of terror. Few men walked away from SIOP at night thinking the nuclear chess game would stay inside a computer forever, year after year, generation after generation. But the men—and then the machines that held the final thread in the weave—had failed so suddenly and so totally. In many ways the machines had been the greater faith of his generation of military men. They had asked for larger, more sophisticated submarines. And got them. Faster, more ingenious airplanes. And got them. Smarter, more deadly missiles. And got them. Then they had asked for more sophisticated, faster, smarter machines to control their machines. Computers to do the instant calculating and communications satellites to pass the instant orders. Encrypters to veil the orders and decoders to unveil them. Radios to talk underwater and through space. Scramble phones that, at the touch of a finger, instantly connected commanders and troops, friends and adversaries, on opposite sides of the globe.

Now, at the touch of another finger, all the machines that controlled the machines had died. SIOP had died predictably along with Icarus, vaporized in one of thousands of explosions each brighter than a thousand suns. The others had gone less predictably. Inside the greatest surviving communications machine in the world, this airplane, the admiral had watched the computers die, the radios go dead, the telephones fall silent, the mechanical eyes go blind. His staff had patched desperately and brought part of the system back to life for the man now sitting across from him. Losing. You bet we are, Mr. President. But not the way you mean it. Harpoon glanced at his watch—1012 Zulu. They were running out of time.

The successor watched Harpoon nervously look at his watch, then glance up at him. The man's mind spun in a clutter of nagging, clawing, personal questions. Was his wife alive? Were his kids okay? Had the radiation already begun to burrow into his bones, chew into his lymph nodes? Every fiber of the man's soul demanded answers. But he would not ask. In the agony of his journey through the Louisiana backwoods he had steeled himself to take control as quickly and decisively as Harry Truman. If a haberdasher could do it—a simple, unprepared tailor from Missouri—he could do it, too. History demanded it. His country, bushwhacked by godless tyrants in the middle of the night, demanded it.

The man shuddered involuntarily, tried to hide it, and sank deeper into his bright blue swivel chair, seeking some comfort from its fresh luxury even as the aircraft bounced erratically on the runway. He brushed at a cobweb tangle of wispy but tenacious Spanish moss still clinging to his jeans. The silken moss refused to dislodge, so he turned his attention instead to a bur snagged in his shirt. He tugged it loose and flicked the little irritant away, propelling it to a landing between the high-gloss black of the shoes across from him. Lord Almighty, losing's not the issue. Truman would have ass-kicked this guy farther than he booted Mac-Arthur.

Harpoon ignored the flight of the bur, taking in the strange scene around him. It was not reassuring to a man accustomed to military order. The takeoff delays were less reassuring. The plane bumped violently, then stopped, the engine whine falling off to a low rumble. He reached toward the white telephone console, so many of its button lights connected to dead ends now. The engine whine accelerated again and the plane edged forward. He thought better of a call to the cockpit—the pilot had enough troubles—and settled back into his seat, one of four clustered near the phone in the command plane's presidential quarters.

On the admiral's right sat the backwoods judge who had rescued the successor from obscurity with a Bible and a quick oath and whom the successor had insisted on rescuing from the bayous. On the successor's left sat the director of the Fish and Wildlife Service, an old friend. He looked a mess, his face flushed, his pudgy fingers tapping their grime nervously onto an armrest, his belly heaving in irregular swells over a barely visible silver-and-turquoise Indian belt buckle.

Behind the Louisiana judge and the admiral stood two Secret Service agents, the survivors of eight sent out from the Baton Rouge Treasury office to collect the man. Their business suits, the discounted flannels favored by young stockbrokers and government agents, were disheveled and torn. Mud caked their trousers,

and splotches of dry dark red spattered their jackets and shirts.
They clearly had been quite efficient. They still held their Uzi
submachine guns at what passed for port arms. The guns made
Harpoon still more edgy. The plane bumped again.

"How bad's bad, admiral?"

The man's words seemed to carom out of nowhere, breaking an
awkward conversational lull and jolting Harpoon out of his tem-
porary preoccupation. He struggled to put his thoughts together.

"Come on, man," the successor said, the drawl back. "Come
on."

The plane cut left, then right. The pilot was zigzagging around
the aprons like a drunken driver. Harpoon wanted to wait now,
give up a few precious minutes to get the plane in the air and the
man downstairs where he could be led with detail rather than
misled with the awful, abbreviated facts.

"You still there, admiral? I do think we got a war goin' on."

"Sorry, sir," Harpoon said slowly. "You are in acute danger. I
want to get airborne."

"Been in acute danger for four hours, admiral. It's mean outside. People are like animals."

"I know, sir."

"Well?"

"Sir?"

"How bad's bad, admiral?"

"Sir, it's extremely complex and technical. You need the fullest
briefing possible."

"Psshaw!" The successor pulled angrily upright in his seat.
"Complex. Technical. Full briefin'. Doggone you, admiral, you
sound like every cotton-pickin' bureaucrat in Washington. We got
no time for that kind of talk."

Harpoon winced. It took them months to break in a new President. How did he do it now in minutes? "No, sir," he said cautiously, "we have very little time."

"Then get on with it, man. Just give it to me. One. Two. Three.
I'm not stupid. How many warheads did the commies hit us
with?"

"About two thousand, sir."

"Two thousand."

Harpoon searched the man's face for a reaction. "Yes, sir. Probably twenty-five hundred megatons." React, damn you. "One

megaton is about fifty times the explosive power of the Hiroshima bomb."

The successor stared at him coldly. "Don't patronize me, admiral. I know damn well what a megaton is. What did we hit them with?"

"About the same, sir. Somewhat less megatonnage."

"Our stuff's better. Always was." The successor prided himself on the show of knowledge.

"More accurate, sir. It was a relatively even exchange." Harpoon shifted uncomfortably. The engines ebbed again. Harpoon started to reach for the intercom button.

"How many dead?" the successor asked.

Harpoon drew his hand away from the phone. "Millions."

"Of Americans."

"Yes."

"And Russians."

"Yes."

"A relatively even exchange." The man harrumphed and went silent, his gaze drifting around his new quarters. The drift stopped on a far blue wall where the portable Seal of the President of the United States stared down on its newest possessor. A clutch of olive branches sprouted from one set of talons on the emblem's proud eagle. An array of arrows jutted from the other.

The man felt a great debt to that eagle and the country it represented. The only son of a dirt-poor Oklahoma farmer, he had gone into the oil fields when he was fifteen, sunk his own well when he was twenty-two, and brought in his first when he was twenty-five. A year later he had his first million dollars and found the Lord about the same time, seeing each as a reflection of the other and both as a reflection of his country's gifts. The Oklahoma City *Times* called the young oilman an American classic—a man who talked hard, worked hard, prayed hard, and had all the rewards to prove it.

In his late thirties, during the continuing OPEC crisis, he merged his successful independent oil company into one of the majors, accepting a fortune and a vice-presidency. It became the unhappiest time of his life. He didn't trust multinational oil, didn't trust anybody who placed as much value on a Persian sand dune as he did on good American soil. He edged into politics, mostly fund-raising. He played the game hard and, some said, mean—skewering candidates who failed to see Americanism his way, pouring cash into the campaigns of those who saw the dream as he saw it.

The last recipient of his cash had been elected President. And the invitation to join the Cabinet was like a prayer answered, particularly when the President-elect told him the first order of business was energy independence to help put the squeeze on the Russians. His mind drifted back to the meeting at which the President-elect had offered him the job. The new President had talked grandly and seriously of the great social responsibility that went with the appointment, emphasizing the chance he would get to move a nation on issues that would carry his imprint far beyond his lifetime. It was a chance to give back to his country part of what his country had given him. He had accepted without hesitation, and the President had thanked him warmly.

"How'd the President get it?" the successor asked quietly, his eyes still fixed on the Seal.

"In *Nighthawk One*, sir," Harpoon replied. "His chopper."

But it soon became clear the President had wanted him for other duties, too. He had become the administration's sonuvabitch, the man who did the balls-slicing while the President smiled, a political lightning rod who drew the bolts meant for the man in the White House. Even those well-schooled in the alley-fighting of Washington politics were surprised at how well he performed those chores. Behind the leather chair in his office on the sixth floor of the Department of the Interior hung a sign that read: "Don't Get Mad, Get Even."

"The chopper started for Andrews. The crew saw they couldn't make it and tried to run."

The successor pulled his eyes back into sharp focus on the Presidential Seal, his Seal now. Above the talons clutching both arrows and olive branches, the single rock-hard eye of the eagle glinted at him in challenge. An eye for an eye. A relatively even exchange.

"We assume the chopper was crushed in the blast wave."

The successor's eyes swung abruptly away from the eagle, taking the glint with them. "Assume?"

Harpoon stared back at the man. He wanted to get him off this subject. He wanted to get the plane off the ground. "Sir," he said evenly, "you don't go looking for bodies in this kind of war. You don't find them." Harpoon paused very briefly. "We haven't heard a word from any political or civil authority since we got the message to come for you." He paused again, adding, "Four hours ago."

The successor looked at him strangely. "Can't all be dead."

"No, sir. Not all. Our communications system is dead. You were out there. In a safe area. Nothing's working."

The successor stiffened. "That's why I'm in here, admiral. We spent a billion dollars protectin' these planes from nuclear effects."

Harpoon stifled a sigh. "You looked in the window downstairs, sir," he said. "We've got our gear back up to ten, maybe twenty years beyond Alexander Graham Bell. Doesn't do us much good if there's nobody at the other end of the phone."

The plane swerved sharply, causing one of the Secret Service agents to stagger. His Uzi wobbled menacingly.

"Sir, those men must sit down," Harpoon said in alarm. "If one of those weapons goes off inside this aircraft . . ."

The successor ignored him. "You tellin' me the President of the United States is inside his command post and he can't talk to his troops, can't talk to his commanders?"

Harpoon glanced worriedly at the agents. "Right now, sir, we're having more luck picking up a disc jockey in Walla Walla."

"Don't you be sarcastic with me, admiral," the successor bristled.

"Sarcastic?" Harpoon forced himself to keep his voice calm. "I'm sorry, sir, but I'm deadly serious. We're picking up a few distress signals and some garbled messages. But communications? We're getting primitive messages through to a handful of bombers. Through Alice." He immediately knew he shouldn't have slipped into the lingo yet. "That is it," he added.

"Alice?"

"The *Looking Glass* plane, sir. The Strategic Air Command's airborne command post. It's a thousand miles north of us and our only tie to anything now."

Harpoon thought he saw the first real flicker of fear cross the man's face. The engines had stopped whining again. Jesus, get this plane out of here. The flicker faded.

"Harpoon they call you?"

"My code name, sir."

"Well, Harpoon, you and Alice better get your act together fast." The man sounded as if his television set had gone blank and the answer was to plug it in again. "If you think this President is going to let this stop at a relatively even exchange, you speared the wrong fish."

"Let it stop?" Harpoon fought the exasperation out of his voice. "We don't know how to stop it, sir. You have a damned tough decision to make. But it may be like the tree falling in the wilderness. If nobody hears it, did it make a sound?" He held a rock-hard gaze on the man. "This war, sir, is completely out of control."

Suddenly the plane turned hard left, then lurched to an abrupt stop. The man with the turquoise belt buckle moaned. The judge firmly closed his eyes. The younger of the two agents lost his footing, careened into the back of the admiral's seat, and lost his grip on his Uzi. The small gray riot gun slithered over the admiral's shoulder, bounced off his knee, and landed on the floor between the officer and the successor. Harpoon reached over, but the successor clamped his foot on the weapon. Pure fear finally gleamed in the man's eyes. A small white light blinked urgently on the telephone console between them. Harpoon retreated from the weapon and lifted the phone, listening. "Crap," he said after seconds. "The *Looking Glass* saw it? Then go, man, go!" He listened further, his craggy face rapidly contorting in anguish. "Oh, my God," he breathed into the phone. After a moment he said bleakly, "Take it over the top of them." He stared at shoes still polished to a duty-night sheen and slowly ground an errant bur into the rug. "Dammit, pilot, take it over the top of them!" Harpoon cradled the phone softly.

"Give the gun back."

The engine rumble rose rapidly into its piercing takeoff whine, the plane edging forward, then rolling.

"Give the gun back, sir."

Harpoon's voice was patient but persistent, as if he were talking to a child. The successor stared at him numbly, holding the submachine gun loosely in his lap, then slowly handed it up to the agent, who stood precariously behind Harpoon.

"Do you understand what's happening, sir?"

"Troops should've cleared the crud off the runway," the successor said in a blank monotone.

"The crud on the runway . . ." Harpoon strained to keep his voice even over the engine roar. "My troops, sir. Your troops. They're the crud on the runway. On their bellies. Shooting the animals. Clearing a path for this aircraft. They're shooting their own people, sir. Your people. People so sweat-stinking scared I can smell the terror in here." The plane bumped. "Thanks, marine."

The nose of the giant plane lifted. It tilted left as one set of wheels left the ground. *Whump!* The plane tilted right. *Whump!* The admiral heard the flaps curl back into the wings as the *E-4* climbed. "You've got a decision to make very soon, sir. Do you understand SIOP? Do you understand transattack deterrence theory? Do you know how to issue nuclear orders? Do you know who I am? Do you know who TACAMO is?" He stopped, feeling the weight press down on him as the plane reached for altitude. "Do you want to be briefed?"

The successor sighed. Harpoon felt uneasy. He knew that most of the military officers aboard this aircraft shared his views about the next steps. He also knew that not all of them did. His mind saw the colonel—the Librarian, they called him, a Russian expert whose bespectacled eyes were forever magnified in that if-you-knew-what-I-know look.

Harpoon looked at the successor. The man's face was certain again. Crap. He shoved his own fear back down into the pit of his stomach. The little white light was blinking urgently at him again, and he reached over to pick up the phone.

"Hey, Radnor?"

Radnor ignored Tyler, staring instead into the flickering radar screen that showed the Canadian coastline giving way to the frozen reaches of the Beaufort Sea and then the Arctic Ocean as they moved north toward Russia again. "Radnor?" Keep the sonuvabitch out of your head, Radnor. He's gonna drive you over the edge, take you with him. Blank him out. Focus on north, north toward the bastards who stole your dream. Stole Laura.

"Hey, Radnor. I'm serious. Really serious."

Radnor's eyes bored into his radar screen. His world narrowed to the edges of the scope. He had no peripheral vision. Tyler would be in his peripheral vision. O'Toole would be there. The world would be there. His wife. His dream. His future. "Radnor." Keep out of my head, damn you, Tyler.

"I'll go halfway with you, Radnor. I'll say it happened. I will. I promise you. But you gotta go halfway with me."

Block him. He's the threat now. "Talk to me, buddy. Radnor.

Talk to me. Please." God damn you, Tyler. Shut up. Live in your own screwed world. Stay out of mine. "Radnor!"

"Shut up, Tyler," Radnor said quietly, fingering the broken pencil.

"Radnor, go halfway with me. Just say Timmie isn't dead. Forget my wife. Radnor, please."

Radnor turned slowly and looked into Tyler's grotesque and mournful face.

"Just Timmie. You don't have to say anything about my wife, Radnor."

Radnor felt dizzy. He forced the jagged edge of the broken pencil against his palm, hard, till it hurt, till the skin broke and blood appeared. "Forget my wife." Radnor burst. Laura! The pencil became a dagger, the palm a fist. The fist rose high, then lunged downward.

Upstairs, the red of the flight panel throbbed hypnotically and Moreau stared into the glowing gauges as she mechanically completed a course correction. Her mind felt flooded with novocaine, half struggling with the aircraft, half struggling to untangle the befogged memory of her father's schedule in semiretirement. Thursday night. Friday morning. Was this a lecture day at the Academy in Colorado Springs? You're dead then, Dad. Dead under the megatons that caved in Cheyenne Mountain and brushed the dust of the Academy up into the clefts of Pike's Peak. Or are you home in Steamboat Springs, sheltered farther back in the mountains? The dancing red fallout clouds moving slowly east across the desert from the wasteland of San Francisco and Sacramento. The fog rolling south from the missile fields of Wyoming, sweeping over the white tops of the Medicine Bow Mountains, crossing the Continental Divide, oozing through the high cut of Rabbit Ear Pass. Be there, Dad. Please, Daddy. Be where you can fight, dig, run, hide, struggle to live. Don't be dead. . . .

Radnor's shriek cut through the earphones in the B-52. Moreau jerked to attention. Kazaklis lost his thoughts of Sarah Jean. Halupalai sat bolt upright, startled out of the farewell to the fifteen-year-old daughter he had not seen for years.

Downstairs, Radnor's fist smashed into the worktable in front of Tyler, blood from his own hand spattering across the navigation charts. Tyler reared back in his seat and sat frozen, tears streaming down his face. "I spanked him, Radnor." Radnor picked up his hand and slammed it down again. And again. He felt nothing.

Out of the corner of his eye, in the unwanted peripheral vision of Tyler's broader screen, he saw the first white intrusion. Then the second, and a third creeping forward. He fixed his eyes on the screen, then relaxed his hand until the bloody pencil released on the console in front of Tyler. Radnor pulled back to his own position. "Incognitos," he said calmly into the all-channels radio. "Incognitos at twelve o'clock."

The admiral's brow furrowed. He clutched the white phone tightly to his jaw and stared intently past the successor. "Forty miles?" he repeated. "Then thirty-six?" He frowned. "No buck-shot pattern? Smart little bugger, isn't he? Thirty-one. Twenty-four. Crap." Harpoon let the phone edge imperceptibly down his chin and brought his eyes into hard focus on the successor. "Sir, would you fasten your belt, place your head in your lap, and brace yourself?"

The man stared back at Harpoon blankly. The admiral's eyes moved away again.

"Dancing 'em up our tailpipe, huh?" His eyes twitched slightly in thought, his mind taking him deep beneath the sea into a more familiar world. The old submariner saw depth-charge patterns. "At what intervals? Crap. Do we know if it's a Yankee-class boat?" He listened. "It better be. Yeah, they've got sixteen tubes. No, with multiple warheads he'd crisscross us." He knew the Soviet submarine captain would fire from all his missile tubes. The heat from one launch set off enemy detectors as surely as the heat from sixteen. You didn't hold back in this kind of war. If you did, you sank with unused missiles. "Nineteen miles? Dud? Mr. President, get your head down!"

The successor looked totally confused. This was not part of the game plan—move quickly, act decisively. What the devil was going on?

"We can figure on two, maybe three duds in the sixteen." Pause. "You got me there, pal. It's Russian goddamn roulette. Fourteen miles?" The admiral's free hand pulled at his open collar. He tried to calculate the pattern marching on them—a string of detonations, probably sixty miles long, cutting slightly diagonally right to left across their takeoff route.

"Mr. President. Please. Do you realize what is happening? A Soviet submarine has launched missiles at us. They are patterned to cross our route. Exploding every fifteen seconds. Do you understand?"

The successor's eyes narrowed warily. He seemed frozen.

"Dammit!" the admiral erupted. "Get your fucking head down!" He reached over and shoved the man's head down to his knees. "Ten miles?" he repeated into the phone. "Port side, aft?" he asked, slipping into more comfortable lingo. He started to order hard right rudder. "Get those damned guards down! Propped up against the bulkheads! Hands off weapons!" The successor glanced indecisively upward at the agents. They looked at each other and began to move.

"Seven miles," Harpoon whispered into the phone. Then he barked: "Hard right! Full power, hard right!"

Suddenly, the presidential compartment turned on its side. The admiral quickly lowered his head into his lap. He felt a weight slam into the back of his seat, a body tumble over his back. Next to him he heard a thud, a whoosh of air, and a muffled chugga-chugga-chugga. He shuddered, but he was counting. Three . . . four . . . Someone screamed. Five . . . six . . . He felt the first ripple, like a sudden squall at sea, and the plane lurched up, then down, metal groaning. He braced himself and waited for the next. Five seconds passed. Ten. Fifteen. Metal ground against metal as the pilot struggled to level out. Twenty. Twenty-five. Without raising his head, the admiral reached for the loose telephone receiver. "What gives?" He slowly pulled himself upright, eyes closed in relief. "I'll be damned." Then he said, "Take her all the way up."

Harpoon sighed. As if to himself, he said, "We got the empty chamber." For a moment he was oblivious to his immediate surroundings, the tension oozing out as he tried to absorb just how lucky they had been. They had survived a dozen rounds—World War Three rounds at just under a megaton each. Then the awful other reality struck him, the low, undulating airport moan echoing in his memory. Baton Rouge had just paid an incredible price for tonight's strange and unheralded presidential visit.

Harpoon opened his eyes slowly. Across from him an unconscious agent, apparently the one who had tumbled over his seat, lay limp over the successor's knees. At Harpoon's side, the judge still slumped forward in the crash position. The new blue fabric of his swivel chair was shredded, white stuffing edging out of three small craters. The seat padding, absorbing some of the impact of the bullets, had saved the aircraft from a perhaps-fatal skin-piercing decompression. The padding had not saved the judge. The back of his shirt was red. The Bible had skittered just out of reach of a hand that dangled loosely to the carpeted floor. Behind the judge's chair, the other agent rose shakily from his knees, staring numbly at the machine gun he had jammed into the back of the seat as he fell.

Harpoon felt ill. Being a submariner himself, he doubted the Soviet commander had fired on direct orders from Moscow. The poor bugger must have been cornered, an American sub on his tail. The orders had come out of sealed contingency plans written years ago in some Soviet think tank, just as similar contingency plans had been created by bright young Americans in the sterile offices of the Rand Corporation and the gingerbread rooms of the Hudson Institute. Harpoon's mind drifted to his last undersea command and the sailing orders he had carried. Don't sink with the nukes. Cornered? Fire. At any available target.

Harpoon finally looked at the successor and saw dumbfounded shock and horror. Damn. He wanted the man scared, but not this way. Leaders were not supposed to see blood. It made them erratic and irrational, stalling some, drawing a need for vengeance out of others. Computer dots representing neutered millions were much safer. The innocent-looking dots insulated the mind. Harpoon shuddered. He had a helluva sales job ahead of him.

"Incognitos like hell," Kazaklis snapped. "Not up here. Them's bandits." He adjusted his helmet. "Distance," he demanded. "Velocity."

"Hundred miles," Radnor snapped back. "Fast. Mach two-plus. Darned near Mach three."

"No, no. Check again." The pilot's voice sounded dubious, not alarmed.

"Affirmative. Eighteen hundred miles an hour. Three, correction, four bandits."

"Battle stations!" Kazaklis ordered. "Helmets! Oxygen! Defense!" He did not wait for responses. "Jamming! Chaff! Shovel that stuff like hay, gunner. Decoys ready?"

Kazaklis glanced quickly at his copilot. "Honored?"

"They cared enough to send the very best," Moreau responded, snapping her oxygen mask.

"Too good. Too fast for an old bucket of bolts like us. MIG-25

Foxbats. They must be very hungry. And suicidal. No way those gas-guzzlers can get back home."

"Makes 'em meaner."

"Meaner than us? You got hemlock in your canteen, too, pal. This is the joust of the kamikazes."

In the softened lights of the corporate-bland and distractingly spotless briefing compartment, three computerized maps glowed on the wall behind Harpoon's chiseled features. One showed the United States, another the Soviet Union, and a third displayed, in Mercator map distortion, the world. The vibration of the aircraft, and the tiny imperfections of the computer's microdot drawings, caused small but mind-bending warps in such familiar outlines as the Florida spit and the Puget Sound cut. Less familiar outcroppings and indentations such as Kamchatka and the Black Sea also wobbled slightly out of tune with reality. But the Mercator distortion, that mapmaker's deformity that enlarged the northernmost parts of the world by creating a squared globe, was the greatest. The landmass of Asia seemed to overwhelm the rest of the world. The successor saw that first.

Harpoon had led him silently down one level into the half-light of this room. The man had been unable to speak during the introductions to half a dozen somber Air Force generals and a single prim colonel. To cover, he had stared stonily into each set of grim eyes and clasped each outstretched hand too firmly.

The officers sat now at an oval boardroom table, the generals seeming to stare at him like vultures in the gloom, the colonel's eyeglasses glinting eerily. The successor had seated himself intentionally to the side, away from them. In his lap he held the portable Seal, which the uninjured Secret Service agent had carried from the other room. In front of him Harpoon seemed to glow luminously in front of the maps. The maps confused him. They pulsed at him—circles and starbursts and pinpoints, some in blue, some in red; clusters of starbursts in some places, huge blank pieces of nothingness in others.

Harpoon struggled for a place to begin. He had stood in front of these maps a hundred times, confidently talking the modern-war code language of Counterforce and Countervailing strategies, of Slickems and Tercoms, of ICBM vulnerabilities and Circular Error Probables. He had listened to experts, talked as an expert, poising nudets against Moscow in the twentieth century's greatest bluff. Until a few hours ago the pinpoints and starbursts and circles had been no more than shrewd computerized chess moves. Now the game's pawns were grandmothers in Boston, school kids in Tucson, peasant farmers in Staraya Russa, pink-cheeked students in Gorki.

Harpoon stared for a moment longer into the successor's expectant face. He had to take time to flesh out the awful realities—give this unprepared man more than knee-jerk knowledge, knee-jerk knowledge being deadly dangerous. How could he explain that all the blustering talk of the past thirty years meant nothing now, that the few elite insiders had worried about just one thing: how do you turn the monster off once you've turned it on? How could he explain that, even now, both nations still were bluffing? Bombers bluffing submarines, submarines bluffing Soviet ICBM reserves in a plan started and not stopped by dead computers? That each new call of the bluff raised the stakes until the last of the world's fifty thousand nuclear weapons took out the last pea patch in Arkansas, the last hog wallow in Uzbekistan? How did he explain that the blue chips were great cities? That the cities were hostage to each other? New York for Leningrad? And New York would go first because that was the way they had built the system? In planning it had seemed to have a certain bleak logic. In reality it took on a grotesque surreality.

"Harpoon," the successor said, suddenly breaking his silence, "you do seem to have a propensity for waitin' for World War Four."

All eyes turned toward him and he drew the Presidential Seal in tighter, like a shield, certain that his fear and uncertainty had screamed out of their hiding place and into his voice. To the others the words sounded as if they had been fired from a cannon. The colonel stifled a chuckle.

Harpoon felt ill again. World War Four? Maybe he should be laughing along with the colonel, he thought bleakly. That was the first joke he'd heard all night. "Major," he said to an unseen officer in a separate cubicle, "will you dim the Soviet Union and the world so we can take a closer look at the United States?"

The compartment grew slightly darker, but the United States loomed boldly in a crazy quilt of red and blue splotches that made the successor's skin crawl, partly because he knew what it must mean, partly because he didn't understand at all. Harpoon stepped slightly to the side, so the entire country was in view, and brushed the light pointer across wide regions.

"What you are seeing, sir, gives you a fair representation of the present condition of the United States," Harpoon began. "In a moment you will see that the Soviet Union is in roughly the same condition. The red markings indicate targets that have been hit. In the first exchanges, all of which took place within the first hour, both nations expended about a third of their arsenals but exercised some restraint. The objective was to do our best to disarm each other, concentrating on missile fields, military installations, and communications facilities. Of course, we could not disarm each other. Therefore, both nations also randomly hit some cities that were not primary military targets. The theory is that randomly striking a few major cities, such as New Orleans, which you were near"—the pointer skittered several hundred miles south of their present location—"makes the threat of the next strike more intimidating."

The successor's eyes froze on Baton Rouge. To the north, Shreveport, the home of a bomber base, was red. To the south, New Orleans was red. He began to sweat. He could feel the crud eating at him.

Harpoon sensed the man's fear, it being so normal. "It is unlikely that the radiation harmed you, sir," he said quietly. The successor slumped, humiliated. *Damn you,* admiral. "Major, bring up the Soviet Union." The top of Asia sprang back into the room.

"For New Orleans, we took Odessa," Harpoon said quickly, flashing the pointer at a red starburst at the top of the Black Sea. Then the pointer fluttered back to the United States. "We were surprised by the attack on Los Angeles, because it is such an attractive hostage for the second strike. When it became clear Los Angeles was lost"—the pointer skittered to Asia again, and the successor's mind began to wobble with it—"the computer suggested we take out Kiev. Some cities were military targets or so near them that the distance was irrelevant. That accounts for the destruction of cities such as Seattle and Vladivostok. So, as you can see, both nations have a few areas of almost total destruction, other pockets of major destruction, but large regions that remain basically untouched."

Harpoon paused and looked at the man. His eyes were riveted on the United States, his face blank. To Harpoon, he did not appear to be listening closely. Harpoon was wrong. He was listening quite closely. But he was confused. He saw far too much blue, and he didn't understand.

"The blue ovals. . ." the successor began haltingly. "The blue represents cities that were not struck?" His voice was disbelieving and slurred.

"That is correct, sir," Harpoon replied. "Not struck in the first attack."

Harpoon watched the man's eyes flicker across the map, left to right. On the West Coast the Puget Sound area was a red mass, as was the eastern part of the state of Washington near Spokane. Oregon was untouched. The red continued again in the Bay Area, spreading from San Francisco east beyond the B-52 base at Sacramento. Los Angeles was red. The destruction began again, with a few gaps, in Montana and the Dakotas, spreading in intensity through the missile fields of the Plains states south into Texas. To the east, New England, an advance staging area for the bombers, was a checkerboard of red. Washington, D.C., was a muddle of red and blue, as if the Soviets had tried to carve parts of it away while leaving other parts. Still, throughout the country, blue dominated. Denver was blue, although a huge red starburst glistened just to the south in Colorado Springs. Minneapolis, Chicago, Indianapolis, Atlanta, Philadelphia, Miami, many major cities including New York, all were blue.

"New York . . ." The successor's voice was dull and distant. "What's happening in New York?"

Harpoon's white eyebrows rose uncertainly. "You saw Baton Rouge, sir," he replied. "Same thing, I imagine, except much worse. We have to assume civil disorder is rampant in the blue areas."

"We can just as easily assume," the colonel cut in abruptly, "that our civil-defense program is efficiently evacuating the blue areas at this very moment."

Harpoon shot an amazed glance across the compartment. "Jeezuz, colonel," he rasped. "New York? In the middle of the night? With no electricity?"

"Just as we should assume the Soviets are evacuating their cities, rapidly and efficiently," the colonel continued undaunted.

Grunts emerged from the generals. The successor seemed to miss the entire exchange. "But it wasn't hit . . ." his dull voice interrupted the grunts. "Why?"

"New York is a hostage city, sir," Harpoon answered simply. "The blue cities are being held hostage."

"Hostage?" The voice went from dull and disbelieving to incredulous.

"Sir, American cities are being held hostage and Soviet cities are being held hostage. That is the system we built. We are holding each other mutually hostage, just as we were before the war. We left Leningrad, holding it hostage. We are saying to them: You take New York and we will take Leningrad. In the second strike. Or the third strike."

"Leningrad is standing?" The voice turned guttural. He had not yet focused on the map of the Soviet Union. "Four hours after a sneak attack on the United States, we have left Leningrad"—the voice broke in anger and dismay—"untouched?"

"That is the system, sir." Harpoon swore under his breath. He was sounding like a damned New England schoolmaster. But he didn't know how else to answer.

The successor's eyes darted past Harpoon to the map of the Soviet Union. Across the top of the Eurasian continent, the same mix of red and blue dotted the landmass. He had fewer reference points in a land he had never visited, but the middle of the continent, from east to west along the Trans-Siberian Railway line, was a long red string where the main missile fields had been. Red starbursts blossomed out of Kamchatka and the Arctic coast near Murmansk, which he assumed were submarine bases. He knew from Cabinet meetings that Plesetsk and Tyuratam were missile- and satellite-launching centers. They were red. So were Vladivostok and Odessa, as promised, as well as Sverdlovsk, Tbilisi, and a handful of other major Soviet cities. Moscow was dotted in red, but blue interrupted the blood color. Leningrad, Minsk, Smolensk, Riga, and other metropolitan areas remained blue.

The successor moved his eyes away from the map and toward Harpoon. Shakily, he started to rise, clattering the Seal to the floor. He sat back down. His face was ghostly white and his mouth moved several times before the words came out. "Treason . . ." he muttered grotesquely. "Ungodly . . . insane . . ." The words trailed off.

Harpoon felt the plane tilt slightly as the pilot maneuvered in the random pattern of evasion he had been taught. Around the briefing table, the officers swayed with the aircraft, eyes cast downward, light coughs interrupting the rhythmic silence of the moment. Only the colonel, outranked by all but here because he was the command plane's expert in Soviet thinking, nodded almost imperceptibly.

Harpoon floundered. He looked at his watch. Damn. "Insane, perhaps," he said wearily. "Ungodly, for sure. But not treason. It is the system we built to protect ourselves. It is the system the Soviets built to protect themselves." He paused very briefly. "It isn't working very well."

"Isn't working very well," the successor repeated in a drone. His mind was weaving with the aircraft. "Loco," he said, the word momentarily jelling his thoughts. He spat the next words: "We runnin' this war from some ward at St. Elizabeth's, Harpoon?"

Harpoon sagged, then drew himself up again. "Sir," he said plaintively, "it is crucial that you quickly learn the system so you have some chance of dealing with it. If all of America is destroyed, the Soviets have no hostages and we have nothing to protect. The Soviets don't want that. If all the Soviet Union is destroyed, we have no hostages and they have nothing to protect. We can't possibly want that. Then there is no *reason* to stop. Ever."

"Stop," the successor repeated.

Harpoon watched the man closely. He had watched men go crazy dealing with this in peacetime.

"Who started this, Harpoon?" he asked.

Damn. There's no time for this crap. "The Soviets, sir."

"How long ago?"

"Four hours. Almost precisely 0600 Zulu." Harpoon felt his fears turn to exasperation. "That's Greenwich mean time, sir. One A.M. in Washington. Midnight in Omaha."

"Winter morning in Moscow. Dark." The successor's words were detached. "Out of darkness. Into darkness." His eyes drifted into the gloom of the briefing compartment. His mind drifted, too.

Now Harpoon felt woozy. Out of darkness, into darkness? Was he quoting from the Bible? He struggled through misty childhood memories of Revelation and Matthew and John. He shook his head.

"Wintertime," the colonel intoned seriously. "A time when the Russian psyche is its darkest, its most depressed, its most paranoid. They are so preoccupied with the cold darkness of their long winters that Russian authors have written novels about the theft of an overcoat. Tells you a lot." Harpoon looked at him in amazement. The colonel paused and then intoned seriously, "It also tells us that if those people were paranoid enough to start this, they are paranoid enough to go down to the last missile."

The admiral stared at the Librarian. You little prick. Spent your whole life burrowing through Russian papers looking for the most belligerent statements to use as ammunition. Then Harpoon cursed himself again. They had all used men like that, kept them around to pry more money out of Congress. Just as the Russians had kept men busy collecting the rashest of the American statements, crap from the John Birch Society, nutty statements from half-baked right-wing congressmen with no more influence than Jerry Falwell. *Damn.* Harpoon continued to stare at the colonel, but he wasn't sure whom he was damning most. The colonel stared back.

Harpoon shook his head once more and turned toward the successor. The man's face was gone again. He felt like he was wrestling with Jell-O. Harpoon tried to fight down the wisp of a memory, the kind he had successfully suppressed during the total involvement of the past four hours. His eleven-year-old grandson pulled at his sleeve, tugging him back into playfulness after one of those periodic lapses far off into his SIOP world. Earth to Gramps, the boy said. Come in, Gramps. The admiral's grandson had been in Seattle. He winced. The admiral fought back the memory. Earth to the President. "Sir, can we please get on with this?"

The successor saw the wince. "I see no point," he said.

"No point?"

"I want our remaining ICBM's fired at the blue circles immediately."

"Sir, please . . ."

Even the colonel was shaking his head now, and a pang of fear flashed through Harpoon. The Librarian had no respect for this man at all. For years the colonel had been the used. Now he was going to be the user.

"Fire them," the successor said.

"All our ICBM's were launched or destroyed hours ago," Harpoon fumbled.

"Why don't you just get to the point, admiral?" The colonel cut in.

"Because he needs to know what is at stake, dammit!" Harpoon flared.

"At stake?" the colonel bored on. "We were attacked. The sovereignty of the United States is at stake. We can give up, or we can use the bombers. To cut the head off the chicken."

"Shut up, colonel," Harpoon said flatly. They were talking as if the successor had left the compartment. But the successor was not listening anyway, tracking on his own course now.

"Precisely how many Americans are dead?" the man interrupted.

"Twenty to thirty million," Harpoon said, swiveling his glare away from the colonel and into the blank face. "More will die from radiation, riots, disorder. Maybe forty million total. If we can stop now."

"Russians?"

"Fifteen, twenty million. Maybe thirty million with the side effects. If we can stop."

"So we have lost."

Harpoon sagged in despair. "Sir," he said desolately, "this isn't victory by body count. Can't you understand? It isn't over, for God's sake. Our bombers are under way for a second strike. Our submarines have been given predetermined orders for a third strike. We can't talk to our submarines. We can't talk to the Russians. Between us we have more than forty thousand warheads left. We don't know how to stop it." He slumped further, feeling trapped and helpless. "It isn't over," he repeated hauntedly. "It's out of control."

"Eighty miles," Radnor's voice droned into the cockpit. "Seventy."

"Foxbat!" Kazaklis demanded the specs on their adversaries.

"Top speed, Mach two-point-eight," Moreau replied. "Range fifteen hundred miles. One way. Toughest in high-altitude dogfights. Most sophisticated—"

"Armaments?" Kazaklis interrupted. He knew the Foxbat was sophisticated—maybe too sophisticated—and he already had begun calculating that to his advantage, the tortoise plotting against the hare. The fighters were three minutes away. If they missed on this run—and they could, because they were approaching too fast—their speed would take them on a long looping turn, giving him invaluable time.

"Four AA-6 ACRID air-to-air missiles," Moreau replied immediately. "Warheads nonnuclear. Heat-seekers, range fifty miles.

Radar-guided, range twenty miles. They'll try 'em both ways. Gun pack, two twenty-three-millimeter machine guns."

"Sixty miles."

"Evasive action," Kazaklis ordered. His words were distant now, as if they were trailing several moves behind his mind. "Close air intakes. Hokay, buddies, let's see how the cossacks like their eggs fried in their own grease."

Moreau began the swaying, groaning maneuver back into the radioactive cloud. "Fifty miles," Radnor said. "Forty miles. Missiles launched! One. Two . . ." He paused. "Six launches!"

"Decoys out!"

"Decoys dispatched." Halupalai instinctively placed his hand on the Gatling-gun trigger, the Vietnam reflex, and then pulled it back.

"Thirty miles."

"Clouds?" Kazaklis wanted the red crud badly, not only because it would spook the racing MIG pilots but more importantly because the dancing radioactivity might clutter the missile guidance systems.

Downstairs, Radnor stared at his radar. He saw six little blips racing at him, four larger ones swooping ahead of the missiles and climbing. From the other direction the fog was creeping slowly across his screen, nearing the center. "Twenty degrees left," he said. "Countdown?"

"No time," Kazaklis barked. "Twenty degrees left," he repeated.

Moreau reacted. Radnor interrupted. "Bandits twenty miles. They're climbing, commander."

"Yeah, they screwed up. They were up our gazoom before they saw us. They're trying to eat speed."

The pilot's voice crackled with tension. But it also carried the slightest touch of satisfaction. He knew that a B-52, once it was found, could be shot down by almost anything that flew. He needed every edge he could get.

The successor had gone silent again. Harpoon peered out at him. He seemed in a daze, so lost and alone. A wave of sympathy flooded through Harpoon, then departed swiftly. He felt alone too, grappling with forces careening out of his control. Suddenly, in the faint light, Harpoon thought he saw in the phallic shadow of the Secret Service agent's gun barrel what Icarus must have seen in the projection of Soviet missiles arching down on him in Omaha. The thought startled him. The pressure was getting to him. Then he saw Icarus sending him away—Godspeed, God grace. He saw the unfrightened face of his young escort turn toward a last gin-rummy game, the vaulted doors sealed below him. He saw the rockets' red glare of a long-ago Fourth of July, the future stretched limitlessly beneath him in the monumental splendor of his nation's capital, and he heard his bride whisper, *Never say good-bye.* And he pulled himself together, signaled the projectionist to bring up the third map, and decided to plod on, his way.

"Sir," Harpoon said, "you should briefly examine how other nations reacted." The successor said nothing. Harpoon flashed a wobbling light on the world. "Most of the less-developed nuclear powers responded reflexively. So did Israel. Only Britain and France held off."

"Our allies," the successor said, his voice still vacant and hollow.

Harpoon ignored him, wanting to hurry through this part. "The Soviets made no move against Western Europe, moved no troops and launched no weapons. Nor did they move against the Middle East, although the Israelis did. The Israelis always have sought buffer zones—the kind they tried to create in the Sinai, the Golan Heights, Lebanon. They also tend to move when the rest of the world is preoccupied. We were very preoccupied." He took a deep breath and added: "They created a rather large buffer zone."

Harpoon's pointer moved quickly through the Middle East. The red splashed erratically. In Syria, Damascus was red, as was Amman in Jordan, Baghdad in Iraq, Tehran and other targets in Iran. Splotches dotted the region of the world's first civilization along the Tigris and Euphrates rivers and through the biblical regions to the edge of Jerusalem and the Dead Sea. The destruction leaped over Egypt to the west but continued along the Mediterranean through Libya. Harpoon's pointer quickly moved back over the Persian Gulf to the Indian subcontinent.

"Others acted completely irrationally." The pointer skirted past red starbursts in Pakistan and India. "Apparently a defective Chinese missile, aimed at Soviet Central Asia, landed in northern Pakistan near the capital of Islamabad. The Paks thought it came from India. They hit New Delhi with the few crude weapons they had. India responded, also with crude weapons, hitting both Islamabad and Karachi."

The successor groped through the maps, his mind inundated, his instincts telling him to take control. Somehow. He remembered the concern about Pakistan when the Soviets invaded Afghanistan. "Sounds like a Soviet conspiracy to me," he blurted. "They always wanted Pakistan."

Harpoon stumbled to a stop. The colonel broke in. "The President has a point, admiral. The Soviets always wanted a warm-water port. Taking Pakistan gives them one."

Harpoon felt like laughing. But he knew the colonel was starting his play for the man. "What in God's name would the Soviets do with a warm-water port after this?" he asked.

"Straight down the Indus River to the Arabian Sea," the successor said with new enthusiasm. *Let them know you understand strategic thinking too.*

"Nothing," the colonel said smugly. "If we stop them."

"Giving them access to the Indian Ocean," the successor said. The two military men were talking around him, but he ignored it. He felt relieved. *Let them know you understand the Soviet mind.*

Harpoon waved the colonel off, glanced hurriedly at his watch, and continued. He moved the pointer far south. "We don't have any notion what happened in South Africa. They had primitive weapons. They exploded them in their own territory. The motives may have been racial."

The pointer skittered back to Asia. "Other than the two superpowers, the Chinese did the most damage and took the worst beating." The pointer moved quickly along the endless frontier from Samarkand to Vladivostok. "The Soviets had about fifty divisions along the border. The Chinese tried to destroy them. They may have incapacitated a fourth of the Soviet border forces. The Soviets used tactical weapons against Chinese border troops, then, moments before we launched our first major wave of ICBM's—" Harpoon faltered again, puzzled, as Alice had been, by the American attack sequence. But he pushed on, not wanting to clutter the problem further— "the Soviets hit Peking and the industrial city of Wuhan with thermonuclear weapons. They appear to have stopped after that."

The successor missed the pause, and the puzzlement. "So only the Chinese helped us," he said.

"The Chinese didn't help us," Harpoon replied more curtly

than he intended. He could feel his caution dissolving, his time compressing. "They tried to help themselves, as did everyone else. Anything that makes the Soviets feel more threatened now should be cause for alarm, not satisfaction, inside this aircraft."

The successor stiffened. "Harpoon," he said in bewilderment, "sometimes when you open your mouth I feel like it isn't connected to my ears. Would you like to say that a different way?"

"No, sir. We are quite pressed for time." The successor looked at him curiously, but Harpoon had decided to bull onward. It was time to lay it on the line. He beckoned to a three-star general sitting at the briefing table.

"The general is expert in nuclear effects and their meaning to civilian populations, political structure, social structure, et cetera. Would you speak as briefly as possible to that subject, general?"

The general rose reluctantly. "Let's try to deal quickly with the rest of the world," he began. "The world has survived plague, pestilence, famine, earthquakes, floods, wars, disasters of immense proportion—"

Harpoon frowned. "General," he interrupted, "keep it short. Please."

"Sorry, admiral, but it is important to understand the context. In the 1920's an earthquake killed two hundred thousand people in Tokyo and Yokohama—approximately the number killed in the World War Two atom-bomb attacks on Hiroshima and Nagasaki twenty years later. We have forgotten the earthquake." He let the words sit very briefly. "My point is simply that the world has absorbed such punishment, natural and man-made, in the past. So when we look at the world map, forgetting the superpowers, we see an incredible amount of damage, grief, and suffering. As it stands now, all of it would be absorbed, even with the radiation effects."

Harpoon shifted impatiently from one foot to the other. "Okay, general, the superpowers?"

"Well, you look at those maps . . ." The general let out a large whoosh of air. "You look at those maps and you see a considerably different picture. Both nations would survive what you see here. I'd also add—pardon me, admiral, but it is worth noting—that the world has suffered similar catastrophes, even worse. In the fourteenth century, when the world's population was a fraction of what it is now, bubonic-plague outbreaks claimed twenty-five million lives in just a few years in Europe and Asia. In this century, the flu epidemic of 1918 killed three times as many as World War One—probably thirty million persons. However—"

"It would be valuable to recall," the colonel interrupted, gazing knowingly over his spectacles, "that the Soviet Union accepted fatalities of twenty million during World War Two. Such is their nature."

"Bullshit!" All heads turned toward Harpoon. He slammed his light pointer onto the table.

"Admiral," the colonel protested. "It is historical fact."

"Bullshit!" Harpoon erupted again. "I've been hearing this crap since I was a plebe at Annapolis and I'm sick of it. The historical fact is that twenty million Russians died. The historical bullshit is to say it is in their nature to accept it."

The colonel looked away unhappily. The successor glanced first at the colonel and then at Harpoon questioningly. "I must say, Harpoon," the man said quietly, "that I seriously doubt the Soviets have the same respect for human life that we do. You disagree?"

"I am saying, sir, that it does us no good to view our adversary as some sort of subhuman species. It is misleading and dangerous. They are our enemy. But they lose loved ones and they mourn just like us. To view them differently not only gets us nowhere, it leads us in the wrong direction. Would you proceed, general?"

The general glanced quickly from the successor to the admiral. He continued.

"However, there is no way to make a comparison between this event and the worst of past disasters. Unlike previous wars, the deaths occurred almost simultaneously over large sections of the two countries. Unlike the largest epidemics, it was accompanied by vast physical destruction. And this event occurred in complex societies which will find it much more difficult to adjust than, say, the agrarian society of China a century ago. The lifeblood of these technological societies—oil, communications, interrelated economic systems—has been destroyed or severely impaired for years or decades.

"Also, it is impossible to calculate the effect that fear of the unknown—particularly radiation—will have on surviving populations. In that regard, we are as primitive as the Dark Ages populations trying to deal with fear of the plague. In those times, terrified families left loved ones to die alone. They ran, panicked, looted, murdered, raped, committed suicide, and rebelled against authorities who often were as fearful as the populace. Radiation, like the plague, is an unseen, unknown menace—"

Harpoon tapped his pointer impatiently. "So, general, please, what kind of society do we have below us if we stop now? Briefly. Speculatively, if necessary."

"It's all speculative," the general protested. But he went on, trying to condense the knowledge he had accumulated over years. "If we stopped now"—and he paused emphatically with doubt— "we have the world's two most powerful nations set back anywhere from several years to several decades.

"We have the world's two superpowers reduced to second-rank powers, perhaps on the level of a Brazil, with their only real influence resting in the threat of their remaining nuclear weapons. That is not a small influence. But we can expect world turmoil, as other countries try to fill the power void. Economies will collapse everywhere. Starvation will be common before spring throughout the United States, the Soviet Union, and the world. Some areas of the United States and the Soviet Union will not be habitable for a century or more. I am not an alarmist on radiation effects. It does not mean the end of the world. But millions more will die, even if we stop, and still further millions will perish from medical epidemics of a nonnuclear nature, from hunger and from civil disorder.

"Allow me just one example. We had more than one thousand intercontinental missiles buried primarily in the Plains states from Montana, Wyoming, and the Dakotas to Missouri and Arkansas. The Soviets had even more in the central regions of their country. Most were double-targeted. The only way to destroy those missile installations is with direct-hit ground bursts of fairly large megatonnage, digging them out in the craters. Such explosions cause the most intensive radiation damage, the dirt from the craters pulverized and kicked into the atmosphere as fallout. In one of our complexes, we had two hundred silos scattered in a hundred-mile radius around Great Falls, Montana. That area alone, according to our preliminary data, received at least three hundred ground-burst explosions in the one-megaton range. The area is so radioactive that men will be unable to live there for at least a century. The area contained the headwaters of the Missouri River, which feeds into the Mississippi. Worse, far worse, the fallout from those detonations plus others throughout the region naturally wafts east on the prevailing winds. It will drop most heavily on the breakbasket regions of the Midwest, the richest farmlands in the world. Crops will grow again there, but certainly not this year. This will cause starvation throughout the nation and probably the world. Ironically, even the Soviets depended on this breadbasket to feed their people."

The general paused.

"Still, to be an optimist, the United States would survive. The Soviet Union would survive. Neither would survive comfortably." The general stopped uncertainly.

"Thank you, general," Harpoon said quietly. "And if this war continues?"

The general's face paled immediately and he snapped his eyes at Harpoon.

Kazaklis glanced at his altimeter. It was spinning. Thirty-seven thousand feet, thirty-six, thirty-five. Moreau, without orders, had begun taking the plane down. Smart little wench. The pilot's stomach was falling up again. He liked the feeling. In front of him, on the red television screen, he could see the MIG's climbing, desperately trying to slow down. They disappeared off the top of his screen. Other white images remained, moving rapidly toward him. Then others appeared, diving on the aircraft.

"New missile launches!" Radnor's voice was losing its artificial calmness. "One! Two! Four missile launches!"

"Radar-guided missiles approaching!" Kazaklis barked. "More chaff!" Alone, in the back of the upstairs cabin, Halupalai dumped more tinfoil. His palms sweated. One hand lurched again at the gun trigger, the other closing over the ejection lever. He swore at himself again for his inability to break the habit. The Buff groaned in its sweeping dive through the fallout cloud. Moreau began rocking the aircraft in evasion.

The first white intrusions were almost upon them. The plane rocked rhythmically. On Halupalai's screen the first blip poofed. Then the next and the next in rapid order. Halupalai felt the airframe shudder ever so slightly. Briefly the gunner was puzzled. Then he saw the last of the first intruders dart left, suckering into the phony heat of his decoy flare—poof!—and he let out a wild whoop. "Hot shit!"

"Hang on to your muumuu back there, ace," Kazaklis drawled. "Four more coming."

Halupalai's exuberance faded instantly. His screen was a clutter now of radioactivity and dancing snow from his tinfoil patterns. The four images sped raggedly at him through the snow. Suddenly they broke crazily away, skittering randomly after the tinfoil ghosts he had created. He sagged back into his bucket seat.

"Let 'er rip now, gunner," Kazaklis exulted. "You just made it to the Super Bowl."

"Hot shit," Halupalai said without enthusiasm.

Up front, Kazaklis and Moreau looked at each other. Kazaklis shrugged. They still had four MIG's out there, with six missiles and a handful of other ways to stop them.

The pilot forgot Halupalai immediately. The Russian pilots had made the first mistake. But they could afford mistakes. He could not. He glanced at the altimeter—ten thousand feet, nine thousand, eight thousand—and then at his screen, on which the Arctic Coast crept back toward them. The fog was gone, the fallout cloud behind them. Kazaklis leaned forward and pulled the flash curtain open at its corner. Below him, starlight shimmered off ice and snow. He felt the tension surge into him, the silver captain's bars rise on his shoulders, the Strategic Air Command lightning bolt stretch tightly on his arm. The percentages were not good. But they were better where he was going. He was not depressed at all. He was going down to low level, where he liked it, where he could take those bastards up against the canyon wall. "I'll take it now," the pilot told Moreau.

"Dammit, admiral, I don't know how to answer that," the general said.

"The hell you don't. We've been studying it for years."

"And all we came up with is imponderables."

"Bullshit. Just plain bullshit. Just because we don't know precisely what happens to the F1 level of the ionosphere as opposed to the F2 level doesn't mean a damn now. Just because we didn't tell the public diddly-squat about it doesn't mean we don't know a lot about it. Tell him what General Jones told Congress."

"Christ, anybody could figure that out. I don't know why people were surprised."

"Start there."

"General Jones, the chairman of the Joint Chiefs late in the Carter administration and early in the Reagan years, testified in 1980 that if both countries emptied the whole shooting gallery . . ."

The general stopped.

"Come on," Harpoon pushed. "Get on with it."

"He testified that the deaths in the northern hemisphere would be in the hundreds of millions."

The successor sat rigidly watching. His face had paled. He felt as if he had been spun up and down like a yo-yo since boarding this plane. This is not what he had planned during his trek through Louisiana. Off to his side the director of Fish and Wildlife, who had not uttered a word since takeoff, sweated like a lathered quarter horse. The remaining Secret Service agent stood with his legs crossed, as if he were faced with a problem of imminent bodily evacuation.

"Thank you," Harpoon said. "Now, go on."

"Go on where, admiral?" the general asked wearily. "We simply don't know."

"We know enough, general. We're in the middle of it. We've got the man sitting here. He may not be able to stop it if he wants to. But he has a right to know. A need."

"Sir, you haven't even told him how the SIOP plan works yet."

"I will, general. I'd like to get to it before it's too late."

"I'm sorry, admiral. It's just that the range of unknowns is so great."

"I know, general. I'm sorry, too. Give him the most optimistic reading."

"Optimistic." The general's voice trailed off. Then he came to stiff attention. He began speaking in clipped tones. "End of the northern hemisphere as we know it. United States would go first, Europe almost simultaneously, Soviet Union shortly thereafter. Whether the hemisphere would remain habitable is conjecture. Radiation, natural epidemics, starvation, postwar hostilities would reduce the number of survivors by a factor of five, ten, twenty within months or a few years. Optimistic . . . Small bands of roaming survivors. Tribes with no political connection to one another. After a few decades, life might become similar to life in the Middle Ages. Fiefdoms. Tribal rivalries. Survivors would have severe problems with solar as well as man-induced radiation. The atmosphere's ozone layer, which protects life from natural solar radiation, will be seriously damaged, perhaps destroyed. At least temporarily. It might rebuild itself in twenty, thirty years. Much would depend on activity in the southern hemisphere."

The general stopped. "Pessimistic," the admiral demanded.

"Pessimistic," the general repeated. "Nobody knows. The explosions and the radiation won't kill everybody. A new ice age is possible from the atmospheric dust shielding the sun. Just the opposite is also possible. If the ozone layer is depleted too greatly, man won't be able to handle it even in the southern hemisphere. Then, in theory, the species will die out. Like the dinosaurs. In that sense, it could be *On the Beach*. But from solar radiation. It took two billion years to build the ozone layer and allow life on this planet. We can totally destroy it in the next few hours. . . ."

The general stopped and stared vacantly for a moment. Then he sat down slowly. The only sound was the slight whir of the *E-4*'s engines, barely perceptible through the insulation of the briefing room.

After a moment, the successor rose suddenly from his seat, his face not quite ashen but distinctly pallid. "I need a moment by myself," he said.

Harpoon stared at the man with both impatience and bleak understanding. "We have very little time, sir," he protested half-heartedly.

"I need a moment by myself," the man repeated unequivocally.

Without further ado, the successor moved quickly out of the compartment. Not even the Secret Service agent followed. Harpoon shifted from foot to foot, briefly bewildered and uneasy. Little time? They had no time. He looked at his watch—1042 Zulu. But as he looked up to see the successor's back disappear out the doorway, the admiral felt a new wave of pity for this overmatched man. He also held a glimmer of hope that the briefing had penetrated. If so, a moment's delay might be worth it.

Outside the briefing room, the successor moved hurriedly down unfamiliar hallways till he found the staircase. He climbed it and reentered the presidential quarters. Inside his own compartment, he knelt quickly. He needed a briefing from a higher source than Harpoon. He prayed deeply and with a low burble that echoed eerily in the lonely room. The prayer lasted only a moment, and then, with a solemn amen, he rose confidently, the pallor gone from his face.

NINE

Kazaklis brought the B-52 back toward the North American coast-line at one thousand feet, temporarily trading deception for speed. He was in a sprint now, with the unseen Foxbats looping high and around toward him, the old bomber screaming low and vulnerable over the last jagged crags of the ice-locked Beaufort Sea. The B-52 gulped gas ferociously, *Elsie*'s precious gift taking them in the wrong direction, the only direction. The pilot's own fuel, adrenaline, pulsed rapidly through his body, deftly tucking questions and fear in some side pocket of his mind. He subconsciously reached for his groin, arranging his vitals for the crunch, and barely caught the urge to remind his copilot to do the same. Instead, he went to the all-channels intercom.

"Hokay, you guardians of democracy," Kazaklis said, "secure the family jewels. We're goin' in for the ball-buster."

The bravado sounded tinny over the tortured scream of the engines, eight jets pushed to their limit. The speed gauge read Mach point-nine-five, just over six hundred miles an hour, just under the speed of sound. The altimeter held briefly, then began to drop again precipitously. At the pilot's right, Moreau helped Kazaklis control the creaking, bumping bomber, forgetting the navigational charts balanced on one knee. In front of them their red screens danced crazily, the night cameras in the Buff's nose picking up the last ice tangles of the sea and converting them into

220

a maze of computer images. Just ahead lay the western mouth of the Mackenzie, where a winter that began in September had petrified the competing forces of the river and the sea, forcing them up into a rock-hard barrier that loomed on the screen.

"Hard left!" Kazaklis barked. The ancient plane moaned as it banked, then leveled out again. "Landfall?"

"River delta," Moreau replied. "Ice jams in the mouth. Broad outlets beyond. Flat tundra. No landmarks." It was not an ideal place to do what Kazaklis needed to do.

The altimeter read three hundred feet and wobbled downward.

"Coming up on twenty seconds," Moreau continued. "Ready . . . now."

Kazaklis braced himself. The altimeter spun down from two hundred feet, bouncing as badly as the plane. The screen showed the ice barrier moving right.

"Five seconds. Hang on."

The B-52 struck the roiling coastal winds like a flat rock on water, bellying up, then sagging down precariously, old rivets and younger bones jolted and complaining under the strain. "Jesus!" Moreau blurted involuntarily. "Fifty feet!" Kazaklis said. "Get it up!" The charts bounced unnoticed off Moreau's knee as she helped the pilot tug frantically at the flailing bomber. At fifty feet, she knew well, they were in severe peril. The long, sleek wings flapped like a seagull's, drooping so much on a routine takeoff the designers had given them wingtip wheels. This was not routine, the ice jam still menacing on their right, the Foxbats menacing somewhere unseen. Moreau agonizingly helped Kazaklis nudge the balky plane back up to one hundred feet. He held it there.

"Cut it a little close," Moreau said brittlely. Then she removed the edge from her voice. "Nicely done, Captain Shazam."

"Umm," Kazaklis responded, preoccupied. "What's ahead?"

Moreau reached for the charts. The plane bumped violently again.

"Hands on wheel!" Kazaklis said urgently. "Forget the charts. That's why we got the boys in the loony bin." He glanced quickly to make certain he had switched to private.

"Flat as a pancake. Dozen arms of the Mackenzie."

They both knew Arctic rivers were so wide and shallow that radar couldn't pick up their banks.

"Great place to hide," Kazaklis said sardonically.

"Be lucky to hide a snowball down there."

"Wanta park it on the river and toss snowballs at 'em?"

Moreau said nothing.

"What about the mountains?"

"Richardsons. We got better charts of the Verkhoyansk."

"Figures."

"Maybe twenty miles to the foothills. Low, treeless. Not much better."

"Book say Foxbats got look-down radar?"

"Says maybe. They were working on it."

"Shit. Anybody tell the spooks at Langley about eternal vigilance?"

"Foxbats were designed to go after other fighters, not look down on us."

"That's our edge."

"Not much."

Kazaklis eased the speed back to Mach point-eight-five. The Buff was rattling like his pa's old Ford truck. Last flight of the *Polar Bear,* he thought. Still, he didn't want the rivets popping just yet. He switched to all channels.

"Anybody talkin' soprano down in the basement?"

Downstairs, in the navigation compartment, Radnor was on private. He was sweating and bleeding, and he held hard eyes on Tyler. "Don't fuck this one up, Tyler," he said menacingly. "I want these bastards. For Laura. You got that, buddy boy? For Laura."

Tyler stared back at his crewmate. The navigator's face twisted grotesquely, but it wore a look of vague understanding. "Yeah, I got it, Radnor. For Laura." Tyler had tears in his eyes. He brushed them away with a fireproof glove and switched radio channels. His voice squeaked in a forced falsetto, a forced joke. "Radnor says I ain't gonna need my jewels anymore, commander." Radnor swore at him silently, then felt the tears welling in his eyes, too.

"You okay down there, navigator?" The pilot's voice was very concerned.

"He's okay," Radnor said flatly. The radio fell silent for a moment. Radnor's eyes continued to lock on Tyler. Both men were crying.

"Well, give me a reading, fellas," Kazaklis said blandly. "Come on."

Tyler turned toward his screen, its rotating arm stretching out one hundred miles, far beyond the nose cameras available to the pilots. "High terrain sixteen miles," he said professionally. "Dead ahead. Five hundred feet elevation, rising to fifteen hundred. Knobs rising eighty, a hundred feet along the way. Watch 'em."

In the cockpit Kazaklis shook his head at Moreau. Tyler's emotions were bobbing up and down like a weekend sailboat in a storm.

"Bandits?" the pilot asked.

"Not yet," Tyler said firmly now. "Screen's clear as a bell."

Kazaklis relaxed briefly, even as the wheel tugged harshly at his forearms. Clear as a bell. Suddenly he drew bolt upright. "Gunner!" he yelled. "You got the jammer on?"

In the rear of the compartment the commander's alarmed voice jolted Halupalai out of a morose daydream. He stared, panicky, at the confusion of unfamiliar switches in front of him. Briefly, he couldn't find the right one. Then he flicked it, sending out the powerful beams that helped hide them. He turned to see Kazaklis craning his head toward him. Halupalai looked away quickly. Shit, Kazaklis thought. The whole damn place is a funny farm.

"Bandits," Tyler broke in. "Southeast. Eighty miles. Just over Mach one."

"Shit," Kazaklis said. "Shit, shit, shit."

The successor strode into the briefing room with a new certainty, and Harpoon, who had presided over the deathly silent group during the several minutes of the man's absence, felt a sudden shiver of concern.

"Are you a believer, admiral?" the successor asked abruptly.

"A believer?" Harpoon repeated, mystified.

"In the Lord."

Harpoon blinked at him.

"Admiral?"

"There are no atheists in foxholes, sir," Harpoon said limply. "We are in one very large foxhole."

"Good." The successor beamed. "I hope you took advantage of this lull to pray. I did. I feel much better."

Harpoon looked around the room for help. He found none. The successor shifted gears rapidly. "Okay," the man said, "now that you gentlemen have finished with the melodrama, how do we win this war?" Harpoon made no reply. His mind spun. He stared into the man's calm and confident face, trying to keep the consternation off his own, and turned slowly back to his maps.

A deep and foreboding sense of futility swept over the admiral. He felt trapped between the successor's dangerously simple certainty, which had returned so abruptly, and the system's dangerously complex certainty, which never changed. Harpoon was losing to both—and he knew it. He also knew the stakes.

"SIOP," he began slowly, "was devised shortly before the Cuban missile crisis. It means Single Integrated Operating Plan and was devised to coordinate all the nuclear forces at our command. We could not have a submarine striking a target that a bomber had struck earlier or a bomber attacking a target that had been destroyed by an ICBM. Over the years, as both the Soviet and our forces became vastly more complex, the system necessarily became highly computerized."

The admiral heard an impatient rustle behind him. "Don't need a history lesson, Harpoon," the successor said curtly.

"You may need everything you can get, sir." Harpoon surprised himself with the directness of his reply. He continued without turning from the maps.

"By the beginning of this decade, we had more than forty thousand targets and innumerable combinations of options programmed into the computers. Clearly, no man or staff of men could possibly handle such complexities in the minutes available in a nuclear crisis. We had serious doubts that a national leader could make a decision to respond at all, let alone order a balanced response, in the time available to him. Indeed, that is what happened. . . ."

"Are you tellin' me that the President . . ."—the successor fumbled—"my predecessor did not respond . . . ?" His voice had gone sullenly incredulous.

"I am saying, sir," Harpoon replied, and now the impatience was creeping into his voice, "that the President had four minutes. He was aware that our early-warning system had sounded many false alarms. He was faced with a somewhat confusing attack without absolute confidence it was real. He absorbed the first missile landings. From our vantage point in Omaha, he responded slowly. In retrospect, I believe he acted reasonably."

"Reasonably." The successor's single word cut through the purr of the engines, and all eyes in the compartment swung toward Harpoon.

"Yes, sir," Harpoon replied, his voice unyielding. "We have a partial transcript of a hot-line message—perhaps a disingenuous message—from the Premier. You might want to read—"

The colonel cut in abruptly. "I would be happy to help you interpret it," he said.

Harpoon turned with methodically slow intimidation toward the jarring voice. "Colonel," he said icily, "I would appreciate it if you would allow me to proceed uninterrupted. The message was quite simple. Perhaps simple-minded. I cannot judge that. I doubt you can, either." Harpoon shifted his gaze to the successor. "The Premier contended that the more militaristic elements within his government were pushing him into a total preemptive attack on us. He chose a limited attack on military installations instead. For what it's worth, and I certainly don't know what to make of it, he offered to accept an equal amount of damage in the Soviet Union." Harpoon immediately regretted his phrasing.

"A relatively even exchange," the successor interjected caustically.

"It was a damned foolish and incredibly dangerous thing to do," Harpoon tried to recoup. "I can't assess his motives. He claimed that our government had squeezed the Soviets too long and too hard and that they couldn't—or wouldn't—accept it any longer."

The colonel could not control himself. "You are describing our national policy, admiral," he blurted. "It surely is not an un-civilized one. It is in man's nature to cage a dangerous animal—to lock up a sociopath, whether a single political assassin or a nation of geopolitical assassins."

Harpoon made a half-turn back toward the colonel, leveling his light pointer at him. The beam glittered off one lens of his glasses. "You and I are not politicians," he said briskly. "I do think we can safely make the observation, without engaging in pseudo-Freud-ian analyses of long winters, that caging a nation with twenty thousand nuclear weapons was a policy with some risks." The admiral heard a mirthless chuckle behind him. His shoulders tightened.

"The colonel's observations seem to make you nervous, Harpoon. I believe I could use the advice of a man who is expert in these matters."

Crap. Expert in Dostoyevsky and obscure Kremlin right-wing-ers. "You are the Commander-in-Chief," he replied as evenly as he could. "You may have the advice of anyone aboard this air-craft—or anyone we can reach on the radio, damned few that they are at the moment. Would you like to be briefed by someone else?"

"Oh, no, not at all." The successor's words cut through the admiral. "I am learning far more than I expected."

Harpoon stared into the red splotch that had been Seattle and, across Puget Sound, the Bremerton-Bangor naval complex. He had spent one long shore-duty tour there and his only son had fallen in love with the Nordic beauty of the alpine mountains and the fjordlike waters. After college, the boy had returned. To make missiles for Boeing. And make his only grandson. The missiles had given them a house on the water, a sailboat, annually recycled automobiles, and a carefree future in the place his son called the Land of the Lotus Eaters. Carry on, Gramps.

"It became clear long ago that the SIOP computer could not be secured from any major attack. Therefore, we began programming it to devise multistage responses that would be carried out twelve to twenty-four hours after its destruction. After the death of the President, for that matter. And after the destruction of most of our means of communicating with our forces. That meant we could issue orders that would be carried out after the disappearance of both our national leadership and our national communications system. It was a major advance. A rather dangerous one. But not all that much more dangerous than the hair-trigger system we already had in place. All our strategy, after all, was a bluff. The escalation of SIOP's responsibilities was the ultimate bluff. The Soviets, as they always did, developed a similar system."

Harpoon paused very briefly, taking a deep breath.

"Tonight, the strategy was relatively simple. Our ICBM's were launched in two waves more than four hours ago. We held our weapons in Europe, awaiting any Soviet move. Those are programmed to go on provocation. Their launching, of course, would mean the total retaliatory destruction of Western Europe. Our bomber forces were ordered into the air as the first wave arrived. They constitute our second strike, a rather limited one. The surviving bombers will arrive on target in four to six hours. The bulk of our submarine forces, in which we carry most of our destructive power, was placed on hold for fifteen hours. They constitute the third strike. Their instructions are to hit their targets massively unless they receive contrary orders, the assumption being that if they can't hear us, we're still at war. That would complete the destruction of the Soviet Union."

Harpoon stopped and turned to look at the successor.

"You find fault in that, Harpoon?" the man asked. "The caged animals, as the colonel put it, attacked us first, did they not?"

"They have a system of their own, sir."

"And?" The successor sounded now as if he were humoring Harpoon, but the admiral decided to ignore it.

"For various reasons," he continued, "the structure of their system is somewhat different. They placed the bulk of their nuclear weaponry in land-based missiles. Many of those silos remain unused and undestroyed. The Russians are extremely defensive in nature. They spent billions on elaborate defenses against our bombers. This drained off resources for submarines. We abandoned serious air defenses decades ago, spending the money instead on a submarine fleet vastly superior to theirs. Frankly, we thought they were suckers. If the game was a bluff, it was better to bluff with offense than defense. The bombers clearly were the weakest part of our system."

The colonel caught a downturn in Harpoon's words and interrupted again. "The Soviets," he said, with a slight touch of condescension, "have been invaded by Tatars, French, Germans . . ." He turned aggressively toward Harpoon. "You are quite right that they are defensive in nature. We quite wisely exploited that tendency." He paused for emphasis. "And what you call the weakest part of our nuclear system may prove to be the Soviets' Achilles' heel."

Harpoon angrily jabbed his pointer again, knowing what the colonel was approaching. "Colonel," he growled, "will you please keep your goddamn mouth shut till I'm finished?"

"I'd like to hear what he has to say," the successor said quietly.

"He can wait. He'll make quite certain you hear him."

"Unless you harpoon him first, admiral," the successor said, gesturing at the pointer.

"The temptation is growing."

"I imagine."

The colonel smugly sank deeper into his chair. Harpoon continued.

"The difference in forces somewhat dictates the timing. It means the Soviet second strike, by their bombers, will take our cities first. Our third strike, by the submarines, will take theirs shortly afterward."

"Malarkey!" The successor started to rise out of his chair. "Even I know the Soviet bombers are so old we could knock 'em down with a peashooter."

"Admiral," the colonel blustered in again, "those Model T

crates are so vulnerable the Minnesota Air National Guard could do the job."

Harpoon finally exploded. "If you're so damned smart, colonel, go to the yellow phone and order 'em into the air. I can't even get through to Minneapolis. Every transistor, every piece of copper communications wire in Minnesota is burned out. We got 150 Model T's coming at us, most of them so old they still have propellers. We can't stop half of 'em and you damned well know it. Every one of them is carrying more than a megaton of thermonuclear weapons. In a few hours they're going to be roaming at will across this country. And they're going to pick off their targets one by goddamned one. New York. Philadelphia. Denver. Minneapolis. Till they get down to Waterloo, Iowa. Waterloo, colonel. You remember Waterloo?"

"And our bombers will do the same thing," the successor said. It was not a question.

"No," Harpoon answered, trying to calm himself. "Their bombers were in the air when the attack began. Most of our alert force was caught on the ground. We have about twenty bombers flying."

"Twenty!"

"Twenty can do a lot of damage, but—"

"But what! What other juicy news do you have for me?"

"At this moment, some of our bombers are under attack by fighter interceptors."

"The Soviets can attack our bombers and we can't attack theirs?"

"Sir, they had the element of surprise. They spent their money on bomber defenses, as we wanted them to. The B-52's are a suicide squad."

"So how much of our vaunted second strike will get through?"

"Maybe a dozen will get past the interceptors. The survivors then have to thread their way through the best bomber defense ever devised. A bit chewed up, but the best. We never expected them to get through. We wanted to mousetrap the Soviets into wasting money on defense for a war with no defenses." He paused and cast a rueful look at the colonel. "We were successful," he added.

"How many?"

"A couple. A half-dozen if we're lucky."

"And we sit idly by while the commies nuke their way through America."

"Sir, for God's sake, we're hardly sitting idly by. In the end, it will equal out. Our submarines will do infinitely more damage. There will be nothing of value left of the Soviet Union, just as there will be nothing of value left of the United States. And it won't stop there. The weapons in Europe will go. The remaining Soviet ICBM's. That's the system we built. It really doesn't make much difference, does it? The Russians simply get the first crack. . . ." The admiral's words trailed off.

"Harpoon, you will roast in hell."

"Probably. But not for telling you the truth, sir."

The successor stared at Harpoon, his gaze almost hateful. "How many warheads we got in our subs?"

"About seven thousand, sir."

"Launch 'em," the man said simply.

Harpoon stared at him silently.

"SIOP be damned!" the successor thundered. "This is the most cockamamie, defeatist, godless thing I've ever heard. Give the bastards the works. Now!"

A wisp of an unhappy smile touched Harpoon's craggy face. He put his pointer down quietly. "I understand your frustration, sir," the admiral said. "I truly understand your frustration. It is a sick system. Even sicker than I've described."

The successor's stare turned raw. "You're patronizing me again, Harpoon. I'm your Commander-in-Chief. I've given you an order."

"An impossible order."

"You refuse a direct order?"

"I can't order the submarines to do anything. Nor can you. We're rebuilding our communications slowly. But even with pre-war communications we couldn't talk to them. They are invulnerable, the perfect final bluff, because no one can find them. Not even us. They received their orders hours ago as the first missiles landed. Those orders were to run silent and deep, away from detection or communications, for fifteen hours. Then the main part of the fleet will come back near the surface to listen. If they hear nothing, they will fire. That's the system. The Soviets know it as well as we do. They know that if their bombers strike, it they send off more ICBM's, they are dead. Because there will be no one and no reason to talk to the submarines."

The successor's eyes dropped slowly. For a moment he seemed lost in thought. Then his eyes rose again, avoiding Harpoon, and moved around the conference table at the silent Air Force officers. The successor whipped his gaze back at Harpoon. "You are telling me," he asked, his words coming in a hauntingly detached cadence, "that the fact of our nation . . . rests in the hands . . . of a dead computer?"

"The fate of the world," whispered the general whom Harpoon had forced to be both optimistic and pessimistic.

Harpoon sighed. "That isn't quite true," he said slowly. "First it is important to understand—and, in our dependence on machines, we often forget it—that SIOP is . . . was . . . no more than the accumulation of the wisdom and foolishness of several generations of our brightest men. Almost all of them well-meaning. Almost all of them scared."

"Do you believe I am well-meaning?" the successor asked.

"I believe so, sir."

"Do you believe I am scared?"

"You were a few moments ago, sir. I hope you are now."

"I'm scared, Harpoon. But only scared of losin'."

"I'm sorry to hear that. I'm so scared I could use a change of skivvies. Few of the men who devised the war plans, on both sides of the world, were total fools. We built the fear quotient, which we saw as our only salvation, into SIOP. The Soviets did the same. Both sides knew that if this mess ever got started, we would have tremendous problems with ego, national pride, animosities, misunderstandings, communications. Why do you think our world, our hemisphere at least, is not destroyed by now? We certainly had the ability to do it faster. It is now almost five hours since Jericho began."

"Jericho?"

"Sorry. Jericho is code for a full-scale nuclear war. When we looked at Jericho, we knew communications would go. We knew leaders would die. We saw a system that could be out of control in minutes. So we built in pauses. To some degree, we even matched the equipment to the pauses. The bombers are very slow, which built a natural pause into the war. We are in that pause. Nearing the end of it, though."

"And the pause was designed by these brightest men," the successor said, derision in his words, "to do precisely what?"

"To give us time to patch our communications, sir. And to give you and your Soviet counterpart time to stop bluffing and make the Jericho decision."

Off to the side, Harpoon saw the colonel rise abruptly out of his seat, wagging his head frantically.

"The chicken!" he shouted. "Tell him about cutting the head off the chicken or you'll . . . you'll be remembered with Aaron Burr!"

Harpoon looked grimly at the colonel. Crap, he mouthed silently.

The Foxbats were on their tail now, fifteen miles back, gaining steadily, holding their six remaining missiles for a certain kill. Kazaklis seemed to ignore them. He gave no orders, said nothing. Only the methodical, droning voice of Tyler broke the radio silence. Okay, high terrain three miles, and it's significant. Up a bit. Down a bit. Little more. Hard left. Good. Kazaklis followed each instruction machinelike. The lightning bolt on his shoulder patch tilted in flawless rhythm with each banking turn around each rolling mountain corner. The white captain's bars rose in perfect harmony with the aircraft as he lifted it over each mountain ridge. His buttocks swayed in their parachute harness to the geometry of each maneuver. He was good. The Foxbats followed his every move.

"Bandits twelve miles and closing," Tyler radioed, his voice devoid of emotion. "High terrain at twelve o'clock. Lift it. Dead ahead. Lift it." Effortlessly the pilot lifted the plane, the captain's bars also rising. In front of her, Moreau's screen filled with ominous red clutter. On the right of her screen the yellow groundtracking altimeter, a little thermometer-like image displaying the plane's height over the ground, plunged rapidly. It bottomed out at twenty-five feet. Ka-*whack!* The brittle, cracking sound came from the bomber's spine. Moreau shuddered. The thermometer darted back up, even as Kazaklis nosed the bomber down over the other side of a ridge into a long, shallow valley. She glanced quickly at the pilot. His face remained impassive, his eyes glued on his own screen as they had been since the beginning of the ducking, darting roller-coaster ride through the mountains minutes ago. "Too close, pilot," she said. His eyes held unblinking to the screen. He's part of the damned computer too, she thought. The Foxbats followed. "Bandits ten miles and closing."

Kazaklis dropped the aircraft low into the valley. He had taken his pursuers on a long zigzag chase through the frozen mountains. He was back now, almost where he started, one ridge from the delta. In front of him the red screen still danced in leaping signals of danger, a vivid tableau he read as naturally as he had read the green screen just hours ago, taking his toy aliens up against the canyon wall. His mind was blank, as it had been then, his various other worlds excluded. No room to think. Thinking caused fuck-ups. Thinking would tell him that it was him or them, perhaps even bring in the emotion of fear. So his mind read the computer and sent light-speed signals to the fingers adept at so many tasks. He had taken the aliens up against the wall. He knew their secrets. But they never stopped chasing.

Long ago Kazaklis had accepted the inevitability of succumbing—somewhere—a minor slip, a SAM battery in Tiksi, a MIG roaring out of some niche in the Baikals, suicidal in its determination to save kids and lovers and parents in the city on the lake. Or simply sputtering engines, *Elsie*-style, and a crash somewhere in the wilderness short of the Chinese escape city. But not in a bleak and frozen valley in the Canadian Yukon, which he saw only in red computer images. "Bandits eight miles and closing." He felt very tired.

"We've lost, Kazaklis," Moreau said softly.

He stared into the red screen, a vivid computer-game house of horrors now. The last flight of the *Polar Bear*, his mind said, thoughts finally invading its sanctum. He turned and looked at her, pain but not fear in his eyes.

"They're taking their own sweet time, aren't they?" Moreau's voice was soothing and also unfrightened. She was readier than she thought, and had been, she realized, for some time.

Kazaklis broke his silence, still blustering. "You shovelin' decoys back there, Halupalai?" Then he went on private, his voice dreary. "Cat's got the mouse, Moreau, and he's playing."

"You gave it a classy run through the hills, Kazaklis."

The pilot ignored the compliment. "They really screwed up on the first pass. They'll close a couple more miles. All they gotta do is stay away from Halupalai's guns."

"Don't imagine that has them terrified."

"No. Not four of 'em with six missiles left."

They went quiet again, the bomber noise rattling through their silence like a tin can full of loose pebbles as it raced along the valley floor. Kazaklis tapped the throttles, edging the speed back up toward Mach point-nine. His sweeping, swaying evasive maneuvers turned halfhearted, seeming to invite the missile launches. Then he reached over and nudged his copilot. "Maybe we oughta give 'em one more thrill," he said, his voice impishly childlike.

Moreau looked at him and saw the brown eyes twinkling again, the perfect white teeth gleaming. "Don't give me that sucker-bait Boom-Boom Room smile of yours, macho man," she said. But she smiled, too.

"Bandits seven miles and closing," the radio squawked.

"What if I put this hunk in a loop and came back on top of 'em?" Kazaklis chuckled. "Maybe they'd all die of heart attacks, huh?"

"Jesus, Kazaklis," Moreau said, smiling at his childishness. "The wings would snap like twigs."

"Maybe the shrapnel would get 'em."

"Yeah. Maybe."

"Sure surprise the shit out of 'em." Kazaklis continued chuckling quietly, then peered sheepishly around the corner of his helmet. "Not such a good idea, huh?"

"Kazaklis, you really are a case," Moreau said. "Born a couple of generations too late. You should have been a barnstormer, the Great Waldo Pepper defying death and deformity for the hayseeds in Iowa. Till you piled in, a legend."

"Woulda lived longer," he said pensively. But his voice changed pitch almost immediately. "The Great Kazaklis. Yeah. With you strapped to the struts of my Sopwith Camel."

"Then you'd have to share the glory. You wouldn't like that."

"Naw, suppose not." Then he laughed uproariously. "With your knockers, lady. Share the glory with your knockers. Them horny old farmers would just be a-twitchin', waitin' for a look at the tits when your blouse blew off."

Tyler cut in. "You have significant terrain at ten o'clock. High terrain at three o'clock. High terrain seven miles dead ahead." The valley was closing around them. Moreau faded off. Their Loony Tunes navigator finally sounded as if he were navigating, their gunner was silently defending them with gum wrappers, their pilot was buried, as ever, in boobs. But she liked them, all of them. Suddenly she became very angry.

"Goddammit, how we screwed up!"

The mood change jolted Kazaklis. "The odds were a hundred to one," he said defensively.

"Not you," she said. "The fucking world. All of us. Anybody could have seen this coming. Why the hell didn't we see this coming?"

Kazaklis sighed. "The world's always been a dangerous neighborhood, Moreau. It became a very small neighborhood when we started packin' around zip guns that could snuff any city or cave in any mountain."

"High terrain five miles ahead," Tyler said.

Moreau froze.

"Or Tyler's high terrain," she thought aloud.

Kazaklis looked at her strangely.

"Arm the first bomb," Moreau said slowly. Kazaklis did not respond. "Arm bomb number one, dammit!"

"That's crazy."

"Not as crazy as doing a loop, Waldo. Do it fast!"

The pilot's mind began racing again. He did not need to tote up his weaponry—six Short Range Attack Missiles tucked under his wings, four one-megaton hydrogen bombs stashed in the bay just fifty feet behind him. He ruled out the SRAM's immediately. He could make them turn circles, twist into figure eights, slip around a corner, and strike a target thirty-five miles behind him. But they were too difficult to reprogram quickly. The bombs were a different story.

Kazaklis had never seen inside the bulbous gray packages he carried, but he had a working knowledge of their innards. They were a complicated piece of machinery, maybe too complicated now. They certainly were not designed for Moreau's sudden brainstorm. The brutes were so powerful they required a nuclear explosion to set off the thermonuclear explosion. So they contained a plutonium trigger to set off a small nuclear bomb that ignited a Styrofoam explosive that finally detonated the thermonuclear explosion. The temperature inside reached twenty million degrees before the casing went. But the bombshells held far more than explosives. They contained altitude and velocity sensors, a drogue parachute to slow their descent, a delay fuse to give him a few extra seconds to escape. They also contained extraordinary safety devices. Hydrogen bombs had careened off the top of ICBM's, fallen out of B-52's, rolled off aircraft carriers, disintegrated in space launches. But none had ever exploded accidentally.

Briefly Kazaklis cursed the safeties—six coded interlocks known as the Permissive Action Link. The PAL was no pal now. He would be in one helluva hurry. Still, he had the codes. He did not think long. It was a long shot, but Moreau's cockeyed plan was not that cockeyed. It would require exquisite skill, exquisite timing, and exquisite luck. And those self-assured Russian fighter pilots would have to be so cocky they'd hold off a few minutes longer. Would he be that cocky? Yeah, he answered himself. If he were given a little more bait, which he intended to give the Russians, Kazaklis the Great would be that cocky. He smiled.

"Moreau," he said, "you're too fucking smart to die so young." Without pause, he continued: "Tyler, are the Russians flying in formation?"

"They're closing fast, commander." Tyler now sounded confused and scared.

"Are they flying in formation, dammit!"

"Yes, sir," the navigator flustered.

Kazaklis smiled again.

"Hokay, you guardians of democracy," he exulted into the intercom, "secure the family jewels again. Our buddy with no jewels to lose has come up with a *real* ball-buster!"

Kazaklis immediately banked the plane left toward the last ridge between him and the river delta. He punched the bomb code into the little cipher box next to him, unlocking the interlocks and arming one bomb. His mind sprinted through timing calculations. Thirty seconds from release to detonation. Thirty seconds at six hundred miles an hour. Five miles. He would have to be damned lucky to catch the MIG's roughly that distance behind him. He did not bother to ask if they had followed his banking left turn. He didn't need to ask, feeling their lust for a crack at him in the wide-open Mackenzie flats. They'd wait for that shot. Just as he would, if he were on the chase.

"You may sit down, colonel," Harpoon said evenly. "Mr. Burr will yield the floor in a moment."

The colonel hesitated, fussily adjusting his glasses, and slowly seated himself. The others, with the exception of the admiral and the successor, shifted uncomfortably. The two men stared at each other wearily. The successor spoke first.

"Do you want to be remembered as an Aaron Burr, Harpoon?" he asked.

"Of course not, sir. I've devoted my life to my country. I love it. I will fight for it, as I am tonight, to the death."

"You don't seem to be sayin' that."

"Sir"—Harpoon felt an overwhelming sense of foreboding—"I'm not simply being asked to fight to my death tonight. I'm being asked to fight to the death of my country."

"You sayin' we've been wrong?"

Harpoon thought for a moment, not to resolve doubts but to

find the proper words. He looked at the row of clocks. They had thirty, perhaps forty-five minutes.

"We don't have time for apple pie, sir. In any normal sense, we are the wronged party tonight. This is not a normal night." He paused. "No finer nation has ever been conceived on this earth. We have tried to correct wrongs within our own borders. We have tried, with less success—and often using our own standards—to correct them outside our borders. I believe we, like few nations, have tried to do our best by the world." He paused again, and swept his eyes around a quietly vibrating compartment in which all other eyes were cast downward except those of the successor and the colonel. "No nation is always right. We've made mistakes, yes. Our largest was the relentless accumulation of the weapons we are now using. There will be no winners tonight, sir. But perhaps, just perhaps, we can find the wisdom to salvage a touch of the humanitarianism of which our country has been so justly proud."

Harpoon stopped, somewhat embarrassed, and there was silence in the compartment. He stared at the successor without challenge and the man stared back with curiosity. Mistakes. God forgive them, they had made so many. God forgive him, he had participated in so many.

"So you want me to be remembered as an umbrella-totin' Chamberlain, buying peace at any price?"

Harpoon felt helpless. After all the combativeness of the briefing, he once again felt empathy for the unprepared human being in front of him. Perhaps he was asking too much, asking him to break out of a lifelong mind mold in mere minutes. In the seventies he had spent several months at the War College in Washington. One of the lecturers was a stooped old professor of philosophy from a liberal Ivy League college. One of Rickover's perverse tests, he and his officer colleagues had concluded. The professor had pushed them about the tree in the wilderness and they had perfunctorily debated whether it made a sound, missing his point. On his final day, the old man told them they were all left-siders, playing chess and war. Right-siders play different games and survive. In his final message—and Harpoon recalled each word now—the man said without enmity: "This generation of men may be the most shortsighted in history. It not only consumes the earth's resources, robbing the future of its heritage, it also toys childlike with a power that could rob the past of its existence. Chess is a simple game, gentlemen." Only now did Harpoon realize that the tree was the earth.

"No, sir," Harpoon said, "I want you to be remembered."

The successor looked at him without understanding.

"I don't like you, Harpoon."

"I know that, sir. I'm sorry, but it's not important."

"Didn't say I didn't respect you."

Harpoon was surprised, but he said nothing.

"We're down to it, aren't we?"

"Yes, sir. We have about thirty minutes."

"And now you're going to ask me to surrender. Can't do that, you know."

Harpoon looked at him with both consternation and compassion. "Surrender, sir? No. I want you to try—simply try—to use the pause. Try to turn this thing off till we can talk to the Soviets, talk to our submarines."

"Talk to the Soviets." The successor shook his head slowly at the thought, and his drawl disappeared immediately. "Dammit, Harpoon, we have been trying to talk to the Soviets for fifty years, and what good's it done us? Hell's bells, mister, we couldn't even talk to them during the Second World War. And they were on our side then. How the devil am I supposed to talk to them? You say I can't even talk to Minneapolis."

"You can't talk to them now, sir. You may be able to in four or five hours if we don't blow the ionosphere to smithereens again and suck the guts out of our radios and computers."

"Harpoon, you amaze me. Downright amaze me. You just said I got thirty minutes."

"To talk to our bombers. Before they go down to low-level and the best communications system in the world couldn't get through to them."

Harpoon paused once more. He felt the beads of sweat pop on his forehead. The map's blue ovals pulsated at him mockingly. Behind the successor the arms of the Zulu clock formed a haunting smile, the second hand relentlessly sweeping onward. He scanned the faces of his colleagues. All knew what was coming, but none, except the colonel, met his eyes. The colonel stared back in a mix of challenge and curiosity. Harpoon stared at his rival. My God, was this a chess game too? The colonel smiled. It was now or never. He drew his eyes away and riveted them on the successor, whose blank face seemed to miss the import of the moment.

"Bring them back, sir," Harpoon said simply.

The words seemed to carom off the fluxing computer maps and echo in the sudden silence of the briefing compartment.

"Bring the bombers back," Harpoon repeated quietly, trying to keep the pleading out of his voice.

The successor stared at Harpoon, briefly bewildered. Then his face slowly broke into a thin smile. "Now, that's a real good plan, Harpoon," he said, his voice cutting with sarcasm. "You want me to call up the Soviet bombers and send them home too?"

"If we're lucky, very lucky," Harpoon replied slowly, "the Soviets will do that themselves. If someone is in control over there. If they can see us. There are many ifs."

"Yes, mister, there damned well are. And the biggest if is if I feel like surrendering. Which I don't."

"Surrender?" Harpoon asked, his voice even despite his despair. "How in God's name is that surrender? You still have your submarines. Sixty percent of our strategic weapons are in those boats. Seven thousand city-killing warheads. Maybe, just maybe, bringing back the bombers would get us a truce."

"Now it's a truce. That's a damned fancy word for surrender. Those uncivilized bastards started this and kicked the pucky out of us, Harpoon. We kicked them back. A relatively even exchange. Except there's ten million more Americans dead. Except we had a damned sight more to lose than those barbarians did. They just brought the United States of America down to their level, Harpoon. Now they'll just go out there and rebuild from the same point as us." The drawl crept back, as if for emphasis. "That means losin', dang you. And quittin' means surrenderin'."

"Good God, sir. Nobody's going to rebuild without outside help. Who would you rather be, us or them? Would you like to ask Poland for aid? Czechoslovakia? Hungary? Afghanistan?"

The successor looked around the table. The colonel still rolled his eyes. The others looked at him in solemn anticipation. He turned back toward Harpoon.

"Rebuildin' isn't the point anyway," he said. "You tell me we only have twenty bombers left and maybe only a couple will get in. They got a hundred and fifty coming at us, soon to be roaming at will over our country, you say, because we haven't got any consarned peashooters. You're the military man. Would you make that trade?"

Harpoon sensed his last chance. "The bombers aren't the point either," he said. "Even a couple could take care of Leningrad and what's left of Moscow, plus odds and ends. The subs are the point. They know we've got them. They know we'll use them. You're the politician. Would you take a chance to make that trade, saving your country from total annihilation?"

"A damned Indian smoke signal," the successor said angrily. "That's what it is. Sounds like we're back in the nineteenth century already."

"We are, sir."

"And that's the Jericho decision? To call the bombers back and hope the Kremlin follows suit?"

"To use the pause in any way possible, sir, to settle things down."

The successor slumped. He caressed the Seal, rubbing the lettering as if it were braille. "What lunatic designed this madness?" he asked disconsolately, the words directed at no one. "There's no way to win."

"There never was, sir," Harpoon said quietly.

Harpoon relaxed briefly. Foolishly, he recognized quickly. On the admiral's flank a clatter interrupted the silence as the colonel rose suddenly, pulling himself up so portentously the eyeglasses slipped on his nose. He cleared his throat in a high wheeze.

Harpoon looked at him with a wan smile. "Looks like the colonel has found the stolen overcoat," he said.

The colonel glared at him. "Are you, or are you not," the officer demanded, "going to tell the President about cutting the head off the chicken?"

Harpoon continued staring. "Promised to save that honor for you, colonel. Mister Burr will now yield." The admiral handed him the light pointer.

Quickly the colonel signaled the projectionist, then turned his full attention to the successor. The map of the Soviet Union fluttered once more, a set of green dots appearing. Many were clustered near Moscow and Leningrad, but others were scattered in more remote regions.

"Unlike the admiral," the colonel began, "I will keep my words brief, clear, and devoid of defeatist philosophy. Victory is possible, sir, and it is not that complicated."

Harpoon's wan smile faded. Little bastard's got balls, he thought. Too bad somebody planted them between his ears instead of his legs.

"To call back our bombers would not move the Soviets. They would see it as a sign of weakness. They exploit weakness, as they did at Yalta and countless times at Geneva. But what if they did respond and turned their bombers? You observed, quite accurately, that we have lost. The Soviets have reduced us to their level. Their system and their philosophy are still intact. Is that an acceptable outcome for an American President?" He paused, peering in challenge over his glasses.

"Sir, it has been the well-conceived policy of this government to squeeze the Soviets until they collapsed from within. President Reagan predicted that fall. Your predecessor pursued the policy still further. The attack on us is the very proof that the policy has been working. The Premier's message to your predecessor, intentionally deceptive, acknowledged as much. You, sir, now have the opportunity to put the final nail in the coffin of aggressive Soviet communism."

Harpoon looked at the colonel in fascinated disbelief, struggling between silence and grim laughter. Nail in the coffin. He's got his symbols right.

"I predict, sir, as President Reagan did, that the Soviet people will now throw off the yoke of totalitarian dictatorship which has oppressed them so long. They will do it as surely as they overthrew the czars during the First World War."

Harpoon could not control himself. "In the next half-dozen hours?" he erupted. "For Christ's sake, colonel, they won't even be able to find them."

The colonel turned toward Harpoon with a look of triumph. "No, admiral, they will not. But we will. And you want to withdraw the very weapon with which we can do it." He abruptly turned away and directed the light pointer at the map.

"Mr. President, the green dots represent Soviet leadership bunkers. Inside those bunkers are the party hierarchy, the Presidium, KGB leaders, the military command, and almost surely the Premier or his successor. They are the head of the Soviet chicken. Cut off that head, and the body dies. The system dies. Forever."

The colonel paused, gazing expectantly at the successor.

"You telling me that a handful of B-52's can do that?"

"The perfect instrument, sir." The colonel smiled. "Those bunkers are hardened much like an ICBM silo. Submarine missiles are not accurate enough to take them out. B-52's are manned. Most of them are carrying at least four one-megaton bombs plus SRAM or cruise missiles. They can drop those babies right down the smokestack. One aircraft could take out half a dozen bunkers, probably more."

Harpoon studied the successor's face carefully. The man seemed deep in perplexing thought. Suddenly he turned toward the admiral. "Harpoon?"

"It's madness, sir."

"Well, it seems we just got madness piled on top of madness tonight, admiral."

"The theory's been examined thoroughly and discredited thoroughly."

The colonel blustered in, his voice venomous. "Discredited by men who insist on keeping communications lines open to bandits and murderers and assassins. Men who want to send smoke signals"—the words oozed animosity—"to barbarians who have perpetrated the most despicable, the most heinous act in the history of mankind."

Harpoon shook his head. "Men who want some remnant of America down there when this plane lands, colonel. We can't stay up here in our splendid cocoon forever. For God's sake, man, what about the *Soviet* bombers? What about the thousands of warheads they have in land-based reserves?"

"Victory has its price, admiral," the colonel replied coldly. "The Soviet forces are a reality. Your smoke signal isn't going to stop them. And, frankly, I believe you've been duplicitous about the Soviet bombers."

"Duplicitous!" Harpoon started to move on the colonel, then retreated.

"They are not due for five hours. Our communications should be functioning at least minimally by that time. We *do* have some fighters. We also have thousands of commercial jets available. Use them."

"You're joking."

"Ram the bastards."

Harpoon slowly seated himself. "Colonel, I cannot believe you are serious. I really cannot. Do you actually believe this country—a country full of panicked Baton Rouges—is in any condition to put together a plan like that?"

The successor suddenly stiffened. "Harpoon, are you implyin' that ramming is a possible defense against bombers? Damn you, are you saying that's possible?"

Harpoon was beginning to feel woozy. "Sir, for God's sake—"

"Are you saying that, damn you?"

"In isolated cases, sir," Harpoon said wearily. "But a hundred and fifty bombers coming in low level from all directions? With our radar out? Even if we got ninety percent of them—which we wouldn't—do you know what fifteen bombers would do? Fifteen of those blue circles"—Harpoon gestured despondently at the map of the United States—"would instantly turn red."

"Harpoon," the successor said, his eyes gleaming angrily, "I don't think I've been getting the whole story. I don't cotton to that thought. Don't cotton to it at all."

Harpoon bristled. "What you're getting now, sir, is maniacal nonsense. What the devil does the colonel want to do about the ICBM's? Call the goddamn CIA? Get all our moles to run around Russia putting their fingers in the silos? Good God, man, there is no defense against this stuff."

The colonel methodically tapped the pointer against the map. "The defense," he said confidently, "is the Soviet people. Take away those green dots—take away their oppressors—and they will stop the ICBM's. The defense is to cut the head off the chicken."

Harpoon took a long, deep breath and then riveted his gaze on the successor. "You're a westerner, sir. Raised on a farm?"

"You find that a disqualification, Harpoon?"

"Not at all, sir. I'm a farmboy too. Kansas. We raised chickens. Got them ready for my mother's stewing pot with one stroke of the hatchet."

"Done it myself. Very effective."

"Yes, eventually. As a boy, I hated it. The chicken didn't die right away. It flapped around, headless, splattering blood all over the barnyard."

The successor smiled thinly at Harpoon's analogy. "Then it collapsed, Harpoon, and ended up in the pot. This here chicken's already been spreading a lot of blood around."

"The world's the only barnyard we've got, sir. I can't believe you would risk it. Are you saying that's your decision?"

The man reached over and picked up the Seal. "Nope," he said, smiling enigmatically. "I'm sayin' I finally got me some options. I also have a few minutes. I'm going to think on it."

With that, he stood and began to leave for his quarters, pausing briefly to ask: "Would you like to join me, Colonel?"

Beneath him, tugging perversely, Kazaklis could feel the strong drag of the bomb-bay doors. The shifting winds of the low Arctic mountain ridge buffeted at the open panels, swirling up inside the cavernous hold and changing the aerodynamic flow in ways he had not felt before. No practice-run radio chatter interrupted his concentration. Just the quiet drone of Tyler's drained voice. They were past the thirty-second mark—*ready . . . ready . . . now*—heading directly at the hastily determined drop point—*on the racetrack* —just over the top of the next and last ridge.

In front of the pilot new lights glimmered. The Master Caution light, reacting to the buffeting, flickered on and off, Moreau punching it with a gloved forefinger each time it warned them of what they already knew. The other lights remained on, three yellow squares in a sequence of four, only the third still dark. Bomb Doors Not Latched. Bomb Doors Open. Bomb Doors Not Closed and Locked. On the red screen, computer-scrambled, Kazaklis could see the last ridge racing at him. *Significant terrain, twelve o'clock. . . .* Not so low this time, pal, no belly-scraping, no spine-snapping on this one.

"Bandits five-point-five miles and closing," Tyler radioed. Kazaklis reached for the red lever, pulled it in sequence with two of his four crewmates, releasing the last safety mechanism.

Briefly the pilot wondered if the Russians could see the looming doors, spot them somehow in the glimmering white starlight, pick up a minuscule distortion on their radar screens. The thought faded, the commitment made. The ridge filled the screen, the ground-tracking thermometer plummeting as the frozen slope raced up at them. Two hundred feet, one hundred, seventy-five. That's it. Ka-*whack!* The plane shuddered again, less agonizingly this time. The ridge disappeared, the red screen opening to the flat panorama of the river flats. Kazaklis nosed the aircraft over slightly, taking it down the far side, where it would disappear briefly from the eyes of his pursuers. He counted down the last seconds, a fireproofed thumb poised on the release button. Briefly he and Moreau arched the B-52's nose to give the weapon one small lift before gravity caught it. The pilot depressed his thumb.

A split second of unholy silence pervaded the airplane, blotting out the engine roar. Then the five crewmen felt a slight lurch, sensed an eerie weightlessness, imagined the low groan of the bomb rack rotating to move the next weapon into place.

"Bomb away," Kazaklis said. The fourth yellow light glared at him from the flight panel. Bombs Released. No duds, Kazaklis prayed silently. Oh, God, no duds.

Briefly, as her mind's eye had seen on the mission drill, Moreau saw the bomb lift heavenward, hover, and then roll over for its short descent, the drogue parachute popping to slow its fall. She began the turning, lifting escape maneuver and felt the controls tugging back at her, a hand on her arm. She turned toward the pilot.

"Not this time," Kazaklis said. "Straight at the river mouth. Low."

Moreau stared at him. Then she understood and her skin crawled. The Russian pilots, suspecting or unsuspecting, still had almost thirty seconds to launch their missiles. Kazaklis wanted no telltale escape maneuvers to tip them off. She drew in her breath. The winds from a one-megaton explosion would whip unimpeded across the open flats, tailing off from more than five hundred miles an hour at the ridge to better than one hundred miles an hour five miles away. The blast wave—a moving wall of crushing pressure—would be worse, far worse. Kazaklis was playing the odds on outrunning the effects rather than outrunning more missiles. Percentage baseball. Moreau accepted that.

In the back, Halupalai sat alone, feeling helpless and useless. And empty. Downstairs, Radnor alternately watched his screen and his crewmate. Since the flailing outburst with the broken pencil, followed by the tearful threat, Tyler had lapsed into a near-catatonic state. He said nothing to Radnor, his only words coming in mechanical and scrupulously precise instructions to the cockpit. Radnor felt no fear, either. Just a deep and pervasive sadness he found impossible to shake. On his screen he saw the four Foxbats racing relentlessly toward the ridge, following their path. "Plus fifteen seconds," the wooden voice said. "Bandits five miles and closing." Radnor watched Tyler's eyes move quickly to the little Kodak print above his console, seeming to see nothing, and then dart back to his screen. "Plus twenty seconds . . ." Radnor also turned back to his screen.

In the cockpit both Kazaklis and Moreau were counting silently. Tyler's voice synchronizing perfectly. "Plus twenty-five . . ." No launches, Moreau pleaded under her breath. No duds, Kazaklis beseeched. "Plus thirty seconds . . ." Kazaklis shuddered. Come on, baby, come on. "Plus thirty-five . . ."

"Goddammit!" Kazaklis shouted. "Blow, damn you, blow!"

"Detonation," Tyler droned.

Kazaklis and Moreau jerked simultaneously. "Climb! Climb! Climb!" Kazaklis yelled, but Moreau had already begun, the two of them pulling together.

"Launches?" Kazaklis demanded of the crew downstairs.

"Plus forty seconds . . ."

"Bandits?" Kazaklis asked.

"Plus forty-five . . ."

"Tyler!" Kazaklis thundered. "Damn you! Bandits?" The pilot looked at the altimeter. Five hundred feet, six hundred.

"Plus fifty seconds . . ."

Kazaklis groaned in frustration.

"It's not Tyler, sir." The awestruck voice of Radnor came on. "Oh, God in heaven . . ." His voice faded briefly. Then he murmured, "There's nothing to see, commander."

In the navigation compartment, Radnor's eyes were glued to his screen. In the center half a white ball expanded furiously, like a malignant brain. The fireball was almost two miles wide and seemed burned into the screen, for Radnor's senses knew it had expanded and disappeared already. A ghostly plume began emerging from the top, almost as wide, rising a thousand feet a second. The remainder of the screen warped in dancing lines like heat rivulets in the desert. Radnor knew the rivulets were the blast wave, rolling at them just beyond the speed of sound, and also just beyond the speed of the aircraft. "Plus sixty seconds . . ." It was going to be now. Radnor braced himself.

Kazaklis and Moreau held the craft at twelve hundred feet, their knuckles aching. Suddenly they seemed weightless again. A feather wafting in splendid silence. Then the thunder crack snapped at them. The feather lifted high, sank, and lifted again. Kazaklis could hear the rivets groaning. Then it was past. "Friendly little kick in the rump, huh?" he asked, jauntily trying to cover the crack in his voice. Moreau said nothing. "Bandits?" Kazaklis asked again.

"Nothing came through that, commander," Radnor said very quietly. "Nothing."

The admiral sat alone in the briefing room, the maps blank now. He picked up the yellow phone. A thousand miles north, the *Looking Glass* general picked up his black phone instantly in response.

"Alice? Harpoon."

The line was remarkably clear. Harpoon thought he could hear the general's sigh of relief.

"You made the snatch?"

"Condor's nested and fed."

"You had our dongs shriveling, Harpoon. Rough down there?"

"Ummm. How many Buffs we got left?"

"We might be moused."

"Alice, old friend, we're having enough trouble hearing ourselves tonight."

"Suppose. Hard to say. Baker's dozen? They used Foxbats. Strange. My hunch is they were leading the Bears and Bisons in, looking for our advance interceptors. Found some Buffs instead. Musta surprised 'em. Next surprise is for their bombers."

"Alice?"

"When we start throwin' rocks at 'em."

"Ummm. Plan down here is peashooters and Delta Air Lines."

"Delta Air Lines?"

"Skip it."

"Must say SAC produced some damn good crews. One of 'em nuked the buggers. Four Foxbats comin' right up their tail. Made a perfect bomb run. Laid the egg—a megaton, for God's sake— right in front of 'em. Poof. No more Foxbats. How's that for a new air-to-air weapon system?"

"Used a bomb, did they? Maybe it saved the Soviet postmaster."

"Harpoon?"

"I think I snatched a chicken-eater."

In the *Looking Glass,* Alice paled. He looked at his primitive wall map, covered with multicolored dots. All he saw was green.

Until the moment just past, the crew of *Polar Bear One* had never dropped a live bomb—never seen a nuclear explosion, except in films. They operated almost entirely on theory, having studied the sterile statistics of escape velocities from both incident and reflected shock waves as well as the punishment their communications and navigation gear might sustain from gamma rays, X rays, skyflash, EMP, ionization, and other phenomena.

Kazaklis did a routine damage check, expecting none and finding only minor radio static as the atmosphere ionized above them. EMP was not a threat from this kind of blast, its effects coming only from extremely high-altitude explosions. He was mildly surprised that EMP hadn't struck them hours ago, shortly after takeoff. But he assumed that, located in the far Northwest corner of the country, they had been outside the rim of the EMP circle, and about that he had been correct.

Except for the routine damage-control checks with each crew station, not a word had been spoken since Radnor's quiet confirmation that the MIG's no longer existed. The altimeter read six thousand feet and Moreau silently pushed the craft higher and higher, back on the northerly course. About four minutes had passed.

"Bank it left," Kazaklis said.

"No."

"Bank it left."

"No. I don't want to see it."

"Bank it left." There was no command in the pilot's voice, just persistence and a haunting echo of curiosity. She banked left and Kazaklis slowly drew back the curtain.

The shock of the light stunned Moreau, and at first, she threw an arm up over her good eye. The moonless Arctic night was not dark at all, and the glare, even four minutes later and now forty miles away, overwhelmed all images. Then slowly, over the barrier of her arm, shapes formed and colors bloomed. In the kittywumpis tilt of the aircraft window, the horizon cut diagonally one way and the majestic stem of the cloud the other. Lightning strikes, purple and violet, darted throughout the pillar. The radioactive gases and debris and water vapor churned inward on each other, over and over, the full twelve-mile length, snakes coiling on each other, devouring each other, and then emerging in ugly anger again. It was satanic. As she looked upward at filaments burning at the edge of the troposphere, the power seemed to touch heaven and holiness itself. It was godly. But as she looked down, where the drogue parachute had floated and the mountain ridge now floated in tumult unimaginable, the power seemed to emanate from other regions altogether. No training film, no lecture, no mathematical equation—no amount of psychic numbing—would prepare someone for this.

Kazaklis could not remove his eyes from the mountain ridge. It was gone, gouged out, and in his mind he saw volcanic Mount St. Helens near his boyhood home and he saw his father and he saw his father's belief in the eternity of nature, and he tried to believe in his father's belief. But his father had never seen this, and Kazaklis doubted again. One flick of a finger, his finger, had caused this. He knew that thousands of fingers were poised now over thousands of unnatural volcanoes, unnatural suns. In the distance

he could not see through the crud to the center where he had
caused the temperature to soar to 150 million degrees. But he
could see the beginning of the flood. He could see where the heat
of his own unnatural sun had cooled to the point where it no
longer vaporized the northern ice into clouds but melted it instead, creating a gushing and raging new river, miles wide, that
raced toward him across the once-frozen Mackenzie delta. He had
turned Arctic winter into tropical summer. He cringed. And he
doubted.

Moreau looked high toward the heavens once more, where the
vapor cloud now stretched laterally away from both sides of the
mushroom cap. And she knew that in the heights the ice vapor
was cooling again, turning to water droplets that fell and froze
once more into crystals and flakes. In the once-clear night sky she
could see snow swirls falling from her cloud, a Christmas cloud
with Christmas swirls from a Christmas gone. She felt ill and she
brushed a fireproofed hand past another fireproofed hand also
reaching forward, as the pilot and copilot pulled the curtain
closed, together, mutually deciding that their psyches must be
numbed again. Quickly. They sat mute, pushing their aircraft
higher and away.

"Oh, Kazaklis," she murmured a moment later, "it was so easy."

"Yeah," he said softly.

"Would it be so easy on a city, too?"

"Yeah." He sounded like a little boy lost.

The return of the successor startled Harpoon. He had cradled
the phone moments earlier and drifted off into a mélange of
disconnected thoughts. He looked up, momentarily confused,
and saw the Uzi first, then the professionally blank expression of
the agent, then the unlined face of the successor, and finally the
Cheshire-cat smile of the colonel.

"Need to send the orders, Harpoon," the successor said.

"You've decided, sir." It was not a question.

"History won't wait."

Harpoon looked at the man sadly. "I hope history hears you."

The man stared at Harpoon, uncomprehending again, not
knowing whether to take umbrage.

"Be careful with the insults, admiral," the colonel said. "It
sounds like losing to me bothers you more than losing to the
commies."

Harpoon looked at the colonel without expression. "You're a
fool," he said calmly. "An incredibly dangerous fool." The man's

smug smile dissolved. He took a half-step toward Harpoon. Harpoon stood abruptly. The agent wobbled his Uzi between the two military men. "Why don't you put that away, sonny," Harpoon said. "It isn't going to stop this riot."

The successor looked on silently while Harpoon reached down and picked up the satchel he had carried out of the blue bunker in Omaha.

"Good luck, sir," he said, and began to leave.

"You think I'll need it, Harpoon." The man had no rancor and no question in his voice.

"Oh, yes, sir. We all needed it tonight. A very large dose of it."

"Past tense?"

"Sorry, sir."

"Where are you going?"

"To my quarters."

"We need to lock you in?"

Harpoon paused thoughtfully. "I've fired all my weapons," he said after a moment. The words had a strange ring, even to Harpoon. He turned to leave. The brittle words of the colonel interrupted him.

"Haven't you forgotten something, admiral?"

Harpoon cocked his head back at the group. The colonel was smiling again, as he gestured at the satchel.

"The card, admiral."

Harpoon stopped, placing the satchel on the table, and opened it. He withdrew a blue-and-red plastic card, charge-plate size. He looked at it briefly. Across the top was a series of random letters and numbers. In the center, the card said: "TOP SECRET CRYPTO. NSA." At the bottom it said: "SEALED AUTHENTICATOR SYSTEM."

"You'll need this," Harpoon said, handing it to the successor. "Orders to the bombers must go through the *Looking Glass*. The code at the top will prove you are authentic. The colonel will give you the word codes."

The successor looked briefly at the card, then raised his eyes to the admiral. "You really forget to give me this, Harpoon?"

Harpoon looked at the man but felt his eyes glaze. The disconnected thoughts, interrupted by the group's arrival, rattled erratically in dark crannies of his head again. If the earth falls in the wilderness, does it make a sound? Did a Beethoven ever make music, a Shakespeare poetry? Out of darkness, into darkness. If you deny the future its existence, did you exist? Chess is such a simple game. "I'm really not sure, sir," Harpoon said, and walked away.

Ten

1130 ZULU

The *Looking Glass* general withdrew a pack of Pall Malls from their normal niche, a cubbyhole to the right of the red lockbox and below a small countdown clock no larger than a starter's watch. The cigarettes were a ritual. He smoked now only on *Looking Glass* nights, his wife frowned on it so. Each time he drew the duty, he conducted the preflight briefing, stopped at the vending machine en route to the runway bus, bought a single pack, and slipped it into his flight jacket. Aboard the aircraft he always placed the pack in the same cubbyhole, as if to hide them here, too. At the end of the eight-hour flight he conducted the debriefing, breaking cover by smoking one last cigarette on the ground, and then discarded the pack in a litter can before the drive home into the suburbs. The discarded pack invariably was three-quarters full.

The general took a single cigarette now, caressing it as he might a fine Havana, tapped it twice on the Top Secret papers in front of him, and snapped a match. The match's flare coincided with the flashing white light of the black phone. He stared at the phone, expecting its signal, and finished the ritualistic lighting of the cigarette as he lifted the receiver.

At first he heard nothing, which was unusual, so he said, "Alice here."

The pause continued briefly and then he heard in a slightly awkward drawl: "Condor speakin'."

"Day word?" Alice asked.

"Cottonmouth."

"Command word?"

"Trinity."

"Action word?"

"Jericho."

"You have your card, sir?"

"I do."

"In the upper-left-hand corner, you see a row of digits and letters. Please read the fourth from the left." In front of him, near a tin-cup ashtray, Alice examined a small blue-and-red plastic card, charge-plate size.

"Seven."

"In the right-hand corner, please read me the final three digits and/or letters."

"Seven C Two."

"C for what, sir?"

There was a pause and a slight grump. "Charlie."

"On the second line from the top, please read me the middle sequence."

"Six D Six Two."

"D for what, sir?"

"Dawg, dammit. All you people waitin' on World War Four, Alice?"

Alice started to chuckle, then looked at the papers in front of him and lost the laugh. "You wish to issue order changes, sir?"

"Sure as hell do."

"Harpoon gave you the signal code?"

"Harpoon's temporarily incapacitated."

Alice took a long burning drag on his Pall Mall. "Sir?"

"Code's Two One Zebra. Zeee-bruh."

"Repeating, Two One Zebra."

"Yes."

The general paused, catching his aide staring at him. Sam's eyebrows lifted. They had known it would be 21-Z, Harpoon telling Alice as much in the brief call earlier. Where the devil was Harpoon? The general felt uneasy. "Would you like some advice, sir?"

"Been gettin' plenty down here."

Alice decided to ignore the warning. "I'm sure, sir. But the situation's fluid."

"Fluid. Been everything else tonight. Might as well be fluid. What's that mean?"

"We found another eye, sir. That's three satellites now. Also received our first message from the ground. Garbled. But coded and scrambled. Means it's part of the system."

"Where from?"

"Not sure, sir. Washington region."

Now Condor paused. "That's good news," he said after a second. "What's it got to do with Two One Zebra?"

"We're getting things back, sir. Slowly. I'd orbit and wait."

"Wait." The line was silent for a moment. "Don't see the point, Alice, but I'll ask the colonel."

Alice sagged. The colonel, for Christ's sake?

The voice came back. "Colonel says they ain't got the gas for a loose fart, Alice. Wants to know the battle order."

Alice didn't know how to answer. The baker's dozen had slipped from thirteen to eleven. Especially with satellite eyes and radio ears opening, even if it was no more than a blink and a peep so far, he was being more cautious than he had been with Harpoon. "Dallas Cowboys," he finally said.

"What the hell's that mean?"

"This is all extremely sensitive, sir. Ask your aide."

Alice could hear muffled talking on the other end. He pulled on the cigarette, dropping ashes on the papers beneath.

"Okay," the voice said. "Implement Two One Zebra."

"It'll take a few minutes, sir."

"You stallin', Alice?" The voice bit. "Had just about enough of that tonight."

"No, sir. We have to do a hand sort. Assignments. Priorities. Alternates. It's tight. I have to put them in orbit briefly, so none of them goes over the side."

"Over the side?" The voice sounded suspicious.

"We're saying too much, sir. Out of listening range."

"Okay." Condor's words turned steely. "Now, you get your tail movin', Alice. I want this workin'. Fast. Hear?"

"Yes, sir," Alice said. He also heard the phone click off. He felt Sam's eyes on him and looked up at his old friend.

"We got ourselves a new White House military aide," the general said. "The Librarian."

"You're kidding? Jesus, no wonder we got 21-Z."

"Yes. Well, send out the orbit orders so we don't lose any of 'em in the weeds. Figuring this out is going to be like wrestling with Rubik's Cube."

"The crews will think we're going nuts back here."

The general looked at Sam. "Well?" He felt the cigarette burning his fingers and he snuffed it out in the tin tray. He turned his attention to the papers on his desk-console, brushing away the Pall Mall's fallen remnants. He glanced down the top sheet, his eyes stopping on:

CHEREPOVETS: Construction, 1977. Cover, Rybinsk Mining Works. Thirty-five miles southeast town Cherepovets; 240 miles north Moscow. Intelligence data: Primary relocation site (timing option one) Soviet Premier, Chief KGB, Minister Defense, Commanding General Soviet Rocket Forces, etc. Hardened at least 1,000 psi.

Okay, Alice in Wonderland, the general said to himself. Start there. He shook his head. The Librarian. Good grief.

Genocide was a twentieth-century word. That he knew. Immediately after the Second World War, at about the time of the Nuremberg trials of the Jew exterminators, they took the Greek root word *genos* and put it together with the Latin suffix *cida*. The word had been misused regularly ever since, man's technology having overtaken man's perversities before the word was conceived. They had no proper word now. Genocide meant the discriminate destruction of one genus of the species, not the indiscriminate destruction of the species itself. They should have a proper word for it. That bothered him. He struggled with proper prefixes for *cida*. Specicide? Humanuscide? Anthropocide? The little compartment to which he had withdrawn was very confining, the weight pressing on him. He stared at the single phone, feeling an abounding need to share his problem. There was no one to call. Except Alice. And Alice was busy doing whatever you call it. Then he realized that words were for the living, connectors between anthropoids, connectors between the past, the present, and the future. If it works, they won't need the word. It it doesn't work completely, someone else could figure it out. At some place like Nuremberg. Tierra del Fuego. That's it. They could figure it out in Tierra del Fuego. Harpoon felt very guilty. He closed his eyes.

*   *   *

Alice had problems. The first orders to the B-52's, briefly and tersely instructing them to orbit and hold, had gone out. Now he had most of his staff, including many whose expertise had no relationship whatsoever to their new assignment, working on the target changes. They struggled with the fuel loads and locations of the eleven remaining B-52's. They struggled with coordinates for the green dots. They struggled to arrange packages of dots for each aircraft, trying to keep the packages practical while pushing the practicalities to the limit. They struggled to assign priorities within each package—which dots were important enough for a direct bomb run, which were secondary enough to risk a looping shot with the highly accurate but less-powerful missiles. A few, such as the choice morsel he had assigned to *Polar Bear One,* were double-targeted with a bomb run by one aircraft and a missile launch by another. It was a given that not all the Buffs would get through.

It also was a given—and Alice wasted no thought on it now— that the intelligence reading was reasonably accurate. For almost two decades neither nation had dug anything larger than a well without an electronic eye watching. The ruses—this one's a mine, that one's a waste-storage facility—had been unraveled by spies and dissidents in both countries. Who would go where and under what circumstances had been the job of moles who had begun their burrowing a generation ago. There were few secrets, and no places to hide.

In a way, as he plodded through the special task he had taken on as a personal obligation to an old friend, Alice felt a profound sense of relief. This, after all, was the decision he had not wanted attached to his soul. And until Harpoon had swooped into Baton Rouge and rescued the man with the western drawl, it had been Alice's to make. One way or the other. Still . . .

Alice tapped his ruddy fingers on the set of targets he had drawn up for *Polar Bear One.* Cherepovets plus five. A grand tour, sneaking in the Soviet back door and plunging at the heart plus a handful of major arteries.

Alice reached for a computer printout sheet of the targets struck by the Soviets. A cursory glance confirmed what didn't need confirmation. They had not struck the most sensitive new American bunker in West Texas. They had not struck Mount Weather, the ancient bunker in Virginia so well-known the press wrote about it. They had taken a crudely surgical slice at Washington, messing up the city pretty badly in their attempt to isolate out military targets. But they had not totally destroyed the capital. He shook his head in dismay. He didn't like this, didn't like it at all.

Alice looked up and saw Sam watching him curiously. The general quickly looked back down at his papers. Dammit, Sam, don't you be my conscience. You follow orders in this business or the business doesn't work. If you're aboard the *Enola Gay*, you fly over Hiroshima and forget it. If you're ordered to drop incendiaries on civilians in Dresden, you do it. And forget it. If you read later that the people raced screaming into the sea, burning phosphorous glued to their backs and burning underwater, you forget it again. That's modern life. Modern war. Very goddamn modern.

"You about ready, Sam?" Alice asked brusquely.

"Yes, sir. We have the orders plotted."

"Then send 'em, dammit."

And so they began sending the new orders. Slowly. On the reliable, low-frequency teletype.

The audio alert startled everyone. Kazaklis quickly stubbed out a cigarette. Moreau craned her neck toward the small teletype and watched in puzzlement as the machine started and stopped almost immediately. Halupalai, the pacing expectant father earlier, lumbered slowly out of the back and pulled the one-line message from its reel. Without glancing at it, he handed the paper to Kazaklis. There was a moment of silence as Kazaklis examined it. Then he handed it back and said, "Tell me what I already know."

Halupalai read it aloud, methodically decoding in his head. "Orbit. Await orders." The gunner paused and added, "I'll take it downstairs, commander."

"Don't bother."

"Commander?"

"Don't bother!" Kazaklis repeated, a frustrated touch of meanness in his voice. Halupalai shrugged and slouched back to his isolated seat.

"Take it easy on him," Moreau reproached the pilot. "You'll have the whole crew ready for the rubber room."

Kazaklis stared into the instrument panel and then turned angrily on her. "Do me a favor, Moreau. Bank the Doomsday Express left. Then shut up for a while, will ya? Huh?"

Moreau bristled, hardly having spoken since the detonation, and began placing the plane in orbit again.

Kazaklis glumly took a reading on their position. One hundred fifty miles into the Arctic Ocean. He glanced at his luminous watch. The minute hand had crept past 1100 Zulu. Five hours that seemed like five years. And they still didn't know where they were heading. He turned toward Moreau and saw the woman wheeling the aircraft intently, professionally into a slow orbit. He tried to drive the agitation out of himself.

"You ever kick your dog, Moreau?"

"I don't have a dog, Kazaklis," she said tersely.

"I love my dog."

Moreau looked at him, shook her head, and said nothing.

"You get the feeling we're going around in circles?" he asked, the lightheartedness sounding artificial.

"You get the feeling we shouldn't complete this circle?" she asked. Her voice carried a strange mix of hostility and pensiveness. It so caught Kazaklis by surprise he briefly went wordless. He forced a laugh.

"Reminds me of a Polish joke."

"Oh, Christ, Kazaklis."

"These two Polish pilots get into trouble. So the pilot says to the copilot, 'Let's do a 360 and get out of here.'" Kazaklis laughed. Moreau didn't. Kazaklis went silent again.

"I think the Polacks have taken over the *Looking Glass,*" he continued after a second. Now his voice was pensive. "Do a couple of 360's and then move ahead one square." He paused. "What do you make of this crap?"

Moreau thought for a second. "Maybe they're going to pull us back."

Kazaklis looked at Moreau, tucking his chin into his Adam's apple, his eyes peering mockingly out of the bottom of his eyebrows. "Oh, yeah, Moreau. I can hardly wait."

"I can think of reasons."

"I almost forgot you're a general's brat." Kazaklis immediately wished he had kept his loose tongue tucked away.

"Shove it, Kazaklis."

"I kick my dog a lot, Moreau."

She looked at him in curiosity, then shook her head again.

"Well, Moreau," the pilot continued, "you can explain the strategic reasons to me when we're at low level over Baikal."

"That's one place we're not going now."

"I know."

They dropped off into silence again, the Buff curling into its holding pattern, the hum of the engines deceptively lulling after the bone-jarring rumble with the Foxbats. Both retreated into their private worlds, trying to sort out the tangle of new realities forced upon them in the few short hours since the klaxon's wail at Fairchild, the bombs bursting in Spokane, their own bomb bursting behind them.

"You really don't think about the reliability regulations, do you?" Moreau suddenly broke the silence.

"Oh, God, Moreau, don't start on PRP now."

"Why don't you think about it?"

Kazaklis sensed danger. His head told him to cut Moreau off. Quickly. But he didn't. "Because it's crazier than what we're doing," he said sullenly.

"About even-Steven, I'd say. They had to come up with something. They invented the bomb and they had to give it to somebody. So they gave it to the politicians. The politicians kept building the fuckers—you do have me talking locker-room, Kazaklis—so they went out and found themselves thousands of kids to hold them. Kids. God, we're the old-timers. What are you? Thirty-one? I'm twenty-seven. Radnor's twenty-five. Even Radnor's an old-timer. They had twenty-year-olds fiddling with them."

"It wasn't the kids who finally let it all go."

"Probably not. Maybe we should thank PRP for that. There was no Personnel Reliability Program for the politicians. You ever hear of a Nixon or a Carter or a Reagan going down to San Antonio to take the test? You think the Politburo got psychological screening, whatever the hell they called it over there?"

"Not a one of 'em woulda passed."

"No. The whole thing was an attempt at a rational answer to a problem with no rational answer. The shrinks got ahold of it and devised a system that required perfect people. Not many of them around. None of us passed tonight."

Kazaklis grew nervous. He tried to divert her. "Oh-oh!" he said, throwing up his hands. "Here comes the Boom-Boom Room routine." He battered her with a staccato recital. "Air Force Regulation 35-dash-99. Section two-dash-three. Figure two-dash-one. Personality and Behavior Factors That May Affect Reliability. Paragraph III. Factors Related to Awareness or Level of Consciousness." He paused. "You know they spelled 'consciousness' wrong? Left out the first 's.' Little reminder that the people looking for perfect people weren't perfect."

"Dated 14 April 1981." Moreau smiled sadly. "You have read

the PRP regulations, you phony." She thought a moment. "A little random reminder. They might miss a digit in a code someday. They might get a random electric pulse in some computer. You think that's how it started?"

"That, pal, we'll never know."

"No."

Kazaklis turned thoughtful. "Moreau?" She looked at him. "Did the Boom-Boom Room thing really bother you that much? All the flyin' we did together?"

She looked at him a moment longer. "Sure it did. Who wants to fly with somebody who's been up all night boozing?"

"God, I'm surprised everybody in the outfit wasn't juiced to the gills," Kazaklis said, melancholy creeping into his voice.

"A lot of 'em were. The brass went nuts trying to trace the marijuana roaches in Minuteman launch capsules. The Soviet Rocket Forces had a vodka problem that made you look like a Mormon. You were all right. A pig, but all right."

Kazaklis grinned broadly. "Moreau, you're getting downright friendly in your sunset years."

"Hours."

"Don't get maudlin. It violates PRP."

"Everything violates PRP. Paragraph I. Suspiciousness. Arrogance. Lack of Humor. Inflexibility. Preoccupation." She paused. "Then comes Sensitivity. Now, that *is* dangerous. We sure didn't want sensitive people around the bomb. Paragraph II. Impulsiveness. Destructiveness. You like that one? Destructiveness."

"Maybe I oughta message San Antonio that we've been showing destructive tendencies. Pull us off the duty."

"Temper Tantrums."

"Whoops."

"Excessive Talking."

"There goes the general's daughter."

"Decreased Talking. Then in Paragraph III we have Daydreaming lumped in with Alcohol and Drug Intoxication, your favorite."

Kazaklis grunted.

"Oh, I'm not taking another zing at you, Kazaklis." She smiled, a faint and distant smile. "You were always full of more shit than booze."

Kazaklis finally laughed uproariously.

"Unusual Happiness," she said. "Paragraph IV. Unusual Happiness is followed by Unusual Sadness. And Suicide."

The drone of the engines cut through the pause. Then Moreau went on quietly, still quoting from the regulations: "Suicide: Particularly significant when accomplished through the deliberate detonation of a weapon. . . ."

Kazaklis stared hard at her. She seemed far away, and briefly, he felt angry again, not being able to sort out his own new uncertainties.

"Moreau," he said slowly, "you and I both chose this path. You signed up for this trip. You signed up for the saki-and-bow-to-the-emperor squad." But he knew she wasn't talking about her suicide. He knew she was talking about distant decisions made by others that meant the world now must absorb fifty thousand of the gray packages the crew of *Polar Bear One* had discharged in the wilderness of the Richardson Mountains. She was talking about a world that was taking the kamikaze oath. His skin tingled. Then the audio alert startled him again.

"Here come the orders to return to Spokane," he said blandly. "You think we'll get a ticker-tape parade?"

In the *Looking Glass,* the black phone lighted again. The general reached for it quickly.

"Alice?" the voice said. "Harpoon."

"Good grief, man, how are you? We were worried."

"I need a word."

"Hard to talk now."

"A word." The voice was insistent.

"Take it easy, Harpoon. What's on your mind?"

"Never mind. I have it."

"Hey, buddy, what gives?"

"Call them back." The voice was plaintive.

"Call who back, Harpoon? What the devil are you talking about?"

"The bombers, general. Please."

Alice reached for another Pall Mall, not caressing it at all this time. "Harpoon, the orders are out. Under National Command Authority. Condor's authority."

The phone seemed to go dead for a moment.

"Harpoon?" Alice asked.

The phone connection suddenly sounded very weak. "Never mind," Harpoon said faintly. "I've got it. It's anthropocide. Yes, that's it. Anthropocide." Then Alice heard Harpoon click off.

The general looked up at Sam with deep concern. "I don't think Harpoon has both oars in the water," he said bleakly.

Halupalai spent several painstaking minutes decoding the latest orders while Kazaklis and Moreau fidgeted up front. At last he handed Kazaklis the message, and the pilot flooded it with his red-filtered flashlight. Moreau watched his face grow tight as he quickly scanned the single long sheet.

"Jesus H. Christ," he said, his voice rising slowly in disbelief. "They want us to run all over Russia. . . ."

REF TWO ONE ZEBRA. IMPRO PATTERN ONE. PRECISE DELIV-
ERY TO COORDINATES MANDATORY. TARGETS HARDENED.
STRIKE ALL TARGETS. PRIORITY CHEREPOVETS. REPEAT. PRI-
ORITY CHEREPOVETS. CAUTIONS. MOSCOW REGION PARTLY
INTACT. LENINGRAD REGION WHOLLY INTACT. NO COVER.
SOVIET COMMUNICATIONS BELIEVED NEAR ZERO. REF TWO
ONE ZEBRA.

Next came a sequence of six targets and coordinates, fuel-depletion estimates, and specific weapon assignments for each. Cherepovets was second on the list, the first being a twin-SRAM attack on a target that by the pilot's rough reckoning was somewhere in the Urals perhaps a thousand miles east of the coordinates for Cherepovets. He didn't recognize any of the place-names, including the priority target. Behind the coordinates for Cherepovets the orders read, in brackets, "RYBINSK MINING WORKS." The four other targets were located in a cluster less than one hundred miles apart and, from the locators, appeared to be in the vicinity of Leningrad but not in the city itself. That gave them a clear run out over the Gulf of Finland to an escape field north of Stockholm, with Helsinki as a nearer but clearly less desirable alternate. However, it was obvious at a glance that the designer of improvised pattern one had made extraordinary assumptions, all optimistic, about fuel consumption. The entire flight was to be made at low level.

"What the hell is Two-One Zebra?" Kazaklis demanded in befuddled anger. "Where the hell is Cherepovets? And why the hell are we runnin' clean across Russia to bomb a friggin' mine?"

Moreau already had reached for the master book, through which she was flipping rapidly. But she sensed the answer and felt her despair plunge toward despondence. She stopped in a rarely studied appendix, read briefly, and let out a long, low whoosh of air. So it's come to this, she thought, and she turned almost in challenge on Kazaklis.

"Damn you, Moreau," the pilot pushed her, "what's going on?"

"The grand tour," she said evenly. "That's what's going on, Kazaklis. You were right. All over Russia, carving 'em out in the craters."

Kazaklis stared at her. "Carving out what, Moreau?" he asked with a touch of hostile impatience. "What?"

"Not what," the copilot replied evenly. "Who." She turned back to the book. "Twenty-one—Precision nuclear bombardment, hardened emplacements." She paused. "Zebra—Political-military infrastructure." She turned the page, broke a plastic-tape seal intricately engraved with the faint outline of an eagle, and glanced hurriedly through contingency instructions they never before had been allowed to read. "Cherepovets (Rybinsk Mine)— Caution. This is not an opportunity target. Strike only on direct orders NCA. Relocation area, timing option one, Omega."

Now the air whooshed out of the pilot. His gloved forefingers slowly tapped at the wheel. "Leadership bunkers," he whispered. "So they really want us to go after the big banana."

"More like somebody's gone bananas," Moreau replied. "Somebody who didn't go to San Antonio for reliability training. Somebody who didn't read the suicide regs. The world suicide regs. They want us to get the leaders, Kazaklis. The only people who can turn this fucker off." She stared hard into the pilot's face. "Request confirmation," she said flatly.

Kazaklis lost his blank look and shot her a withering glance. "You just get promoted?" Moreau looked back at him stone-faced. He shrugged and motioned to Halupalai to send the brief confirmation request. Kazaklis felt his mind turn muddy. The message told him far more than he ever expected to learn. Timing option one confirmed what he already knew—the Soviets had started it. The orders themselves told him what he also had guessed—the pattern of bunker targets was stretched so thin it was obvious the B-52 fleet had been chewed to pieces on the ground. Soviet communications near zero. Both nations had used an EMP attack. Not surprising. Leningrad standing, Moscow partly destroyed. Mildly surprising. They had given him that information because he needed it to defend himself. But the *Looking Glass* also was telling him indirectly that major cities still stood in the United States as well. Otherwise the subs would have been ordered to clean out the Soviet cities.

But if it hadn't all gone in one spasm, if the war was progressing in stages as he would have expected, why were they getting orders like these? Moreau was right, damn her. This meant the end, the whole shooting match. Omega. Omega was a catch-all code. No holds barred.

Kazaklis felt woozy. They were asking a handful of Buffs to stab the king—and not wound him. That was taboo, drilled into them time and time again. The crews had joked sourly about it. Politicians protecting politicians while we nuke the folks. But the instructions had been explicit. If the boss gets caught in the office, so goes it. The Omahas and Cheyennes of Russia would go. But no overt political targets. No accidents, no stray runs, no open alternates, no targets of opportunity. We need somebody to talk to, the Air Force had drilled them. His mind spun. He didn't like this. He also didn't like her staring at him, probing him.

"You find a wart on my nose, Moreau?" he blustered.

"You know, Kazaklis," she said.

Kazaklis fought back an involuntary shudder. He stuck his chin out. "I know it means we don't have to go in and drop a million tons of concentrated TNT on a bunch of kids, Moreau. Isn't that better, for God's sake?"

"You mean more satisfying?"

"Damn right it's more satisfying." Kazaklis choked a gurgle out of his voice. The roiling, churning horror of the plume over the Richardsons flashed before his eyes, then quickly disappeared. "Maybe it'll get it over faster."

She continued staring at him, her lip curling upward. "Faster," she said.

"Damn you, Moreau." Her face settled into a granite shield. "Moreau," Kazaklis said plaintively, his voice taking on a low, painful whine. Behind him, Halupalai hovered again. He handed the pilot another brief message: "CONFIRM TWO ONE ZEBRA. NCA CODE HENHOUSE."

Kazaklis handed the message to Moreau. "Look up 'Henhouse.'"

Moreau did not bother to look at the message. She stared silently at Kazaklis, who returned her stare with uneasy stubbornness. The steady roar of the engines pounded at their ears in an escalating staccato—not a drone now but a racing pulse of explosive individual heartbeats. "They want us to vaporize the Premier,

Kazaklis," Moreau said steadily. "And the Presidium. And the head of the KGB, who controls the warheads. And the head of the Rocket Forces, who controls the missiles. Everybody with any control."

Kazaklis stuck his chin out. "The bastards started it."

"The bastards have to stop it. Nobody else can."

"Look up 'Henhouse.'"

Moreau held her steady gaze on him silently. His eyes twitched and he tried to cover the sign of his uncertainty. His chin jutted out further. "You want us to nuke kids instead, huh?" he snapped.

She stared. Kazaklis began to bluster defensively.

"It always was a bunch of bullshit, leaving the leaders alone. Bunch of fucking politicians protecting another bunch of fucking politicians." His voice cracked and he tried to cover it by blustering again. "Assholes. Sittin' down in their holes, flying around in their safe airplanes, pushing their fucking dominoes this way and that way over millions of people. Fuck 'em. They got us into this mess."

"Somebody's got to be at the other end of the phone, Kazaklis." Moreau's voice quavered now. She had spent her adult life trying to prove she belonged in this bomber, that macho wasn't just male.

"What fucking phone?" Kazaklis snapped. "You think they're talking to each other and sending out orders like this?"

"Leningrad's still standing," Moreau said, her voice dropping off. "Moscow's partly standing. Something's still there. Somebody's back home to send out this insane crap. Somebody's over there to take it."

Kazaklis turned away from her, staring into the flash curtains, the commander in him wrestling with the man who had reached to the curtain and stared into the face of a megaton meant for Irkutsk, who had murmured bye-bye, mamushka. "Look up 'Henhouse,'" he said.

"You know what comes next," Moreau said, barely audibly. "Some poor spooked sucker of a second lieutenant lets the chemicals go in Europe. Unlooses the anthrax spores because he's scared. Some colonel in Korea sees a shadow in the night and fires every tactical missile he's got." She sat silently for a moment, the engine sound torturing her. "Submarine commanders will roam around for days, weeks, months—popping one here, popping one there—until they just say screw it and let 240 warheads go at the commies in Nicaragua."

Kazaklis exploded in frustration. "What the fuck do you want me to do? Write my congressman?"

"Till every last nuke is gone." Moreau's voice seemed far off and ghostly now. "Every last biological spore." She stopped again. "Nobody can turn it off after this. Not ever. Not before everything's gone."

Kazaklis felt every muscle, every tendon, turn rigid. "Look up 'Henhouse,'" he said.

"No," she said.

Kazaklis looked at her strangely. She stared straight ahead, not a muscle moving. He didn't know what to do. He felt cornered, trapped in a mad maze from which escape was impossible. His voice turned raw with agony. "It won't make any difference, Moreau."

"I know."

"Nothing will change. Somebody else will do it."

"I know."

"Cherepovets will go. Irkutsk will go. Ulan-Ude. Everything will go anyway."

"I know."

He paused. Her good eye seemed as distant as her bad. "New York, Coos Bay, everything in between," he said slowly, pausing very briefly. "Steamboat Springs."

The good eye glinted at the thought of her father. Then it glazed again. "I know," she said quietly. "But I'm not going to do it. I can't."

"Can't?"

"Won't."

Kazaklis turned away from her, staring into the dirty gray ripples of the flash curtain. "You weren't going to Irkutsk, either," he said, knowing that the decision had been forming well before the doomsday orders for the grand tour had arrived.

"They gave us too much time to think."

"You'd have turned a Minuteman key in the first five minutes." It wasn't a question.

"Yes."

"Bitch," he said. The ripples mocked him. He saw for the first time that the folds of the curtain were rank with dirt and crud, trapped off years of sweaty and eternally vigilant hands. His soul ached, as if he were deserting all those who had come before him, all those who had kept this aircraft poised and ready, all those who had believed. "Cunt." His voice carried no emotion. He flexed a fireproofed hand, then reached forward and ran a gloved index finger down the grime of a generation. "Damn you."

Kazaklis sank back in his seat, tightening his glove slowly into the mailed fist he wore on his shoulder, and suddenly pounded it, over and over again, into the crud of the curtain and the Plexiglas behind it. He stopped and looked again into her unmovable face.

"What do you want me to do?" he asked. "Shoot you? Eject you? Put you down on the ice?"

She stared ahead.

He reached behind his seat for his gray-green alert bag, pulling it forward into his lap. He tugged at the soiled glove, removing it. He placed his bare hand inside the bag, rummaging past the candy bars, the Russian money, the Chinese money, the first-aid kit, and the .45. He withdrew a small canister, roughly the size of an aspirin tin, and snapped it open. He handed its singular content to Moreau. She took it, looking at the white capsule without curiosity. *Melech hamafis.* She shifted out of her seat to go downstairs with O'Toole. She felt a hard hand on her wrist, twisting. The cyanide pill popped loose and rolled innocently into the darkness of the cabin. She turned and looked at Kazaklis. "That's one PRP violation too many, captain," he said.

For a moment they were silent, the engines droning on, their drumbeat a drumroll now, Moreau poised halfway into the aisle-way.

"I can't go either," Kazaklis finally said with neither passion nor sadness.

"I know," Moreau said, and shifted back into her seat.

"Damn," Kazaklis finally sobbed. "Damn, damn, damn."

"So what's next?" Moreau asked quietly.

"I dunno," Kazaklis replied emptily.

Kazaklis rummaged again through the alert bag, extracting a roll of medical tape. He tore two strips and attached them to the glove. He taped the glove to the red screen in front of him. All fingers were folded down except one.

"Up theirs," he said. "Let 'em do their own killing."

Then he began banking the aircraft out of the endless circle in which they had been flying. Moreau helped him.

Down below, Radnor felt the first almost imperceptible turning of the aircraft. He should have found that more unusual, because he had heard no request for course corrections and had not ob-

served Halupalai bringing down order changes for Tyler's confirmation. But since the race with the MIG's, in which he had
played no significant role, Radnor had retreated so deeply within
himself that he had observed almost nothing. He quickly glanced
sideways at Tyler, catching a camera-flick image of his crewmate's
still-twisted face. Radnor just as quickly turned away. He did not
want to see Tyler at all, so the young radar operator slipped easily
back into the dismal swamp of his own private sadness. Had he
looked closer he would have seen that Tyler's face had changed
somewhat, that it had taken on a look of brutally raw anger. He
also would have seen that Tyler was listening intently to someone
else's conversation, his radio switch fixed to the private channel in
use by someone upstairs.

The *Looking Glass* lurched left. Alice, who had been stretching
in the aisle, lurched with it, his hand landing on Sam's drooping
shoulder. He could feel the wetness seeping through the rumpled
blue cotton of the colonel's shirt.

"Sorry, Sam," he said. "Bumpy trip."

Sam looked up, brushed his forehead, and nodded. "Smitty's
really threading the needle tonight, isn't he? Ducking in and out
of the clouds like a fighter pilot."

"Let's hope he's just ducking." The general smiled wanly. Sam
said nothing. "All's well up north?"

Sam shrugged. "They all got the orders, sir. We sure had 'em
automated."

The general looked at him inquisitively. "How's that?"

"Only one asked for National Command Authority confirmation."

"It's not required."

"No."

"Who asked?"

"Polar Bear One."

The general's gaze drifted away from Sam, up the aisle of his
wounded command plane. Kazaklis and Moreau. Figures.

"Would you have asked, Sam?"

The colonel thought for a second, probing back into the youthful days when he had flown B-52's. "I don't know, general. Probably not."

"I don't know either," Alice said. "I'd sure as hell like to think I
would." The general clenched the colonel's shoulder in cama-

raderie and started to move away. "Think I'll take a look up front."

"General," the colonel called after him, "I think you were right about the Foxbats."

"Sam?"

"We're picking up confirmed Soviet bomber sightings. They're coming in squadrons. Most of 'em are heading for the East Coast. But we got about fifteen Bisons coming straight at *Polar Bear*. The Foxbats had to be leading 'em in."

Alice shook his head slightly. Small world. They can wave at each other on the way past. The bombers all had bigger fish to fry than each other. He moved up the aisle, patting shoulders as he went. He looked at his watch. The hands had moved past five A.M., Omaha time. But Omaha was a bit of an anachronism now, so his watch read 1110 Zulu. He wondered where they were. Knowing Smitty, he could make a pretty good guess. The pilot would have them over the safest place in the United States. And the last place any of them wanted to be. He pushed through the cockpit door, his eyes quickly adjusting to the red glow of the night lights. Smitty sat in the left-hand seat, staring at his radar screen. The copilot sat on the right. Unlike the B-52's, the *Looking Glass* had flash panels that fitted snugly into the cockpit windows, a peel-back patch about one foot square in the center. The silver panels flashed almost disco magenta in the strange light.

"You're handling this old 707 like an F-15, Smitty," Alice said.

"Oh, hello, sir," the pilot responded. "We've got some pretty hot clouds out there, general. How're things in the back of the bus?"

"Sweaty."

"Found the boss, huh?"

"Yes, we found the boss." Alice paused for a moment, staring into the panels. "Where are we, Smitty?"

The pilot hesitated.

"Over Omaha?"

"It's safest, general. The cloud is blowing east. And the really dirty clouds from the missile fields won't reach here for a few hours."

The general paused again. Then he said. "Open the hole, Smitty."

"You don't want to, general."

"Open it."

Reluctantly the pilot reached into his flight-jacket pocket and pulled out a black eyepatch. He fitted it snugly over his left eye, making sure the copilot had done the same. He handed another to the general.

"They aren't going to hit us again here," Alice protested. "That's why you've got us over Omaha."

"Just put it on, sir." There was no give in the pilot's voice. Alice strapped the patch over one eye and the pilot slowly peeled back the opening, the Velcro sealers scratching through the engine hum like angry cat's claws.

Briefly the shimmer of a million stars brought goose bumps to the general's arms. It was so incredibly beautiful up here at night. Then he leaned over Smitty and peered down at the ground forty thousand feet below. His hands began shaking violently. Oh, God, Madge, I'm sorry. Below him, there was nothing but blackness. No lights. No landmarks. No movement of pinprick headlights. Miles away, in a near-perfect arc, orange flames still licked at the edge of the dark, empty circle. Beyond, sporadic fires burned in the prairies. Beyond the fires, not even a Nebraska farmhouse light shone. Even the snow was gone. The far horizon glowed slightly red and he knew it was not the sunrise. He felt a lump build in his throat. He remembered how much his wife had hated Omaha, with its hayseed social life and the isolation of its long winters. Suddenly he felt terribly embarrassed. Smitty's wife had been down there, too. And the copilot's.

"Close it up," he said. Walking back through the main compartment, he couldn't look at Sam. Alice was pondering how many more cities, how many more wives, he had condemned to that.

Kazaklis took it on himself to inform the rest of the crew and, as commander of a now retreating strategic penetrator, decided it was best to do it face to face. He laid his helmet aside, adjusted the radio headset, and unsnapped the connector above him. With the radio wire hanging loosely, he pulled himself up from his seat, laid his hand on the copilot's shoulder, and edged his way down the short walkway toward Halupalai. He sat down in O'Toole's seat, and even before he made the radio attachment, Halupalai's baleful eyes told the commander that he already knew. There was no argument in them, just a bleak look of failure, and Kazaklis winced at his friend's discomfort.

"You done great, champ," Kazaklis said weakly, placing his hand on the gunner's arm. The pilot groped for words, feeling as wretched as Halupalai looked. "There was no purpose in it, old buddy," the pilot said plaintively. Halupalai's round face softened, as if to say he understood lack of purpose above all, and then he wordlessly gestured for Kazaklis to leave and tell the others.

The open hatch to the lower compartment lay just behind Halupalai's seat, and Kazaklis shuddered as he squinted down into the dark redness in search of a foothold on the ladder. Below him, he saw five legs. He drew in a deep breath and backed down the ladder, stepping over the pretzel twist of O'Toole's body, which had jammed forward into the back of the downstairs seats during the low-level race through the mountains. One of O'Toole's legs was bent at the knee between Radnor and Tyler. The other had wrapped itself formlessly around the far side of Tyler's seat. The discordant scene in the downstairs compartment was far worse then Kazaklis could have imagined, even considering the irrational radio conversations of the past five hours. The two small desktop workplaces, usually scrupulously neat, were a jumbled disarray of navigation papers, some bloodied, and broken pencils.

Neither of the two crew members seemed to notice the disarray, Radnor oblivious even to the pilot's presence and Tyler craning his neck to watch him suspiciously. Kazaklis stared at Tyler briefly and then pulled O'Toole back to his resting place facing the locked bomb bay. In the little alcove, temporarily out of Tyler's sight, Kazaklis leaned his forehead against the bulkhead and rubbed his eyes. Then he stepped back over the body, came around the corner, and knelt between the two men, attaching his radio wire.

"Tough down here, huh, guys?" Kazaklis asked, placing a hand on each man's knee. He felt Tyler's muscles tighten. Radnor felt as lifeless as O'Toole. Kazaklis cringed and struggled for the right words. But Tyler spoke first.

"I am EWO ready," he said. His voice was eerily hollow—and menacing—as if it had been reinforced in an echo chamber. He firmly pushed the pilot's hand off his knee.

"I know you are," Kazaklis said softly, trying to make the lie soothing and convincing. "We were all EWO ready, nav. We've been EWO ready for a long time." Kazaklis looked compassionately at his deranged crewman and then glanced briefly and mistakenly at the little Kodak icon above the navigator's console.

Suddenly an elbow ripped viciously into his rib cage and he

bowled backward onto his rump, the radio wire whiplashing at his neck. He looked up groggily and saw Tyler place one hand over the photograph as if to hide Kazaklis from the boy instead of the boy from Kazaklis. The other hand darted at the pilot's radio wire, wrenching it out of its socket and pulling the headset painfully down behind his neck. Tyler jerked at the wire, then relaxed it, then jerked again.

"*EEE . . . WOE . . . Red . . . dee!*" Tyler screamed hysterically over the roar of the engines, jerking the wire between each tortured and disconnected syllable. "*Ready! Ready! Now!*" The whiplash pain stunned Kazaklis and he shook his head in an attempt to free it as Tyler's becrazed outrage disintegrated into a jumble of unrelated mutterings: *on the racetrack . . . cottonmouth . . . Radnor's wife . . .* At the mention of his wife, the young radar operator turned for the first time to look expressionlessly at the scene. He made no other move. Tyler screamed again. "Coward! Coward! Coward!" The words were a tearful wail now, but he jerked at the wire again, and again. Kazaklis, the pain searing at his neck, jammed a steel-plated flight boot into Tyler's shoulder. The pilot bolted upright, grabbed Tyler around the arms, and shook him violently. The navigator slammed his elbow into the pilot's ribs and Kazaklis struck him swiftly, a judo chop to the neck. Tyler slumped to the side.

Kazaklis slowly took a step back, the radio wire hanging from his neck like a loose noose. Radnor looked at him strangely but serenely, with the detachment of a man whose soul had taken leave for a more blissful place. He also quietly mouthed unheard words into the radio. Kazaklis took his hand and felt warm, wet blood. The pilot's taut body drooped. My God. EWO ready . . .

After a second, Kazaklis forlornly hooked the radio wire back into its socket. "We are not going, Radnor," he said simply.

Radnor looked at him without chastisement, without any emotion at all. Kazaklis felt a deep, abiding heartache. Radnor was so young, so innocent, his wide eyes blank among a teenager's harvest of freckles.

"My wife was a cop, commander," the boyish radar operator said tonelessly.

"I know, Radnor." The despair in the little basement of his aircraft began to engulf Kazaklis. "A good one."

"She protected us, commander."

"I know she did, buddy. You should be proud of her."

Radnor turned back toward his radar screen. "Who protected her?" he asked vacantly.

Kazaklis choked back the tears again. The red walls closed in on him. He wanted out. Badly.

"I dunno, Radnor," he said. Then he turned and slowly climbed the ladder back upstairs. It was only after he had returned to his seat, avoiding Moreau's questioning look, that he realized that not even Halupalai had asked where they were going now.

He also realized that he hadn't asked himself.

The lights were simply intolerable, so bright, one in each eye, that it took him a fuzzy moment to realize how cold he was. In the background he could hear a pervasive whine. Air-conditioning equipment? Operating-room equipment? Oh, Christ, they had him on the table again. He struggled to remember what it was this time. But he was so cold. He panicked. So this is the way it felt. An icy hand doth taketh. The fear chipped away at the mind fog. Dammit, he had the best doctors in the world. He fluttered his eyes and fought it. The operating-room lights were so strong, moon strobes that bored through his eyes, closed or open. He groaned and felt a hand on his arm. "Doctor?"

"It's Sedgwick, sir," a voice replied. "You've been out a very long time."

"Sedgwick?" He didn't have a doctor named Sedgwick.

"Hang tough, sir. You really got clobbered."

The President strained to see the man talking to him, but saw only the lights. He heard a distant popping noise. Far off. Much farther off than the chaotic clatter during the race across the South Lawn. Sedgwick. Oh, Jesus. Sedgwick! He tried to pull himself up, and the pain speared through his legs. He felt Sedgwick gently restrain him. He fought through the pain to focus his eyes on the young military aide, but the piercing lights blotted out everything.

"Where am I, Sedgwick?"

"I honest to God don't know, sir," Sedgwick answered apologetically. "Somewhere in Maryland. Not that far from the city. We're down in some kind of gorge. You were very lucky."

The President put his arm over his eyes. His mind felt rubbery, as it had toward the end in the White House, aboard the chopper. "The lights, Sedgwick," he said desperately. "I don't understand the lights."

"Lights, sir?" Except for the small fire, and the far-off glow of the burning city, their encampment was quite dark.

"The lights, dammit!" The President groaned in pain.

"Both your legs are broken, Mr. President."

The President moaned again.

"I believe you watched the detonation, sir," Sedgwick said softly. "I believe you are blind."

The President shivered, but not from the cold. He remembered the full moon. He remembered it blooming, bursting. He remembered the rare beauty of it. Blind. . . . He started to whimper and pull deeper under the blankets. Then, abruptly, he steeled himself. "How long have we been here, Sedgwick?"

"Five hours, Mr. President."

"We're near the city and it's not destroyed?"

"It's burning, sir. Took several small nukes, I believe. In and around the town. Andrews obviously. The Pentagon. I'm not sure what else."

"But Washington's not destroyed?"

"I don't think so, sir. Or we'd be in more trouble out here."

"You have to get me out of here, man. Do you understand?" The blurred words in the helicopter—*after our response to their attack on the Chinese*—now seemed tattooed in his brain, haunting in their new and awful clarity. "Do you understand how badly I screwed up?!" Then the blur began to return, the pain taking him again. "You *must* get me out . . ."

"I know, sir," Sedgwick replied. "But I don't know quite how, Mr. President. Both my legs are broken, too."

ELEVEN

1200 ZULU

In the good old days, six hours ago, a motorist on the ice-powder streets of Fairbanks could have spun his radio dial randomly and, if the crystalline currents of the winter atmosphere had flowed purely with his dreams, found himself wafted away ever so briefly by the siren strains of another world. The fickle radio waves would have teased him with the canary-soprano lure of the Orient, taken him for the most wonderful moment far from his cares and woes, and then without so much as a by-your-leave or a sayonara, dropped him off again in his own world, Yokohama gone, Fairbanks back, driving his Chevy to the levee and the levee was dry, the upper regions huzzing at him in playful am/fm mockery. Those were the good old days. Now, six hours after thousands of preternatural solar flares had shattered the crystalline carriers of man's words and music, the mockery remained for those left to listen. But the playfulness was gone and capriciousness replaced it.

In the *Looking Glass* the chunky communications officer examined the data that told her something had gone awry over the Arctic Ocean. But she withheld it from Alice, reworking it instead, certain that the currents were playing tricks again.

In a small underground bunker in the farmlands near Olney, Maryland, a civil-defense technician despondently unzipped the

273

heavy white suit he had worn outside to check his radio antennae. He showered to remove any lingering radiation, dressed hurriedly, and returned to his radio to send out his message again. The antennae, which he had popped up out of their concrete-and-copper silos after the EMP explosions, seemed to be working. But he received no reply.

In a much more elaborate bunker, south of the town of Cherepovets, a gray-uniformed cryptographer sweated furiously. His superiors were pushing him. But what was he to make of the garbled message he had intercepted from the outskirts of Washington? He assumed, rightly, that it had emerged from a tomb like his and merely acknowledged that men were there, as he was. He read the same data the *Looking Glass* woman had read and was equally suspicious—an American bomber had turned?—but he passed it along because the pressure was on. He had unscrambled part of a confusing conversation between two American command planes. It made no sense at all. He finally sent the mystifying code word off to his superiors, too. It was beyond his ken. Let them worry about anthropocide.

Inside *Polar Bear One,* heading in an unplanned and undefined southwesterly course across Alaska, the messages were mocking and capricious indeed. The music sounded tinny and hollow, and it came in dirges. It invaded helmets and souls alike, but it was not balm, not the siren strains of another world but the mournful gasp of a world departed. Suddenly the rigidly trained occupants of *Polar Bear One* had no world—neither the kamikaze world for which they had been programmed nor the world they had left behind. For the moment, none of them could cope with the latest change.

Downstairs, Radnor and Tyler withdrew still deeper into their isolation, even from each other. Upstairs, Halupalai, trying to make some sense of his latest failure, had rigged the radio once again for commercial broadcasts. That was a mistake. But Kazaklis, since his return from the tombs almost a half-hour ago, had retreated into silence. He grunted into the intercom just once. The grunt came when Halupalai, in spinning across the radio bands, landed on the cadenced monologue of a distant radio-pulpit preacher: *There are three strata of the heavens . . . the first is the atmosphere . . . the second is the stars, and that refers to the planetary system where our solar system resides . . . the third is the abode of God, where we shall spend eternity . . . it is not heaven, for remember the Bible says heaven and earth shall both pass away . . . the abode of God cannot pass away . . . we will be taken there in the Rapture. . . . In this series we will study the timing of the Rapture . . . the Rapture . . . the Rapture. . . .*

When the messenger of God's tape stuck, echoing the Rapture over and over inside the pilot's helmet, Kazaklis finally let out a disapproving grunt, no real thought attached to it, and Halupalai quickly swept through the capricious currents, finding an offering of ballads and doleful love songs instead. The Crazy Eddies were gone now, headed for the hills, and the Oxy-5 jingles, too, in final acknowledgment that acne was not the problem. *If a picture paints a thousand words, then why can't I paint you? . . .* There were no station call letters, no pauses for news, no whining interruptions from the Emergency Broadcast System. Just a tape left running, while others ran, too.

Kazaklis took no heed of the music. He stared silently into the red-haloed silhouette of his one-fingered glove and tried to balance its certainty against the haunting assault of Tyler's maniacal words—coward, coward, coward. He thought of *Elsie* trading her last drop of fuel, and everything else she had, to give them those precious extra miles. To what? Palm trees on a South Sea island? And the lonely man at Klickitat One, passing up the Jack Daniel's at Ruby's, waiting for the ash instead to give them one more eye on bandits approaching over the Pole. He thought about vengeance for the millions dead. Could they be avenged—should they be?—by killing millions more? But he could not answer his own question. He sidetracked it, as he did the music, in some obscure niche in the honeycomb of his mind.

Flying aimlessly south over central Alaska now, only Moreau made an attempt at communication. When the radio came on, she cast a concerned glance over her shoulder at Halupalai's intently hunched back. She placed a hand on the pilot's shoulder, shaking it lightly to share her sense of danger. But Kazaklis kept his eyes on the silhouette of his rebellion and his mind on its bleak and guilty wanderings. He gently removed her hand in an unspoken reply that said if north toward nowhere had no purpose, south toward nowhere might have less. She briefly called downstairs to determine if Tyler had been badly injured. The voice came back at first with surreal calm. "I have no injuries, captain," Tyler responded. Then the voice turned almost cadaverous in its haunt. "I am EWO ready," he said.

Moreau's head rattled with the decisions they had to make.

Where were they going? Anywhere? Or were they simply turning their part in a mass suicide into a nice, simple, private ceremony? What did they do if American fighters, half-brothers of the MIG's, came up after them? Someone had to go down and give Tyler a hypo to knock him out, but she was not up to it yet. Radnor was already out, flying solo now. Could they go anywhere without navigators? They needed to do fuel calculations and examine their options. They also needed to get rid of the weapons. The bombs were wasted weight, the SRAM's aerodynamic flaws burning precious fuel. The questions bounced without answers through her head. The music bounced, too.

If a man could be two places at one time, I'd be with you. . . . The music was gnawing at her, an invitation to emotional disaster. *Tomorrow and today, beside you all the way. . . .*

She started to turn toward Kazaklis to protest, warn, plead. She knew the lyrics. *If . . . If . . .*

Downstairs, the two isolated crewmen had come full circle. Tyler babbled wildly at his crewmate, crazily muddling duty and flag and courage with Radnor's wife. Radnor seemed not to hear him.

If the world should stop revolving . . .

Tyler shook his crewmate ferociously and Radnor turned toward him, his placidly happy face meeting Tyler's hideously tortured mask without fear. Radnor smiled blissfully.

Spinning slowly down to die . . .

He serenely placed a finger to his lips, shushing the navigator. Shhhhhh, Tyler, the music.

I'd spend the end with you. . . .

Upstairs, Moreau reached over and shook the pilot desperately. "Good God, Kazaklis!" He looked up in surprise. She turned in desperation toward Halupalai, whose back was still hunched, oblivious to all.

And when the world is through . . .

Radnor's smile spread peacefully across his face. He happily showed Tyler the small object he had withdrawn from his alert bag.

One by one, the stars would all go out. . . .

Calmly, he placed the white capsule in his mouth, appeared to bite once, and started to swallow. His face was rapturous.

Then you and I . . .

The young radar operator slumped forward, his freckled forehead gently coming to rest below his scope, its tracking arm spinning slowly through the night, slowly above his mussed sandy hair.

Would simply fly away. . . .

Tyler watched in stuporous wonder. Far away, in some abandoned radio-station studio, a tape spun silently between songs. Tyler reached over tentatively and lightly nudged his friend, receiving no response. The tape whirred into the next offering. *A long, long time ago* . . . Tyler leaned back the other direction and reached into his own alert bag . . . *I can still remember* . . . withdrew a different object . . . *how that music used to make me smile* . . . stroked it and made sure the clip was full, reached up toward the Kodak icon and patted it reverently . . . *can't remember if I cried* . . . and then unhooked his radio headset, the second before the music died, and started up the steel ladder, his .45 in hand.

Had Tyler been intent on anything else, had he been watching the tracking arm spinning through the night on his own radar scope, he would have seen a most remarkable sight. He would have seen a squadron of incognitos, at least fifteen strong, edging into the corner of his screen. Had he stayed but a few seconds longer, he would have seen a still more remarkable sight. He would have seen the incognitos begin to maneuver. But Tyler no longer had an interest in incognitos. As a consequence, no one in *Polar Bear One* saw the approaching Bison bombers. And no one saw their maneuverings as they made a gracefully sweeping and symbolic turn.

"One of our bombers has aborted, general."

Alice swiveled in his chair and looked at the communications officer as if he had not heard her correctly.

"*Polar Bear One* turned, sir. South. Southwesterly, actually."

"No." Alice frowned at her and shook his head.

"I'm afraid so, sir. I checked the data three times."

Alice swiveled slowly away from her, staring slightly upward at the countdown watch. Briefly, anger and frustration coursed through him and he slammed his beefy fist into the high desk in front of him. Then he slumped in weariness. "Southwesterly?" he asked quietly.

"Yes, sir. Across Alaska toward the North Pacific."

Alice did not look back at her, but he felt her steady gaze. Sam's too. He grew pensive in his weariness, his mind drifting back to

the early days of the cold war when he had been assigned to the
spanking-new B-52s. It had been a great youthful adventure then,
not quite so suicidal, not quite so total. Simpler. The rightness
more certain. He also remembered the islands. They all had an
island, their own private preserve in paradise, and they argued
about them, rambunctiously, outrageously, in bars and locker
rooms and during parties in the little apartments a captain's pay
could afford. They'd pull out the maps of the South Pacific, figure
their fuel loads and headings, and bicker endlessly. Ponape?
Tough luck, buddy. That's ours. One crew to an island. You can
have Bikini and roast your balls. They'd laugh and laugh. The
wives never laughed. It's a joke, Madge. Dammit, it's a mean and
dirty business and we need to laugh about something. But he'd go
to sleep at night, as the rest of them did, and the dream warp
would take him low over the last reef, the surf cresting into an
azure lagoon, his sleek new B-52 cruising toward beckoning
palms. While the rest of the world fried. And he would snap out
of the dream, snap out of the joke, and go back to work. As they
all did.

"We have to bring them down, sir," Sam interrupted.

"Now, that is a joke, Sam," Alice replied wistfully.

"Sir?"

Alice swiveled a half-turn this time and stared into the map on
the far wall. The little pasted ridge seemed to rise as high as the
Urals themselves, the green dot of Cherepovets throbbing at him
just beyond the seam, the blue expanse of the Pacific divided at
the edges of the world.

"We have to inform Condor, sir," Sam continued.

Alice paused thoughtfully. "Yes," he said vacantly, "I suppose
we do."

Something touched me deep inside . . . The tinny resonance reverberated through Moreau's skull. *The day the m-uu-zik died* . . . She
wanted to scream again, shriek the dirge out of her head. *So bye-
bye, Miss American pie, drove my Chevy to the levee but the levee was
dry* . . .

"Ha . . . lup . . . a . . . lai!"

Them good old boys was drinkin' whiskey and rye . . . She and
Halupalai turned toward each other simultaneously and suddenly
froze. In the dark ten-foot walkway between them, the shadowy
figure of Tyler loomed. He stood at the top of the ladder, his back

to Halupalai and slightly out of the Hawaiian's reach, his face and his intent concentrated on the cockpit. He stood in a slight crouch, almost a policeman's crouch, both arms thrust forward. *This'll be the day that I die . . .*

Moreau could see nothing but the form in the darkness, but she instinctively reached for Kazaklis, trying to shove his head down below his seat's headrest. Halupalai moved as quickly, lurching so suddenly out of his seat and across the open hatch that his radio wire snapped clean, whiplashing Don McLean's lyrics back into the void as the singer inquired *did you write the book of love?* slamming an old scatback shoulder into Tyler's kidneys, reaching a hand around as they had taught so long ago on the campus in Westwood, rousting the arms in search of a fumble.

Halupalai felt, rather than heard, Tyler's grunt. The navigator started to go down, but Halupalai went first, one of his legs plunging into the open well to the basement. He teetered briefly, gave one last painful wrench at the handgun, and lost his balance, careening backward into the steel seat braces. He heard the gun clanging faintly as it skittered across the metal floor. For a moment his head spun foggily and he couldn't move, his leg tangled in the ladder, his back aching where the two sharp-edged braces—the ejection tracks—stabbed into his shoulder blades.

Groggily, he saw Moreau wheeling out of her seat and Tyler on his hands and knees between them, groping for the weapon. Halupalai let out a wild, animal yell and flung himself at Tyler, catching him by the collar. He pulled with such desperate strength that the young navigator flipped backward in a half-somersault, his legs flailing upward, his head crashing down over the edge of the open well. Halupalai heard the crack, even over the engine noise. It was not the noise of a collarbone snap on the playing field, not the curdling crack of the Buff's aging back as it roared over a ridge. It was a crack he had heard only in his youthful imagination—the quick, clean spinal snap of a haole caught in a wave he had not been meant to ride.

Moreau stood at the front of the plane, staring vacantly at the scene. The music clawed through her helmet, scratchily huzzing in and out as the beam faded and reemerged. *Helter-skelter . . .* huzz . . . *birds flew off to the fallout shelter . . .* huzz . . . *got up to dance . . .* huzz . . . *never got the chance . . .* She pounded at the helmet with two clenched fists. Stop it, stop it, stop it!

Slowly she bent over into the darkness behind the pilot, retrieved the .45, removed the clip, and dropped both on her seat. Kazaklis looked at her desolately. *Generation lost in space* . . . "Four little robots," Moreau said emptily. *No time to start again* . . . Moreau reached to pull the radio plug. *Jack be nimble, Jack be quick, Jack Squire sat on a candlestick* . . . Then there was only the roar of the engines, and she started down the narrow walkway.

It was clear at a glance that Tyler was dead. His head wobbled loosely but peacefully in the open well, only the vibration of the aircraft stirring him now. She examined him most briefly, then looked up at Halupalai. The big Hawaiian stood with his back pressed awkwardly against the far wall of the defensive station, his arms spread slightly. Moreau reached out to comfort him, but Halupalai pushed back more tightly, as if he wanted to withdraw beyond the barrier. Moreau smiled wanly at him—poor, lost, gentle friend—and knelt beside the well hatch. She carefully took Tyler's lolling head in her hands, edged it over to a resting place on the deck, and started down the ladder.

She first saw O'Toole stretched tranquilly in the alcove, his body faintly luminous in the red light. Then she turned toward Radnor and her knees buckled. She grabbed Tyler's seat to support herself, then sagged into it. She laid a hand on Radnor's sandy hair, tenderly stroked it, and gently moved him upright, briefly catching and then forever avoiding his faint smile.

Moreau shrieked. "No-o-o-o-o-o-o!" In the aircraft no one heard her. She plugged in the radio cord. *In the streets the children screamed, the lovers cried and the poets dreamed* . . . "No-o-o-o-o-o-o!" *Not a word was spoken, the church bells all were broken* . . . She pulled herself erect and switched the radio to all channels, so she could speak through the dirge.

"Three little robots," she said dully.

"Moreau?" The alarmed voice of Kazaklis cut through the hollow rhythms.

The three men I admire most, the Father, Son, and the Holy Ghost, they caught the last train for the coast, the day the music died . . . Moreau lifted a leaden arm to disconnect the radio. *They were singing byebye, Miss American pie* . . . And the sounds were gone again, the endless drone back, and Moreau stared into Tyler's screen, its whirling arm seeing no high terrain, no pulsing clouds, no incognitos. Moreau placed her head in her hands, and she cried.

"So what do you folks do, Alice, when one of your crews goes gutless?"

Alice floundered. He looked up from the black phone, his eyes pleading with Sam. Sam shrugged.

"Sir, there's no precedent—"

"Hell with precedent! No precedent for nothin' tonight!"

"Normally, sir, we'd send up interceptors," Alice said weakly, "and try to bring them down."

"Shoot 'em down?"

"If necessary. We'd try to force them to land first."

"Land." The scorn cut across the distance. "Then you'd shoot 'em. What's the difference? Deserters are deserters. Shoot 'em down."

"Good God, Condor—"

"And stop callin' me Condor, dammit. This is your President speakin', not some damned dyin' bird."

Alice felt the blood rise in his face. "Sir, ears are opening. They can mouse us. We can mouse them. We're getting the first bits of messages moving inside Russia."

There was a pause. "You don't think you should've told your . . . me . . . about that, Alice?"

"Sir, we can't make sense out of it yet. It's snatches. Bits and pieces. All we can determine is they're rattled. Just as we are."

"You think we're rattled?"

Alice sighed. "Yes, sir." The general felt someone hovering at his elbow. He impatiently brushed the figure back.

"I'm gonna tell you somethin', Alice. Straight out. Thing that's rattlin' me most is my own damned military geniuses."

Alice took a deep breath. "In this one, sir, there are no military geniuses." The figure tugged persistently at his sleeve. He turned angrily and saw his communications officer waving papers at him. "Excuse me a moment, sir," Alice said, cupping the phone. He could hear protests squawking out of the receiver. "For Christ's sake, lieutenant, I'm talking to your Commander-in-Chief," he snapped at the young woman.

"He needs to know this, sir," she replied, unyielding. "The Bisons have turned. Shortly after *Polar Bear One* turned, the Soviet squadron approaching them also turned."

Alice looked at her in disbelief. "You positive?"

"Positive?" The woman shrugged. "Tonight?" She shrugged again. "I'm as sure as I am about *Polar Bear One*. Same data. Same source."

Alice scanned the readouts hurriedly. "And the rest of them?" he asked.

"Proceeding, sir. As before."

Alice stared into the black phone, from which he could hear a persistent babble tugging at him. To the general it seemed an eternity before he spoke into the phone again.

Beneath the Maryland farmlands, the dismayed radio operator ran his fingers through his still-damp hair, massaging the roots thoughtfully. He could hear the hum of the giant turbines, one floor below, methodically cleansing their air. It wasn't that dirty out there, he thought. Yet. He glanced at the bank of telegraph machines to his left, leafing through the last printouts. Routine stuff until almost an hour after his midnight shift had begun. A string of the usual fifteen-minute communications checks in Greenwich mean time: "NORAD COMM CHECK 0500 CHEYENNE . . . NORAD COMM CHECK 0515 CHEYENNE." The last had come at 0545, followed by a gushing volume of increasing status alerts, urgent alarms, and finally the list of impact areas. Then the machine stopped at 0630 and the paper roll was blank. He glanced at a clock marked Zulu—1204. Four minutes past seven. The sun would be coming up soon. He turned to the tall balding man watching him.

"I just don't understand it, sir," the technician said. "Half the time I can hear the *Looking Glass* talking to the *E-4*. But I can't hear the *E-4*, and neither of them seems to hear us."

"Keep trying," the man said halfheartedly. "We don't have a helluva lot to tell them anyway, do we?"

"Maybe not. But one more EMP whomp and we won't be talking to anybody."

"Son," the man said, "after the next whomp we won't be talking to each other."

The technician slumped in his government-issue secretarial chair. "Dammit—pardon me—but wouldn't they want to know about the signals from Russia?"

"Hmmph," the older man grunted, unimpressed. "Moscow calling."

"It's not Moscow. It's north of there, in the dingleberries. But they're directing the messages at the United States."

"Son," the man said patronizingly, "you're listening to some spook from the CIA trying to tell us we left a bridge open over the Volga. We know that."

The technician returned disconsolately to his radio. His superior, a retired brigadier general now running the Central Atlantic regional civil-defense program, wandered slowly out of the room. As he left, he glanced at a wall map of the Washington metropolitan area with 466 pinpoints for the air-raid sirens he had triggered at 1:10 in the morning—after the first missile had landed. Shit-pot full of good they did, he thought, moving on into the empty briefing room. The plans called for the governors and leaders of a half-dozen states to relocate here. Not a one had arrived. Neither had his staff of forty. He was stuck down here with the normal nighttime crew of seven, plus two. The only outsiders who had shown up were two young nurses from the standby list. The way they looked when they showed up—bruised, clothes torn—he figured they had been more worried about being raped than nuked. Not even a doctor had shown up. He felt very left out.

"As I said, sir," Alice replied, slightly irritably, "there are no geniuses in this one. I don't know what this means. I can make an optimistic guess."

"A smoke signal." The voice was contemptuous.

"You might call it that."

"Alice," the successor said slowly, "Harpoon told me all about smoke signals. So fifteen Russian bombers turned around. I read this little war chant as sayin' we got one deserter and they got fifteen. You read it different?"

Alice took a long deep breath, letting the air out slowly. "Yes, sir, I believe I do."

"Maybe you want to believe it more than you do believe it."

"Perhaps, sir."

"I ain't into wishful thinkin'."

"Please, sir. Turn the bombers." Alice closed his eyes, embarrassed. He thought he sounded more pathetic than convincing, and he didn't like those near him to be listening. "See what happens. We have so little time."

The general waited through a brief pause. Then the successor continued. "Alice, lemme ask you somethin'. You say ears are openin' up and we're hearin' folks and folks're hearin' us?"

"Yes, sir. Not very well."

"Wel-l-l-l, Alice, I truly hope the Premier is eavesdroppin' right now. 'Cuz he can shove his Bisons right up his rosy-red bee-hind. He started this and he better start duckin'. And you hear this, general. You put another bomber on the henhouse. Damned fast. Got that?"

Alice clamped his eyes tightly closed. He saw the black hole of Omaha, the surf crashing over a reef forever forbidden to him. "I hear you, sir," he said.

"And if there's ears out there, Alice, some of 'em's ours. So you send out general orders, right now, to shoot down *Polar Bear One.* No questions. Just shoot. Hear?"

Alice could feel beads of sweat popping on his forehead. He brushed at his face with a sleeve that was already damp. When he spoke, his own voice sounded foreign. "I hear you, sir," he said again.

"Don't sound very convinced, general."

"I don't believe I am, sir."

The pause was quite brief. "You tread careful, Alice, or you'll find yourself in deep shit. Deep shit indeed."

"Yes, sir."

"We can send out the orders from here."

Alice thought only for a split second. "I'd suggest you do that, sir."

"I hear you right, Alice?"

"Yes, sir."

There was a moment of silence. Then the phone connection clicked and huzzed out.

"You get the duty, Kazaklis," Moreau said. Kazaklis looked into her ghostly white face and the wet smudges she had tried to blot away. "Or we'll be down to two little robots."

"I know," the pilot said.

"Send him up here first, will you? He's really a case."

"Help him, Moreau," Kazaklis said in tones more tender than she had ever heard him use.

The pilot then swung slowly out of his seat and started down the aisle. Tyler's boots rested pigeon-toed a few feet behind the cockpit, his body pointing directly down the middle of the walkway. Only his head was out of line, crazily crooked, where Moreau had moved it from the well which had broken his neck. It rested at the foot of the jump seat on which the red code box sat, and directly behind Halupalai's seat. Halupalai, however, still stood frozen against the instrument panel, his arms stretched outward almost in a crucifixion stance, little yellow gauge lights glowing around him. Kazaklis moved carefully past Tyler and placed a hand on Halupalai's elbow.

"Come on, old boy," Kazaklis said soothingly. "Go up front with Moreau." The gunner didn't move. Halupalai's arm was leaden. Kazaklis tugged at it lightly before noticing the shredded radio wire. He reached up and gently eased Halupalai's helmet off his head, dropping it into O'Toole's seat with one hand and softly massaging the tight tendons of his friend's neck with the other. He leaned forward and placed his mouth near Halupalai's ear. "Please, ace," he whispered. "Go up with Moreau for a while. You know how women are. She's a little twittery. She needs you. Please."

Halupalai slowly turned his head, fastening big and mournful eyes on Kazaklis. The eyes blinked once, transmitting the briefest subliminal message of the kind that could pass only between friends. It said: Stop the con, Kazaklis. Then the eyes went balefully blank again and the pilot's heart sank. "Get your ass up front, sergeant," Kazaklis said with quiet firmness.

Halupalai smiled faintly, almost unnoticeably. "Where you gonna go, commander?"

The question had an eerie ring, and it sent an alarm through Kazaklis. But he forced the super-con, Boom-Room Room smile anyway, tightened his brotherly grip on Halupalai's taut neck, and said cheerily, "You can pick the island, beachboy." Kazaklis felt Halupalai's tendons grow tighter.

"I didn't mean to hurt him," the gunner whispered, haunted.

"I know, pal," Kazaklis said. "I know, I know." He took Halupalai by both arms and pulled him away from the wall.

Kazaklis watched as Halupalai moved toward the cockpit, edging his way in a crab-walk, his back to the bulkhead, his arms still outstretched to feel his way, his eyes held unseeing far above the form beneath him. He saw Halupalai lower himself uneasily into the pilot's seat and reach out tentatively to touch the one-fingered glove. Then Kazaklis went about his business, which was body stacking. Kazaklis struggled to get Tyler's corpse down the narrow ladder, thinking briefly of simply dropping it, and then, out of respect, dismissing the thought and doing it the hard way. At the bottom he dragged the limp heap, trying to avoid looking at the lolling head, and placed the navigator next to O'Toole. Then he moved Radnor, building a bleak pyramid in the narrow space leading to the sealed chamber holding their remaining bombs. He turned and went to Tyler's seat. He sat down, and for no reason, sorted out the mess, stacking the jumbled papers, wetting his fingers and trying to erase the now dried spatters of blood. His eyes fastened unexpectedly on the hallowed Kodak print, a little boy staring round-eyed and worshipfully at him.

Suddenly he felt exhausted. He laid his head down on Tyler's desktop and drifted into a fitful half-sleep. He saw Sarah Jean—rah! rah!—her breasts now tight little mailed fists flouncing beneath a soft sweater, her hand reaching toward his groin, clasping, pulling at a red lever. Nikko turned scrawny and old, taunting him with a lightning-bolt tongue. A little boy shivered in the rain, scrounging among the beetles, digging the life-giving pitch out of rotting hulks in a primeval swamp, feeding his precious find to the giant insects, and the pterodactyls devoured the white capsules he offered, swooped over the rubble of his splintered forest, arched triumphantly over the pulverized cities of his adulthood, their giant wings shrouds now, casting widening shadows as they dived into a flawless crater in which Halupalai lofted a perfect pass and Moreau leaped as the spheroid soared higher and farther—rah! rah!—and a little boy placed a match to a perfect tepee frame of the bulbous gray firewood the world had given him, and he built a fire in the rain.

"They'll shoot you, general."

"Sam." Alice looked deeply into the troubled face of his colleague, seeing great pain, which he appreciated, and great doubt, which he understood. "Sam, I should find such an angel of mercy."

The general turned briefly away, reached into the satchel at his side, and withdrew the special-issue revolver he had carried since he won his first star. He looked at it fondly. It was a general officer's tool never used. He felt every eye in the *Looking Glass* on him now, but he had no sense of embarrassment at all.

"You know, Sam," Alice said thoughtfully, "they tell us at West Point that every war is made up of a million private wars. They tell us only once, because no officer likes it that way. Not very disciplined, private wars." He paused and sighed. "I've just fought mine. As God is my witness, I don't know if I won or lost."

"Ten of our bombers, general," Sam said quietly. "What does it mean? You can't call back the submarines. You can't hold the rest of the world together." The voice turned beseeching and Alice knew that Sam's war was raging now. "It won't change anything, general."

"Change anything?" Alice sounded detached, even to himself. "I don't believe that's what private wars are all about, Sam."

Alice felt the finely etched security of the gun handle in his palm. Then he flipped the weapon neatly, catching it by the barrel, and placed it atop the code box. He stood, perfectly erect, and held unflinching eyes on his friend and subordinate.

"I just gave you an order, Sam," he said firmly. "Just disobeyed one, too. First in more than thirty years. I'm tired. I'm going back to lie down." He started to turn. "I'll understand, warrior," he added. Then he walked out of the compartment, into the aircraft's rear cabin, and lay down on its single cot, his back turned toward a doorway intentionally left open.

"It wasn't your fault, good friend," Moreau said in a voice that washed over Halupalai in the same massaging rhythm of the airplane's vibrations, the same rhythm of her fingers.

Halupalai was unaccustomed to the front seat and equally unaccustomed to the comfort of a woman's hand. When he first came up front, he had said nothing. Then he had begun to babble, gushing all the guilt of a lifetime at the woman kneading his shoulders. But now he sensed that Moreau was having no easier time than he. That added to his guilt, but he tried to pull himself together.

"I didn't mean it to be that way with Tyler," he said, painfully firming up his voice.

Moreau looked at him in anguish. Halupalai had sensed correctly that she was having trouble, and not simply with the task of calming him. "You saved us," she said. The words sounded hollow, even to her. In some unfathomable way, she was finding the turnabout run more difficult than the plunge into Russia. They had programmed her to die, not to live, not to deal with the new problems of surviving. She tried to finish her thought. "Tyler went crazy."

Halupalai looked at her with a strange childlike expression. "Is it all right to kill crazy people now?" The look on Moreau's face turned from anguish to raw pain. Halupalai floundered. He wanted away from the subject. He wanted to tell her something else, but he didn't know how.

"Moreau . . . ?"

She sighed and squeezed his shoulder lightly.

"Moreau," he continued tentatively, "you shouldn't fight with Kazaklis all the time. He's really okay."

Moreau's fingers tightened noticeably on his shoulder, but he went on.

"He's got a side he never lets you see."

She said nothing.

"Please, Moreau. It's important."

"I know," Moreau finally replied. "We've all got that side, Halupalai."

"Please," he insisted.

She stared hard into Halupalai's open face. He sounded as if he were writing his will. She shivered, and then she nodded and patted his shoulder reassuringly. He smiled. They both went silent, each into a separate world, and Moreau felt the shame and guilt well up, only to be replaced by fear—a great fear of a new unknown. Until now her future had been ordained and simple—a robot pilot's death in the death of a doomed world. It no longer was quite that simple, and the simplicity suddenly seemed cleaner, preferable. What kind of void was she entering now, with what kind of shadow of a man? Could she survive in this new wilderness? Did she want to survive? Did she want to walk into the new emptiness with a man whose other side she had never seen? She shuddered, realizing shamefully that her mind had cut Halupalai out of that world. She reached for him. But he was gone, having shuffled silently back to his proper place in the dark redness. She was very afraid. Where was Kazaklis? He seemed to have been gone forever.

Sedgwick felt something jabbing at him. He didn't want to awaken. He was very comfortably, sleepily cold. He brushed at the irritant, the pain from his hands racking him out of his grogginess. His hands hurt more than his broken legs now. Near him he heard brush crackle, snow crunch, as something suddenly withdrew from him.

"You soldier?" a frightened, squeaky voice asked.

Sedgwick forced his eyes open. The light had changed to the difficult shadows of a murky false dawn. Or perhaps the fires had moved closer. He had trouble focusing his eyes. He saw a small form pulling away through the winter-barren skeletons of the underbrush.

"Don't go!" Sedgwick pleaded, stretching a bloodied hand outward.

"You American?" the voice asked suspiciously.

Sedgwick forced his eyes to focus and saw a young boy, perhaps eight years old, black and cherub-faced. The boy backed slowly away, holding a stick in defense.

"Don't go," Sedgwick said again. "Please."

"Soldiers nuked us."

"Get your daddy. Please."

"M' daddy's dead."

"Please, boy"—don't call him boy, Sedgwick, you klutz—"please get someone. Your mama." Sedgwick's head was swimming, pain overwhelming desperation, then desperation overwhelming pain. "The President is down there." The boy said nothing. Sedgwick despaired at the very absurdity of what he had said, and he began to slip away again, his mind fuzzily telling him not even a child could believe him. "Your mama," he whimpered one more time, his head falling back into the snow.

"M' mama doan like the President."

Sedgwick lifted his head and reached out again—and the Queen said to Alice: Why, I've believed as many as six impossible things before breakfast—but the boy was gone. Sedgwick slipped back into semiconsciousness at the top of the gully up which he had pulled himself hand over hand.

Kazaklis snapped abruptly out of his nightmare, sitting bolt upright in Tyler's seat. For a moment he was disoriented, the claustrophobic red lights closing in on him, his head swaying ever so slightly with the radar arm in front of him. The arm swept over a tongue of land, which they were departing, then over ice-free sea, and then, in the distance, over the ragged coastline of a fairly large island. He looked at his watch: 1225 Zulu. He shook his head, not remembering precisely when he had come downstairs. "Where the hell are we?" he bellowed. In the mirror reflection of the screen he could see the faint outline of the bodies stacked behind him, a pyre glowing in the redness. "Where the hell are we?" he shouted again. No answer. He felt very alone. He shuddered and stood, starting to unhook his radio connection. Then he sagged back in the seat, cursing himself. Anybody would go nuts down here. The radio wire hung loosely, never having been connected as he completed his grim chores. He attached it to

Tyler's outlet and, a trifle sheepishly, asked: "Where the hell are we?"

Moreau's voice cut icily into his earphones. "You seem to like navigating, commander. You tell me."

How long had he been down here? Ten minutes? Twenty? Thirty? He would have been furious with anyone else. "How's our friend?" he asked defensively.

"Spooked," Moreau spat back. "Do you mind coming back up here? We do have some problems." He started to snap at her—this had not been the night's most pleasant assignment—but Moreau continued. "See if you can snitch Halupalai's alert bag on the way by."

Kazaklis heard the radio click off abruptly. A pang of fear rippled through the pilot. He rose quickly, unhooked, and took one last look around. He did not want to come down here again. His eyes halted on Timmie. Reverently he pulled the photo loose from its simple plastic-tape frame. He walked to the alcove, tucked the photo into Tyler's flight-jacket pocket, and zipped the pocket shut. Then he hurried up the ladder.

Halupalai sat inertly with his back to the stairwell. Kazaklis reached quickly for the bag, placing it behind his back, and squeezed the gunner's shoulder. Halupalai woodenly turned a now ancient face toward him. The big Hawaiian's hollow eyes slowly dropped toward the half-hidden alert bag, then moved knowingly back up at Kazaklis. He shook his head slightly, as if to tell Kazaklis it was foolish to worry about the cyanide pill, even more foolish to worry about the .45. The pilot clenched Halupalai's shoulder once more and moved up front.

"Welcome back," Moreau said acidly, forgetting her unspoken promise to Halupalai.

Kazaklis ignored her. "He doesn't seem any better."

"He's blaming himself for everything from Vietnam to Radnor's wife."

"Jesus."

"Shoulda known O'Toole was freezing to death. Shoulda tapped Tyler on the shoulder and asked for the damned gun. Shoulda shot down some bloody SAM's fifteen years ago in Vietnam. Shoulda this, shoulda that, shoulda, shoulda, shoulda!" Moreau was beginning to sound hysterical.

"Hey, take it easy, pal."

"Take it easy, bullshit! Everybody's going bonkers! You disappear, Halupalai babbles, the world's committing fucking suicide. Dammit . . ." Moreau's voice trailed off.

Kazaklis softly placed a hand on her shoulder. She shook uncontrollably from rage and frustration.

"Get your damned hands off me!" she shrieked. "Go back downstairs and jack off—or whatever the hell you were doing. That's all the world's been doing for forty years." Her voice sagged again. "You deserve each other."

"Hey, Moreau," he protested feebly.

"Then help me, Kazaklis. Play your silly percentage baseball. Give it your fancy barroom hustle. Do something. Anything. But don't mope and don't disappear for half an hour." She paused and slumped in her seat. "Halupalai says there's a side of you I don't see," she said quietly.

Kazaklis said nothing for a moment. He was tired. He had been trying to hold this plane together—this crew together—for more than six hours. He peered around the side of his helmet, peekaboo style. "My backside, maybe?" he asked impishly.

Moreau lunged at him in her fury, pounding her fists into his shoulder. "Stop it, damn you!"

Kazaklis took it for a second, then pushed her back gently but firmly. "Fuel load?" he asked professionally.

"Two hundred one thousand pounds," she replied, equally professionally.

"Weapons load?"

"Just under twenty thousand pounds."

"We have to jettison the weapons."

"Yes."

Kazaklis quickly ran the numbers through his head. By flying upstairs instead of down in the weeds, they would gain a thirty-five-percent fuel saving. If they didn't push it, if they cruised at an optimum altitude of forty thousand feet or higher, they would burn twenty thousand pounds of fuel an hour. Dumping the bombs—the three of them were the only payload worth carrying now—and eliminating the drag from the missiles tucked under their wings would give them still more efficiency. With a few breaks they could stay up ten, eleven, twelve hours. This old brute still had at least six thousand miles in it.

"Where are we?" Kazaklis asked.

"Navigation isn't our strong point."

"We'll make do. Halupalai wouldn't last ten minutes down in that pit. It's an Edgar Allan Poe horror story."

"I know."

"So where are we? You been drivin', lady. I saw a peninsula and an island before I came up."

"South of Anchorage. What was Anchorage. They sure didn't want interceptors coming at them from the Alaskan Air Command."

"Neither do we, pal. Only favor the cossacks did for us."

"Yeah. Some favor. It's the Kenai Peninsula, with Kodiak Island coming up."

Kazaklis didn't bother with a map. Like every B-52 crewman since the fifties, he had played this game with the same fervor that an English pubgoer played darts. He had the board memorized, all its fanciful targets etched in his head. Not once had he taken it seriously. But he could draw the circle in his mind, each degree of latitude another seventy miles south. From Kodiak, at fifty-eight degrees, the equator lay four thousand miles distant. Tahiti, Moreau's once-prankish fantasy island, lay 1,250 miles beyond, almost due south of their present position. Tonga, Fiji, and a thousand islands of a thousand dead fantasies lay inside the arc.

The engine roar had become a purr now, its roar their silence. They let the silence sit. Then Kazaklis looked at Moreau, her face moon-framed in its white helmet, the stress lines washed out by the night-light red, the nuked eye appearing natural now.

"Having doubts?" she asked.

"No," he replied, then checked himself. "Sure I am, Moreau. I was just thinking that our world is dying out there and we haven't seen a thing, haven't heard a thing, don't have the foggiest notion why, and probably never will. Yet we were the killers. We saw a couple of MIG's, dropped a bomb in the wilderness, had our own little civil war. But even if we had gone, we wouldn't have been part of the world's agony. We wouldn't have seen any more, known any more."

"We weren't supposed to, Kazaklis. That's why people like us could do it."

"Maybe. I'm not so sure. We humans can be a mean bunch of critters. Give us a creed—any creed—and we'll shove people with other creeds into ovens. I guess that was our special talent—building bigger and better ovens. Till we finally built one big enough for all of us."

The purr filled the cockpit again, both of them staring into the mesmerizing maze of their flight panel.

Kazaklis felt awkward and he suddenly switched the radio from private to all stations. "Hokay, mutineers!" he whooped flamboyantly. "Rarotonga! Bora Bora! Hiva Oa! Papeete for the lady! We're goin' for the blue lagoon! Sound okay to you, Halupalai?!"

Only a low grunt came from the rear. Moreau turned worriedly toward Kazaklis and asked privately, "Where are we really going?"

Kazaklis shot a worried look back. "I'm not sure."

She looked at him curiously. "You're going to fly over Hawaii, aren't you?"

"It's a natural navigational pivot point," Kazaklis answered, much too quickly.

"Pivot point, my ass," Moreau said quietly.

"We have to see it, Moreau."

"Him too?" Moreau asked a trifle aggressively as she motioned toward the back.

Kazaklis stared straight ahead. "All of us. We can't live in some other world without seeing why we had to leave. We'd be nuts in a month. He wouldn't last a week." Kazaklis sounded very certain.

"You know what it will look like."

"Yes."

They flew on silently for several moments, the engine roar filling their voids.

"He already asked," Moreau broke the silence.

Kazaklis turned on her abruptly, a strange look in his eyes.

"I said maybe," she answered defensively. "He was coming apart at the seams. I didn't want four people stacked downstairs." She paused. "Maybe five. What *were* you doing down there?"

Kazaklis allowed a faint smile to cross his face. "Sleepin'," he drawled.

"You sonuvabitch," Moreau said. "Kazaklis, you are the most hopeless person I've ever met."

"Yeah," he acknowledged. "But I may have met my match."

The persistent rapping startled Harpoon, his mind having drifted so far away. Out of ingrained habit he leaned over in his chair, used the forearm of his starched white shirt to do a quick buff of his shit-polish shine, and then rose quickly. At the door he was greeted by the fat man whom he had pulled aboard with

Condor in the chaos of Baton Rouge. The man still sweated profusely, as if he had jogged on this errand, and the turquoise belt buckle was loosened to make more room for his heaving stomach.

"The President would like to see you," the man wheezed.

"Why, of course," Harpoon replied, surprised but curious. He reached for the jacket he had draped so neatly over a second chair.

"You won't need that," the man said, and Harpoon shrugged, left the coat, and followed him into the hallway. They walked, not quite briskly enough for the admiral, up the spiral staircase and into the presidential quarters. Inside, Condor and the Librarian sat talking intently. The blank-faced Secret Service agent lingered in the background, still cradling his Uzi.

Harpoon drew his shoulders back smartly and snapped a salute. "Sir!" he said.

"Admiral," the successor acknowledged. He did not invite him to sit down. "We got ourselves a situation here. Need a little more information on our naval forces. Colonel says we got nukes floatin' all over the place."

"That's true, sir. Most of the surface fleet is equipped with both nuclear and conventional weapons. Everything from surface-to-surface missiles to depth charges. You name it. Both fleets, ours and the Soviet."

"What they doin' out there now?"

Harpoon's brow furrowed. "Jockeying, I imagine. I wouldn't want to be in a surface ship now. They're just no match for the submarines."

"What kind of orders they under?"

"General orders. Respond if attacked. Take out any enemy vessels they can find. Especially submarines. They won't get many. I imagine they're trying to stay alive to see if the situation settles. If they've got any sense, they've scattered. We debated that a lot. Navy likes to cluster to protect the carriers. With nukes, that doesn't work very well."

"And we can't talk with them?"

"It would be disastrous, sir. They're sitting ducks. It would bring in the attack subs like sharks."

"Can they hear us?"

Harpoon was growing confused. "I can't imagine what we would want to tell them at the moment. They know what happened. Their cut of the pie, their operating space, is very small. Even the carriers."

"Dammit, Harpoon, just answer the question." Until now, the successor had not turned to look at the admiral. His head swiveled toward Harpoon, eyes blazing. "Can they hear us?"

Harpoon stared back, perplexed. What the devil was this man up to now? "Some vessels might pick up a satellite patch," he answered warily. "It would be very hit-and-miss. I doubt they would answer, or even try, unless the situation were one of extremis."

The successor turned away again. "Okay, enough of that," he said, quickly dismissing the issue. "Can your friend Alice"—his voice had a ferocious bite on the words, *your friend*—"issue orders to the submarines?"

Harpoon looked at the colonel, who smiled thinly. What was this all about? The colonel knew most of these answers. "Any command post, including the *Looking Glass,* could serve as a communications relay," Harpoon replied. "But the Air Force can't issue orders to the Navy. Ask for support, offer support, coordinate. But not order."

"Even if he counterfeited the codes, so it seemed to come from me?"

Counterfeited? Now Harpoon's heart was racing. Something very big had happened. "I don't see how he could do that, sir," the admiral flustered. But Harpoon did see how, with the bogus use of an authenticator card and access to other codes.

"Seems pretty good at doin' it with the Air Force," the successor said venomously.

"My God, sir, what's going on?"

The successor ignored him. "Navy's got its own command planes over the Atlantic and Pacific?"

"TACAMO," Harpoon responded in a whisper.

"They did get airborne?"

"Yes."

"But we haven't talked to them."

"No."

"Don't think the Russians shot 'em down?"

Harpoon's mind was spinning. "Only if they were suicidal. TACAMO's the best link we have to the submarines. The Soviets know that. They also know that even if the SIOP orders didn't get through, the subs had a preexisting strike plan. They sail with standard contingency orders. I can't imagine the Soviets would want the submarines out there without their communications umbilical, firing at will and whim for days, weeks or months after an attack."

The successor stared at him. "Now, Harpoon, I called you in for just one reason. You've been down in those submarines. You've been up in TACAMO planes. What would happen if the TACAMO planes got conflicting orders?"

The reality of what had occurred sizzled through Harpoon with an electric jolt. Alice had turned the B-52's. A surge of hope—and curiosity—filled him. "How did the Soviets respond?" he asked slowly.

"Answer me, Harpoon," Condor commanded.

Harpoon tilted forward in amazement. "You can't even be considering that now, sir."

"Answer me."

"Do you realize what the Soviets have done? Most of their bombers won't even get back. They don't have our range. They'll run out of fuel. The Soviets couldn't make their intentions clearer. Someone over there is talking *directly* to you."

The Librarian cut in abruptly. "And signaling an incredible strategic error," he said, his tone authoritative and confident. "It is now our entire submarine fleet versus their remaining ICBM's. It is the greatest shift in the strategic balance in the history of the cold war."

"Cold war!" Harpoon gasped.

"Alice, through his treason, has built us the perfect mousetrap," the Librarian said triumphantly, his eyes narrowing to slits behind his spectacles. "We now can win. Do you understand that word, admiral? Win."

The successor angrily brushed the colonel into silence. He also motioned to the Secret Service agent, who half-reluctantly turned his gray Uzi on the admiral. Harpoon stared, dazed, into the snub-nosed barrel a dozen feet distant. A remote thought tugged at his mind but did not penetrate the crazy clutter of his emotions.

"What would happen if TACAMO got conflicting orders?" the successor asked once more.

Harpoon clipped off his words as if he were automated. "If both commands had the proper codes, they would be confused.

They would suspect the Soviets had spoofed one set. They would not know which. They would allow the original orders to stand."

"That's all, admiral. You're dismissed."

"Please, sir . . ." Harpoon's words wavered in a feeble, pitiable sound.

"Dismissed."

Harpoon turned and shuffled slowly out. At the top of the staircase he gripped the railing for support, trying to force his mind to function properly. Random thoughts collided with random thoughts. He remembered his tour with the Joint Chiefs during the Watergate crisis, when the Defense Secretary had issued quiet instructions to report "unusual" orders from a presumably irrational President. He remembered reading years later that John Ehrlichman, seeking to end all his personal agony, and the national agony as well, had posed at the cockpit door of *Air Force One*, fighting down the urge to rush it and crash the plane. Harpoon took a single step toward his quarters. Then he pulled back and moved rapidly down the hallway toward the flight deck.

Kazaklis felt the final tiny lurch, the Buff seeming to waft airily free like a feather in the wind, the sensation more in his mind than in reality, as the third and last of the unarmed gravity bombs fell toward the Gulf of Alaska forty-four thousand feet below. One by one the yellow bomb-bay lights flashed off, the giant doors closing again. He began the procedure for scuttling the SRAM's, popping them harmlessly off the wings. He jettisoned one after another, the flow of the aircraft altering slightly as each disengaged and began its long downward tumble. On the sixth and last missile he hit the release mechanism a second time, then a third. "Dammit," he muttered. "Shake loose." For the next several minutes he rocked the aircraft, jiggering the release mechanism, finally trying unsuccessfully to fire the missile to get rid of it. Then he looked at Moreau and shrugged. She shrugged back. They trimmed the aircraft for the slight imbalance of one SRAM that refused to dislodge and flew on, the added weight and drag an irritant more than a problem on the long, uncertain journey ahead of them.

The awesomeness of the dawn's first light stunned Harpoon. He paused briefly, taking in the breathtaking if unnatural beauty of the panoramic scene through the now unscreened cockpit windows. Venus winked at him mockingly, the morning star hovering at eye level low over the horizon's haze. The sun peeped over the earth's curvature somewhere to the right, out of sight but casting endless tongues of fire-opal reds through strata of clouds both normal and not. He felt ever so fleetingly that man had improved on God, and then he knew that he had not. He slipped forward past the busy cockpit crew and toward the left-hand seat. The pilot turned, a black patch strapped diagonally across one eye, and smiled comfortably at him. "'Morning, admiral," he said. "You really should wear a patch, even in the daylight."

"I'm sorry, major," Harpoon said.

The pilot's single eye looked at him strangely, then darted over the admiral's shoulder. "What the hell?"

Harpoon began to lunge. He felt a strong hand clasp one of his biceps from behind. He felt the Uzi barrel jam painfully into his midvertebrae. The remote thought that eluded him in the presidential cabin broke decisively through the old barriers. He prayed with quick fervor: Please, God, let him pull the trigger and bring this plane down, too. He felt the Uzi withdraw, the grip tighten on his bicep, damp and jellylike flesh press in where the gun had been. He heard the pilot scream. "For God's sake, no!" A glint of turquoise flashed in the periphery of his vision. A belt tightened around his neck. Gray metal whipped at the side of his head. He heard himself gurgle and groan. He saw one last spectacular flash of color—the rockets' red glare of a nation he had guarded, the sun's bright spasms of a strange new day—and then Harpoon neither saw nor heard nor felt anything.

Twelve

1600 ZULU

The probing irritated Sedgwick greatly this time, for his dreams had become blissful voyages deeper and deeper into a more serene world. He lashed out without looking up and felt a swift, hurtful kick in the ribs. "Doan do that," a surly voice, upper-Fourteenth Street tough, growled at him. He rolled painfully onto his side in the thin mantle of snow and saw the cherub image retreating again. He also saw, through eyes still half-tracking on his dreams, three larger images looming around him. The light was much brighter now, although it hung in the dull burnt-orange color of smoke. In the background a soft, soulful wind whisked eerily through the canyon.

A different voice spoke. It was deep but rich, mellifluous and feminine. "My son says you has the President down in the hollow." The voice was time-worn and suspicious. Once again, Sedgwick forced his eyes to focus. Gradually the outline of an immense woman took form. Beside her stood two muscular and sullen teenage boys, perhaps sixteen and eighteen years old. "The Man," the younger said, his words skittering toward a high, hostile laugh. "Who else you got down there, mofu?" he gibed. "The First Muthah?" The teenager cackled and started to kick Sedgwick again. The older youth grabbed his brother and the woman spoke again in a quiet but confident matronly command. "Zachary, you

299

keep your filthy street mouth shut. You very close to your Lord this mornin'.'' The boy pulled back. The woman looked down at Sedgwick with large and unsmiling brown eyes.

Sedgwick reached toward her gratefully. "God bless you for coming, ma'am," he said feebly.

"Lord's not blessin' us for much of anything today, young man," the woman said with a weariness that had begun long before this day. "Now, what kind of foolery you been tellin' my son?"

Sedgwick drew a deep racking breath and began to explain a story so strange his words sounded unbelievable to himself. But the woman listened quietly and patiently, as if she had seen too much to discard anything. She watched him without expression as he concluded the story of a President lost and injured for many hours, Sedgwick not being certain of the time any longer. He pointed shakily through the light haze. A few hundred feet away, wrapped in splintered trees, the forward section of the Sikorsky helicopter lay mangled at the lip of the gully. The skin of *Nighthawk One* was broken jaggedly, creating a jigsaw puzzle of the words "UNITED STATES OF AMERICA." The woman gazed only briefly at the wreckage. Then she firmly directed the two older boys, who seemed far more intent on salvaging the helicopter, down into the ravine.

Sedgwick sagged back in relief, slipping toward his dreams again. He shook himself, drawing deep on his will, and forced himself to remain alert. "Where are we?" he asked.

"Ya'all didn't get far, young man," the woman replied. "Fell down in Rocky Gorge."

Sedgwick looked befuddled.

"The reservoir. The President fell down in the reservoir. Lucky it's winter. Ya'all mighta drowned." Sedgwick still looked befuddled. "Doan know your way around much, do you? Skaggsville's over the gorge. Ednor's a mite closer. Brown's Corner, too." Sedgwick shook his head despairingly. He had never heard of any of these places. "Lordy me, young man, you really doan know your way around. We's kind o' out in the toolies here. But Baltimore's just over yonder. Washington's only a frog-hop away, maybe a dozen miles." She wagged her head sadly. "Not that ya's goin' there."

Sedgwick struggled, fighting the mind fog for some rough fix on where they were. "Fort Meade," he said suddenly, remembering that the Army post, headquarters of the National Security

Agency, was somewhere near the Baltimore-Washington Parkway.

"Yessir, yessir, Fort Meade's over the gorge too." The woman wagged her head again. "Was. They had a ba-a-ad Fourth of July, young man."

"Ma'am," Sedgwick began to plead, "the President must get to a military base, with radios and a hospital. I can't exaggerate how important it is."

The huge black woman looked down at Sedgwick and smiled for the first time. "Doan imagine you can exaggerate anything today, mister. Jus' can't see how we's goin' to do it. Doan look like you're gonna walk far." She paused. "A world full of trouble out there, too," she added with great melancholy.

Sedgwick slumped back to the ground, the memory of the wailing and the shooting and the godawful race across the White House lawn filling his mind. "Riots," he said dully.

"O-h-h-h, no, no," the woman's mournful voice continued. "Time for that's gone. Can't you hear it, young man?"

Sedgwick listened. He heard only the soulful wind, ebbing in a low haunt as it passed through the naked stands of trees, then flowing in a distant shriek as it rushed down the gorge. It was a horrible wind, and his flesh crawled as the woman's silence let its sound immerse him. He stared at her in confusion.

"People," she said in a hush. "That's the sound of people, young man."

Sedgwick felt very nauseated.

"Oh, they did their riotin', the big, fancy cars racin' at us one way from Baltimore, the other way from Washington, crashin' inta people, crashin' inta houses, crashin' inta each other till there was no room t' crash no more. Then they was shootin' and when they got tired o' shootin' they jus' started walkin'. Walkin' and moanin', moanin' and walkin'." She looked at him curiously. "Your man start it?"

Sedgwick buried his head in the ground. "No, ma'am," he whispered.

"Don't make no never-mind. Comin' anyway. Preacher tol' us. Teevee tol' us. Plain sense tol' us."

Sedgwick heard thrashing behind him and saw the cherub boy dart away. Then he watched the two muscular teenagers approaching through the woods, carrying a limp form. Sedgwick's heart sank. The President, still wrapped in the blankets like a mummy, looked quite dead. The teenagers placed him carefully on the ground and the woman hovered over him. "So that's the Man," she said solemnly. "Doan look so mean now. Doan look so good, either, do he?" She poked at the quiet form. "Alive. Always knew he was a tough cuss." She beckoned to her sons. "You boys gonna carry these men over to the hospital at Olney."

Sedgwick's mind fuzzed on him again. "Olney?" he muttered.

"Hospital there. Leastways, there was yesterday. It's four, five miles. Best we can do."

Sedgwick reached up toward her, grasping at a worn woolen coat. "FEMA," he said desperately. In his muddle, he couldn't think of anything else to say. "Out past Muncaster Road." He pulled hard at her coat. "FEMA," he repeated weakly. "Please understand."

She took his hand and released it from her coat. "I's not stupid, young man," she reproached him. "I teach m' boys. I read the papers. You talkin' 'bout civil defense." She stopped, the disdain spreading across her face. "They's been real helpful folk. Yessir, real helpful." Sedgwick began to whimper in pain. "Calm down, young man. Everybody in these parts knows the place. Out past the feed store. The Man ever wakes up, you tell him he can't keep a place secret if'n they's always poppin' radio aerials up 'n down out of cee-ment holes."

Sedgwick faded then, somewhere in the realm between consciousness and unconsciousness. He seemed asleep, but his dream-visions were far less blissful. The soulful winds turned woeful and he saw shadows of people walking, empty-faced and hunched, down country roads strewn with smashed cars and rubble. The wailing followed him through suburban yards deep in shattered glass and decapitated azaleas. It trailed him across farmers' fields where cow eyes watched him dolefully, accusingly, from the tangled debris of crumpled barns. Then his visions went totally black.

The flight south was a dreadful drone. The B-52 cruised economically but uneventfully at just over forty thousand feet in a slightly southwesterly drift edging them slowly west of the 150th meridian. Kazaklis had cut off all radios except the intercom, and it was rarely used. For the most part, except for the engine noise, the plane had become deathly silent, its occupants keeping their thoughts to themselves. The make-work chores were unnecessary and undone. It was a bus ride.

Kazaklis and Moreau had had no further discussions about a final destination, but they both knew they were not going to her fantasy island. They were moving west of Tahiti, and while they could cut back later, it was not the place for them. Gauguin's velvet had turned to acrylic long ago. If civilization were busily killing itself off, as they assumed it was, they had no desire to land among overweight, hysterical tourists whose last dream had been to bring home a silicone-covered conch shell. Nor did Kazaklis want to land among provincial French gendarmes casting about for the guilty ones in the destruction of the far-off republic which, even to French provincials, was the world. He had no wish to spend whatever time he had left in a stinking tropical bastille.

Kazaklis had few illusions. In the vast expanse of the Pacific their options were mostly paradises lost or paradises never there—bleak little atolls on which a living might be scrounged while they waited for God knew what. Radiation, solar or manmade. A half-crazed exodus of survivors from a totally wrecked world. Naval patrols from a half-wrecked and angry world. Nothingness. . . .

If they had options. The Air Force had not been considerate enough to provide accurate charts for the turncoat run. They had no navigators. They were heading into a blue desert as intimidating and untracked as the Sahara. In the tedium of the flight south, the pilot's mind wandered into a thousand thoughts. But one occurred—a faint memory of a history lesson about Magellan sailing ten thousand miles through the atolls and islands of the mid-Pacific without spotting a rock until he stumbled onto Guam far on the other side.

Kazaklis glanced over his shoulder into the murk behind him. Halupalai had not moved in hours, his back stooped as if he had aged a year for every hour since they left Fairchild. The gunner had not fled into the destructive schizophrenia that had consumed Tyler. Nor did he seem lost in the utterly morose and suicidal inwardness that had killed Radnor. He had stopped the guilt-ridden babbling. He answered questions rationally and sensibly. But the answers returned without life. Kazaklis worried about him. The pilot turned back toward the flight panel and looked at his watch. It read 1555 Zulu—more than three hours since they had passed over Kodiak and less than an hour to the rendezvous with Halupalai's islands. Moreau's pensive voice interrupted the pilot's thoughts.

"Sunrise," she said.

The single wistful word did not connect and he turned slowly toward her. Moreau stared straight into the flash curtains, still drawn against the night, still drawn against the chance of a blinding explosion.

"It's almost time for sunrise." Her voice filled with quiet awe, as if she had made a remarkable discovery. Her hand reached childlike toward the curtain and tugged at a dirty corner. Through the peephole, stars still twinkled enticingly at them. But the stars no longer shone out of inky blackness. Their background carpet had turned to a deep, regal purple. Local time in their ocean wilderness was about six A.M. In a few minutes the sun would pop suddenly out of the subtropical sea. Moreau slowly let the curtain return to its place and sat back in her seat.

The two of them were silent for several moments, entranced by the same thought. Destiny had granted them a night flight—a 10 P.M. departure from Spokane, a journey through the winter Arctic darkness over a slowly spinning earth that turned man's clocks toward an identical 10 P.M. appointment at a faroff city. There, they were to ignite a man-made sun they would not see and make a final nocturnal run toward oblivion long before their own life-star rose again. They had changed that destiny, if only in the most fleeting way. They sat in respectful silence now, uncertain how to accept the simple blessing of a sunrise. Kazaklis spoke first.

"Just thinking about it stops you in your tracks, doesn't it?" he said quietly.

Moreau turned and looked at this man beside whom she had flown for so many months and seen only in one dimension, just as she had acted out her own life in only one dimension. "I don't know if I want to see it, Kazaklis," she said. "It's as if it might promise me too much." Kazaklis thought she sounded embarrassed.

"It promises you another day, Moreau. No more. No less. Be glad it's there. Be glad the sea's there. Be glad something's there we couldn't screw up." His voice choked, almost imperceptibly. He paused, thinking of his father, thinking of the love-hate, thinking of the brute innocence and the raw wisdom, both of which he had rejected, but both of which had left their indelible mark. "I'm glad. I'm glad Halupalai's there." He paused again, not looking at her. He seemed far away. "I'm glad you're there," he said very quietly. "Here," he added in a whisper.

Moreau felt the tears forming again. She fought against them and lost. Beneath the sleeves of her flight jacket the hair tingled on her arms, bristling against fireproofed fiber. She was shaking. She reached out, unthinking at first, and touched his arm. Then she clenched it. Then she clambered suddenly, awkwardly, half out of her steel seat, one leg tangling in the steering column, the other snarling itself in the mesh of the eight white engine throttles between them, her arms stretching past Master Caution lights and Bombs Released lights. She wrapped both arms around him, tucking a white helmet beneath a white helmet, and held him tightly. He fumbled briefly, shaking, too, and then he held her. For a moment—the quickest flutter of time not measured in Zulu—they embraced and the solitary shuddering of the one absorbed the lonely shuddering of the other till neither shuddered.

Then, as abruptly as it had begun, Moreau withdrew. She stared, frightfully embarrassed, into the grungy curtains. Numbly she took the wheel and pressed the raw trembling out of the bomber as they had pressed the trembling out of each other.

"I'm sorry," she murmured.

"Why?" he asked.

The question was put with such utter simplicity it required no answer. The bomber droned south, both of them staring into the dirty curtains. Minutes passed before Moreau asked, "Do you think we'll see another sunrise?"

"I don't know, Moreau," Kazaklis replied. "I think we've both missed too many sunrises—too many days—already." Together they reached forward to draw back the curtains.

Neither of them spoke. The scene was flawless—as if man had never touched it. On Moreau's side of the aircraft the sky, stretching west toward Asia, remained the deeply regal purple of their earlier glimpse, stars still twinkling. But as their eyes passed left, toward the east and home, the sky and the stars faded into violet and then soft mauve and then faint blue. Slightly above them, wisping freely at perhaps forty-five thousand feet, a few delicate strands of cirrus clouds caught the first fiery hints of day. Below them the ocean spread endlessly in surreal ripples. After a moment, to the far left of Kazaklis, the orange arc of the sun peeped out of the sea, then emerged rapidly. It was, without question, the most beautiful sight they had ever seen, the searing rays dashing along the horizon, the sun springing back into their world.

"Hey, Halupalai," Kazaklis radioed into the back of the compartment. "You have to come up and see this, buddy." Halupalai's voice returned evenly. "No, thanks, commander. I'll wait." The pilot's heart sank.

Kazaklis watched a moment longer, until the sun sat like a great orange egg on the edge of the earth, the planet's atmosphere seeming to hold it back briefly, compressing the orb into an ellipse. Then it burst free, full and round. Kazaklis turned and pulled the red filter from his viewing screen, replacing it with green for daylight flying. They would fly with the windows exposed now. They needed to see. He carefully stripped the medical tape and his one-fingered glove from his old filter and placed it on the new. He edged the plane slightly right, keeping it in its southwesterly drift. Moreau watched and then replaced her filter, too. She chuckled lightly, although no humor was attached to it. "Green filters," she said. Kazaklis looked at her questioningly. "The green screen reminded me of you and your silly computer game."

Kazaklis grinned. "Space Invaders. I felt like killing you in the alert room."

"Why'd you take it so seriously?"

Kazaklis shrugged. "Passed the time."

"It was more than that."

"Yeah, it was. It was a lot like life. Like what we're doing. I wanted to beat it."

"But you couldn't."

"No." Kazaklis paused thoughtfully. "That was the hook. You could never beat it." He paused again briefly. "You said it. The better you got, the better it got. So you just kept feedin' it quarters. Funny, I think I had that damn computer game's secrets figured out better than the Jap who programmed it. I got to the point where I lost only to random malfunctions. They were programmed into it, too."

"Programmed malfunctions?"

"Yeah. The shits, huh? How do you beat programmed random malfunctions?"

Moreau stared out the window into the false peace of the Pacific. "You think that's what we're in now?" she asked quietly.

"Sorry?" Kazaklis missed the subtle shift in direction.

"You think the world's in a programmed malfunction?"

Kazaklis stared at her but said nothing. He understood. He had no answer.

"You learned everything about that game except the ultimate secret, Kazaklis," Moreau said without rancor. "You never discovered the secret of the narcotic."

Again Kazaklis said nothing. But he had sensed that secret, too.

"You just keep shoving money into it, getting better and better, discovering new secrets, developing new strategies, escalating your ability, escalating your mind's technology." Moreau paused. Her voice grew still more pensive. "Every time you escalate, the other side escalates. You advance. The adversary advances." She slipped almost unnoticeably into a language of equal-versus-equal, man-versus-man. "You got better. He got better. You cracked one secret. He sprang another. You slugged in money. He responded. But the escalation never stopped. You could never win, Kazaklis, no matter how good you got. That was the secret. The only way to win was to stop."

"And if you didn't stop, the malfunction got you." Now Kazaklis sounded wistful. "Pretty smart little college girl, aren't you?"

Moreau felt tears forming again. "Not that smart," she said. "My father explained it to me. It took him a lifetime to understand the narcotic." She sniffled and tried to hide it. Kazaklis reached out and squeezed her elbow in support. "He must have been quite a guy," Kazaklis soothed. "You loved him very much, didn't you?"

Moreau spun toward him, shuddering, the past tense jarring her sensibilities. Kazaklis understood instantly. "I'm sorry, Moreau," he said quickly. "I didn't mean it that way. There's a good chance he made it."

"Not a good chance," she said flatly, pulling herself back together. "A chance. If he was home, he made it through the bombing. Now the fallout's coming." She paused, but the tears were gone and the strength back. "He lectured a lot at the Academy. If he was there . . ." She thought of Christmas again. "I think he was ready." She looked at Kazaklis. She knew so little about him. "Your family?" she asked.

Kazaklis glanced at his watch, seeing it was eight A.M. along the Coos. "My pa," he said. "Mean old bastard. Tough as the Oregon woods. The old fart will fight it all the way." The words were harsh but the voice soft and full of wonderment. Moreau had never heard Kazaklis speak quite that way.

"You also love him deeply," she said.

A perplexed expression spread across his face. "Love him?" he asked vacantly. "My God, I guess I never thought I did. The old bastard." He turned away and gazed thoughtfully into the eternity of the ocean. "I don't suppose the fallout's made it to Coos Bay yet." He paused. "Another day. Two maybe."

"What will he do?" Moreau asked softly.

Kazaklis turned back toward her with an ear-to-ear grin, no rascality in it at all, only pure pleasure. "If anybody will make it, Pa will make it," he said with certainty. "The old coot wouldn't mind goin' in a flood or a forest fire. Anything natural. But he'll fight this shit like he'd fight the devil himself. Shoot a deer, find a cave, send out for all the whores in Coos Bay, and start himself a new master race."

Moreau could not prevent herself from laughing, Kazaklis having presented the image of his father with such bizarre exuberance. "A master race?" she sputtered through her laughter.

"Sure!" Kazaklis exuded, and he was laughing harder than Moreau now. "Just look at me!"

The two of them broke down into hysterical laughter, venting all the guilt of *Elsies* and Klickitats and duties and fathers left behind; venting all the fears and sorrows, the griefs and uncertainties, too. In the back of the cabin, Halupalai heard the strange sounds over the roar of the engine. He turned to see them convulsed in mutual laughter. He nodded appreciatively. He liked that. It was a good sign. Going home was, too, and they were getting close now.

Long after the two injured men had been hoisted across the teenagers' muscular backs, and long after the perilous trek toward Olney had begun, Sedgwick emerged from his mind's blackness. He had no idea how much time had transpired. The scene made no more sense to him than the crazy half-dreams of the ghostly trip across the countryside. He awoke to see the large black woman present herself regally to a man in a hooded white suit. She announced, quite authoritatively, "We has brought you the President of the United States."

A hollow and tinny voice responded from inside the white

hood. "Sure thing, lady," it said, "and the Pope's knocking at the back door."

Kazaklis and Moreau had stopped laughing and were checking vectors. Halupalai's islands lay forty-five minutes away.

Moreau's mind had trouble focusing on the work. It raced with a dozen questions about the dead world they were about to pass over, still more about the unknown world that lay beyond. "I wish I had gotten to know you better," she said suddenly. Kazaklis looked up from his plotting, surprised. "We don't even know each other," she continued. "None of us. Do you think we can survive, locked together in some *New Yorker* cartoon of a desert island?" Kazaklis turned away. His voice went very quiet. "We can't do any worse than the four billion people locked together on that big island beneath us. I like our odds better."

She shook her head slowly. It was not a very optimistic reading. "Percentage baseball, huh?" she asked forlornly.

"To hell with percentage baseball," Kazaklis said without emotion. "At some point, Moreau, you have to get out of Yankee Stadium and back to the sandlots."

"Yes," Moreau said. She gazed for a moment into the fluttering yellow gauges of the flight panel and the life she had chosen. "The roar of the madding crowd gets hard on the ears," she said wistfully. "After a while that's all you hear and you can't understand the person next to you." Kazaklis turned back toward her. "I still wish I had taken the time to know you better," she said. He looked at her a moment longer. Then he said, "Check the vectors, will you?"

Moreau methodically returned to work, cross-checking their course. After a moment she looked up and asked, "We're really going to make the overflight?"

"Yes," he replied tersely. But it was clear he was worried too. "Moreau, take a look out there." He gestured disconsolately at the spectacularly clean and serene panorama that immersed them. "The world doesn't look that way anymore. We have to see the world once."

She nodded in understanding. But she still asked, "And Halupalai, too?"

Kazaklis drew bleakly inside himself, not answering. Halupalai's islands had controlled this entire ocean. They had been the repository for more of the gray instruments of control than any other place in the country whose flag *Polar Bear One* flew. They had contained submarine pens and air bases for rapid dispersal of the weapons throughout their realm. They had contained the headquarters of CINCPAC and the Pacific fleet, satellite-tracking stations and elaborate communications bases to tie the control together. In Halupalai's paradise, grass-skirt hula dancers had fluttered talking hands at hidden megatons. No war would be fought without taking out Hawaii.

"Maybe Tyler was right," he said. "This is all a bad dream. A great hoax. A test we failed." He touched his symbolic glove and paused. "It's the height of the tourist season, Moreau. The gonzos will be cruising the curls off Waikiki and the flower shirts will be guzzling maitais at the Ilikei." His voice trailed off.

"I understand, Kazaklis," she said.

"I had a buddy once . . ." Kazaklis grew distant. "Did grunt duty in Vietnam. Halfway through, they pulled him out of the mud and the crud and the blood, stuffed him aboard Pan American, and twelve hours later they dropped him in paradise. Six days of rest and recreation on Waikiki. He chased poon and watched the fat flower shirts swillin' martinis like there was no mud and crud and body bags anywhere. For the flower shirts, there wasn't. Then the Army collared him and took him back. Jesus." Kazaklis grunted. "Hell to heaven. Heaven to hell. All he did was duck after that. Said Hawaii was the reason we lost the war. Half the Army was waitin' for R and R and duckin'. The other half was rememberin' and duckin'." He grunted again and stopped.

Moreau kept her gaze trained on him.

"How the hell do I know, Moreau?" he asked, finally answering the question about Halupalai's needs. "I just know we can't run forever from something we haven't seen."

She stretched her arm out toward him again. "I'll go back and talk to him before we make the approach," he said. Then he went silent again, staring out the left-hand window at a sun ballooning upward into a perfect sky.

IV

JERICHO'S WALLS

I am not proud of the part I've played in it. . . . I think we will probably destroy ourselves, so what difference does it make?

—Admiral Hyman Rickover, father of the nuclear submarine

Thirteen

1700 ZULU

The fog of war blurs all human conflicts. It hangs in a heavy mist, clouding men's minds and warping their judgments. It is a strange phenomenon, causing some men to vacillate disastrously, others to move with an equally disastrous certitude. It instantly transforms enemies into beasts and sadly human errors into methodically inhuman calculations. In a moment of desolate passion an infantryman, unable to cope with the horror surrounding him, mindlessly performs the machine-gun stitching of women and children. The infantryman's distant leaders view the mysteriously ruthless response of husbands and fathers and, through the fog of war, see the new act as that of a barbaric enemy requiring swift retribution. So goes it. And goes it.

At 1600 Zulu on this winter day, as the pilots of *Polar Bear One* watched the sun pop out of the deceptively undisturbed expanse of the Pacific, the fog of war hung heavy indeed over the rest of the battlefield. Just five hours remained before the American submarines would rise, attempt to penetrate the fog, and almost certainly deliver the penultimate retribution for lost wives and children. A few moments later the Soviet ICBM reserves would respond in kind. Remaining throughout the world, of course, would be thousands of additional weapons, the arsenals were so large and well dispersed. These weapons would be expended

313

without any semblance of even semicivilized restraint over the
next days, weeks, months. Their use would be somewhat redun-
dant.

Among the elite few who had even a lottery player's chance of
altering the events, the miscalculation, and confusion were almost
total. They were making assumptions that were logical but wrong.
They were treating truths as falsehoods and falsehoods as truths,
and acting on both. In fact, in all the beleaguered world, not a
single person had the access or the wisdom to understand the
swirl of events engulfing them.

Nor did the events of the last several hours, since the bombers
had turned, help lift the fog. In the Soviet Union two more cities
had been destroyed. Pushkin, a medium-sized town just outside
Leningrad, had been leveled by an American submarine cornered
in the North Sea. Nadhodka, a Siberian port city, had been hit by
a trapped outrider cruising beneath the Sea of Japan. In the
United States the Raleigh-Durham area of North Carolina had
been sprayed randomly, like Baton Rouge, by a Soviet submarine
off the Outer Banks. All three attackers had been losing deadly
chases by enemy hunter subs. They had unloaded on available
targets, as their orders dictated. So goes it.

Limited communications gradually were returning. But as
often as not, the sketchy information caused as many problems as
it solved, creating as much fog as it dispelled. Nor did it help that
in Cherepovets the Soviet Premier now had gone more than
thirty-six hours without sleep. Nor did it help that in Olney two
frightened but dedicated young nurses, steeped in the sister-
hood's time-honored tradition of giving solace and relieving pain,
were adding their own brand of fog to the intravenous solution
they had begun feeding through the forearm of a hurting and
semiconscious American President. Nor did it help that the American government appeared to have two Presidents and that only
one man—a bureaucratic second-level civil-defense director—
held that information.

In the massive underground labyrinth south of Cherepovets,
the Soviet Premier popped another amphetamine. He had been
taking the uppers most of the day to keep himself alert. He was
taking an occasional vodka as well, to settle his racking anxiety. He
glanced quickly about the sterile room to see if anyone had observed him taking the pill. Already today he had quelled the inev-

itable coup attempt, employing methods far more sweeping than those used in the cockpit of the *E-4*. Still, his political control was tenuous, at best. The loyalist advisers and military officers with him in the multilevel bunker were edgy and doubtful, even about him. Little wonder, he grumped. His grand plan—he had been completely honest with the American President—had lurched nightmarishly out of control. Had he been a fool to think it would not? But why? Why, after the Americans had reacted so rationally to an attack on their own territory, had they acted so irrationally to such a minor event in China? Were the Americans that protective of the fuck-their-mother Chinese? The little yellow devils had obliterated fifteen of his Red Army divisions! So the rebellious commanding general of the Rocket Forces had struck back at Peking and Wuhañ. Against his orders. And starting the coup. Also starting, he presumed, and he shook his head in despair at the thought of it, the spasm launches of ICBM's bursting out of the American prairies. Then the rebellious general's response out of the steppes. Then the prairies again. Then the steppes again. He groaned, swallowing hard to get the amphetamine all the way down. Could he control anything now? Anyone? He glanced about the room. There were only three other persons here—a radio operator, a decrypter, and the new commanding general of the Rocket Forces, whom the Premier had appointed only hours ago after dealing directly—and finally—with the man's predecessor. All seemed preoccupied except the general.

The Premier moved his eyes to a clock—1600 hours, Greenwich mean time, ten hours after he had begun this lunacy. How much longer could he hold it together? He had one newly rebellious ICBM wing commander in control of the isolated Zhangiztobe field in the south-central deserts. The man's wife and children had been in Pushkin. The Premier shook his head wearily, fought to stifle a yawn, and felt a powerful hand land lightly on his shoulder.

"Comrade," the general said, "why don't you get some sleep? We will awaken you."

"Sleep," the Premier replied. "Sleep is for the innocent, comrade general."

The general's broad brow knitted in concern.

"Figure of speech." The Premier smiled without conviction. "And the Rocket Forces? No change?"

The general shrugged. "They will go, if necessary." He paused.

"They will be somewhat more difficult to stop." The general probed the Premier's face for hidden messages. "If necessary," the general added.

"Zhangiztobe?" the Premier asked bleakly.

The general shrugged again. "Even getting through to them is difficult, Comrade Premier. And threats have little effect to-night."

The Premier sighed in acknowledgment, flicking his fingers to dismiss his military commander. He was having extraordinary difficulty communicating with the surviving Rocket Forces. He was having extraordinary difficulty communicating with anyone. Why couldn't he get through to the Americans? He looked at the arched back of his radio operator and cursed silently.

The Premier brushed the wetness from his forehead and tried to review what he knew. The American President was dead, his command plane not having made it out of Andrews. The death was most unfortunate and unintended. He felt no love for his old antagonist and still blamed him, rightly or wrongly being irrele-vant now, for pushing them both into this disaster. Still, the Pre-mier was a practical man. He had not wanted to deal—if any dealing could be done—with a leaderless country out of political control. Nor had he wanted to deal with an amateurish successor drawn out of the insignificant ranks of the American Congress or the President's Cabinet. But a successor was in charge. The sketchy information intercepted from conversations between the *E-4* and the *Looking Glass* was incomplete and incomprehensible. Still, orders of some kind were moving back and forth. And that confirmed it.

So. He was dealing with a faceless man. He had no clue as to his identity or his background. But, to his surprise, the Premier had developed a tremendous respect for the man already. It had been beyond reasonable hope to find such a sophisticated man drawn out of the lower reaches of either of their governments. But the chess moves with the bombers! Masterful! Turn one bomber, wait for a response, and then turn the others! Ingenious! The man had reinvented the carrier pigeon. It had bought them some time. The Premier slumped in his seat. Perhaps not enough, he thought bleakly. Pushkin. Nadhodka. He knew the system. He knew the orders to take his cities had not come from the *E-4*, just as the decision to hit Baton Rouge had not come from Cherepovets.

It further amazed the Premier that the presidential successor had shown such wisdom after that bit of insanity. The Premier had issued orders to have the idiot submarine commander shot if he ever made it back to the motherland, which was doubtful. The American submarine commander had shown far greater wisdom as he prepared to die in the North Sea. Had he unloaded his missiles on Leningrad instead, there would have been no controlling the people in this bunker, loyalist or not. The Premier knew people. He knew that neither side could tolerate many more Pushkins or Baton Rouges. His hands were shaking. He reached for another small vodka to settle his nerves. The American had sent him a sign of good intentions. Still, even with the best intentions, the Premier knew the system he once thought he controlled was hanging on by a most slender and fraying thread. He was certain the new President had the same problem—especially with the submarines. Those infernal American submarines. He absolutely had to talk with the man.

The Premier swirled down the vodka. He lifted himself ponderously and moved toward the radio operator. He harangued the man unmercifully—*Durak!* Fool!—and ordered him to bull his way through the mangled atmosphere to the American *E-4.* The technician frantically went through the motions again, but with no success. The only place in America from which he heard regular signals—signals that were neither directed at them nor understandable—emerged from the location in Maryland that the KGB had identified as an obscure civil-defense bunker. The Premier, unable to control himself, thumped his fist down angrily. He was not interested in chatter among low-ranking American bureaucrats. He needed to talk only with the President.

"Large hematoma on the right thigh . . . abrasions, contusions. Whole area's edematous."

"Ummmm. Legs crushed. Do we have any ice around here?"

"Good God, his eyes are gone. Severe retinal burn."

"Nothing we can do about that. Just make him comfortable. Get the ice, huh? Let's get his legs splinted."

The President moaned unintelligibly.

"Just relax, Mr. President. You'll feel better in a minute. Just relax, sir."

"Shocky."

"Little wonder at that. What's with the I.V.?"

"Normal stuff. L.R. Lactated ringers. Two milligrams of morphine."

"Yeah. How long ago was that?"

"Let's see. Ummmm . . . twenty-five minutes."

"Let's give the poor man two more milligrams. Damn, I wish we had a doctor here."

"Well, we don't. Tough bugger, isn't he?"

"Tough, but he's no youngster. And he's hurting, sweetie. Two more milligrams of morphine."

"Got it right here. They stocked this place with enough to keep every junkie in Washington going for a year."

The President groaned again and tried to say something.

"Just relax, sir. You're doing fine. You'll feel better in a minute."

Sedgwick already was feeling better—much, much better. He floated rapturously, not a care in the world, two angels in white hovering over him and his friend. Life was splendid and the nurses' words washed serenely over him. The room was white and bright and warm. His friend lay next to him. His friend . . .

The young naval officer sat bolt upright in his bed, the pain from his legs searing through his serenity. He ripped at the intravenous tubing attached to his arm, causing one of the nurses to rush at him.

"No morphine!" he screamed, lashing out at the nurse.

"Hey, hey, hey," the nurse soothed. "Calm down. You'll be okay, soldier."

"Sailor," he corrected her, more calmly, the drug taking him again.

The nurse chuckled softly. "Okay, sailor boy, take it easy."

"Two aspirin and call me in the morning," the President mumbled woozily.

The nurse laughed. Sedgwick floated back into his angelic world.

Off to the side, in the small white hospital ward buried near Olney, the civil-defense director watched the scene without interrupting. He had trouble absorbing what suddenly had happened in his obscure little niche in the bunker world. He had almost refused the President entry, the scene outside had been so unlikely. A man arriving battered and bruised, dressed only in a tattered bathrobe and pajamas, wrapped in blankets, carried on the back of a street tough he could barely understand. Unconscious and with no identification. It was only the military aide's NSA card, with the little coded dot that gave him admission anywhere, that finally convinced him.

Earlier, the bureaucrat had seen the instructions from the computerized Presidential Successor Locator sending the *E-4* after the Secretary of the Interior. Now, for the first time, it occurred to him that the United States actually might have two Presidents. It also occurred to him that he was the only person in the world who was aware of that awkward possibility. However, he didn't have the vaguest notion what to do with the information. There was no one to tell—not even this President, who was semiconscious and loopy on the painkilling morphine. It did not occur to him that it might be unwise to allow the nurses to administer the morphine.

Nearby, the Olney radio operator was growing increasingly frustrated, downright angry at times, with his superior's casual indifference to the radio traffic he now was receiving. Dammit, they had the President of the United States back there, even if the poor bastard was in no shape to talk to anyone.

Transmissions were moving between NATO countries, although he couldn't hold them for reasons that were beyond his understanding. The radio traffic between the *Looking Glass* and the *E-4* had fallen off to rare, brief messages and he still had not been able to get a response from them. But it was the stuff out of the Soviet Union that fascinated him. Maybe the source was a CIA spy, but he certainly had access to good equipment. He was trying everything under the sun—very high frequency, ultra high frequency, very low frequency. It all seemed directed at the Midwest, perhaps at the command planes. And now the spook had tapped into a Molniya II satellite. The radio operator shook his head on that one. Molniya II was the Soviets' hot-line link. The hot line was deader than a doornail. He would have sworn that Molniya, a satellite with a perigee of only three hundred miles, was dead by now, too. But it wasn't. The guy was one smart spook—and desperate, too, using the Soviets' own satellites.

On his own, without informing his uninterested boss, the radio operator tapped out a brief response. "This is Pit Stop Two," the low-frequency telegraph message said. "Do you read?"

In another of the world's modern mole holes, beneath Cherepovets, the harassed Soviet communications operator felt a brief moment of extraordinary excitement and relief. Then he sagged in despair again. The American message, still encoded, had come from the insignificant bunker in Maryland. He angrily kicked at his radio. *Prokliatia mashina!* Damned machine! He despondently handed the message to the equally harassed cryptographer. The cryptographer, perspiring so steadily he had begun taking salt tablets, worked hurriedly over the short message. He turned wearily toward his colleague and arched his bushy eyebrows. *Pit Stop Two?* But they moved the message up channels, knowing they would feel the Premier's wrath whether they moved the message or whether they didn't.

"Halupalai?"
In the lonely seat in the back of *Polar Bear One*'s upper compartment, the big gunner turned slowly, his eyes straining in the redness for a look at Kazaklis. Halupalai smiled and the pilot smiled back. "We're almost there, aren't we, commander?" he asked.
"Almost there, pal," Kazaklis replied. The two stared at each other, Kazaklis probing for anything in his friend's face that would flash a warning that the risk was too great. He saw nothing. "We've been worried about you, old buddy," Kazaklis said.
"I know, commander. I listened to part of it. Sorry."
Kazaklis shrugged at the admission of the eavesdropping. "Should we be worried, pal?"
"No, commander." His voice was calm and certain.
"It's going to be awfully beat up, Halupalai. Like nothing we ever saw before."
"Honolulu wasn't my home. Not even on my island. Please don't worry, commander."
The pilot continued staring into the Hawaiian's tired but open face. "Kauai," Kazaklis acknowledged, and Halupalai's face brightened like a birthday child's.
"We take one quick look-see?" Halupalai asked expectantly, his voice reverting to the simple, chanting tones of the islands. "It's the charmer, boss."
Kazaklis tightened. "No," he said flatly.
"Won't be beat up like Honolulu," Halupalai pleaded. "No way will it."
Kazaklis felt an alarm run quickly through him. "No," he repeated, with a bite this time. But Halupalai did not protest further.
"Okay, commander," he said. "You're the boss-man." The smile faded slightly and the sad brown eyes held on Kazaklis. "You

didn't need to take my alert bag, commander," Halupalai said reproachfully. "I wouldn't hurt either of you."

"We know that, pal. We aren't worried about us," Kazaklis looked at him closely. "We're worried about you."

Halupalai smiled again. "Thanks," he said, and he meant it. No one had said that to him for a long while. "Don't you worry about me. I'm okay." His smile grew wider and he gave Kazaklis a friendly fist jab in the ribs. "Now get your ass back up front, Kazaklis," he said, "and do what you have to do."

Kazaklis reluctantly turned back toward the cockpit. The worry still nagged at him faintly, but Halupalai seemed nothing like the two crazies he had dealt with earlier. And, about that, the pilot's perception was accurate. Halupalai was neither violent nor spooked. He just wanted to go home.

The *Looking Glass* flew almost aimlessly now, no bombers and no missiles left to command. Alice and Sam talked to each other vacantly, each having fought his own private war and each arriving independently at the same outcome. But they had developed a deep sense of mutual embarrassment, as if the other's eyes were a mirror reflecting a man who had violated the most elemental rule of the code by which he had lived his life.

After abandoning all his West Point training by openly defying his Commander-in-Chief and taking it onto himself to turn the bombers, Alice made a few halfhearted attempts to call the *E-4* and reason with the successor. Each time, the reply returned tersely: "You're in deep shit, Alice." Then the phone clicked off. He had searched his soul desperately for a feasible way to prevent the submarine launchings but could find none. His only hope was Harpoon, but their last conversation had been hours ago and nearly incomprehensible. Almost four excruciatingly long hours after his decision, Alice was quietly despondent, as was Sam, who had gone along with the mutiny.

Aboard the now impotent SAC command plane, only two other members of the crew of twenty spoke to Alice unless he spoke first. Smitty, the pilot, understood the decision in some deeply forlorn way. He occasionally tried to make small talk. And the communications officer reported to him regularly, but she averted her eyes as she spoke.

Communications were improving methodically but slowly. They had intercepted some clear messages moving within Eu-

rope, including some between NATO facilities. Alice was not sur-
prised. Europe had received minimal physical destruction and
that made the electromagnetic damage from the high-altitude
EMP explosions somewhat easier to repair. The Soviets had used
EMP in detonations high over the NATO nations, just as the
United States had used it over the Warsaw Pact countries.

What did confuse the general was the nature of the occasional
direct communication they now were able to establish with a few
NATO bases. The conversations were as abrupt as those with
Condor. And the operators at the other end, even though they all
understood English, spoke to him only in their native languages—
German or Norsk . . . or Flemish. Where were the American
commanders, for Christ's sake? Alice also knew Condor had to be
making the same connections. If he were so single-mindedly determined to hit the Soviets, why wait for the submarines? Why not
order the NATO forces into it, even if that meant the suicide of
Europe? The successor's decision meant all was lost anyway. And
he could always follow with the submarines.

The lieutenant also reported that garbled messages now were
arriving from a handful of sites around the country. She had
identified the site of the original messages as a regional civil-
defense bunker in Maryland. Those messages, still garbled, were
arriving more regularly now. Alice waved her away. He simply
wasn't in the mood to worry about a lonely civil-defense station
wet-nursing a few governors. If they got through, fine. If not,
fine.

The Zulu clock stood at precisely 1700 hours, four hours before
the submarines would unleash most of America's remaining nuclear arsenal, when Alice finally realized that winning his own
private war simply wasn't enough. The realization arrived
abruptly as he stared at the perfectly synchronized hand of his
watch edging relentlessly past the marker. He knew it would move
just as relentlessly past the next hour markers, till it passed 2100,
and then it would stop. All watches would stop.

The general harbored no illusions. If Condor were somehow
taken away, there would be no one to talk to the submarines and
the result would be the same. If he tried to fake contradictory
orders from the *Looking Glass,* at best TACAMO would be confused and go with the original SIOP plan. It was a hopeless dilemma. Nevertheless, as he watched the second hand move
steadily onward, Alice concluded that at least he could remove

control from one totally determined man and place it in the lap of fate. Fate seemed equally determined. But he decided, quickly and simply, that he liked the second option better. Even so, Alice reached one more time for the phone.

"Ummmmm?" the voice responded impatiently.

"Alice here, Condor."

"You're in deep shit, Alice."

"Don't hang up." The general's voice was a command. "You will not allow me to dissuade you?"

"No."

"You will not allow Harpoon to dissuade you?"

"Harpoon's dead."

The general's hand tightened, white-knuckled, over the phone. But he did not pause. "It is beyond debate?"

"You and I will settle up on the ground, Alice."

"I think not, Condor." This time Alice disconnected and turned immediately to Sam, who had watched the drama closely.

"Where is the *E-4*, Sam?" he asked. "Precisely."

"Four hundred fifty miles southeast, sir," Sam answered immediately.

"Order a new course for an intercept point," Alice said routinely.

The two old friends locked eyes for a moment. Sam's mind spun. Intercept point, hell. The general was asking for a collision point. He could not see how that would do any more good than turning the bombers. But Sam did not think long. Just as routinely, Alice's old friend replied, "Yes, sir," having also concluded that a private war was not enough.

Condor was furious. The abortive NATO conversations had been going on for an hour now. The *E-4*'s radio officers reported that whenever they broke through the garbles to a NATO facility, a clearly military voice would speak briefly in a NATO-country tongue and then the conversation would break off. The words were always the same, regardless of the language: "Sorry, sir, we are instructed to say nothing to you."

Finally, at shortly after 1700 hours, Condor took to the radio himself in exasperation. A proper Italian voice babbled at him in a short sentence he didn't understand. "You little wop bastard!" Condor exploded. "This is the President of the United States talkin' to you! Who do you think bought your fancy fuckin' uniform? You talk to me in English and put an American officer on! On the goddamned double!" The Italian did not hesitate, breaking from his native language into flawless and unalarmed English. "Your officers are not available, sir," he said. Then the man disconnected.

Condor, his mouth gaping open and his face almost apoplectic, turned toward the Librarian. The Librarian's face furrowed grimly. "Frankly, sir," he said, "I believe the Europeans have our boys in the tank." Condor continued to stare at him, his mouth still agape. "It was damned foolish of us to tie up NATO in a nuclear war," the Librarian continued. "Now the Europeans seem to have it tied up for us. At least part of it."

Condor seethed. He was fully committed now, and the frustration left him barely able to speak. "Those ingrates!" he finally flustered. "Don't they remember the Marshall Plan?"

"They are playing their old game," the Librarian said. "Trying to protect themselves by not provoking the Soviets. It is a sad, sad error. In the end the Soviets will obliterate them anyway."

Condor stormed out of the compartment, convinced that he could trust no one, that the United States was utterly alone, and that he most certainly had made the correct decision.

In the gunner's seat, Halupalai's back remained to the cockpit window. He had felt the aircraft's first maneuverings but had made no move to go up front. He felt no foreboding. Kazaklis felt the foreboding, but he couldn't pinpoint the cause. Halupalai was neither suicidal nor maniacal. The foreboding had to come from anticipation of the grim new world they had decided they must approach.

The pilot gradually edged the aircraft lower, passing through fifteen thousand feet. The northern edge of Oahu, Kahuku Point, lay perhaps fifteen miles distant, slightly off Moreau's side of the aircraft. Kauai, which Kazaklis was trying to ignore, sat shrouded in the rainy island's usual clouds about seventy-five miles directly out Moreau's side window. He did not like what he could see of Oahu, with Honolulu still forty miles away on the far side. The clouds ahead, usually billowing white playthings or dark gray rain pouches hanging over the leeward side of the island, blew brown and thick in the early-morning sun. They spread over most of the island and wafted high and far to the east, where the westerlies had carried them. Kazaklis looked at Moreau and shook his head.

This promised to be one helluva mess. A moment later they passed over Kahuku at ten thousand feet, catching one quick glimpse of the splendid surf, and then they entered the clouds or smoke and began bumping badly. They came in due south, straight over the center of the island toward Pearl Harbor and Honolulu. The visibility was near zero. Moreau saw the first crater.

"Holy Mary, mother of God," she said, and crossed herself.

Kazaklis banked the plane quickly in an attempt to catch a view. The radiation alarm squawked naggingly behind them. "Oxygen!" he ordered. "Vents closed!" By the time Kazaklis had looked again, they were past Moreau's sighting and the clouds had closed again.

"What was it?"

"A hole in the ground," she replied in clipped, brittle tones. "A very big hole."

Kazaklis looked at her. She had paled.

"That's all?"

"That's all."

They were almost on top of Pearl Harbor now. But even at 7,500 feet Kazaklis saw nothing through the murk. "Halupalai, if you're coming up here, come up here now," the pilot said, more tersely than he intended.

"I'm right behind you, commander," Halupalai replied.

Kazaklis turned and saw the big Hawaiian, his helmet on, his mask strapped, his eyes glazed. He sat in the jump seat at the pilot's back. Kazaklis reached around and patted him on the knee, then clenched it and squeezed. "Where are we?" the gunner asked.

Kazaklis lifted his shoulders in dismay. "I can't see shit out there. We should be right over Pearl, coming up on Hickam and Honolulu International, Diamond Head on the left. Sure as hell hope we don't have company coming in over two airfields in this muck."

"That was Schofield," Halupalai said evenly.

Kazaklis and Moreau exchanged quick and worried glances.

"The hole," Halupalai said as blandly as a bored tour guide. "That was Schofield Barracks."

Kazaklis ignored the alarm bells ringing in his head. The island was so small, the B-52 still moving so rapidly, there was no time to think. "I'm gonna take it out over Mamala Bay, bring it around, and come in lower from the south," he said. "Anybody got problems with that?"

"Let's skip it," Moreau answered quickly. She sounded even more brittle and quite insistent.

"I'd like to go, captain." Halupalai addressed Moreau, his voice so level and unemotional it spooked her. Moreau looked at Kazaklis and shook her head slightly.

"I think we all need to see it," Kazaklis said.

Suddenly the B-52 broke into brilliant sunshine, and below them they caught a split-second view of the flowing Waikiki surf, missing any sighting of the shoreline, and then they were at sea again. "What kind of mountains you got on that rock, Halupalai?" Kazaklis asked. The plane banked hard left now, back toward Diamond Head, and Kazaklis strained for a look out the left-hand window.

"Kaala's the big one, about four thousand feet." The voice remained tour-guide monotone. "Don't worry about it. It's too far west." In the distance Kazaklis could see Molokai, once the island of the lepers, perhaps thirty miles away. "Konahuanui about three thousand, Tantalus maybe two thousand, both should stay to your right coming over the top." Light billowing clouds hovered over Molokai, making it postcard pretty.

The sight mesmerized Kazaklis as he replied, "Hokay, I'm taking it down just under two thousand so we can activate the terrain cameras." Then, through the windows, he saw the debris in the water, enormous gobs of gunk floating toward the postcard image. "Jesus." The stunned hush of his voice reverberated through all three helmets. Amid the crazy clutter of splintered wood and junk he saw tangled bodies, and an occasional arm seemed to wave out of the ocean at him. "Good Jesus." They were halfway through the turn, the first computer images of Oahu dancing nonsensically on the green screens. Kazaklis, being in the left-hand seat, saw the real image first. "No," he said, "no, no."

Moreau moaned. "Get us out of here, Kazaklis," she said, her voice sounding as if she were strangling in her mask.

Halupalai said nothing, his eyes transfixed just to the left of the pilot's helmet as the panorama of Diamond Head, then Waikiki, then Honolulu swept slowly across the cockpit window, the aircraft leveling out and coming straight in, low, at the island's edge.

Diamond Head still stood at the right, and the serene surf of Waikiki, its white curls starting almost a mile offshore, still rolled placidly toward the land. Not even gunk remained to spoil the waters. All else had changed. It was as if a great hand had sliced angrily at the man-made concrete jungle of towering beachfront hotels, creating a desert in its place. On the left, toward downtown Honolulu and Hickam Air Force Base, not even rubble remained. Toward the right and the majesty of the Head, the hand seemed to have grown weary of its task and left the litter in larger and larger mounds. At the end of the once magical Waikiki strip, and the foot of Diamond Head, the mounds were perhaps thirty feet high where thirty-story condominiums had stood. Behind it all, where the island rose toward the low Koolau Mountains dividing Oahu's windward and leeward sides, the smoke and fires began, clouding the view of the interior.

Of the three now silent people in the aircraft, only Halupalai had a real perception of the topography. But as he surveyed it, every nerve ending in his body dead now, it made no sense. Ocean water flowed where Hickam had been, widening the narrow entrance to Pearl Harbor by perhaps a mile. A wall of still-smoldering earth stood at its edge like a levee holding the waters out of the no-man's-land that had been Honolulu International. There was absolutely no human movement in the city area, no sign that anything human had ever been there, and Halupalai drew his eyes away quickly, searching for something, anything, through the rapidly approaching smoke. The brown clouds billowed here, wafted there, depending on what was left to burn. The plane was coming straight in at the Punchbowl, the natural volcanic crater which had been made a national cemetery after the great war in the Pacific. Halupalai, his numbed nerves throbbing again, probed desperately for a sign of the natural crater's edge, seeking a glimpse of the endless rows of plain white markers over the last war's dead. But it wasn't there, the volcanic rim having been pushed over into the crater itself, creating a plateau, burying the long-dead deeper. Then they were in the smoke.

Kazaklis moved his eyes rapidly back and forth between the windows and his green screen. He throttled the plane back, but held it safely at well over stall speed. The altitude reading was eighteen hundred feet. The island was narrow here, eight to ten miles wide, and they'd be beyond it in a moment. Out the window, wind-whipped fires raged in the forests of the edge of the Koolau. On the screen the low peak of Tantalus passed by quickly and Konahuanui loomed above him on the right. The plane bumped badly. The green screen flashed the opening of the mountain pass, the Pali, dead ahead. The smoke gave way briefly, sunlight sparkling in as if it didn't belong, and the scenic wonder of the Pali opened ahead of them. In the pass, a few hundred feet below and just in front of them, they caught a quick glimpse of small and ragged bands of people waving, the sunlight glinting off their frantic signals. The Master Caution light flashed. Moreau punched it. Halupalai whimpered. The light flashed again. Moreau punched it. Out the side window she saw the signals were angry, the sunlight glinting off gun barrels. The violently bumping aircraft popped and cracked and shuddered.

"They're shooting at us!" she shrieked.

And then the people were gone, the smoke back.

"Get us out of here, Kazaklis!"

The pilot wrenched at the throttles and climbed. "We're on their side," he murmured, disbelieving.

"No one is on their side," Moreau said quietly. She hit the Master Caution button. And they climbed through the smoke, three people knowing they had been granted what they came here to get—a new view of the world, imprinted in their minds forever, be that minutes or years.

At Olney, the voice jarred the radio operator into excited attention, even though he didn't have the vaguest idea what the man was saying. The voice sounded scratchy, guttural—and Russian, for Christ's sake. It arrived on an ultra-high-frequency radiotelephone and he had not intercepted it. The call was meant for him. Briefly he floundered. Would he blow the spy's cover by responding in English? Ridiculous. He didn't speak a word of Russian and no one else in this place did either. He frantically waved at a young woman passing his shock- and soundproof windows. "Pit Stop Two," he said into the receiver. "You will need to speak English." He heard a crackling noise on the radio. He saw the woman poke her head in the door. "Get the boss!" he snapped. "On the double!"

"Yes?" a new voice asked. "Am I speaking to the alternate command facility for the Federal Emergency Management Agency?" The words flowed at him in perfectly modulated American English of the kind used by late-news television announcers who had not yet learned the need for the tiny, calculated speech flaw that would set them apart and move them to prime time.

The radio operator floundered again, confused. "This is a priority channel"—that's rich, he thought, not having spoken to anyone all night—"you are required to identify yourself."

"Certainly. I am Pyotr Krilenko, attaché to the chairman of the Presidium of the Supreme Soviet and Premier of the Union of Soviet Socialist Republics. The Premier is with me and must speak to your superior on a matter of utmost importance."

The radio operator blanched. He could hear the Premier's guttural Russian instructions to the interpreter in the background. He turned and saw the director looking at him questioningly. At sixty-four, the Northeast regional civil-defense director was an embittered man, and had been long before 0600 Zulu. He played by the book. The single star given him by the Army, before he also was presented with his walking papers, was a testament to how well he played by the rules. He was not a risk-taker. He never understood that a second star, perhaps a third, might have come with that occasional risk. He took the radiophone matter-of-factly and listened briefly. His brow furrowed before speaking.

"We are at war, sir," he said sternly, struggling for some truly historic response. Nothing occurred to him. "Under no circumstances would I supply such information to you."

At the other end, two persons were on the phone. The first words came in irritable and occasionally angry Russian. Then they were translated flawlessly, but with the emotion removed, in the modulated tones of Pyotr Krilenko. Krilenko spoke in the first person, as if the words were coming directly from the Soviet Premier.

"I repeat, sir, I am not seeking information. I know the precise location of your *E-4* aircraft. It is flying now over Jonesboro in the state of Arkansas." The director flinched. The son of a bitch knew more than he did. "I ask you once again, on behalf of all humankind, to assist me in making radio contact with that aircraft."

The director drew himself up militarily, not forgetting the presence of his young radio operator. "I will not confirm the existence of any aircraft," he said.

"You will not provide a radio patch to the President, whom I know and you know is aboard the *E-4* aircraft?"

"I will not confirm the existence of any aircraft," he repeated, feeling satisfaction well up in him. Nicely handled.

"Will you, for the sake of both our nations, transmit a message to the *E-4* aircraft informing the President that I wish to communicate with him directly?"

The director stared into the awestruck face of his radio operator. "Absolutely not," he said. Then, more for the young radioman, he added: "I don't know who you are. You could be calling from Joe's Pizza Parlor."

There was a pause and then the Russian words continued, more pensive than angry. "I am who I am," the interpreter continued. "You, sir, are a fool."

The director flushed. "I find that . . ." he blustered. "I find that incredibly insulting!"

Again the conversation paused. Then the Premier responded in brief and calm tones. The director could hear the interpreter questioning him quietly in Russian and the Premier responding insistently, *"Da! Da!"*

"What's going on?" the director demanded.

"The Premier wishes it to be said," the interpreter replied, shifting out of the first person, "that he is surprised you find his words insulting. It would surprise him if you could find your rectum with both hands and a hunting dog."

Kazaklis emerged from the smoke at twenty thousand feet as he swung westward around Kahuku Point, trying to avoid the unneeded horror of an outward flight over the floating death in the channel between Oahu and Molokai. In the distance he saw Halupalai's island, Kauai, glimmering flawlessly and invitingly due west and almost directly in front of them. Somehow, he had to thread the needle between Halupalai's personal trauma—a home lost—and the collective trauma of a second overflight of the obscene debris of Oahu—a civilization lost. They may have needed one look at that. They did not need two.

None of them had spoken since the emergency climb away from the Pali. The shock from what they had seen and the unexpected reception from their own dying people had numbed their sensibilities. Kazaklis and Moreau acted by rote. Halupalai, with nothing to do, sat stoically and apparently deep in thought. Kazaklis concentrated on getting the aircraft up and away from the mildly radioactive clouds so he could open the vents and get them off oxygen. Moreau sat rigidly at his right, methodically punching the Master Caution light over and over again like a catatonic resident of some asylum.

"What the fuck's the matter with that thing?" Kazaklis finally asked irritably. "Is it on the fritz again?"

The pilot's abrupt question jarred Moreau out of her trance. She had become so accustomed to pushing the button every time the plane bumped that it had not occurred to her that the light had been flashing since they pulled away from the mountain pass. She punched it again, watching it flicker and light up still one more time. Quickly she began checking the other instruments. She froze. "Something's wrong," she said. "We show a fuel leak."

"Instrument malfunction," Kazaklis said tersely. "Check it again."

"It's only a few minutes away, commander," Halupalai said.

"Double checks," Moreau said. "Wing tank. Number One."

Kazaklis craned his neck to peer out the left window at the wingtip sweeping almost one hundred feet behind him. The tip pointed back toward the floating debris, back toward the grotesque skeleton of Honolulu, and Kazaklis refused to allow his eyes to focus beyond the sleek wing. The surface looked sludgy and gray. That was normal. Inside the wing, the latticework structure contained various interconnected fuel reservoirs. But he could not see anything out of the ordinary on the outside. "I can't see it," he grumbled.

Kazaklis brought his eyes quickly back to the flight panel, oblivious to the shrouded island rapidly approaching from Moreau's side of the aircraft. In his preoccupation he did not see any of the emerald beauty of Kauai, the dark rain clouds hanging over its nearest shore, only a few layered shadows of ominous brown clouds moving toward them. Halupalai saw it.

"Just a quick fly-by, commander. You don't have to go down."

A fly-by? They just made their fucking fly-by. The gunner's quiet request did not register properly in the pilot's preoccupied mind. He had other problems. Serious problems. Kazaklis checked the instruments. They confirmed a fuel leak.

"I think we took a hit," Moreau said.

Halupalai scrambled out of the jump seat and hunched over the copilot. She could feel the big man's muscles grow tighter as he draped himself against her and pressed his helmet against the side window. "Come on!" Kazaklis snapped in disbelief. "From those little popguns?"

Moreau shrugged and felt her shoulders jam into Halupalai's soft gut. Briefly, his presence irritated her. Then she felt a quick surge of alarm. But it rapidly disappeared into the underground of her mind. "Kazaklis, you know damn well I could shove a pencil through the wing of this airplane," she said, the skin of their aircraft being less than one-quarter inch thick. Halupalai stooped, entranced, over the side window. Far below, clouds obscured the little south-shore village in which he had grown up. "How many pounds we got in that tank?" Normal clouds, he told himself, for his island was the rainy island. "Sixty-five hundred." Halupalai brushed his eyes and looked beyond the clouds. "Seal the connector valve." Waimea Canyon opened to him as it did when he was a child, Kalalau Valley beckoning far to the north with its high cliffs and low green wonderlands. "Done." His eyes glistened, blurring his island and blurring his mind, so that he stood on the shore again and the wave swelled until his neck craned high to watch the sunlight filter through the perfect prism of its massive curl. "Vents open." The wave crashed, thundering with the infinite power of nature, sending swirls of foam and churning coral bits and little messages from distances undreamed up around the small brown feet of a child long since taken into a different world. "Off oxygen." He could feel the great aircraft turning. He leaned farther forward, watching his island slip away around the edge of the window, and then he saw the new crater at Kokee where he had played as a child and where the satellite-tracking station had been built much later. "Dammit, Halupalai, sit down!" He could hear the commander's words, feel Moreau pushing at him now. But he saw another new crater in the desert at Mana, where a child long ago had pressed a small brown face against a chain-link fence to stare curiously into a secret Air Force base. "Halupalai!" The pilot's arm grabbed at him. He saw another crater. And another. The ugly brown smoke drifted up the low green wonderlands of his valley, Kalalau. Halupalai drew himself up and turned around, unaware of his crewmates, and headed back into the privacy of his adopted world's redness.

Kazaklis and Moreau exchanged deeply worried glances. But Kazaklis also was trying to sort out his new problems. He knew their golden circle had tightened by several hundred miles. "So much for Australia," he muttered. Moreau scowled, then turned to look into the shadows at Halupalai. She saw only the arching outline of his massive back. She looked again at Kazaklis and he shook his head slightly in worry. Then they went back to work, honing their new southwesterly course.

Kazaklis and Moreau removed their helmets, feeling the usual sense of relief at shedding the heavy headgear. They also pushed the aircraft upward through thirty-five thousand feet toward an economy altitude they needed more than ever now.

Halupalai had not been back in the redness more than five minutes before he decided to go home. In that short time his mind took a thousand life trips, following a thousand tangled paths all leading to dead ends. Then it returned to the equally dead red cubicle in which he seemed forever entombed. And so he decided to go home, back to a place where the coral bits would wash up around sun-browned feet, back to a world of blue lagoons that made room for dark gray fins and small boys, too.

Quickly and efficiently, as he had done in Vietnam, Halupalai reached for the small green oxygen bottle he would need for the ride down. He attached it, snapped the mask back over his face, and pulled the green ball that released the last artificial air he ever wanted to breathe. It flooded his lungs, causing a brief moment of headiness again. He placed one hand over the ejection lever and used the other to close his helmet visor. He began to disconnect the radio wire so he would not whiplash on the way out. He paused, the guilt and shame enveloping him briefly, and reached for the radio switch. "I'm sorry," he said. Then he quickly disconnected the radio with one hand and hit the lever with the other. Kazaklis and Moreau did not have time to turn around.

Forty thousand feet above the ocean, and thirty-five miles from his boyhood island, the air slammed into Halupalai at almost six hundred miles an hour. He was protected somewhat—by his helmet and the steel seat that had shot out of the top of the aircraft with him. The temperature, even in these latitudes, was seventy below zero. But he did not feel the cold. The jolt knocked him unconscious immediately, and also broke the arm he had used to disconnect the radio wire after his brief farewell. He tumbled, his body tucked in fetus form, end over end, downward. He would fall in that manner for more than thirty-thousand feet. Then, below ten-thousand feet, the parachute would pop. That much was a virtual certainty. The parachute rarely failed. The body often did. In any case, the chute then would waft him slowly down into the cradle of the sea.

In the aircraft, Kazaklis and Moreau heard a tremendous thunderclap, although, in truth, there were two claps, one following the other so quickly their ears could not make the differentiation.

The first came from the small explosive charge that propelled Halupalai away. The second came almost simultaneously from the rapid decompression of the aircraft, the oxygen being sucked out of the B-52 almost as rapidly as Halupalai had left. With the instant change in pressure, all other loose items rushed out of the upper compartment—charts, manuals, alert bags, unfinished box lunches. Tyler's body swept up through the well and out the hole above the gunner's seat. O'Toole's body jammed in the well and kept Radnor aboard, too. In the cockpit, a fog briefly clouded the fliers' vision as all on-board water vaporized. Both the pilot's and the copilot's fingertips began to turn blue, although not from the cold. Almost instantly, both Kazaklis and Moreau began suffering acutely from the symptoms of hypoxia. At this altitude they had fifteen, perhaps twenty seconds to take supplemental oxygen. After that their brains would cease functioning with any rationality. A few seconds later they would be unconscious. Shortly after that, they would be dead. Kazaklis and Moreau were well-trained to recognize the deadly effects of hypoxia, but the condition is subtle and hypnotic, affecting airmen much the way nitrogen overload affects scuba divers. Its symptoms are light-headedness, euphoria, well-being, even eroticism. And so Kazaklis, his tired but now soaring mind recalling the warmth and pleasure of Moreau's unexpected bear hug, reached for his co-pilot's thigh instead of his oxygen.

FOURTEEN

1800 ZULU

Sedgwick glanced fuzzily at the clock—1720 Zulu—flinched, and
then moved his eyes to the President, who lay near him. The I.V.
still hung above the man's arm just as an I.V. hung above his.
Sedgwick shifted uncomfortably in the wetness of his bed. Beneath his buttocks the I.V. tubing dripped slowly and steadily, the
serum solution and the last dose of morphine washing through
his sheet and soaking into the mattress as it had for the past half-
hour. His eyes moved slowly from the President's I.V. bag to his.
The solution was depleting at the same rate. That was a good sign.
He followed his own tubing down beneath the top sheet where he
had moved his right arm. A small spot of blood stained the sheet
where he had pulled back the medical tape and foggily removed
the tubing from his arm. The President moaned slightly and babbled a few incoherent words. Across the room the nurses stopped
their conversation, looked at the man, and began to draw another
small dose of the peace-giving drug they would inject directly into
the tube running into the President's veins. Sedgwick flailed at his
bedsheets and screamed, now wanting to draw attention to himself and away from the President. The nurses moved to Sedgwick
first, one to each side of the bed.

"Hey, there, sailor," said the one on the left, placing a calming
hand on his head.

335

"What the hell is this?" demanded the one on the right, as she prepared to insert the hypodermic into the tubing above the revealing bloodstain.

Sedgwick forced his clouded mind and hurting body to function together. His right hand darted from beneath the sheet and grasped the nurse's wrist, twisting until the hypodermic clattered to the floor. He reared up painfully and lunged at the other nurse, grabbing her by the neck of the dress, ripping the fabric. Both nurses reared back, stunned.

The nurse on the left screamed urgently. "Help us! For God's sake, someone help us!"

Sedgwick lunged again, shredding the front of her dress until she was naked to the waist. He twisted the fabric in a lock around his hand. "Shut up!" he ordered. "Shut up and listen!" He fumbled briefly for the most compelling words. "We're going to die," he said.

"You're not going to die," the nurse on the right said, nervously trying to calm him. "Let us give you something for the pain, sir."

"Fuck the pain!" He could hear the noise of someone approaching from another room. "Listen to me! Stop the President's morphine!" The hurting was beginning to overwhelm him, but he fought it back down.

The nurse on the left whimpered. The nurse on the right persisted in trying to soothe him. "You don't want him to suffer." She brought her free hand down on his chest and pushed. He wrenched at her arm again.

"Screw the suffering!" His words began to gush as he heard others approach. "There's not enough morphine in the world to stop the suffering! Don't you understand? It's better that he hurt! You must understand, damn you! Damn you . . . damn you . . . can't you understand . . . ?"

Sedgwick felt someone roughly pulling his arms away from the nurses. He sagged back, closing his eyes and yielding briefly to the pain. He reopened them slowly. A man held him down. On his left the nurse had withdrawn, sobbing lightly and covering her breasts with her arms. On his right the other nurse stared at him angrily, curiously. Sedgwick's eyes begged now. "Please hear me," he pleaded. "You were outside. You saw. You have no idea what can still happen. He must be able to think. To feel. Please understand. . . ." All the strength began to ebb out of him. "Please . . ." he muttered. The nurse's face blurred. He felt her patting him on the shoulder. He thought he saw her fuzzy face nod comfortingly. But by that time he was well on his way out again.

Alice clenched Smitty's shoulder, and the pilot turned away from the unshielded cockpit windows—away from the smoke and crud floating over the Ozarks—and looked up at his commanding officer. "You doing okay, general?"

Alice smiled. "It's my job to ask you that, Smitty."

"Oh, I'm doing all right," the pilot said. "You ever think it would be this way, sir?"

"Tell you the truth, Smitty, I don't know what I thought."

"No, I guess none of us did."

"I'm very proud of you, old friend. All of you people."

The pilot turned back to his work and said nothing. They were in an extremely hot area, flying directly through the radioactive debris floating away from the crater-gouging attack on the Missouri Minuteman fields. Even with the vents closed, the radiation ate at them now. The general shuddered. It would not kill him. He would go much faster now that his new course was set for a deadly midair meeting with Condor. But he shuddered nevertheless and forced his thoughts back to his crew, of whom he was immensely proud.

Alice had come close to not telling his staff, letting Sam and the cockpit crew know and allowing the rest to carry on routinely. Sam had wagged his head at the thought, and he had been correct. The crew was too tight a group, confined in quarters too small, confined too many months and years in a life too other-worldly for any of them to have missed the dynamics of the decision. Or to have misunderstood—even in the sodden depression that pervaded the airplane after their orderly military world had been shattered by his earlier decision. They had accepted the new decision sadly and fatalistically—but without a single objection. A few moments ago, when the *Looking Glass* passed over the devastated missile fields, the crew had filed into the cockpit one by one. They had peered down into the moonscape of the once pastoral Missouri farmland, saw crater overlapping crater where the missiles had been planted with other crops. Then they had returned quietly to work. He understood their need for that. It gave meaning to this final mission.

"Where is the *E-4* now, Smitty?" Alice asked.

"About a hundred miles away, sir. North of Memphis. Circling over the river on the Arkansas-Tennessee border."

"They'll spot us pretty soon."

"Yes, sir. Figure it out, too."

"Yes, I know."

The pilot of the *E-4* had kept his windows unscreened since dawn, shortly before the grotesque scene with Harpoon. He had a dull, nagging headache. He took the eyepatch off one eye and placed it over the other. He was having a difficult time keeping the aircraft out of the dirty clouds. The flight was becoming more unreal than he had dreamed in his worst nightmares. The sporadic clouds moved to higher and higher altitudes, better for the people below, not good for them. Far below, the Mississippi Valley lay quiet and placid, seemingly as untouched as a day ago.

Untouched. He shivered as he thought of the admiral. The poor bugger must have gone over the side. He didn't know the admiral well, a swabbie in among all the flyboys. But he had seemed like a steady, level man. Christ, this kind of pressure could get to anybody. He double-checked the position of the *Looking Glass*. Was everybody going bananas? Why had Alice brought the plane so near them? They were scarcely a hundred miles away. And closing on him. He tried to radio the *Looking Glass* one more time. No response again. He went to the intercom. On the other end, the Librarian seemed momentarily puzzled. Then he shrieked at the pilot: *"Evade him! Run for it!"* The pilot's head throbbed. Evade him? It made no sense for the *Looking Glass* to crowd them, to come in where one missile could get them both. It made less sense to start a panicky run away from the SAC command plane. Especially in this environment. He took the aircraft out of its circle and headed east. But he did not do it in a beeline. He continued to avoid the clouds.

Something godawful had happened. The aircraft had decompressed. Kazaklis knew that, but he didn't care. He felt too good. She felt too good. In front of him the azure blue of the sky bathed him, soothed him, entranced him. His hand moved slowly on her thigh, incredibly sensitive fingers probing each taut muscle, each sensuous sinew. The sinews seemed to ripple in response, drawing him farther. Five seconds had passed.

She struggled, her senses sending conflicting messages. Her

mind was sludgy, her body not. Her first thought was that the
bullet had done it, illogically, irrationally chewing a hole in the
pressurized crew compartment long after it had been fired. Her
second thought came from a different part of her body, the
lonely, aching part that had reached out earlier. The hand
massaged deadened cords suddenly alive. She wanted to die this
way, in euphoria and ecstasy. She turned and leaned left. Ten
seconds had passed.

Kazaklis turned also, and looked at her. Moreau's face was
haloed and shimmering, her eyes a ravishing match of sparkling
sapphire and uncut diamond. He leaned toward her, brushing
past lightning-bolt jewelry. Her lips were blue. She was dying. He
touched her face. She slumped, raven lady, into his lap.

"No-o-o-o!" he screamed. Frantically he lurched at his dangling
oxygen mask, drawing it to his face first, not out of selfishness but
out of rigid training. If he went, she went, and he was going fast.
He took one breath, then another and another, the raw oxygen
driving ecstasy out and some sensibility in. Moreau's head lay
peacefully between his legs, her eyes barely open. Another three
or four seconds had passed, but Kazaklis had gained a few. He
quickly drew the mask from his face and stretched it down into his
lap, over hers. He pulled her partly upright and looked into her
face. She wobbled back out of insensibility, briefly into the rapture
again, and then flashed pure fear at him. Now he was going again.
He had trouble finding the radio button. He couldn't remember
her name. "Get . . . on . . . your . . . own . . ." Each word required
a monumental effort. He took the mask away, roughly shoving
her back toward her seat. He breathed. His peripheral vision was
gone, narrowed into a tight tunnel, and he couldn't see her. The
aircraft had nosed over slightly, the air speed increasing, and he
pulled back on the wheel to level it. He could do no more. He
breathed deeply and wasn't certain whether the light-headedness
was coming from the hypoxia or the sudden gush of oxygen.
Slowly, so agonizingly slowly, his senses returned. Twenty, thirty
seconds passed. *Moreau.* That was her name. *Moreau!*

He turned suddenly toward her in alarm. She sat with her
shoulders hunched, the mask clasped over her face, staring
straight ahead. They said nothing for a full minute—well beyond
the recovery time, the brain responding almost as soon as the
blood circulated the oxygen upward from their lungs. Then Moreau said, "Unseasonably cold for Hawaii, isn't it?" Her voice was

strained, but together they began to take the aircraft down where they could breathe.

Minutes later, Halupalai's parachute opened at eight thousand feet, jerking him out of six miles of free fall. He did not feel it. He was alive but still unconscious. He awakened minutes later as his boots slammed into the sea, his weight taking him down toward the depths, then his buoyancy popping him back to the surface. His island was gone, lost over the horizon, obscured by the swells. But Halupalai was not looking for his island. He was looking for the choppers. He was not bobbing in the mid-Pacific but in the South China Sea, as he had the last time he pulled the lever so long ago. With his good arm, he activated his rescue beacon. The Air Force would risk fifty men to pull one downed flier out of the drink. Soon the silence would be broken by the distantly accelerating whump-whump-whump of the rescue team. The rope would come down, the divers, too, joining him in the swells. He waited confidently.

Several hundred miles to the southwest, the beleaguered captain of the newly commissioned nuclear carrier *Ticonderoga* heard no distress calls and sent out no search plane. His ship carried the proud name of a mothballed carrier from the previous great war. But the routine shakedown cruise had become a nightmare of a kind that no previous war, no training in Annapolis, could have prepared him for.

Shortly before 0600 Zulu, not long after sunset last night in these waters, America's vast military communications network had filled his radio room with a babble of escalating alert messages. Then they stopped, almost precisely as he saw the first eerie flare of light far over the horizon. Twenty minutes later he saw a second and larger flare, then several more. He knew little of the condition of the world. But he knew that Pearl, his next port of call, was no longer there. He also knew that, for him and his crew of four thousand, Pearl Harbor's disappearance was irrelevant. They would never reach a safe harbor, Pearl or any other. They had spent the night, and now the morning hours, frantically dodging Soviet attack submarines. They had peppered the waters around them with nuclear depth charges. He had sent out wave after wave of search aircraft. But he was losing.

The captain nervously tapped his fingers on the papers in front of him. A weather advisory warned him of a tropical storm approaching from the southwest. Briefly the old sailor in him said run for the storm and its cover. The new sailor told him there was no cover anywhere. He shuffled through the papers, glancing at the single terse message he had received from the outside since 0600. A priority all-listeners order to bring down a stray B-52. He shook his head wearily. What kind of jackasses were running the show up there? He had a nuclear-powered Victor-class Soviet attack sub on his butt. He was a dead man. And they wanted him to look for Buffs in the mid-Pacific?

Sedgwick awakened in a panic. The clock read 1750 Zulu. How much time could they possibly have? He turned toward the President, and his heart sank. The man lay quietly on his back, the I.V. still feeding into his arm. He reached out toward him and felt the tug of the tubing reinserted in his arm. He fell back and groaned in despair. A cool, comforting hand caressed his forehead. "Easy. Easy. It's going to be all right now."

Sedgwick stared bleakly into the nurse's sad smile. "Why?" he asked. "Why can't I make you understand?"

"I do understand," she said softly. "No more morphine."

Sedgwick's eyes darted to the President's intravenous tube, then to his own. His legs throbbed. He looked back at the nurse in confusion.

"Blood serum," she said. "Nothing else. He's going to hurt, but he's going to think."

Sedgwick closed his eyes. "Bless you," he said. "God bless you."

The nurse looked at him desolately. "Is it going to do any good?"

"I don't know, miss. I really don't know." Sedgwick had no idea how SIOP had scheduled the submarines. He was reasonably certain the President did not know either, having had no time for detail before the mad dash out of the White House to *Nighthawk One*. But Sedgwick knew there was a schedule. In his mind he could see them lurking, ready. He was Navy, and there always was a schedule for the submarines. At 1750 Zulu, it couldn't be far off.

"How long before he'll be coherent?"

The nurse wrinkled her forehead. "Half-hour. Forty-five minutes maybe. He'll be pretty rummy at first. He's been off it almost an hour now. You"—she cleared her voice in mock reproach—"you've been off it a while longer." She chuckled. "You're the kind of patient who makes hospital legends, sailor. We get a lot of bed-wetters. But that was a new one."

Sedgwick noticed for the first time that his sheet was dry, changed after he had passed out. People doing their jobs, he thought. All kinds of jobs. As trained.

"Is there anything you can do to bring him around faster?"

"Not much, I'm afraid. We could shoot something into him to hop him up now that we've knocked him down. It'd be very dangerous. And I truly don't think it would do any good. You'd probably have a babbling chimpanzee on your hands. Not the President you need." She paused. "Are we really in that much trouble?"

"I'm afraid so," Sedgwick answered. He felt the nurse shudder and pull her hand away. He looked at her and saw eyes that retreated in guilt, not fear. He reached for her hand.

"I'm sorry we screwed things up," she whispered.

He squeezed the hand he had wrenched a half-hour earlier. "Believe me, nurse," he said, "you aren't the ones who screwed up."

After the sudden and violent gust of wind cleaned out the B-52, the air pressure inside the cabin stabilized with the pressure outside. The wind stopped almost immediately, replaced by the barely perceptible rustle of thin air racing over the escape hole Halupalai had left in the top of the plane. Even as they began their rapid descent, Kazaklis reached forward and stripped his glove off the green screen, his hand becoming infinitely colder even than his contempt for the world that had placed them in this mess. The temperature had plummeted more than one hundred degrees in a split second. The pressure fell to less than three pounds per square inch, one-fifth of normal. The nitrogen in their body fluids began to form bubbles. Unless they descended quickly, they would begin to suffer from ailments ranging from the bends to paresthesia to uncontrollable choking. With the air outside their bodies thinning by a factor of five, the gases inside their stomachs and intestines expanded by a factor of five. The pain stabbed. To deal with this irritation, they had to vent the expanded gases through both available bodily orifices. This they did, without shame. Otherwise, they rode silently downward—each drawn deeply within, each depressed, each having more difficulty with the emotional stress than the physical stress.

Moreau did not look back. Kazaklis looked once, confirming with a quick glance that Halupalai's seat was gone, his buddy gone with it, and that they now had a gaping and irreparable hole in the top of their aircraft. Kazaklis made the rest of the descent feeling as if the hole had been torn through him. They leveled out at twelve-thousand feet, unsnapped their oxygen again, and quietly flew on, wordlessly telling each other that neither was ready to begin the discussion of their new dilemma. Kazaklis finally broke the silence. "The son of a bitch," he said, his words emerging in a low, tormented hush. "The poor, dumb, wonderful son of a bitch. Damn him." He pounded a newly gloved fist into his knee in hurt and frustration. "Why, Moreau? Why?"

Moreau stared straight ahead, unmoving. "He wanted to go home," she said flatly. "He was happy there." She fought against the shivering, still trying to shake the subzero cold out of her bones and adjust to the marginal warmth they had found. "Maybe that's what we should have done, too."

Kazaklis turned to look at her questioningly. She continued to stare ahead, her oxygen mask hanging loosely below a clenched jaw. "Were you happy there?" he asked.

Her brow furrowed briefly, memories of the past Christmas flooding her mind. She had asked her father close to the same question. "I don't think happiness is one of the goals I set in life," she replied, almost exactly as he had.

Kazaklis turned away. He peered out the cockpit window at the vast and vacant sea scarcely more than two miles below them now, its whitecaps clearly visible atop giant swells. It showed no sign of hostility, no sign of tampering, no clutter of crud and bodies. It was pure. Kazaklis, conveniently blotting out the possibility of a faulty and mangling ejection, envisioned Halupalai in it. His friend bobbed placidly in the swells, basking in their peacefulness, no more rejection, no more failure, not bothering to open his rubber raft, not bothering to begin the long and pointless search for a home that was long gone. He knew Halupalai wasn't going home. Kazaklis sighed. "Our lovable beachboy didn't do us any favors, bless his lost soul," he said.

"I know."

"We got ourselves some real problems."

"Yes."

"You serious about going home?" He looked at her intently. He had no intention of making the same lost search that Halupalai had begun.

"Could we make it?"

"How's our fuel? Hundred thousand pounds?"

"Ninety-six."

He ran it through his head for curiosity's sake. San Francisco lay 2,500 miles away. Fiji roughly the same. The westerlies would help them, although not much at this altitude. With the new drag, their fuel would give them four hours, four and a half perhaps. "A chance," he said. "My guess is we'd paddle the last couple hundred miles. Through the crud." He added a bite to his last sentence.

Moreau didn't appear to notice. "Maybe we ought to face reality," she said blankly. Her voice was devoid of all life.

"Reality?" He let the word sit a minute. "If we're lucky, reality's a firing squad, Moreau."

She smiled faintly. "And if we're unlucky, commander?" she asked, the question suddenly abrasive.

"Planet of the apes, pal. They won't even care who we are."

"Shit!" Moreau exploded, stopping the unintentional game.

"Cherepovets," Kazaklis said calmly. "Zebra two-one, Moreau. They went for the gonads. The other guys must be going for ours. Who's going to turn it off? Halupalai's out there looking for an island that won't be there if he ever finds it."

"Dammit." The edge started to back off her voice.

"You know the system better than I do. It has to go. Maybe they'll dig out of the rubble someday." He paused. "I don't want to spend the rest of my life digging."

Moreau lurched across the throttles between them. She pounded tight fists angrily into the pilot's chest and arms. He sat stolidly, allowing the thrashing to continue until finally she slumped back into her seat. "Dammit," she said despairingly. "Dammit, Kazaklis, I feel so guilty."

A stillness enveloped them, the engine roar unheard, the rush of the wind a mere whisper over Halupalai's escape hatch. The whispering sound seemed to whisk ghosts out of the emptiness: the pale, splotched face of the young air controller from the Bronx—*melech hamafis*; the moxie in the last haunted words from *Polar Bear Three*—*get those mutha-fuckahs for us*; Klickitat and *Elsie*, who chose a bleak and different duty; Tyler's tortured soul and lost son; Radnor's blissfully sad decision to join his wife. And Halupalai. . . .

"Did we do anything right, Kazaklis?" Moreau asked mournfully.

"We did what we had to do, Moreau," he said, not answering.

"Damn you, did we do *anything* right?"

"You never know, Moreau," he said slowly. "Not even when it's all over."

They sat silently for several minutes. Then Kazaklis stiffened. "You gonna be okay?" he asked sternly. "Can we get on with it now? Or do I have to do this all myself?"

Moreau turned and looked at him. She smiled, sadly at first, then less so. "You have a couple of holes in your magic carpet, Captain Shazam," she said. "Where do you think that tattered cape will take us?"

Kazaklis grinned from ear to ear, every tooth showing, although a close study would have shown that the eyes were not shining with quite the toothsome gleam. But he covered, as he always did. "Rarotonga!" he exulted. "Bora Bora! Hiva Oa! Papeete for the lady!" He turned quickly away, as if to check the port engines. He would not let her see the gleam turn to a glisten. But Moreau didn't need to look at him to know the cover was fraudulent.

"God, I'm going to miss him," Moreau said.

"Yeah, me too," Kazaklis said quietly.

For a moment the silence returned, the roar and the whir of the wind pounding only at their memories. Then Moreau sucked in a deep breath, resigned to the knowledge that Halupalai had taken his route just as they had taken theirs.

"What kind of chance do we have, Kazaklis?"

"Fiji. Maybe."

"It's as far as San Francisco and a lot harder to find."

He turned and grinned at her again, the teeth telling one story, the eyes another. "There's plenty of palm trees out there, Moreau. We'll find a sandy beach somewhere. If not, it's two in a canoe, kid. A rubber canoe." He reached over and slapped her on the thigh. Half-slap, half-pat, really, making certain it carried some nicely indefinable touch just between the two.

The President grumbled contentiously under his breath. The

advance work was abominable tonight, the protocol inexcusably sloppy. Where the hell was the Marine Band? Band always played "Hail to the Chief" when he left Andrews. No excuse for this. None. But Sedgwick's here. Good man, Sedgwick. Had to get to know him better. Give him a little presidential nudge over at the Pentagon. Never hurt, helping a young officer. Navy's in fine form tonight. Marines are wading knee-deep in trouble. Commandant would find his ass in a sling for this one. God, he was tired. Stairs to *Air Force One* looked like the side of the pyramids. He groaned, then tried to suppress the sound. Smile, buster. Part of the job. Screw the smiling. Screw the job. Sometimes this job isn't worth sour owl crap. He grunted. Then he reared himself up to full strength for the walk, Presidentially, up the aircraft stairs.

"Gimme a hand, Sedgwick," he mumbled. He could confide in Sedgwick. "Feel like I'm walking the last mile."

Sedgwick's hand landed lightly on the President's chest, gently pushing him back into his bed. "Take it easy, Mr. President," the aide said. "We're not walking anywhere tonight." Another, cooler hand caressed his forehead. He felt dizzy.

"President always walks," he protested. "Tradition. Tradition's goin' to hell around here tonight, Sedgwick."

God, he was tired. Where the devil were they going? Slipped his mind. Be careful of that. Nice to be here in Detroit. Except it's Denver. Damned bad politics. Time to turn and wave. Tradition. He raised an arm and arched it slowly across his hospital bed. He heard a soft feminine voice reassuring him. His wife? His wife . . . "Connie . . . ?" He sagged back in his bed and lay still for a moment. "What time is it, Sedgwick?" he asked, perfectly lucid.

"Eighteen-twenty-five Zulu, sir," Sedgwick replied from his own bed. "Twenty-five minutes after one."

"In the afternoon? Jesus Christ. Where are we?"

"In the FEMA bunker at Olney."

"Who's with us?"

Sedgwick's eyes moved around the room, passing the two nurses and landing on the civil-defense director to whom he had just talked and who now stood at rigid attention a few feet away. The military aide lingered a second, then answered, "Two charming and wise nurses, a radio operator, and a half-dozen technicians—and the Northeast regional director of FEMA."

"That's it?" the President asked incredulously.

"That's it, sir."

"Jesus Christ." All the king's horses and all the king's men . . . He felt dizzy again. "What's the matter with me?"

"You're blind, sir. Your legs are broken."

"Fuck that, Sedgwick. I know that." He thought of the nurses. "Pardon the language, ladies. I can't see you so you're not there. What have you got me on? My mind's dancing all over the place."

"Morphine, Mr. President," a female voice answered. "Sorry. We thought it was best. Mr. Sedgwick convinced us otherwise." The nurse looked at Sedgwick and blushed. "Just keep talking, sir, and it'll clear up. You sound pretty clearheaded now."

The President grumped. "Time to be clearheaded was when I came into this godforsaken job." He paused. "So how come we're not all dead, Sedgwick? What the hell's going on out there?"

"I'm afraid we don't have a very good fix on it, sir. Communications are shot to hell. Some of it's coming back very slowly. But nobody's been talking to anyone else, as far as we can tell. We're in a helluva mess."

"Our preliminary data show it could have been much worse," the director cut in too eagerly. "Most of the targets were military. Collateral damage to civilian populations, of course. A few cities were hit intentionally. But I'd say our fatalities are only about thirty million, surely no more than forty million."

The President tried to pull himself up in bed. He felt a sharp pang of pain in his legs but continued to grope blindly toward the strange voice. "Who the hell is that?"

"Bascomb, Mr. President," the man replied. "Director, Northeast region. FEMA. Retired Army. General officer." He reluctantly added: "Brigadier."

The President slumped back in his bed, his mind spinning. "No more than forty million . . ." He struggled to look back in the direction of the civil-defense director. "I'd say you lost a couple of divisions, Mr. Director," the President whispered.

"My point, sir—"

Sedgwick waved the man off. "It's horrible, Mr. President. It's also much more complicated, much more dangerous . . . and probably much worse than the estimated casualty figures."

"Do we have it turned off?" the President asked hauntedly.

"I don't know, sir. No one down here knows. But it certainly doesn't sound like it. We've got a couple of command planes up. We haven't been able to get through to either of them. We can hear one of them. The *Looking Glass* plane."

The President felt his mind wandering again. "So Alice is running the war . . ."

"Snap out of it, sir!" Sedgwick commanded, surprising himself. "I doubt anyone is running the war. If they can't talk, they can't run it. My guess is SIOP's still running the war. And that's bad. Very bad."

"The fucking computer."

"The fucking computer programmed all the orders, sir." Sedgwick hesitated. "You signed off on them. For the ICBM's, the bombers . . . and the submarines. The ICBM's are gone. The bombers . . . I don't know. I assume they're gone, but they go in only with confirming orders through the *Looking Glass*. By someone with National Command Authority. The subs are different. They operate on the reverse principle. They go with the original order unless the order is countermanded."

"Countermanded? Good God, Sedgwick!" The President bolted upright in his bed again, ignoring the pain from his legs. "Communications are shot? Then we can't countermand anything. We can't talk to them."

"I don't believe so, Mr. President. Not at the moment."

The President looked sightlessly into the ceiling. "What about the Soviets, Sedgwick?" he asked quietly. "What are they up to?"

Sedgwick glanced quickly at the civil-defense director. "I'm guessing, sir. From bits and pieces picked up on the radio here. Not too much seems to have happened since the first wave. Their bombers should have been in on top of us by now. We know they held back more than half their ICBM's. They've got some subs left. There is absolutely nothing the Soviets can do about our submarines. I think they're waiting. If our subs go, they'll hit us with everything they've got." Sedgwick closed his eyes. "I hate to say it, but I suppose that's what I'd do."

The nurses took a step backward, expressions of fascinated horror on their faces. The director shifted from foot to foot. The only sound in the room was the whir of the giant air purifiers. "When, Sedgwick?" the President asked with terrifying calm. "When are the submarines programmed to go?"

"We left the White House in a helluva hurry, sir."

"When, Sedgwick?"

"I don't know." The young naval aide clipped his words. He looked at the clock. It read 1830 Zulu. He heaved a great sigh.

"Five minutes? Couple of hours? The only people who know are in the subs. And in the command planes."

The President slowly raised a hand to his face, causing the I.V. stand to teeter precariously. He rubbed his empty eyes. "How?" he whispered. "How could we create such an ungodly monster?"

Sedgwick sighed again. "There's more, sir."

"There can't be much more, Sedgwick." The President's voice was raw with agony now. "Forty million dead? If the rest of those babies go, we'll be lucky if there are forty million alive." He stared into the blankness. "Very damned lucky."

"I know that, sir." Sedgwick resumed slowly. "The Olney radio operator is picking up some traffic. Bits and pieces, as I said. Some from Europe. He received a most peculiar call from the Soviet Union an hour ago. The speaker claimed he was the Soviet Premier."

"The Premier?" The President's mind was whirling now and he was sure it wasn't the morphine.

The director cut in again. "I talked with him, sir. He wanted us to patch him through to the *E-4*."

"The *E-4*?" The President sounded confused. "What god-damned *E-4*?"

"I'm sure he was an impostor. Naturally, I refused, as I would have done in any case."

"Why the hell didn't you let me decide that?"

"You were colder than yesterday's turkey, Mr. President," Sedgwick interrupted.

"Why the hell didn't he get you?"

Sedgwick lifted his eyebrows, spread his palm toward the director, and let him have the floor. "He wanted the *E-4*," the man sputtered.

"Jesus Christ, you two. The goddamned *E-4* went with my eyes at Andrews!"

Sedgwick looked levelly at the director. "Are you going to tell him or aren't you?" he demanded. The director shot an angry glance at the much younger man, but he said nothing. "According to the director," Sedgwick continued bluntly, "an alternate *E-4* made it out of Omaha and picked up a presidential successor in Baton Rouge. The man is aboard the *E-4* at this time."

"A successor?" The President's voice was dumbfounded.

"Everyone thinks you're dead, sir," Sedgwick said. "Including the Soviet Premier, if the call was authentic. I'm inclined to believe it was."

The President was becoming far more angry than confused. He waved both arms toward his unseen underlings, causing one of the nurses to rush to the teetering I.V. stand. "Is anybody going to bother to tell me who the hell the new President is?"

"The director believes," Sedgwick replied, "that the Secretary of the Interior has been sworn into office and is aboard the *E-4*."

"Jesus Christ."

No one said anything.

"Jesus H. Christ."

Sedgwick shifted uncomfortably.

"We got Alice in one plane and the Mad Hatter in the other."

The silence lasted only seconds, but it seemed endless to all in the room.

"Okay," the President said. "Let me see if I've got this straight. You're telling me that everybody thinks I'm dead, that Wild Bill Hickok thinks he is President, that our submarines are about to destroy the Soviet Union, that the Soviet Union then will destroy us, that we can't talk to our own people, but somebody claiming to be the Soviet Premier just called and we told the guy to take a hike. Is that about right? Or is that the morphine talking?"

"I'm afraid that's about right," Sedgwick said.

"Baskin?"

"Bascomb, sir," the director replied.

"What the hell makes you think you were not talking to the Premier?"

"Most improbable, sir," the director replied nervously. "Really, most improbable."

"Improbable," the President said in exasperation.

"He was too rude, sir," the director flustered, "far too rude for a national leader attempting to negotiate with a foreign power."

"Rude," the President said quietly. "We're nuking the be-Jesus out of each other and you think he was rude." Suddenly the President thundered, "You want to see a national leader get rude, you blathering nincompoop? What the hell did he say to you?"

The director started to stammer a reply and then froze.

"Oh, for God's sake," Sedgwick said. "The Russian said the director couldn't find his ass with both hands and a hunting dog."

One of the nurses tittered nervously. The President started to laugh, first in a low rumble, then in a slowly escalating roar, until the pain forced him to stop. "Baskin, off that information alone, I'd bet this little rabbit hole of yours that you had the Soviet Premier on the phone." He paused, then added very calmly, "Now get your ass, assuming you can find it, into the radio room and try to get him back. *Please.*"

The President could hear the man moving briskly out of the room.

"Sedgwick?"

"Sir?"

"You think we have a chance?"

"I don't know, sir."

"It's harder than hell to get through to submerged submarines, isn't it?"

"We often had trouble in peacetime, Mr. President."

Sedgwick looked long and sadly at the unseeing President. "You have one other problem, sir." The President rolled his head toward the naval aide, as if to look at him. "Your authenticator card is missing."

The President took a long, deep breath. "Nurse," he said, "roll me into the radio room, will you please?"

On the bridge of the *Ticonderoga*, the captain grimaced as he sucked on a cup of unusually foul coffee. He watched a young ensign stride toward him. "Sir!" The young officer snapped a salute and handed him a brief message.

"Victor?" the fatigued captain asked, his mind never straying from the Soviet submarine silently hounding them.

"No soundings, sir," the ensign replied. "We still can't find him."

The captain turned away, staring into the western horizon, where dark clouds gathered more rapidly now. He moved his eyes down to the flight deck, where a twin-jet S-3A Viking sub chaser caught the restraining cable, jerking to a halt after another sweeping search. Its two air-launched nuclear-tipped torpedoes still were slung beneath its wings, signaling another fruitless mission. He shook his head gloomily.

The ensign, on his first sea duty, lingered longer than he should. It also being his last sea duty, he also ventured more than he normally would dare. "Maybe Victor has forgotten us, sir," he said tentatively. "Found bigger game." They both knew that an American submarine, packing the nuclear firepower to take out a good part of the Soviet Union, was a far more attractive target than their floating island.

"Then we better start chasing him, dammit!" the captain snapped. "That's our job, mister."

The young officer blushed, and wanted to remove himself quickly. But the captain, in his preoccupation, still had not read the message. "We have an unidentified aircraft, sir." The captain turned and looked at him without expression. "Confusing," the ensign continued. "It has the radar profile of a B-52, sir."

The captain stared at the young officer a moment longer, then dismissed him. He examined the new message, which gave coordinates for a large bomber approaching at a distance of about seventy-five miles. He looked back down at the deck, debating between his F-14's and the newer F-18 Hornet interceptors, both of which were ready. He wagged his head at the sheer lunacy of it. He chose the F-18's.

Even unseeing, the President felt incredibly claustrophobic inside the tight confines of the radio room, his bed angled up tightly against an array of communications gear and other paraphernalia. There was little he could say to the Premier, except to ascertain the man's intentions, express his own, and reopen the lines of communication. The lines had been closed, unfortunately, far longer than the thirteen hours since the missiles flew. He clenched the phone rigidly, trying to will the pain out of his voice, while the two of them moved as quickly as possible through the necessary pleasantries, including the Premier's genuinely amazed relief that he was alive. They dealt hurriedly and bleakly with the misunderstanding over the Soviet launch at the Chinese and the disastrous American response. The Premiere did not mention the coup attempt. The President did not mention the possibility that he had been duped by Icarus. The information was irrelevant now—an irretrievable part of the past like the scores of millions dead and dying. They had no time for the past. The delays for interpretation, which the President had found to be convenient opportunities to plot his next hard-ball response during their past conversations, became almost intolerable irritations now. Both men wanted to move rapidly past the preliminaries.

"I'm afraid I don't have very reassuring news, Mr. Premier," the President said. "I need time—perhaps more than you can grant me. But I'm asking you to give me what you can. May I assume that at last we share a common goal and want to stop this madness?"

The President felt sweat forming on his forehead while his words were translated, the hyperactive voice of the Premier responded, and then the Premier's words were translated.

"Time, Mr. President, is a luxury neither of us has," the Premier's response began. "I will give you what I can. You can be assured we share the same goal. However, I cannot control all events here. My people will not absorb much more punishment. It is not a question of fault now, Mr. President. I will accept the fault, if necessary, and history's judgment of it. You must stop your submarines."

"Yes, yes, I know that, Mr. Premier." The President rubbed his aching eyes, wondering how much to tell the Soviet leader. "At the moment, I might have less control over events than you."

The Premier paused, as if he were pondering the same dilemma about how far to go in this conversation. "You have a pretender aboard your command plane," he said flatly.

"A pretender? I'm not sure that is the correct term, sir. He apparently believes he is President, legitimized by our Constitution."

The President heard a low grunt at the other end. "I had been marveling at the efficiency of your political system. We always considered your system to be your greatest weakness. It is so ponderously slow at times."

"On this occasion it may have been too efficient," the President said. Then he added ruefully, "In more ways than one."

"In translation, Mr. President, that sounds threatening. Do you mean it that way?"

"No, Mr. Premier, most certainly not. I merely mean that my control over events is minimal. I need time to put my house in order."

"This pretender, this other President, he has control?"

"I'm not certain anyone has control here, sir."

"His intentions are the same as yours?"

"I'm not certain, Mr. Premier." The President thought a moment. "Your weapons were very thorough in their destruction of our communications system. I have not been able to talk to him."

Again the President heard a low grunt and then an almost wistful sound in the Premier's voice. "I thought your man had been talking to me," the translator said enigmatically. "Sir?" the President asked in confusion.

"You are aware that your bombers returned home and, in response, I returned mine?"

A great puzzlement spread across the President's face. He desperately wished he could see Sedgwick, who lay nearby in the doorway, to read his face for some indication of how to evaluate the unexpected information. "No, Mr. Premier," he replied after a moment. "I did not know that. It is reassuring news."

"I thought so at the time," the Premier responded. "Unfortunately, the bombers are not the most serious problem. My intelligence officers inform me that your submarine fleet operates on a preprogrammed attack schedule."

"That is correct."

"How much time do we have?"

"I don't know, Mr. Premier."

The radiophone seemed to go dead for a moment. Then the President heard a rapid, brief burst of Russian.

"This is no time to be disingenuous, Mr. President."

"I assure you, Mr. Premier, I would tell you if I knew. You must trust me. I do not know."

The pause was longer this time. The President could hear deep and erratic breathing at the other end.

"We are wasting time we might not have," the Premier said. "I will trust your intentions. I have little choice. Your intentions might not be enough. You are well aware, I assume, that I will not be able to control my ICBM's if you are unable to control your submarines?"

"Too well aware, Mr. Premier."

"Then I recommend that you proceed to, as you put it, place your house in order. Frankly, mine is in some disarray as well. We will talk again, destiny willing. God willing, if you prefer."

"We need both destiny and God on our side today, Mr. Premier. And a good measure of luck."

The President heard the Premier's disconsolate *da*. Then the Russian continued briefly.

"I fear I was somewhat abrupt with one of your advisers. My temper is short today. Please tender my apologies."

The President chuckled, gaining a slight release from the tension, only to have the small laugh send excruciating pain stabbing through his legs. "Apologies are not necessary, Mr. Premier. We are finding the man a mirror."

A babble of confused Russian emerged out of the phone, which the President now had trouble holding. After several short exchanges between the translator and the Premier, the translator asked, "A mirror?"

"Tell the Premier that despite our efficiency, we do not stock hunting dogs in these places," the President said. He was near exhaustion. But he heard a chuckle, also small, emerge out of Cherepovets.

"God be with you, Mr. President."

"And Destiny with you, Mr. Premier."

The pause seemed to linger endlessly this time, as they tried to conclude the conversation.

"I am sorry, Mr. President," the Premier said.

"I am sorry too, Mr. Premier." The President blindly handed the phone upward, felt it taken away, and tried to force his exhausted brain to concentrate on the next step.

Sedgwick, listening from the doorway, glanced at the clock. It read 1900 Zulu.

Fifteen

Framed in the cockpit window, less than two miles away, the *E-4* glimmered majestically in the muted sunlight. It was a handsome craft, the cockpit dome and the presidential compartment bulging white and dramatically out of its spine not entirely unlike the proud head of the eagle it represented. Alice could just make out the lettering—"UNITED STATES OF AMERICA"—stripped in blue across its ribs. The Stars and Stripes flew proudly on its tail, also visible. The *E-4*'s pilot was maneuvering now, swinging the massive tail this way and that in a desperate attempt to outrun his pursuer. But the *Looking Glass* had him cornered. Alice shivered. He grasped Smitty's shoulder and felt the shudder run through him, too. Neither spoke.

Smitty had done a masterful job, one that normally would have been deserving of the highest praise. Alice refrained. The pilot would have been frightfully embarrassed at praise for this grim chore. The general would have found it impossible to give.

The *E-4* was a much newer aircraft and twice as large as the *Looking Glass*. The two aircraft flew at roughly the same velocity, just under the speed of sound, and it was no simple feat to catch an aircraft flying your speed. Smitty, however, had one immense advantage. The pilot of the *E-4* had continued to try to protect himself and his precious cargo from lengthy runs through the

356

radiation. Alice and Smitty had long since abandoned themselves to that risk, cutting directly through the hottest clouds, forcing the *E-4* closer and closer to the fallout so the huge plane would alter its course slightly. On each adjustment, the *Looking Glass* gained. Alice felt a pang of pity for the pilot with the black eyepatch. He was a friend. They were forcing him to choose between the insidious threat of the radiation and the puzzling threat of the *Looking Glass*. The general was not certain which choice he would have made. Would he have played the odds that his pursuer would not have the guts for the final suicidal plunge?

Alice barely heard the figure approaching behind him, and when a hand landed lightly on his arm, he flinched in surprise. He turned to see his communications officer, her mouth agape as her eyes held transfixed to the vision of the command plane looming in front of them.

"Lieutenant?" Alice asked quietly.

The woman shook her head, as if to bring herself back from some far place, and mumbled, "I'm sorry, sir." Her eyes remained on the *E-4*. "The civil-defense station at Olney has made direct contact. They're on the radio now, trying to arrange a patch to the *E-4*."

"Lieutenant—", the general began, subduing his irritated disbelief in condescending tones.

"They want to talk to you, sir," she continued in a monotone.

"Jee-zuz Kee-rist, lieutenant!" Alice suddenly fumed. "Civil defense? Can't you keep those fucking bureaucrats off my back? I'm a little busy!" He drew a deep breath to regain control of himself and then placed a comforting hand on the woman's shoulder. "Lieutenant, it's over," he said flatly. "Go back and handle it for me, will you please? Tell them to crawl under their desks and put a piece of paper over their heads. It's over."

Kazaklis was bone-aching tired, almost giddy from the punishment to body and soul that he had taken now for thirteen hours. In the distance he saw the storm gathering and threatening to cut off their most direct course to Fiji. Their only course to Fiji, he thought sourly. He was not precisely sure where they were. But from the time, shortly after 1900 Zulu, and the rough course they had followed since the decompression, he estimated they were about 10 degrees north of the equator at about 170 degrees west longitude. Ten degrees from the dateline, he thought wistfully.

Ten degrees from tomorrow. The Marshall Islands should be
about a thousand miles west, somewhat closer than Fiji. But the
Marshalls were a dreadful collection of rocks and atolls, scattered
hopelessly, their average elevation a mere five feet above sea level.
The islands also were directly behind the storm. The pilot glanced
left, where the view was more inviting. His eyes moved across the
increasingly frothy ocean, its swells pushed higher and angrier by
the approaching storm. Suddenly his eyes jarred to a stop.

"Whoo-e-e-e-e," he said, nudging Moreau. "Take a look at
that."

Moreau leaned across him. She scanned through the white-
laced blue and then locked on the aircraft carrier. It was a massive
beast, several football fields long. Still, in the distance, it looked
like a child's toy floating in a huge tub. Kazaklis could feel Moreau
tighten.

"Mmm-uhm," Kazaklis clucked. "I always wanted to land on
one of those babies. You think they'd take a wounded old Buff?"

"They'll take us, all right," Moreau replied coldly.

"Turn on the radio and see whose side they're on."

"What the devil difference does it make?" Moreau snapped.
"You think anybody's on our side? We're in deep trouble."

Kazaklis turned toward her and nodded silently, but his eyes
carried no recognition of the threat. He looked exhausted. "Still
think I'll take stars and stripes over a hammer and sickle," he said.

"Damn you, Kazaklis, we're up to our ass in alligators and it
doesn't make much difference if they're commie alligators or
not." She switched on the radio, adjusting it for incoming traffic.
Almost instantly, their earphones were squawking.

"Polar Bear One, Polar Bear One . . ."

"Jesus Christ, we're famous," Kazaklis said in surprise. Moreau
glared at him.

". . . USS *Ticonderoga* calling Air Force B-52 Zero-Two-Six-Six-
Four. Acknowledge. . . ."

Kazaklis froze on the recitation of the identification number of
their tail. He reached quickly toward Moreau, as if to stop her
from replying. "I'm not talking to anybody," she snapped into the
intercom. "I want to hear what they have to say."

". . . Zero-Two-Six-Six-Four, you will ditch in the sea. Escort
aircraft and air-sea rescue have been launched. Repeat, you will
ditch in the sea. We have NCA orders to bring you down or shoot
you down. Acknowledge. . . ."

Kazaklis glanced hurriedly down at the carrier. Two small specks, one after the other, lifted off the deck. He banked the B-52 straight toward the approaching storm.

Alice could feel the ripple of the *E-4*'s wash now. The plane's four immense engines, 747 engines, kicked churning air back at them like a pickup spinning out of gravel. They had closed to about a quarter-mile. The *E-4*'s pilot occasionally bobbed and weaved, feinting a dive, bluffing a turn, but mostly he raced full throttle. They had him and he knew it. The general had a sick, sinking feeling in his gut and he was certain Smitty did, too. They both had spent time aboard the other plane. Alice could envision the *E-4*'s staff still hunched over their machines, just as his people hunched over theirs, doing their jobs even as the end neared— men and women, friends and acquaintances, golf partners and old colleagues who had paused in the halls of SAC headquarters just yesterday and asked: *How's Madge?*

"General?"

Alice did not appear to hear the voice.

"General. Excuse me, sir."

He turned slowly and looked into the worried but determined face of the communications officer.

"General, I've got Olney again. It's important."

Alice ran a beefy hand slowly up his cheeks, gouging, until the fingers squeezed at his eyes. "Damn you, lieutenant," he said with quiet desperation. He could feel the shadow of the *E-4* at his back.

"Sir, it's the President."

Alice dropped his hand abruptly and stared at her in confusion. "Condor?"

"No, sir," she replied. "The President."

"I don't understand," he said slowly.

"I don't understand either, sir. But I have the President on the radiophone. *The* President. He says it's urgent."

Alice turned away and looked out the cockpit window. They were closing methodically on the *E-4*, its towering tail fin seeming to inch toward them. "Break it off, Smitty," he said. Then he added, as he left the cockpit: "Don't let him stray far."

The F-18 Hornets were on them quickly, one off each wingtip so snugly they almost scraped metal. Sidewinder missiles, far superior to the Soviet ACRID's they had evaded over the Arctic, were slung under the wings and tucked tightly near the fuselage of the crack Navy fighter-interceptors. But Kazaklis and Moreau knew the Hornets would not need their missiles to make a fatal sting. Old-fashioned bullets—a quick chug-a-chug-a from the Gatling guns in their white needle noses—would bring the Buff down now. They would not even see it coming. Since Halupalai's ejection, they not only were crippled and defenseless but they had no vision to the rear of the airplane.

Kazaklis swept his eyes across the horizon. The storm was closing in on three sides. But it still lay miles distant and out of immediate reach. He also knew the storm was a dubious haven, that it could prove as fatal to the wounded bomber as the lacing they would get from the made-in-the-U.S.A. machine guns. He turned his gaze back toward the Hornet hovering only a few feet off his wingtip. The fighter tipped its wings like kayak paddles in the universal signal to come down or be taken down. Kazaklis could see the pilot clearly, being not much more than one hundred feet away. He was fuzz-faced in his white helmet, barely out of college, and much younger than Kazaklis. Join the Navy and see the world, Kazaklis thought grimly. The carrier pilot signaled Kazaklis flamboyantly, his gloved hand raised high, the thumb pumping down, down, down.

Kazaklis grinned. "I think that boy's serious, Moreau."

"Jesus Christ, Kazaklis," Moreau shot back, "sometimes I wish your brain were as active as your prick."

"I'm surrounded by hostile forces, threatening from the outside and boring from within," he replied, still grinning.

"Knock it off."

"What the hell do you want me to do? Wave my meat out the window at 'em? You think they'd die of envy?"

Moreau looked at him in dismay, desperately trying to suppress a smile. "Die of laughter, more like it," she said. "The Navy's not intimidated by four-inch guns, Kazaklis."

Kazaklis swiveled his head abruptly toward Moreau, his eyes futilely trying to feign outraged indignation. Instead, he broke into giddy laughter. Moreau began laughing too. Suddenly the cockpit was filled with uproarious, convulsive laughter, the two of them giving way to the exhaustion and hopelessness, venting the repressed fear and loss, easing the incredible tension. The release lasted only a moment. Out of the corner of his eye, Kazaklis caught the first glimpse of the F-18 spitting fire into the emptiness in front of them, clearing its weapons in one final warning.

"I'd say that boy's *very* serious," Kazaklis said, the laughter gone, the eyes glued on the blue-and-white fighter still hovering just forward of his wingtip.

Moreau also had abruptly stopped laughing. "Okay," she said, "so what do we do? Put it down?"

Kazaklis gazed down into the ocean. The carrier was behind them, nowhere in sight. "No," he said. "No, I'm not going that way. Hauled out of the drink by some eager-beaver rescue team on their last drill, plopped down on the deck, grilled by naval intelligence. Then slammed into the brig until some Russky submarine commander pops a couple of kilotons into the hull. No, thanks. That big baby won't make it through the day. Surprised she made it through the night."

Out the left-hand window, the young Hornet pilot gestured toward his face mask. "He wants to talk to us," Kazaklis said. "You think he wants to negotiate?"

"Mmmmm," Moreau grunted.

Kazaklis flicked on the radio, searching the bands until he found them.

"Air Force Zero-Two-Six-Six-Four . . ." the radio crackled.

"That's us, pal," Kazaklis replied. "Our friends call us *Polar Bear*."

"Okay, smart-ass," the fighter pilot snapped back, "our orders are to bring you down or shoot you down. Do you understand?"

"Already got that message, buddy. I think we'll stay up. My friend here's afraid of sharks."

"Roger, Zero-Two-Six-Six-Four. Your choice. You know what a Sidewinder will do to that beat-up crate of yours?"

"Come off it, sailor. You don't need a missile. Save your heavy stuff for the bad guys." Kazaklis paused, turning on his little-boy-amazed voice. "You know I got a lady in the right-hand seat?" He could hear Moreau's groan over the sound of the engines. "Puttin' all that lead in a lady. Now, that's hard to stomach, huh?"

"Bring you down or shoot you down," the radio crackled again. "Your choice, flyboy."

"Hokay, sailor, we sure do understand your problem, havin' orders and all," Kazaklis drawled. "Lemme make it a little easier for you. Now, our navigator's dead, and our radar man's dead,

poor souls. That means we can't see out the back of the airplane.
Our EWO's dead, nice guy he was, too. That means we can't send
out decoys, as if they'd do some good. Our gunner's dead, and he
was the *crème de la crème*"—Kazaklis glanced at Moreau, grinning;
you like my French, Josephine?—"and that means we couldn't
shoot at you even if we could see you. Now, we also got a hole
about three feet square in the top of this gem of SAC's mighty
fleet, and that means we can't go for altitude. So, with the benefit
of all that priceless intelligence, why don't you fellas just wheel
around and pump a few rounds into us, not wastin' too many?"
He stared into the face of the Navy pilot. Then Kazaklis the-
atrically gestured toward Moreau. "You want to say good-bye to
the lady?"

The Navy pilots stared briefly into the cockpit of the B-52. A
voice echoed out of the F-18 off Moreau's wing. "We don't want to
do this, buddy." Then, in unison, the two fighters peeled off into
their turns for the loop around that would bring them back in for
the kill.

"So much for that," Kazaklis said.

"Good God, man," Moreau said, shaking her head in amazement, "is that how you racked up all those scores in the Boom-
Boom Room?"

"Wel-l-l-l," Kazaklis drawled, "in the Boom-Boom Room the
four-inch gun helped."

"Alice here."

Sweat poured off the general, soaking through his clothing. He
had steeled himself, the way a strong man does, for the ultimate
moment. If the last-minute reprieve was a blessing, his bodily
functions did not accept it. The tension release had been too
sudden. All his systems seemed ready to fail now, almost as surely
as they would have flooded in release with the snap-lock opening
of a hangman's trapdoor. His hand shook, his breathing came in
short gasps, his voice quavered, or so it seemed to him, and he was
certain that was why he received no instant reply.

"Alice here," the general repeated, a trifle louder, a touch more
stridently. He had every excuse to feel paranoid, and fleetingly it
occurred to him that he had been had.

"This is the President speaking," a voice said. It was a familiar
voice, with a resonance he had heard hundreds of times. Alice
drew a deep breath, trying to pull his rebellious bodily functions

back into harmony. He instantly fell back on his training. A familiar voice was not enough in his world.

"Day word?" Alice asked automatically.

"I don't think we have time for that, general," the voice said.

Dammit! The unexpected response jarred Alice, steadying him as it also angered him. Now what the hell was going on? Anyone could fake a voice. The President of the United States would know better.

"Listen, pal," Alice barked caustically into the phone, "we haven't had a President since Calvin Coolidge who would've tried that line of shit. I don't know what you are, but you give me the day word. Now. Or you'll find yourself alone in a phone booth."

Alice heard a slight, appreciative—and familiar—chuckle. "Day word's Cottonmouth, general," the voice said. "The command word's Trinity, and the action word's Jericho, bless our tumbling walls. Now you'll ask for the authenticator codes, right?"

"Bet your ass, buddy," Alice said, fingering the small card in front of him.

"I don't have my authenticator card, Alice. It's lost and you either trust me or more than Jericho's walls will come tumbling down."

Alice sagged. "Without that card, you're a phony," he said wearily. "I don't know who you are."

"So what do we do now, general? Check my baseball averages? Play the old Brooklyn Dodgers game? You want Betty Grable's measurements? Or is it Bo Derek this time around? What do we do?"

"We hang up," the general said flatly. "I won't talk to you. I'm disconnecting."

"You . . . hold . . . on . . . general." The sweat from Alice's forehead dripped off his eyebrows, stinging his eyes. He *wanted* to believe. "This is the President of the United States calling you. Authenticator card or no authenticator card. We can play it by the book and blow the world to smithereens. That's what the book calls for. That's where it's taking us. Is that where you want to go?"

Alice didn't answer. The irony of being accused of playing by the book was lost on him, his mind darting down too many dead-end alleys. The perspiration was causing his hand to slide down the receiver. It fleetingly occurred to him—a bolt out of nowhere and departing just as fast—that their greatest mistake had been to expect anyone to act rationally under this pressure. He wanted a cigarette.

"I need a patch through to the *E-4*," the voice said. "I know you can talk to them. We can hear you. We can't reach them from Olney. I know where the plane is. I know who's aboard. The Secretary of the Interior is aboard. He thinks I'm dead. He thinks he's the President. I must talk to him. Fast. About the submarines. Do you understand?"

Alice still said nothing.

"General, for Christ's sake, do you want the precise location? The *E-4*'s flying over Paducah, Kentucky. You're also flying over Paducah, Kentucky. You're damn near on his ass! As your Commander-in-Chief, I'm telling you you're too fucking close to him! One spooked Soviet submarine commander decides to take a potshot, and neither of you will be worrying about goddamned authenticator cards! There won't be any cards! Then where the hell will we be? Answer me, damn you!"

"Where is your card?"

The general heard a pained sigh. "Damned if I know, general. On the South Lawn, which I crawled across on my belly. In the back end of *Nighthawk*, which got blown down in a gully, me in it. Lost in the rubble of somebody's front yard when a kid packed me five miles on his back to this godforsaken hole. In the Olney incinerator with the bathrobe I was wearing when Icarus called." The voice drifted, as if the man were in great pain. "Damned if I know."

"Without the card, the *E-4* won't give you the time of day." Alice looked at the clock. It read 1925 Zulu, one hour and thirty-five minutes to go.

"You let me worry about that, general. That's what I get paid for. I think it's time to earn my pay."

Alice stared into the hands of the clock. "The risk . . ." he mumbled, more to himself than the man on the phone.

"Risk?" the voice bellowed into Alice's ear. "This is a bad time to be talking about risk, general. I'm not asking you for information, though God knows I could use some. Do you think I'm a Russian, spoofing you? Good God, man, they would have read you the numbers so fast your head would spin. They probably have more of our goddamned cards than we do. I just talked to the Soviet Premier. You want me to call him back and ask *him* for the numbers?" The voice shook, wavered, and then returned very wearily.

"Fucking little credit card. Charge-a-war. Damn, it's probably the one thing we did keep secret from the Russians. Or I *would* get it from the Premier. Hell's bells, man, I couldn't read you the numbers if I had the card in my hand. I'm blinder than a bat."

Alice slumped over the phone, rocking slowly.

"It's a bad day for book players, general. I guess orders won't do any good, but I'm asking you to patch me through. Will you do it?"

Alice pulled himself back up to an erect and militarily correct posture. He reached in search of a cigarette. In the private niche the pack of Pall Malls lay crumpled and empty. "Yes, sir, Mr. President, of course I will. I should brief you on a few matters first."

Over the next five minutes, while the clock spun toward 1930 Zulu and Smitty dropped slightly off the tail of the *E-4*, Alice told the President about the extent of the damage to the world, about *Polar Bear One*'s unprompted turnabout made for reasons known only inside the B-52, about his own decision to turn the remaining bombers, about the Soviet response and Condor's reaction, and, most important, about the timing of the submarine attack just ninety minutes hence. The President did not interrupt once.

As Alice concluded, the President let out a low, long whistle and asked, out of genuine curiosity, "What made you believe me, general?"

The general stared into his small countdown watch, brushed at a forehead now dry of sweat, and replied: "Believe you, sir? I'm not sure I do."

"Yes," the President pondered. "I thought as much. Please patch me through now."

"Certainly, sir. I wouldn't count on much, though, with the radio relay coming from the *Looking Glass*."

"General?"

"I was just about to ram him, Mr. President."

"Ram him?"

"Ram him."

The mood inside the B-52 had moved from giddily rambunctious to eerily introspective. Little conversation took place between the two survivors of the flight of *Polar Bear One*. Kazaklis flew directly toward the dark and roiling wall of clouds, but he knew they were out of reach. The storm had edged around the three sides of their visibility and the cockpit had grown dark again. It was not the total darkness of night-light red, but worse— gray and gloomy and foreboding. The light lay behind them, as did their pursuers.

The F-18's had broken off several minutes ago and it would take several more for them to complete the attack run. It would not require more than one pass. The only human noise in *Polar Bear One* was the occasional crackling sound of the two Navy pilots coordinating their maneuvers. Kazaklis had tapped into their radio frequency, wanting to give Moreau time to eject. He had not made the decision for himself.

"*Red Fox One,* this is *Red Fox Two,* into the turn . . ."

"Lost you in the sun, *Red Fox Two* . . ."

In his mind Kazaklis could see the two deadly jets—F-18's were top of the line—sweeping into majestic arcs away from each other to swoop back together behind him.

"About two o'clock. . . . You'll pick me up in a second. . . ."

"Roger, *Two.* Got you now. Let's not get a bloody nose out of this. . . ."

Kazaklis shook his head at Moreau and broke the silence between them. "Bloody nose," he said sarcastically. "Buggers are worried about shooting themselves in the foot."

"Do we have to listen to the play-by-play, Kazaklis?" Moreau's voice was brittle.

Kazaklis shrugged. "You want a black hood?"

Moreau looked at him without replying.

"Have you ever ejected from one of these beauties, Moreau?"

"Uh-uh."

"You want me to throttle it back to a couple hundred knots?" He asked the question compassionately. They both knew airmen who had become instant vegetables taking the windblast head-on. They also both thought immediately of Halupalai.

"No," she said. "Are you going to eject?"

"I dunno, Moreau. Right now I feel like riding the old boy down, if I get the chance. It could blow, you know." He looked at her beseechingly. "Please, Moreau, I'd like you to jump. They'll pull you out."

Moreau started to speak.

"Okay, *Red Fox Two,* pull it in a little tighter," the radio crackled. "You see 'em?"

"Roger, *One.* Got 'em. Three miles."

"Okay, *Two*. Let's go for it."

"Larry?"

"*Two?*"

"Real shit duty, isn't it?"

"Everything's shit duty today, *Red Fox Two*. In we go."

Kazaklis grunted. "Those guys got a lot of heart."

"Duty." Moreau spoke without malice. "Everybody's doing their duty today."

The two sat silently for a moment, their minds retreating.

"Hey, Moreau?" She turned to find him staring intently at her. "I wish I had come to know you better, too." His face wore no con.

She smiled. "My knickers, Kazaklis," she said without hostility. "You wish you had known my knickers."

He grinned. "Oh, those too," he said jauntily. "Pretty nice knickers, they are."

Moreau laughed lightly. "I seem to remember something about better thighs on a Safeway fryer."

He reached over and patted her thigh. "Did I say that? Feels like triple-A to me."

She removed his hand. "But attached to a real bitch, huh?" she said sadly.

"Yeah, sometimes," he said.

"Yeah, most of the time," she said, and they fell silent again.

"One mile, *Red Fox Two*. Take it up a bit and come down on 'em. . . ."

"Moreau?" The voice was urgent and she turned quickly toward him. "I wasn't talking about your knickers."

A shiver raced through her. "Thanks, Kazaklis," she said.

In front of them the black clouds loomed larger, but still out of reach. A flash, like heat lightning, illuminated the leading edge of the approaching storm. A slight shudder rippled through the B-52. *Red Fox One* crackled, "What the hell was *that?*"

The *Looking Glass* patched the call straight through to the white phone, so it was President to President immediately, without the preliminary formality of authenticator cards.

"Condor," the successor said as he lifted the phone.

He heard a vaguely familiar chuckle on the other end. "Good God, is that what they call you?" the undeniably familiar voice asked cheerily. "I don't know if I'd stand for that, Mr. Secretary."

After his conversation with Alice, the President had concluded that he would have severe problems with his Cabinet secretary. So he had decided to approach him obliquely.

Condor, on the other hand, was suffering less than might be expected from the anxiety of the doomsday chase with the *Looking Glass*. Across from him, the Librarian fidgeted. Condor, however, had resolved, in his own mind, that he had made the right decision, a hard and brutal one in a hard and brutal world. He had concluded that his place in history was assured and, perhaps more important, that the events and his role in them could not be changed even if preceded by his death. He had deduced, without further assistance from the colonel, that the mutual destruction of the two command planes assured that the submarines would fire as he wanted. No one would be left in a position to redirect them. He considered that a Divine Irony, and he rather enjoyed it. Condor had made his peace with his Maker—made it long ago, as a matter of fact. So, while not eager, he was ready. Now, in this suddenly teetering moment of doubt, he wondered if Divine Irony had been supplanted by a Divine Joke. "You're dead, Mr. President," he whispered.

The Librarian blanched, then leaped out of his seat. The voice on the phone chuckled again. "Like Mark Twain, Mr. Secretary, I'm afraid the reports of my death have been greatly exaggerated. I'm told, however, that you have done a superb job while I was incapacitated. Turning the bombers was a brilliant stroke."

Condor stared wordlessly across the room, a perplexed look of ambivalence spreading across his face. The Librarian hovered over him, tugging at the arm holding the phone. "Who the devil is it?"

"It was a statesman's stroke, Mr. Secretary. I'm not sure I would have been so cool myself. I congratulate you and give you my eternal thanks." The voice was soothing and calm.

"What the hell is going on?" The Librarian was pulling at him.

"Now we have to work together on the next step, my old friend. We haven't much time."

Uncertainty crept into the successor's eyes. The colonel struggled more fiercely for the phone. "It's the President," the successor said, trying to shoulder him away. The Librarian loosened his grip and shook his head, smiling thinly in disdain.

"We must stop those submarines, Mr. Secretary. It's going to take the two of us."

"This is the oldest trick in the book," the Librarian said, withdrawing a step and continuing to shake his head.

"It's the President," Condor protested feebly.

"Ninety minutes, Mr. Secretary. I need your help. Or everything we both hold dear and holy will be gone forever. I am counting on you."

"My fellow Americans," the Librarian began mockingly, "I come into your living rooms tonight to discuss a matter of the gravest importance . . ." The voice was a near-perfect mimicry of the voice on the white phone. The successor paled.

"We must send out the orders for a cease-fire, Mr. Secretary. Then, together, we can begin to put what's left of our nation back together again."

"Who are you?" the successor asked. The question carried an edge, and beneath the farmlands outside Olney, the President sagged back into his pillow. He could hear bits and pieces of the other voice contradicting him aboard the *E-4*. He knew his bluff wasn't working, the system too stringent, the man and the liturgy—his own liturgy not long ago—too compelling. For a split second the President saw himself long ago on Inauguration Day, still viewing the world in the comfortable simplicity of his election rhetoric. He saw his former self in the man on the other end of the phone. He knew what would come next.

Aboard the *E-4*, the Librarian challenged Condor confidently now. "A thousand Russians are trained to do that. Tape machines. Audio enhancers. They can make the President's voice tell you to fly this aircraft nonstop to Vnukovo Airport for surrender ceremonies. They can tell you your wife's maiden name, your favorite breakfast cereal." He paused dramatically, changing tone and pitch. "They've got turds in their pants. They're scared silly. They're trying everything."

"Mr. Secretary," the phone voice said more sternly now, "I am the President of the United States and you know that very well. You are from Anadarko, Oklahoma. I attended your granddaughter's baptism not three months ago. The child's name is Rachel. She has beautiful blond ringlets."

The successor winced. "You're a fraud," he said painfully. His granddaughter did have beautiful blond ringlets.

"Ask him for authenticator-card confirmation," the Librarian intoned.

The successor withdrew his card and struggled to remember the routine Alice had put him through. "In the upper-right-hand corner of your Sealed Authenticator System card," the successor said, "read me the third, fourth, and fifth letters and/or digits."

"My card's lost, Mr. Secretary. That shouldn't surprise you. You were on the ground. It's not the first time a President's card has been missing. President Reagan's was gone for two days when he was shot. It's a lot messier down here now than it was then." The President drew a breath and continued bluntly. "I'm issuing you a direct command now. Land that aircraft at the nearest available field."

"Lost," the successor said.

"Lost," the Librarian echoed knowingly.

"You're a no-good commie fraud," the successor said evenly.

"You are making a monumental error, Mr. Secretary. It could mean the end of everything."

The successor shook his head at the gall of it, even playing on his love for his granddaughter. He struggled for an appropriate parting remark that would be earthy and memorable.

"Tough titty, comrade," he said, and hung up the phone.

The chatter between the F-18's had stopped briefly. Kazaklis and Moreau looked at each other in confused apprehension. The interceptors should be on their tail now. It had occurred to Kazaklis to send Moreau back to Halupalai's empty station to try to activate their tail cannon. It had occurred to him to try to use the hung-up SRAM, even though that was a thousand-to-one shot. He had dismissed both ideas quickly. Both were pointless. A carrier of this size had many more F-18's and perhaps sixty or seventy additional aircraft that could bring them down. He also had no stomach for shooting his own. Kazaklis gestured to Moreau to prepare for ejection. She shook her head. The radio squawked again suddenly.

"Holy heaven . . ."

"Don't look at it, buddy. . . ."

"But it—"

"Don't look at it!"

The voices warped in and out, half in awe, half in horror. Kazaklis felt a surge of curiosity and thought of banking the plane for a look. He didn't. He plodded on, neither adding throttle nor maneuvering. He stared straight into the approaching clouds, the heat-lightning flare having come and gone instantly. Moreau craned her neck far to the right and out the side window but saw nothing. The clouds seemed to be enveloping them, still miles away but curling up around them. She started to speak to Kazaklis, but the pilot shook his head.

"*Red Fox Two,* I'll take the first pass. . . ."

Kazaklis reached far over, grabbed Moreau's hand, and placed it over the ejection lever, forcing her fingers around it. She withdrew her hand. He looked at her angrily.

"Break it off, Larry," the voice of the wing man, *Red Fox Two,* crackled. But it sounded weepy through the static.

"You take the second pass, buddy. . . ."

"This isn't shit duty now. . . . It's crazy. . . ."

"Get your act together!"

"It's finished, Larry."

Silence huzzed out of *Red Fox One.*

"Let 'em go, Larry . . . let somebody go, for God's sake. . . ."

The empty static roared into the cockpit of the B-52, *Red Fox One* not replying. Then the radio crackled again.

"*Red Fox Two,* this is *Red Fox One.* I'm goin' in. . . ."

"Break away! Break away! Get off 'em, Larry. . . ."

"Closing . . ."

"Ple-e-ease . . . !" The anguished screech, a banshee wail, pounded through the earphones inside the B-52. Then through the radio din came a faint chug-a-chug-a, one short burst. Kazaklis tightened the muscles in his back to prepare for the impact. Moreau hunched forward slightly, then glanced in puzzlement at the pilot. The radio huzzed, then snapped again. "Eject, damn you! Larry!" The raw torment of the voice sliced through the two people in the B-52. "Get out! Hit it, Larry! Hit it!"

"I couldn't order you to do that," the President said. "I couldn't order anyone to do it."

"Order me, sir?" Alice asked. "I was breathing his fumes when you called. At that time, all I had for hope was a prayer to a merciful God. I must say the signs of His mercy were difficult to see."

"There must be some other way."

"Mr. President, I have serious doubt there is any way. With that aircraft aloft, I *know* there is no way. If those subs get conflicting orders—if TACAMO gets conflicting orders—they'll go with the orders they had. It's that simple."

The President sighed forlornly. From his bed, he slowly moved his eyes across the ceiling in a habit that no longer served him. "What do you think, Sedgwick?"

The young naval aide, listening on a separate phone from his bed in the doorway, wagged his head gloomily. He was glad the President could not see his despair. He looked at the clock. The time was 1940 Zulu. Without the two command planes, they would lose their best—probably their only—potential relays to the TACAMO aircraft. Still, Sedgwick thought bleakly, without the general's offer, not even a miracle could occur. "I'm afraid the general's right, Mr. President," he said. "To make anything work, however, the general will have to read me the authenticator codes. Digit by digit. Letter by letter. That's extremely dangerous. We know the Soviets can hear the *Looking Glass*. If they pick them up, they'll have almost as much control over our weapons as you do, sir."

The President's eyes remained open, staring emptily at the ceiling. "Yesterday that would have been high treason, Sedgwick," he said sadly. "Today it sounds like it comes out to zero plus zero."

"It is dangerous, Mr. President," Alice cut in.

"Yes, general, I know damned well it is. But I can't imagine anything more dangerous than what we have right now. I've asked the Premier to trust me. I suppose I'd better reciprocate. Read Sedgwick the codes. I couldn't see them to write them down." He swallowed hard. "Let's pray I haven't lost all my vision."

For the next several minutes Sedgwick methodically transcribed the codes, double-checking each. With the task completed, the President gave Alice his approval for a suicidal collision of America's two premier command planes.

"I don't know what to say to you, general. Except thank you."

"Don't thank me, Mr. President. I don't feel comfortable being thanked. It's time to get on with it. We've lost some ground. It won't be as easy this time."

"Will you call me before the . . . uh . . . ?"

"The end, Mr. President," Alice calmly helped him. "Yes, of course." The general paused a moment. "We did a lot of faulty people programming, sir. Condor's defending God and country too. His version."

"Yes," the President replied. "Yes, I know."

A single F-18 Hornet appeared suddenly off Moreau's wingtip, the pilot pulling in tightly and peering into the cockpit of the B-52. He stared silently at them for several seconds and then the radio crackled once more.

"Good luck, *Polar Bear,*" the pilot said in a voice incredibly young and incredibly sad. Moreau felt a lump grow in her throat. She stared into the F-18, trying to probe the youthful face. But his visor was down, shielding his embarrassment, making him more apparition than man. "Why?" Moreau asked.

The interceptor's wings tipped slightly, as if the apparition were about to vanish, having passed its only message. "Why?" Moreau asked again.

The empty fish-bowl face reflected fading sunbeams at her. "We had nowhere to go," the hollow voice responded. "Maybe you do."

"Your carrier?"

The Navy pilot's voice suddenly choked with anguish. "Just gone," he burbled. "There was a flash. The bow went down in one place, the stern in another . . . and it was just gone. . . ."

"Holy Mary, mother of God," Moreau whispered, crossing herself again.

"We knew it would go." The pilot's voice gathered strength and a certain impatience. "I gotta leave you now." He started to break off and then he leveled out again. "You know anything about home?"

"Not much," Moreau said. "Hawaii."

"Yeah, we saw the flashes last night. We knew it was Pearl. Worse than that?"

"Much."

"Yeah. You'd think they'd stop, wouldn't you?"

"Not sure they know how."

The radios huzzed briefly without words. Then Kazaklis cut in.

"Hey, buddy, why don't you tag along?"

"Palm trees and coconuts and native girls?"

"Somethin' like that."

"It's a pretty empty ocean."

"Invitation stands."

"Negative, thanks. I got a buddy in the drink back there."

"He made it?"

"Oh, yeah. I just whumped him a little one. He got out. He's got his raft open. No fun being alone down there. I'll bet he's feeling meaner than a barracuda right now, too."

Moreau was fighting back tears again.

"Polar Bear?"

"Yeah, *Red Fox?"*

"When the two of us come paddlin' in, you bring on the dancin' girls." The radio crackled. "Hear?"

"You bet, *Red Fox,"* Kazaklis replied, fighting hopelessly against his faltering voice. Moreau gazed into the cockpit canopy through the blur of moistened eyes and saw the pilot snap a cocky thumbs-up at them. "Luck!" she and Kazaklis said simultaneously. But before the word was out, the gleaming fighter was gone and the B-52 plowed head-on into the murk of the storm.

As he reentered the cockpit of the *Looking Glass,* Alice's heart sank. The *E-4* had pulled almost a mile ahead of them again, Smitty having lost far more ground than the general had expected.

"They've decided to take the rads too." Smitty shrugged. "I guess they figure school's out. They've stopped ducking the clouds. Makes it tougher."

"It's more important now, Smitty," the general said.

The pilot cocked an eye at Alice. "Your talk improved the odds?"

"Yes," Alice said with a faint smile. "They're down to about a hundred to one."

Smitty raised his eyebrows. "Shit, general, that's almost a shoo-in." He nudged the throttles, trying to pick up a few knots of air speed.

"I must ask you to hold off until twenty-one hundred hours, Mr. Premier. A little more than sixty minutes. Are you able to do that?"

The nurses fluttered nervously around the President, wedging the radio operator in between two dead teletypes as they elbowed for space to get at the man. His face was mottled and clammy, his body shuddering involuntarily. It was clear he was in extreme pain, although he withheld all complaints. He did not withhold his irritation, batting at them blindly as if he were flailing at two buzzing houseflies. They shot concerned looks at Sedgwick. The man was pushing himself far too hard. Sedgwick shook his head slowly to let them know the man's agony was necessary.

"Do I have a choice, Mr. President?" the Premier asked.

"No, I'm afraid not. I am doing everything I can, but my situation is desperate."

He could hear the Premier grunt and answer in aggravation that was softened somewhat by the interpreter.

"Your situation may be desperate, Mr. President. But need I remind you that it is my people who will be at the receiving end of your desperation?"

The President swatted angrily at a hand that mopped his forehead. "Need I remind you that it was my people who were at the end of yours, Mr. Premier?" he snapped.

A long pause followed and then a much more subdued Russian voice responded, small catches of silence punctuating the words. "No, Mr. President, you do not need to remind me. I fear it was my desperation—although I still see no way I could have avoided it—that placed both our peoples in the path of the dragon. I will spend the rest of my time living with that curse. All of one hour, perhaps. Can we slay the dragon in that time, Mr. President?"

"I cannot assure you of anything, Mr. Premier. I can only tell you that I have taken every possible step and some of my people are making great personal sacrifices—ultimate sacrifices—to give us a chance."

"There are many sacrifices being made," the Premier said after a brief pause. "You do know that both our nations are continuing to lose cities?"

"Lose cities?" The President was staggered. "All the bombers returned hours ago," he said in disbelief.

He could hear a great sigh on the phone. "You did not know," the Premier said sadly. "I regret to be the one to inform you, but your lack of that knowledge may help illustrate my problem. My nation has lost the cities of Nadhodka, Pushkin, and most recently Kursk. Your nation has lost Baton Rouge, Raleigh, and, just moments ago, the city of Phoenix."

The President lay back in his bed, exhaustion eating at him. "How, Mr. Premier? How could such a thing happen now? Why?"

"Mr. President, your submarines and mine have been pursuing each other for fourteen hours. As good as they are, it was inevitable that a few would be caught like fish in a net. When trapped, they operate on the same principle. They fire their missiles before the net closes. Thus far, we have been . . . it is difficult to say, with so many lives lost . . . but thus far we have been most fortunate. The submarine commanders have shown great restraint in choosing relatively minor targets and not spraying their weapons."

Phoenix. Raleigh. Baton Rouge. Minor targets. The President groaned, bringing a nurse rapidly to his side. He brushed her away. "We have created a relentless dragon, Mr. Premier."

"A most relentless dragon. But to satisfy your curiosity about my situation, Mr. President, I must warn you that the dragon's breath may be hotter in my cave than yours. My people are aware of the loss of those cities. They are nervous, and many are mourning the loss of families."

Deep in the bowels of the Cherepovets bunker, the Premier stopped and the translator looked at him expectantly. The Soviet leader pondered whether to tell the President of his own bellicose Condor whom he had to harness in the distant deserts of Zhangiztobe. He knew he also had other rebellious birds, held on a short tether right here in his own nest. The translator cleared his throat to bring the Premier back. "Not all my people are certain of your intentions, Mr. President," he finished.

"Mr. Premier," the President said wearily but firmly, "you are aware of my intentions. You overheard my conversation with the commanding general of the Strategic Air Command. You are aware of his intentions, the personal totality of his commitment." The President paused and took a deep breath. "I have asked you for one hour."

"Mr. President," the Premier said slowly, "I believe in your intentions. I will try to grant you your hour—and guarantee my commitment to it with the same totality given by your general. But I must warn you. The control has largely left our hands. If one of your submarine commanders, trapped in a net, decides Leningrad or Moscow is a more attractive target than another Pushkin . . ."

This time the translator stopped, asking the Premier to repeat his final words.

". . . If that happens, Mr. President, I cannot guarantee you two minutes."

SIXTEEN

2000 ZULU

Around the world, on the various clocks set to Zulu, the hands moved silently past twenty hundred hours. A certain lulling fatalism settled in among the players in the last act. The system functioned.

In the cavernous bunker beneath Cherepovets, the Soviet Premier missed the marking of the last hour. His head nodded from exhaustion. His mind skittered in a dozen foggy directions. His heavy eyelids drooped, then snapped back open again, focusing fuzzily on the small red canister over which he had burned the American codes and shredded the ashes through its rarely used and rusted grille.

His eyes moved ponderously to the blur of the huge display screen from which the symbols of his remaining ICBM's gleamed mockingly. Zhangiztobe, tucked far away in the high plains of Kazakhstan, throbbed rather than gleamed at him. He forced his fatigued eyes away to the next screen, where a handful of computerized white cursors fluttered in a taunting reminder of the tattered remains of his nation's other, and more exhilarating, use for rockets. He sighed. They had beaten the Americans into space—stunned the world with Sputnik, charmed it with the orbiting of the little dog Laika, awed it with the human triumph of Yuri Gagarin. *I am eagle!* They had placed stars in the heavens,

377

but now the stars were blinking out, only a few white cursors remaining as testaments to Gagarin's glory. From its low orbit, Molniya, a survivor, his only link to the American President, winked at him like the setting evening star. Too few others twinkled—a Volna, a Cosmos, another Volna launched into high geostationary orbit in 1980. *I am mole,* he thought despairingly. His heavy eyelids drooped further. The screen blurred. He reached for another amphetamine. His last one, he told himself ruefully. Of that, and only that, he was certain.

In the smaller bunker beneath Olney, the American President lay in the clinic now, eyes closed, neither asleep nor awake, drifting. Occasionally he emitted a loud moan, bringing the nurses rushing to his side, but the occasional moans were not products of the pain. Those, he suppressed. These rose from a deeper source, wrenched out of the depths of his soul as his sightless eyes drifted into new visions of America, its purple-mountained majesties, its fruited plain, its alabaster cities pockmarked like the moon.

Sedgwick manned the radio room, his bed rolled into the cramped slot vacated by the President. He, too, missed the passing of the Zulu clock's hands as he pushed the radio operator through futile probe after futile probe—UHF, VHF, HF, LF, frequency after frequency, dead satellite after dead satellite. He picked up an increasing gaggle of world sounds now—curt Europeans, an excitable Portuguese voice out of Brazil, a New Zealander who babbled incoherently about Nevil Shute, an occasional dirge from some unknown and unmanned American radio station. His frustration was total, the flutter of other radio conversations infuriating. He *knew* the TACAMO planes were there, one having lifted out of Bermuda, the other out of Guam. But they made no sounds.

In the *E-4,* Condor did not notice the passing of the hour. He rested comfortably, even contentedly. Each man is presented with his moment of truth, and Condor had faced his, meeting it to his satisfaction. The Librarian had moved to the radio compartment. If any American communications center had a chance to reach the TACAMO planes, the *E-4*'s chance was best. The communication was not necessary, but the Librarian was an efficient man. He could negate any possible breakthrough by creating a conflict, so he worked as diligently as Sedgwick at reaching the planes.

Of the crucial players aboard the *E-4,* only the pilot was troubled. Just inside the locked cockpit door the Secret Service agent stood cradling his Uzi, the pilot's security against further madness of the kind that had brought Harpoon down almost at his side. He forced himself to accept that Alice, closing in on him again, suffered from the same battlefield malady. It was difficult to believe of men he had respected, but strong men had cracked under far less pressure. He followed orders—just as he followed orders to no longer avoid radioactive clouds. The fate of his nation was at stake.

In the *Looking Glass*, Alice felt the pressure. He gazed out the cockpit window at the shimmering plane ahead of him and saw both his nation and the world slipping out of his fingers. The *E-4* had become desperately artful, racing at full bore, darting into billowing clouds, maneuvering in the opaque vapor, and then darting out in a different direction. Smitty swerved the *Looking Glass* onto the surprise course, only to have the *E-4* swing again. The *Looking Glass* measured its gains in feet. It was not enough. Alice wanted a cigarette.

In the placid depths of the world's oceans, in silently roaming behemoths, American submarine commanders methodically noted the hour. Beneath their feet giant gyroscopes, one of the true marvels of American technology, whirred relentlessly with precision even greater than that of the Zulu clocks. The gyros guided both the submarines and their deadly cargo, inextricably linking the two. With timing measured in microseconds the gyroscopes monitored the submarines' forward progress, their depth, their direction, their turns and pauses. Through huge umbilicals, the gyros fed the data to the missiles, adjusting their trajectories microsecond after microsecond so they were forever trained precisely on thousands of far-off targets. When the time came, and it was scarcely an hour off now, the commanders would turn simple keys from positions at Hold on the left, to Tactical straight up, to Fire on the right. The gyros would send the last microsecond's trajectory adjustment, the umbilicals would fall away, and the commanders would feel a lurching whoosh, whoosh, whoosh. The gyroscopes were called the Ships Inertial Navigation System. Aboard the boats, they were known simply as SINS.

In scores of tiny mole holes across the Soviet Union, pink-cheeked young officers of the Rocket Forces had no way of knowing the significance of the hour change. They waited, locked deep in the frozen earth with their SS-17's and SS-19's. A few sat with rockets designated SS-18's. They were loaded with twenty-five-

megaton warheads, the world's largest—a weapon that would dig a hole, killing everything within a diameter of thirteen miles, igniting winter-dry shrubbery as well as children's clothing twenty-five miles from its target. The young men sat nervously, their imaginations at work. Unlike the submarine crews, they were not yet sure of their role. But they would act, as surely as the submarines. Upon instruction, they would utter the final count: *tri . . . dva . . . odin . . . pust!* On the display boards in front of them, green lights marked with Cyrillic lettering would begin to flick rapidly: Enable Command . . . flick . . . Launch Command . . . flick . . . Launch in Progress . . . flick . . . Missile Away . . . flick.
World away.
Flick.

Aboard the *Polar Bear*, where two stragglers still struggled against the system, the system rebelled against the rebellious. In the B-52, buffeted violently just barely above seas far more angry than the serene depths in which the submarines roamed, the gyros functioned less well, as did the display lights. Torrential rains, whipped by the fury of the tropical storm, flooded through Halupalai's escape hatch. Water pellets lashed into the sophisticated electronic jamming equipment at the rear of the topside compartment, jamming the equipment instead, shorting it out in sizzles and snaps that flashed like devils' beacons in the murk.

Kazaklis turned off the equipment, and the navigational gear downstairs as well, both being useless to him anyway. But on the instrument panel in front of him, which he needed, the yellow lights began to sputter and fail too. The directional gyro went, as did the horizon gyro. So did various of their compasses and altimeters, as well as the fuel-flow indicator. They had almost two hundred gauges and switches, most of which were dead, malfunctioning, or simply lying. They had no idea if they were flying level or descending, although common sense told them the latter. At eye level in front of Kazaklis and Moreau the two green screens still shimmered, the trustworthy nose cameras probing ahead. But the images they fed back told the pilots nothing. They were computer-scrambled green visions of hell.

By no measure—neither the pilot's percentage baseball nor the manufacturer's stress guidelines—could the B-52 survive this punishment. It groaned and shrieked in protest. It fell hundreds of feet in downdrafts, belly-flopping into new air currents that racked human and aluminum bones alike, wrenching at arms, tearing at fragile wings more comfortable in the thin reaches of the stratosphere long since abandoned. After more than half an hour, Kazaklis and Moreau had no idea how high above the ocean they flew. Each time they bellied out, certain they had struck the swells, they bulled the aching aircraft back upward, or so they hoped, through the turmoil. They spoke only when necessary, but they acted as one now.

Kazaklis looked out the window. Through the sheets of water he could not see the wingtip. He could not see beyond the feeble gray outline of the nearest engine. Kazaklis glanced back at Moreau. She stared rigidly ahead, unaware of him, her face quietly intent.

"Fire in Number Three," she said mechanically.

Kazaklis looked back out into the murk but saw no more where one of their inboard engines was giving out.

"Shut it down," he said calmly. She already had done it.

The Librarian grinned broadly, the very audacity of his discovery giving him great satisfaction. The radio-room crew watched him strangely, finding no humor in their predicament. But to the colonel the others were not present. He had found a way to break through to the TACAMO planes, guaranteeing beyond any doubt that the submarines would fire. He congratulated himself for his relentless and unappreciated years studying the Soviets. It now had paid off so handsomely! He would contact the Navy command planes with the Russians' own communications equipment! He chuckled aloud at the triumph, then paused for a moment, testing the wisdom of the idea. Would the Soviets catch on? Probably. Would their awareness make any difference? No. Could they stop him? Highly unlikely. His grin spread from ear to ear. He glanced at the clock. 2015.

Alice irritably ripped off the cigarette filter, concluding that John Kennedy had been all too correct: life is not fair. The Pall Malls were gone and the copilot had offered a Carlton—one of those infernally denatured weeds that threatened to give you a heart attack trying to inhale it. He dragged hard and looked out the cockpit window, furthering his irritation. The giant presidential command plane screamed through the thin air and dancing clouds ahead of them, always just beyond reach. He looked at his watch. 2016. The *Looking Glass* had lost its edge. There was no point in calling the President to tell him that.

The last amphetamine had jarred the Soviet Premier's sensibilities into a jangled alertness again. He sat in the same chair and stared into his display screens. Under the artificial stimulus of the drug, the ICBM cursors appeared to throb rather than gleam, taunting him—Yoshkar Ola field ready, comrade; Zhangiztobe field ready, comrade. Zhangiztobe.

The Premier suddenly felt uncomfortable, a presence hovering near him. He looked away from the screen into the grim face of the new commander of the Rocket Forces.

"The silo doors are open," the Premier said. He had no question in his voice.

"Yes, they are open." The reply was sullen.

"They will fire if necessary."

"It is quite a simple act, Comrade Premier."

"Yes. And closing the doors also is simple?"

The general stared probingly into the Premier's drawn face. He cocked his head, averting his gaze to the map without answering.

"Zhangiztobe," the Premier said forlornly.

The general continued to stare into the map, unresponsive.

"General! Can we stop Zhangiztobe?"

The general turned slowly and looked at the Premier. The general was no fool. He could see the ravages of the man's fatigue. He also could see the effects of the amphetamines and the occasional vodka. "Can the Americans stop their submarines?" he asked, a slight touch of hostility in his voice.

The Premier bristled, then snapped: "Comrade general, I do not need a Viennese psychiatrist answering questions with questions."

"The rocket-base commander is not rational, comrade. His family is dead. Killed by the Americans. He is holding. I do not believe he will continue to hold if we order him to close his doors."

"Not even if the American submarines are stopped," the Premier said. It was not a question and it received no answer. He looked at the clock. 2017. "How many rockets remain at Zhangiztobe?"

"About forty, comrade."

"With multiple warheads?"

"Most of them."

"Their targets?"

"Petroleum facilities and ports."

"But they can be retargeted? On site?"

"In minutes, Comrade Premier."

"And to what targets?"

The general's eyes darted away from the Premier, nervously and evasively. He gazed back into the map of the missile fields over which he had taken command just hours ago at this man's behest. "The retargeting has its limitations." Behind him, he heard a fist pound powerfully into a desk. *Chert voz'mi!* The devil take it! "I am losing my patience, comrade! Can you see the clock?"

"The warheads can be retargeted on most of the major cities in the central and northern United States," the general said rapidly.

The Premier slumped. His tortured nervous system sent electric shocks down his arms and legs. How had he let this sit so long? "Where are our nearest bombers?" he asked.

The general wheeled on the Premier, his eyes narrow and accusatory. "Comrade Premier, you called them back to crashes into the Arctic Ocean. A handful made northern airfields. Zhangiztobe is one of our more isolated fields, more than two thousand kilometers south of the northern frontier—"

The Premier pounded his fist again and again. "Find me an answer, general!"

"You trust the Americans that much?"

"I trust nothing except this infernal system we created!"

Reflexively the general's hand edged over his button-holster sidearm. The two men stared at each other coldly, the Premier's weary face slowly breaking into a half-smile.

"You think that is the answer, comrade general?"

The general sagged in despair. "But how can we do this before the Americans have their submarines under control?"

"Will it do any good afterward? The submarines will still exist. The Americans will have thirty Zhangiztobes floating beneath the sea. With commanders as irrational, comrade, if more of their cities are destroyed."

The general's hand dropped away from his sidearm, but he could no longer hold his eyes on the Premier. "We have several Backfire bombers stationed 150 kilometers away near Ust-Kamenogorsk." His voice was dull and lifeless. He paused and added sadly, "They were deployed against the Chinese."

"They can destroy the command post?"

"Quite certainly."

"That will incapacitate the entire field?"

"With reasonable assurance."

"When?"

"They are supersonic. They could be there in minutes. With the communications . . ."—he turned and stared hard into the Premier's ravaged face—"and the psychological difficulties, it might take twenty or thirty."

"Order them into the air, comrade."

The general's powerful shoulders slumped, seeming to collapse under the weight of the massive array of medals and ribbons strung across his breast. "This is the price of my appointment, Comrade Premier? My first order is to destroy my own forces?"

"Your first order is to save Russia, comrade."

The general's blue eyes had turned gray with agony. He nodded stiffly and left the room. The Premier watched the man's back for a moment, subduing the thought that his own rationality might be as questionable as that of his far-off ICBM wing commander. The devil has taken me, he thought. I have just ordered my own people killed on the remote chance—and it is most remote—that the Americans will not kill them. When such twisted logic makes sense, all hope is gone. He slumped and turned back to the screens. He moved his eyes quickly away from the missile display and escaped to the relative peace of the space-satellite screen. Ah, my stars above, he sighed, how much more pleasurable it was to play with your rockets. And there are so few of you now.

Suddenly his frazzled mind focused perfectly. He cursed the fog that had prevented him from seeing such simplicity earlier. He bolted up from his chair. Simultaneously his radio operator also stood, a look of confused concern on his face. He frantically signaled the Premier. The Premier's heart sank, his first thought being of Leningrad. He looked at the clock. 2021.

"Fire in Number Four," Moreau said.

"Shut it down."

"Done."

"Rudder."

"Got it."

Kazaklis looked left through the horizontal slashes of water on the window. He could see the outline of Number Four, the nearest inboard engine. It appeared to have blackened fire streaks. But by now he knew they were suffering from various optical illusions. The "leans" could have them flying at a tilt to the horizon, the lack of any visual frame of reference making the appearance of level flight an uncertainty. The plane could be nosed up slightly. It could be nosed down, which was more likely. They could fly with six of their eight engines, even lose a couple more in normal weather. But not for long in this mess. "Altitude?" he asked.

"You kidding?" Moreau replied with rigid calm.

"Can we cross-reference?"

"Negative." Moreau tugged on the wheel. "Try the EVS."

Kazaklis switched the green screen from its normal viewing system to terrain tracking. The small yellow thermometers appeared on the right of the two screens, darting up and down. Kazaklis winced. The computer clearly was converting the storm's violence into a false surface. But unless it was lying completely, they were well below two thousand feet, the system's range. The aft section of the plane lurched ferociously in a sudden gust, jerking Kazaklis toward Moreau and Moreau into the side of the cockpit. The tear of ripping metal raged through the other aircraft noise. The B-52 sounded like an old man dying, moaning, creaking, wheezing, in the somber half-light of the last call.

"Shit," Kazaklis said. "We're gonna lose the rudder and the stabilizer. We gotta get some altitude."

"Thanks. Which way's up?"

"Been askin' myself that all my life."

"Very funny."

"Always figured it had to be the other way."

Suddenly, out of nowhere, without a downdraft or a gust, a calamitous whomp sounded in the belly of the plane. The Buff bounced like a flat rock on water. Kazaklis swiveled his head left. The murk had thinned. Far off he saw streaks of yellow in the darkness. He also saw that the two inboard engines, numbers three and four, had broken off and fallen into the sea. And he saw the sea just below, frothy, ugly, gray, and deadly with swells of sixty or seventy feet. He knew that one of those swells had just tickled their belly, and not with a feathery touch.

Moreau looked out her window. "You're right," she said quietly. "It's the other way."

The two of them wrenched at the controls.

"We're not going to make it," Kazaklis said.

"Yes we are."

"Prepare to eject."

"I'm not ejecting, Kazaklis."

"I really want you to make it, Moreau." She looked at him, and he had pleading in his eyes. They both turned to look down from their side windows. She shook her head slowly. Kazaklis nodded and went quiet. She wouldn't make it in that caldron, either. Without conscious thought, rote being his guide now, Kazaklis kept the *Polar Bear*'s nose pointed into the distant streaks of yellow. They seemed very far away.

The Premier stood over his radio operator, babbling almost incoherently. "Jam the swines!" he ordered, his face purple with rage. The radio operator shrank back in fear of the man's wrath. "Comrade Premier," he said with trepidation, "we do not have the capability." The Premier pounded a fist on his subordinate's desk. "Order a submarine attack!" The operator cowered further. "Comrade, you know we can't get through."

The Premier's face sagged. "They can use our equipment to reach their submarines, and we can't do the same to reach ours?" he asked.

"They are communicating with an aircraft relay, Comrade Premier," the radioman replied. "Not with submerged submarines."

The Premier placed his hand on the man's shoulder to assure him the blame was not his, the anger born of frustration. He cursed himself again for a brain so muddled it had allowed the American pretender to discover the answer moments before he made the same discovery. Dejectedly he looked at the intercepted message. It was brief, making contact, awaiting the request for the codes he had just burned. He turned his gaze toward the clock. 2022. He must call the President immediately. Condor, the foul bird, was using his Volna satellites to contact the American submarine-control planes.

The Librarian rushed excitedly around the compartment, patting technicians' shoulders, shaking limp hands, not noticing that few of the others in the room shared his enthusiasm for this coup. He had two brief replies, one from each TACAMO plane, seeking NCA code confirmation and orders. He moved quickly to the phone.

Condor answered somewhat irritably. "You interrupted my prayers, colonel."

"I have the answer to your prayers, sir," the Librarian said.

"Didn't expect the answer by phone," Condor replied drolly.

"Sir, I've reached the TACAMO planes. It's in the bag. You will have to come down with the authenticator card."

The phone went silent for a moment. Then Condor asked, "How in the Lord's name did you do that?"

"Straight through a couple of Soviet satellites, sir!" the Librarian exulted. "How's that for shoving it to them?"

"Be right down, colonel," Condor said, adding: "Man deserves the Medal of Honor for somethin' like this."

The Librarian cradled the phone. It occurred to him ever so briefly that the award would be posthumous. But then, that is the most valorous kind. Still, the thought of death reminded him of the *Looking Glass*. He cast a hurried look at the clock—2024—and reached again for the phone, pushing the button for the cockpit.

"Where the hell is Alice?" he demanded of the pilot.

"Right on our tail, sir," the pilot replied.

"You keep that bastard off us for another fifteen minutes, major," the Librarian snapped. "If you want to win this war."

In the cockpit, the pilot clicked off. A perplexed look spread across his face. Win *this* war? He thought the objective was to end it.

"Alice is calling, sir."

The President lifted his loose hand, raising one finger and wagging it in a silent instruction to keep the general holding while he finished his present conversation.

"Afraid the culture gap is too great to give you any advice on that, Mr. Premier," he said into the phone. "What we do here is pray. . . . I understand. . . . Yes. . . . Thank you, sir. Thank you greatly. . . . Yes, he's on the line now. I'd best get on with it. . . . Good luck to you, too." He handed up one phone and beckoned for the other.

"General," he said, not wasting a second. "The situation?"

"Tough, sir. He's got a half-mile on us and he's evading expertly."

"It's imperative that this happen fast now. Our situation's changed."

"Sir?"

"We've found a way through to TACAMO—"

"Good God, sir," Alice interrupted, "that means we can succeed."

"I'm afraid it also means we can fail, general. The Premier, bless his black little heart . . ." He suddenly remembered the Soviet leader could hear his every word. "Uh, pardon me, Mr. Premier, that's American idiom—the Premier has found a radio routing. Unfortunately, someone in the E-4 discovered the routing a few moments earlier. The E-4 has made contact."

"Shit!" Alice didn't bother to apologize. "Conflicting orders." Alice's voice went quietly somber. "It dooms us, Mr. President."

"Perhaps. Perhaps not. It's in your lap, general. The E-4 got a locator message through. The TACAMO planes have asked for confirmation and codes. The messages don't move instantly. It'll take a few minutes to move the codes. Not many. Can you catch him in five minutes?"

In the Looking Glass, Alice's heart sank. He stared out the window at the tail section of the E-4, so close . . . so distant. The plane's four huge contrails flooded past him, the vapor mixing with dark exhaust as if the man in the black eyepatch were stoking the furnace with everything now. Smitty hung on him, just above the contrails, following every swoop of the gleaming plane, chasing the huge tail into the fog of each cloud and then out again for a zigzag in the fading sunlight. The E-4 yielded a little meaningless space here, a little there. Then the pilot, flying like the best, which he was, took the lost space back. It would take a miracle to catch him in less than twenty minutes, and he couldn't guarantee it even then.

"General?"

"I'm sorry, sir," he replied with great sadness. "It is impossible." The President paused only briefly. "Try," he said.

Alice shook his head dismally. "Of course I'll try, sir."

"General, they should have stocked these damned places with braille watches. What the hell time is it?"

"2034, sir."

"Okay, you call me back in two minutes—2036 on the nose. We're counting in seconds now, but I have to deal with TACAMO, too." He paused. "Everything—*everything*—rides with you now, general," he added quietly.

"Yes, sir. I know, sir."

In the Looking Glass, Alice heard the disconnection. He reached over and grabbed Smitty's shoulder. "I want you to burn out every fan in those engines of yours, Smitty," he said. "We've got five minutes. Or it's all over."

Smitty turned and started to shake his head. But the general no longer was looking at him.

"Will somebody get me a fucking cigarette?"

The copilot offered him another Carlton.

He waved it away. "A *real* goddamned cigarette!"

Condor entered the communications room alone, unannounced, and almost completely without fanfare. Several heads turned briefly, because none of those present, with the exception of the Librarian, had seen the man before. One young officer saluted. He immediately felt awkward. Saluting was an unnecessary formality here, and he had done it out of nervousness.

The Librarian immediately ushered Condor to a telegraph operator. That somewhat surprised him, because he had expected voice communication. But those were the rules, and they were to be scrupulously followed. TACAMO wanted the message on paper and it would arrive in specific sequence or it would be ignored. Any suspicions about the validity and they might come back for voice confirmation. But voices meant nothing with the stakes this high. The message would be sent with word codes first, authenticator codes second, and message last. The message would be simple enough, being just three words: "SIOP PRIME CONFIRMED."

The Librarian already had begun sending the word codes. Sending the information from the Sealed Authenticator System was slightly more complex. As Alice had done earlier, TACAMO had randomly requested several series of letters and digits rather than the entire list. This was a precaution against interception. If someone were listening—as indeed the Soviet Premier was doing in a cold sweat at this very moment—it would do the eavesdropper no good. For the next set of orders, if needed, a different series would be requested. The entire message would automatically be encrypted and decoded by computer—by eye and hand, if necessary—at the other end. It was cumbersome, but these were orders involving thousands of nuclear warheads. With the unconventional relay they were using, it would take perhaps five or six minutes. The Librarian and Condor embarked immediately on the difficult portion, the authenticator codes. The time was 2036 hours.

In the cockpit of the *Looking Glass,* the communications officer also snapped an unnecessary salute. But she did it intentionally, with tears in her eyes, a smile on her face, and a single Pall Mall cigarette proffered in her other hand. Alice accepted the cigarette, snorted through his nose as if he were catching a cold, snapped his hand to his brow in a flawless West Point tribute, and quickly turned away so she would not see the real him, as if she had not already. He stared through his own mist at the other aircraft, still too distant. His people had given him everything. But they were not going to make it. His watch read 2036. He snorted again, trying to cover that tribute to them, too, by giving Smitty an unusually brusque order to futilely push the *Looking Glass* beyond limits already reached. Then he grabbed the cockpit phone to the President, placing the cigarette behind his ear.

On the flight deck of the *E-4,* the pilot with the black eyepatch turned his head away from the wispy clouds ahead of him and probed the shadows in the rear of his spacious cockpit. The Secret Service agent stood at the door with his Uzi, still symbolizing his protection against madness. With a shiver of sadness mixed with surprise, the pilot suddenly saw madness in a different perspective.

"I have the Premier on the other line, Alice. His people are monitoring the transmission. The *E-4* has begun the authenticator codes. You have three, maybe four minutes. That transmission must be interrupted." The President paused, hoping he did not have to ask. "Can you do it in that time?"

Alice stared straight ahead. The *Looking Glass* flew slightly above the *E-4,* Smitty avoiding the five-mile copper trailing wire normally used as a VLF radio antenna. It was out as a snare now, whipping dangerously beneath them. The heat warps from the command plane's giant engines rippled the air between them, causing the massive tail section to wobble like a ghostly mirage, always beyond his grasp. On the side of the stabilizer fin Alice could see the American flag fluttering in the heat rivulets, painted stars wobbling in triumph, stripes flowing as if the nation's proud emblem had been planted atop a hill taken. The hill remained more than a quarter-mile away, and it remained secure.

"No, Mr. President, I cannot," Alice said.

On the phone the silence seemed endless and deafening. Alice could hear his own pulse pounding in the earphone. The President finally spoke, and Alice shuddered at the eerie calm of his voice.

"You understand what this means?"

"All too well, Mr. President."

"It's hopeless?"

Alice held his eyes unflinchingly on the *E-4*. "Another ten minutes, sir . . ." he said quietly. "Another twenty. If the pilot made one false move, one small slip . . ." The general's voice also was eerily calm. "Any man could make that slip, Mr. President. Any man would. Eventually. But I know the pilot. I helped train him. He's good. When I place myself in his position, I . . . I . . ."

Alice fumbled only briefly, his voice catching. Then he continued. "If I place myself in the cockpit of the *E-4*, sir, I see myself pursued by a madman. I see the President of the United States pursued by a madman, with only me between the two." He paused. "I would not slip, sir."

The President's voice turned pensive. "Yes," he said. "Yes, I can see that. Madness takes many forms, general. I'm afraid I can see that more clearly now, sightless, than I did with both eyes. It's a heavy burden to carry out of this world."

Alice said nothing. The floor vibrated beneath him, the engines screaming in the torture of their impossible reach for the giant plane cutting through the clouds just ahead of them.

"General?"

"Yes, sir?"

"Against your wishes, I am going to thank you." The President paused and Alice thought he heard a sniffle on the other end. "Not all our people programming was that faulty."

Alice swallowed hard, blinking his eyes against the increasing mist. He was unable to reply, reaching behind his ear for the cigarette instead. He fondled it, as he might a fine Havana.

"The people," the President began again, his voice curious, as if he had found one truth too late and now sought another, "the crew aboard the bomber that turned . . . who were they?"

The general swallowed again and took a deep breath. They had time now. Not much. But they had no better way to use it.

"I don't know what to tell you, sir," Alice responded painfully. "The pilot was very good. The copilot was the daughter of one of my best friends. You knew him. General Moreau. Devoted his life to this, convinced like all of us that we could prevent it by keeping it ready. That's a tough mistake to take upstairs, too. . . ." Alice found it almost impossible to continue, his voice dropping off to a whisper. "What can I tell you? They weren't average, whatever the hell that means. They weren't that special, whatever that meant in our world. . . . Does it make any difference?"

The clocks ticked past 2038.

"Why?" the President asked. "Why did they do it? Scared—?"

Alice suddenly flared in uncontrollable anger and hurt. "Scared? You're damned right they were scared! Just like I'm scared! Just like you're scared, the Premier's scared, the whole fucking world is scared out of its wits! You want me to say they were cowards? Cowards, sir? Heroes, sir? Mad, sir? Sane, sir? How the hell do I know?!" Alice broke it off just as suddenly. "They gave us a glimmer of hope, Mr. President," he added softly.

"That's why I wanted to know, general." The President sighed. "They gave us, for whatever reason, more than I gave. That's a heavy one to carry, too."

Alice paused. Suddenly he felt as if he had no time and all the time in the world. "Mr. President?"

"Yes, general."

"I saw General Moreau a month ago. I thought he was growing senile. He said we were losing."

The President bristled slightly. He had built every weapon the military wanted. He drew a deep breath. Every weapon you wanted, too, buster, he said to himself. "Losing," he said quietly. "To the Soviets?"

"To the system, sir."

At 2039 Zulu a series of explosions occurred almost unnoticed in the wastelands of eastern Kazakhstan. The world's sensing devices did not record them, and their relevance would have been puzzling in any case. The ground-burst explosions carved craters nearly a kilometer wide and more than fifty meters deep in the place known as Zhangiztobe. Of the crews of the two Backfire bombers flying over the isolated region, one intentionally failed to pull up and out. The other flew home.

Condor and the Librarian calmly supervised the methodical tap-tap-a-tap of authenticator codes soaring upward toward two

Soviet satellites orbiting over the earth and back downward toward two American aircraft orbiting over the oceans. The clock read 2039 Zulu, the codes more than half delivered, when they looked at each other in confusion. They felt the sharp lurch of their command plane as it banked hard left.

At 2039 Zulu, Alice withdrew the cigarette from the cranny above his ear. The general's reach was subconscious, so mesmerized was he by the marvelous aircraft racing untouchably ahead of him. In some deep and entrenched way, he admired the pilot who was beating him. The man was so good, trained to be entrusted with the President of the United States, trained to lose an eye to a man-made sun and blithely take the protective patch off his good eye, exposing it so he could fly onward, the President secure.

Behind the two aircraft, in the late afternoon, the winter sun was setting again now, casting fiery beams across the white plateau of clouds through which the fruitless chase continued. The *E-4*'s wing sliced gracefully through a pink cotton-candy cloud bubble, cut majestically through the ebbing blue of a fading day, dashed easily toward the darkness of a last night.

To Alice, buried now in dreary thought, the hopeless race seemed to be taking them both beyond the clouds, beyond the sun, and over the very edge of their earth. He snapped a match to light the cigarette. In the flare, he lost the first move. Smitty lost it too, so suddenly had the hunted made himself vulnerable.

In front of them, the giant aircraft turned broadside to the *Looking Glass.* Alice dropped the match and the cigarette, tightening his grip on the phone. Smitty froze, ever so briefly, in puzzlement. The *E-4*'s wings tipped slightly one way and then the other in an invitation and also in one man's acknowledgment that he understood. It would happen very quickly now.

Smitty nudged the *Looking Glass* into a shallow, banking dive to the left. Alice's eyes flooded. His knuckles turned rigid on the phone. "Mr. President," he said quickly. "Do better next time, sir." He did not hear a reply.

In the windshield, the blue letters spelling "UNITED STATES OF AMERICA" swelled instantly. Without pause or thought, Smitty veered his prow into the loop of the U just forward of the *E-4*'s wings, just aft of the presidential plane's pilot.

In that final microsecond, the one that turns infinite for each being, Alice was certain he saw a vision from the left-hand seat of the other aircraft's flight deck. In the side window he saw a man in a black eyepatch snap a perfect, academy-taught salute. Alice was equally certain that, from the cockpit of the *Looking Glass,* the salute was returned with proper flair and suitable honor.

The explosion, high over the black and rich earth near the confluence of the Ohio and Mississippi rivers, was small by the standards of the day. It was measured in neither kilos nor megas but merely in tons. It emitted no rays harmful to man's programming, mechanical or otherwise.

Six hundred miles to the east and north, in a hole in the ground, the President of the United States said "Alice" once, but not twice, into the huzz.

V

ETERNAL VIGILANCE

The unleashed power of the atom has changed everything but our way of thinking.

—Albert Einstein

Epilogue

2100 ZULU

At 2040 Zulu, Sedgwick's transmission reached the two TAC-AMO aircraft through the Volna satellites.

At 2044, the codes were completed, followed by the encrypted instructions: "CEASE ALL HOSTILITIES IMMEDIATELY."

At 2046, Olney received a message requesting further codes because of the confusion over the interrupted transmission from the *E-4* command plane.

At 2049, the second message was completed.

At 2052, Olney's telegraph clattered with the beginning of the incoming message: "CONFIRM CESSATION OF HOSTILITIES." Sedgwick watched expectantly as the machine hummed in a brief pause, as if to interject its own emphasis. Then it clattered its conclusion: "ALERT STATUS MAINTAINED."

The young naval officer stared at the last words. Suddenly and overwhelmingly, his relief dissolved into a great and unexpected wave of depression. He shuddered involuntarily, his eyes riveted on the system's final statement. Then he shook his head slightly, tore the message off the telegraph, and read it to the President.

At 2054, the leaders of the two nuclear superpowers spoke one last time.

The President lay in his hospital bed in the radio room at

397

Olney, the short telegraphic message resting on his stomach. He could not see it, but Sedgwick's reading still rang in his ears. As he spoke into the phone, he found his voice extraordinarily weary and desolate. "There may be aftershocks, Mr. Premier. Are you prepared for them?"

"Another lost city, Mr. President?" The President could hear his own despondence reflected in the tired Russian voice. "Two cities? Three?" The President knew the Premier had the same message in front of him, its Cyrillic lettering glaring at the Soviet leader with the same haunt. "We will cope," the Premier continued somberly. "As will you."

"Yes, we will cope with lost cities," the President said. He shifted uneasily in his bed. "Those are not the aftershocks that concern me, Mr. Premier."

Labored breathing undulated across the distance between them. "No . . ." the Premier continued slowly. "The world will awaken tomorrow with one hundred million people dead and still more dying. It also will awaken with the same differences it had yesterday. Will we cope with them?"

The President peered into the empty whiteness. He felt tears forming in eyes that would forever see the sun. "It also will awaken with forty thousand unused nuclear weapons, Mr. Premier," he said. "Will we cope with them?"

"We will cope with one or we will cope with the other, Mr. President. We were blessed with great luck today."

"Luck. . . ."

A long silence followed, as both men burrowed far within themselves, dwelling, as they so rarely had before, on the same thought.

"Do you believe"—the President finally broke the quiet—"that we will draw any benefit from this, Mr. Premier?"

The Premier said nothing.

"Do you think that our one hundred million dead will become the symbols that will bring the world to its senses?" the President continued. "That would be luck, Mr. Premier. We will need much more of that precious commodity."

The Premier sighed. He spoke in the same fatalistic voice the President had heard in their only personal meeting, and he uttered the same fatalistic words. "We now return to our world of men, Mr. President."

The memory of their one meeting filled the President's mind.

"Yes, we now return to our world of men, Mr. Premier," the President repeated quietly into a phone linking two mole holes a planet apart. "Do you think we can control such a place?"

The President heard nothing for a moment, and he shifted uncomfortably, sending the short message relayed by Volna fluttering toward the floor. Near him, Sedgwick watched tears streaming from his Commander-in-Chief's eyes. He averted his gaze, even from the sightless man, and followed the paper as it wafted to the floor between their beds.

"I do not know, Mr. President," the Premier finally answered.

Sedgwick leaned out of his bed, tugging against the umbilical system of the intravenous tubing.

"Nor do I, Mr. Premier," the President said.

Sedgwick leaned farther, pulling against the system. His hand stretched toward the paper—his fingers hovering for a moment just inches away from "ALERT STATUS MAINTAINED"—and then he fell back into his bed, the system holding him, and he closed his eyes.

At 2058 Zulu, the commander of the Rocket Forces ordered the closing of the silo doors throughout the Soviet Union. He then completed the unbuttoning of his holster, withdrew his service revolver, and shot himself. In the concrete wombs beneath two dozen fields stretched across Asia, the young pink-cheeked men waited patiently. A shift change was long overdue, but the flickering green lights could not be left unmanned.

At 2100 Zulu, the American submarines emerged from the depths of many seas. They lingered briefly, protected just below the surface, and listened. A moment later they returned to their safe haunts and waited, eternally vigilant.

In the mid-Pacific, the storm's fury gradually ebbed. The grayness gave way to the distant streaks of yellow, and the yellow began to fill with growing patches of blue. Kazaklis relaxed slightly as the tumult eased and left *Polar Bear One* flying in a precarious but steady washboard bump.

"So now what?" Moreau asked.

Kazaklis squinted into the bright sunlight. The storm was disappearing in the void behind them. The ocean emerged in the void ahead.

"Rarotonga?" he said.

He looked out the side window at the battered swept-wing remnant of his old world. A gouged scar remained where the turmoil
had torn away the engines, two of man's useful tools. Next to the
scar's emptiness another of man's tools, the sleek white missile he
couldn't shake, filled the vacuum. It held itself snug, a survivor
like them.

"Bora Bora?"

The remaining engines held them precariously several hundred feet above the sea. He strained to look over the side, watching the past rush to the rear. He turned to look ahead at a horizon
too low, the future unseen somewhere beyond its edge.

"Hiva Oa?"

He glanced at his watch. It read 2100 Zulu by a time that no
longer had meaning. He ran his eyes across gauges and dials and
switches that told him nothing.

"Papeete for the lady?"

"Kazaklis!"

"Two in a canoe?"

"Kazaklis!"

He squinted again into the sun, trying to relate it to the time he
was abandoning and relate both to the gauges that had abandoned him. He knew only that they were somewhere near the
equator and somewhere near the 180th meridian, the artificial
line civilization used as its dateline, the artificial intersection man
had marked as the very center of his earth. It was the place where
yesterday became tomorrow and tomorrow became yesterday and
today didn't exist. As far as Kazaklis could see, nothing was there.

He reached for the first switch that had failed, as if something
should change as they entered a new day. He flicked it aimlessly
and felt a slight shudder. But the missile stayed with them.

So now what?

"I don't know, Moreau."

He reached toward Moreau's thigh and took her hand instead.
It shuddered but stayed with him, settling into his. Quietly they
absorbed each other's shuddering as they also absorbed the shuddering of the fragile craft that held them so precariously above
the void.

"Welcome to tomorrow," Kazaklis said.